WRITTEN BY
BRADY J. SADLER

Copyright © 2025 by Brady J. Sadler

www.bradyjsadler.com

Cover Art & Design by Evan Simonet
Additional Graphic Design by Brady J. Sadler

ISBN: 979-8-9910250-2-7 (Hardcover)
ISBN: 979-8-9910250-1-0 (Paperback)
ISBN: 979-8-9910250-3-4 (eBook)

This one's for you, Dad.

I'd say that I miss you, but I don't think I ever really let you go.

For the time you bought me my first drum set behind Mom's back
(man, she was pissed).
And all the times you blared Phil Collins.
I dedicate this story about a father and son, doing
everything they can to set things right, to your memory.

Love you, Pops.

The Days of Astasia

Eve of Corruption (2012)

The Malice of Light

The Acrid Sky (2023)

The Withered Roots (2024)

The Smoldering Vein (Forthcoming)

In Short Order (2025)

Emerald Decay (2025)

Relic Meyers

Relic Meyers & The Rhythms of Ruin (2024)

Relic Meyers & The Harmony of Hexes (2025)

PROLOGUE

LARAMIE, IN. 1998.

S teven couldn't tell what time it was anymore.

Since moving to third shift at the factory, his weekdays had been a groggy blur of microwaved meals and short afternoon naps. He supposed he could have done the sane thing and slept immediately after getting off work—maybe allowing him to get a full six or eight hours of rest—but he was always too wired to go to bed just when freedom called.

Not even spending seven hundred and twenty-two days trapped in a hellish dimension, playing drums nonstop for over seventeen thousand three hundred and twenty-eight hours could diminish the thrill he got from clocking out at his dead-end job.

It was the end of June on a Saturday, and Steven guessed it was around 6am, but he never wore a watch, not even before getting imprisoned outside of time. The Indiana humidity had settled in, and even this early in the morning, Steven had to wipe the sweat from his brow several times.

As he sat there waiting for Adratheon's call, he wondered if he should tell his son about the deal he had made. Lydia Thompkins was still in the dark, which meant Rothen most likely had no other mediums—if anyone at the company knew, there's no way they'd still be trying to recruit Steven to their security team.

Sipping his stale McDonald's coffee, Steven was forced once again to question his refusal of Lydia's third and "final" offer.

"We can't keep waiting," she had told Steven last week at the Thompkinses' big summer cookout. The kids were playing catch with a frisbee while Dina and Calvin chatted with the new neighbors, Karla and Phil McArthur, leaving

Steven to be pulled aside by Rothen's most persistent executive. "This kind of offer won't last."

Steven took a sip of his beer, struggling to think of new ways of telling the woman he wasn't interested—even though his interest was actually growing stronger each day.

"I'm not a soldier," Steven told her quietly. "I've seen the ex-cops and Navy SEALs that the Corps hires, and that ain't me, Lydia. I can barely even hold a drumstick anymore after everything that's happened."

She rolled her eyes, bringing the remnants of her margarita to her lips. "We have plenty of soldiers, Steven. You have something much more valuable." She tossed back the rest of her drink. "Besides, you'll get the proper training."

"Anyone want another burger?" Russ Thompkins called from the grill.

Steven raised his can of beer. "I'll take one, chef!"

"You bet, Stick!"

"I'm fine, hon," Lydia called. Keeping her eyes on Steven, she added in a quieter voice, "No one has been where you've been. And with Marshall acquiring DeMono Tech, we're going to need your expertise to avoid a hostile takeover."

Steven took another drink of his barely chilled beer, buying himself time to strengthen his refusal.

Lydia must have sensed it and added, "You will be well compensated, Steven. As I've assured you before, you can pretty much name your salary."

"Heads up!"

Steven turned just in time to catch a pink frisbee that almost clocked him in the head. His reflexes were more than just back, they felt nearly superhuman.

"Sorry, Dad," Relic said, breathless and smiling as he jogged over. "Bree's aim needs work."

"That was right to you, man!" Bree called from the other side of the back yard. "Don't blame me for your lack of coordination!"

With a flick of his wrist, Steven tossed the disc back to his son. As the kid ran off to resume playing catch with his girlfriend, Steven's eyes drifted to Dina, who flashed him a wide smile before returning to the conversation her fiancé was having with the McArthurs. Another happy couple.

"Can I at least tell them you're interested?"

Still watching his disjointed family enjoy a rare, breezy summer day, Steven gave a sardonic smile, as if Lydia were suggesting something preposterous. "No."

Relic shouted again after seeing Bree dive and catch the frisbee between the tips of her fingers.

"Steven—"

"Look, Lydia," he said, trying to quell the annoyance he felt brewing in his gut from the woman's constant pressure, "I wouldn't be here if it weren't for my son—he's really all that matters to me anymore."

"And you don't think I'm considering my daughter with everything I do for Rothen?" Her voice was steady, but Steven could tell he had inadvertently struck a nerve. "You may have protected your own family by traipsing across Europe with your band for the last decade, but I've lost count of how many wide-scale tragedies I've diverted while you toyed with the Widow."

Steven seethed, but said nothing. He knew he couldn't tell her what happened in Europe or the bargain with Adratheon that instigated all of this. Also, she was mostly right—he had done it all to protect his own family.

Lydia sighed. "I didn't want it to go this way, Steve, but this hardball shit is getting old." She turned to screen Steven from the other guests, her gaze cold. "Your old buddy on the force, Keith Barnes, stopped coming around your apartment, hasn't he? Since that partner of his got canned for not staying out of Rothen's affairs, it seems like he's lost interest in you, yeah?"

Steven narrowed his eyes on her. He had guessed the company had something to do with the cops not following up on his disappearance or Valentine's supposed murder, yet her confirmation still managed to rattle him.

There was no joy or victory in her smirk. "Rothen protects its interests. I'd suggest you remain interesting to the board."

"Hey, hon," Russ called as he approached. "Can I get you a refill?"

"You certainly can, doll," Lydia said in a completely different tone of voice. She handed over her empty cup and gave Russ a kiss on the cheek.

"Here ya go, Steve." Russ handed over a burger on a greasy paper plate.

"Thanks, man." Seizing the opportunity, Steven took the burger and retreated from Lydia.

The payphone rang, returning Steven's distant gaze to the present. Despite the bright clear sky, a haunting chill settled in, freezing his legs in place.

The phone rang again. Nobody else was around to hear; the cashier inside Village Pantry was playing a handheld video game. A lone car drove by. But as that phone rang again, Steven felt more alone than he ever had.

His first step forward took him back to 1987, to the fateful night when he could have called Dina and maybe saved their marriage (even if it meant angering a godlike entity that he was indebted to). Thousands of doubts ran through his mind as he reached the phone on the third ring, clenching his fingers before lifting the handset off the hook.

"Hello."

There was fuzzy silence on the other end, but Steven knew Adratheon listened. He was always listening.

"I can't keep this up, man. I just want out—to be normal—"

"Normal?!" the voice roared, crackling with static.

Steven recoiled from the handset, feeling pins in his brain to emphasize Adratheon's fury.

"Consider yourself fortunate that you know what normal is, mortal." The entity's breathing sounded demonic, but Steven knew there was something darker on the other line, and it was clearly still pissed at him.

"Look," Steven said, tossing his coffee cup to splatter its contents against the Village Pantry's brick wall, "I don't know how many times I have to tell you: I tried to stop it. How was I supposed to know your daughter was hiding in another tape?"

"We had a deal," Adratheon said, his rage still simmering, but his voice gaining a human quality, "and like every other human, greed led you to betrayal. Now the son shall suffer the consequences."

"No!" Steven looked around to make sure nobody heard his outburst, but he was still alone. He gripped the handset in both hands to help control his rage. "You leave him alone. He's been through enough. This is between us!"

Adratheon laughed. "It seems fitting, does it not? The hexes that have guarded this place for so long, protecting it from the wretched world beyond, shall now be its undoing. And the boy will usher in the new era that you failed to deliver: the age of Adratheon."

"You bastard!" Steven screamed now and no longer cared who heard him. "You wanted me before, take me! Come and get me! Leave my son alone!"

The dial tone signaled that Adratheon—wherever he really was—had hung up.

Steven slammed the handset back into the cradle, picking it up to hammer it back in place again. Then again. And again.

"Hey!" The cashier with the GameBoy held the store door open. "Knock it off or I'll call the cops."

Steven let go of the phone, taking a deep breath to clear his thoughts. He needed to think this through carefully, before jumping into a solution like last time—a solution that got him stuck in Alternus.

But instead, he grabbed the phone again, slipped in a quarter, and dialed the first number that came to mind.

After a single ring, Lydia picked up. "Hello?"

Unexpectedly, the sound of her voice pulled Steven back to that summer cookout. He remembered Relic smiling, joking with his girlfriend during their game of catch, enjoying a simple, quiet life. Steven owed everything to that kid.

"Hello?"

Steven opened his mouth to tell her, "I'm in," but in the split second it would have taken to say those words, he saw himself being ripped out of his son's life again, joining an elite squad of soldiers employed by the most shadowy corporation imaginable, and inevitably destroying any semblance of a normal childhood for Relic.

He couldn't do that. Not again.

Closing his mouth, Steven hung up the phone. His next call was to Gate.

"It's time, man," Steven told him. "We gotta slay the dragon."

Lydia kept her hand on the phone, expecting it to ring again. But she was left with the familiar, sterile silence of her office. Running her finger down the headset, she imagined Steven Meyers sitting at home in his shitty new apartment wrestling with the decision to call her back and beg for the job.

Not that Lydia considered herself a petty or vengeful person, but she'd be lying if she didn't admit to a certain subtle satisfaction in Steven's suffering; she never handled rejection well.

Lydia jolted at the soft tap on her door. "Step louder, Justin! Walk like a normal goddamn person so people can hear you coming." She glared at the door that remained shut. "Jesus," she mumbled as she got up and strode around her desk.

Justin Garrison jerked back slightly when Lydia pulled the door open. It was hard for her to even look at the kid without getting annoyed. He was a handsome young man with a promising future, but he made a habit of looking like a lost lamb, which drove Lydia crazy.

"Why are you here so early?" Lydia asked her assistant when he just stared at her expectantly.

Justin clutched a leather planner to his chest with one arm, motioning over his shoulder with the other. "You wanted me to check on her first thing."

"Right," she said, rubbing her temples. *Jesus, have I been here for two straight days?* She checked her watch, groaning at the early hour. *I need to call Russ and let him know I haven't been called away again.* "Yeah, you go check on her—we don't want the doctors poking around in there."

"That's the thing," Justin began.

Lydia waved him away, turning to reach for the bottle of water on her desk while wondering where she put her aspirin. "Just take care of it, Justin. I need to call Benson and figure out how to tell the board that both Valentine and Meyers might be lost causes."

"Mrs. Thomkins. She's awake."

Grumbling, Lydia pushed past him, abandoning thoughts of painkillers for the headache that was brewing. She needed all her faculties. "Next time lead with that, Justin."

She nearly jogged down the vacant, fluorescent-lit hall with Justin following silently in her wake. Like most Rothen facilities, this one was half corporate office space and half medical labs, and Lydia's office was just down the hall from their patient's room.

The metallic clang of a tray hitting the tiled floor could be heard, and Lydia quickly scanned her keycard to open Delilah Crane's recovery room.

"Where am I?"

Lydia held her hands up to calm the girl down while speaking quietly over her shoulder. "Justin, please wait outside."

Delilah's head jerked toward Justin as the door gently clicked shut. She snapped back to Lydia. "You're Bree's mom..." The tension in the girl seemed to lessen then, her dark eyes taking in her surroundings. "Is she okay? Is Relic okay?"

Lydia adjusted herself, considering how to break it to the girl. After only a slight hesitation, she took her usual approach: brutally direct. "You've been in a coma for over two months."

The girl looked down at her Rothen medical gown—a much more fashionable version of what she had worn when Lydia had found her recovering in St. Regis with her father—and then inspected the IV in her arm. When Delilah reached to pull it out, Lydia stepped forward.

"Wait."

The girl looked up and Lydia saw something curious in her eyes: not anger or suspicion, but fear. It reminded Lydia that this creature was just a girl like her own daughter, scared and overwhelmed by all the chemical imbalances of a teenager. Lydia felt the urgent need to suffocate the sympathy that was rising within her, because this was business and her career was on the line.

"Where am I?"

"This is a Rothen facility," Lydia explained. "You were recovering from the events at the Chambers High battle of the bands when we became worried that

Marshall Crane had…" She looked down at her Rothen keycard, wondering how much to tell the girl. "We worried that your adopted father would not provide the care you needed."

Delilah swayed on her feet, reaching for her head. Lydia stepped forward, motioning to the bed. "Sit down. Even a…someone like you needs a little time to recover."

As she eased herself to the bed, Delilah looked up from the IV still taped in place on her arm, anger replacing the fear in her eyes. "What did you do to me?"

She knows, Lydia thought, straining to keep her composure. She realized none of her usual smoke and mirrors would work on this one. Lydia sighed as she sat down next to Delilah on the bed.

"A long time ago—well before my time at Rothen—there was a project called VANDAL."

"Vandal?"

"Vitality Amplifying Neural-Derived Adrenal Liberator," Lydia explained. "The goal was to create a steroid compound that could not only enhance physical regeneration, but also prevent psychotic disturbances in subjects, especially those prone to hallucinations or schizophrenia." She turned to look at Delilah. "Even I don't have all the details regarding those early tests, but I do know they all ended in disaster."

Delilah looked back at her IV. "Until now?"

"You were exactly what we needed," Lydia said, reaching into her pocket and drawing out a vial of green fluid labeled *VANDAL Serum*. She placed it into Delilah's hand. "And it was exactly what you needed."

The look in Delilah's eyes told Lydia that the girl knew exactly what she held.

Their fates—their very lives—now depended on each other.

"Dina, go home!" Rook bellowed, tossing a heavy pan into the sink. "This is the last time I'm gonna tell you!" He picked up a huge carving knife to see if it needed sharpening.

The front door chimed as a group of chatty teenagers left the diner.

"Alright, alright," she replied with a laughter that Rook still wasn't used to. "Let me just drop their check off. Last table, I swear." Dina pushed her way through grimy kitchen doors as she flipped through several receipts.

Rook didn't fail to notice the wad of cash curled in her fist. He smiled, glad that she was at least making good tips despite business slumping so hard over the summer. The dinner rush was dying down, and Rook was ready to get down to cleaning the grease traps early so he wasn't going to be stuck there all night.

"That goes for you too," Rook snapped at Beverly as she picked up her last order from the window overlooking the front of house. "I'm not paying you to wait on any stragglers. I can handle 'em." He carefully put the knife back on the cutting board, impressed with how well the thing held its edge.

"Cheapskate," Beverly replied through a snap of her gum, but any acid from the words were soothed by the flirty wink she gave him.

Rook couldn't help but smile. Bev wasn't exactly his type, but it didn't stop them from flirting through just about every shift. If there was one thing that Rodney "Rook" Warren never learned, it was that women only ever led him to trouble.

With that thought, he flipped off the big flat top and made his way to the small back office adorned with the glories of his past. The peeling walls inside the closet-sized room were strewn with pictures of a young, hale catcher in the green and yellow uniform of an Oakland Athletics ballplayer. However, the pictures didn't show the drunk driving charges or the woman who betrayed young Rodney Warren when he lost his big league paychecks. Everyone still called him Rook because he blew his rookie year in the show.

And they'll never let me forget it.

The front door chimed again, indicating another guest had left Rook's Home Plate Diner.

Taking a seat, Rook's knees popped and his protruding belly strained against his dirty white shirt. Unimpressed with what he saw in the reflective glass of his picture frames, he pulled open the drawer of his meager desk and produced the near-empty bottle of whiskey that would make his nocturnal maintenance more bearable.

"See ya, Rook!" Dina shouted from up front. "Last table just left! I'm going to go pick Relic up from practice."

"Tell him to learn some Journey for me!" he called back. "That metal shit is too loud!"

"Will do," Dina said with a laugh.

Beverly poked her head through the window. "Need a hand tonight?" She wiggled her eyebrows.

Rook scoffed kindly. "Appreciate the offer, babe. Another time. It's nasty back here."

"Your loss, old man." She popped her gum as she waved goodbye.

The door chimed.

Rook polished off the bottle of whiskey, thinking back to when he first bought the diner off his father. The Warrens weren't a wealthy family, and he and his brother were raised to earn their own way. There was no inheriting the family business, Rook remembered bitterly. The only way he could get a lifeline from his old man was to buy one, deeply discounted at least.

He stared into the empty bottle, thinking about how he should probably thank his brother for blowing any shot he may have had at taking this place over. Ricky Warren was even more of a failure than his older brother, and that was saying something.

The alcohol hit him unexpectedly, and Rook nearly fell asleep in his desk chair. But the chime at the front door snapped him awake.

"Sorry," Rook called as he struggled to his feet, "we're winding down for the night. All we got—"

Narrowing his eyes, Rook observed a vacant counter and empty booths. The front doors were firmly closed. He leaned his head out to survey the rest of the diner, seeing nothing but the dusty baseball decorations that adorned the walls.

"Damn wind," he grumbled, pushing his way through the flimsy kitchen doors and locking the front entrance. He flicked the *Open* sign off, even though it wasn't even 8pm. Rodney Warren was done for the night.

Returning to the kitchen, he cracked his knuckles and prepared for the slimy job of degreasing his outdated appliances.

But the door chimed again.

Feeling uneasy now, Rook made to retrieve his trusty knife that never seemed to lose its edge. There wasn't much that rattled him these days, but seeing his knife no longer atop the cutting board where he had left it sent an icy chill down his spine.

Get a grip, he told himself. In the last twelve years he'd been running this place—and in the decades his father, Stuart Warren, had run it prior—there had never been a robbery or an intruder. However, he couldn't shake the feeling that he wasn't alone.

Rook stood still for a moment, waiting to hear any movement. The drip of the leaky sink was all he got for his trouble. Feeling paranoid, he went about his work, casting another glance toward the entrance just in case—still secure.

"Gonna cost me an arm and a leg to get that thing fixed, I'm sure," Rook complained, undoing the locks on the wheels of the grill. But his heart stopped as he heard the kitchen door groan slightly. He spun around and was almost even more shocked to see Ricky Warren, lead singer of Unknown Oath and pathetic excuse for a brother.

Ricky's eyes were distant, not staring at Rook, but still seeing him. "Hey, bro."

Rook didn't fail to see his knife in Ricky's clenched hand. He wore an old denim jacket as if it were still 1987, the year he had first bailed on the family when they needed him most. Rook wasn't sure what drugs his little brother was on now, but he was clearly whacked out of his skull.

"How'd you get my knife, Ricky?" The news from last fall—about how his brother had killed the singer for Gator Sponge in Boston—replayed in his head. Was Ricky here to kill his own brother now?

Looking down at the blade as if for the first time, Ricky seemed to snap out of his weird trance. He looked at his older brother. "It's just in case she comes."

Rook swallowed, subtly considering what objects in the kitchen he might be able to use to fight off an armed addict. "In case who comes, Ricky?"

He raised the knife as he stepped forward suddenly. "Her!" Ricky shouted. "The chick that followed us?"

It sounded like a question, but Rook didn't have the answer. "Just put it down, man. Let's talk. I'll make you some coffee."

Ricky inclined his head, as if he didn't understand a word Rook said. But then he looked down at the knife held between them and laughed. "What the fuck..." Ricky dropped the knife on the counter and reached up to push his long hair back. "She, uh... Sorry, bro, I, uh... She does this, ya know? Keeps following me, making me paranoid."

"Who you talking about, Ricky? A cop?"

Shaking his head, Ricky began nervously tapping the counter where the knife lay as if to emphasize a point. "No, no, no...the cops can't help, man. We tried that. Just makes it worse. I just need to find the damn book. Stick said he left it in the studio, but Gator Sponge was the only other band that used it after us before it burnt down...and Holden was one of them!" Ricky's tapping fingers curled into a fist and he began slamming the counter as if he held an invisible knife, jamming it into his victim. "He was one of them, bro!"

Knowing he would lose his opportunity if he didn't take it, Rook made his move toward the knife, hoping to get it away from his deranged brother. But the motion sobered Ricky right up, who quickly snatched the knife back up and held it between them again.

"His kid!" Ricky's eyes were wide with revelation. "His kid's gotta have it, man! We can stop her, bro. Rick and Rod, man, just like the old days."

"You talking about Meyers? Relic Meyers?" Rook asked, keeping his hands where Ricky could see them. "Dina's kid?" The mention of Stick made things a little clearer to Rook now. "What do you want with him? He's just a kid. The cops are already after you, man! I'm not going to let you get the kid mixed up with you."

Ricky's eyes were still wild. "The kid's already mixed up with it, man. She can't kill him, but he can! And I know how to stop him!"

"Him who?!" Rook demanded, losing his patience.

Ricky looked at the knife. "His dad, man. Steven fuckin' Meyers."

CHAPTER 1

R elic's hand shook as he checked his watch. It was a cheap timekeeper—a simple chrome disc set into a studded black leather bracelet—but it was the first real gift he had gotten from his father, so Relic cherished it.

That didn't prevent him from groaning as he stared at it, noting the time.

"Dammit, Dad," he hissed, shaking the nerves out of his fingers.

"He'll be here," Bree said before brushing his cheek gently with her lips. "Just make sure you don't play 'Child of the Damned' as fast as you did at practice."

Relic smiled, his nerves already slightly calmer.

"And you can't spell misery without me!" Becca Reynolds' voice gave out as she screamed the final chorus. The rest of Habitual Void thrashed around on the small stage, making up for their lack of musicianship with plenty of energy and destructive tendencies.

The crowd filling The Voodoo could certainly get behind it, Relic noted, wondering if the rowdy teens would be able to appreciate Altar Stone's more structured performance after something so raw and untethered. That idle worry brought the nerves back, and Relic put his arm around Bree's waist, pulling her close as she tuned her guitar.

He looked out across the small venue, seeing mostly college students and locals, with a smattering of people Relic recognized from school. It felt surreal to him that he was about to play his first real gig with his first band, and the electricity that realization brought on balanced out the nervousness that his dad had told him would be inevitable.

"You'll always get some sort of stage fright, man," he had said last night after watching their rehearsal. "I remember James Hetfield told me in Stockholm back in '92: the night you're not giddy to go on stage is probably the night you should hang it up."

Relic spun a drumstick through his fingers as he smiled and tried to appreciate the moment—he was actually annoyed at his father for being late to *his* band's show. The situation would have seemed like a fairytale to Relic just last year, yet here he was getting upset over something so freaking normal.

Habitual Void's final chords finally quieted to a static buzz and the crammed audience roared in approval.

"We love you, maggots," Becca snarled into the mic, the black spikes of her hair falling limp due to the sweat pouring out of her on the hot stage. "We are Habitual Void and we have CDs in the back. Stick around for Laramie's own little oath keepers." She gave Relic and Bree a condescending grin.

Relic inwardly seethed at the mockery. "They're just jealous," his mom would always tell him, but it never helped soothe the rage he felt when other local bands continued to dog on Altar Stone just because of who he was.

"Someone's a little threatened," Bree said under her breath, echoing Dina's sentiments as usual. She turned around and pressed her cheek against Relic's so she could whisper in his ear—a move that nearly caused his legs to give out. "Whatever you do, don't make their drummer regret ever sitting behind that three-piece kit."

Chuckling, Relic pushed himself away from the wall and followed Bree toward the side of the stage where their own gear was stashed. As they walked past The Voodoo's main door, Relic began hoping his dad wouldn't even show up. Even though this was Atlar Stone's first real gig, and he'd always dreamed of his dad cheering him on, the presence of Unknown Oath's miraculously returned drummer would certainly cast a shadow over his own band's moment in the spotlight.

Despite all that, Relic was still annoyed over the absence. His dad had been more present over the summer than Relic could have hoped for, but these last couple weeks had felt off. Maybe it was the move to the night shift at work, or helping Gate with—well, Relic had no clue what the two of them were actually up to lately. Whatever it was, Relic's dad was becoming much less present, and that naturally unsettled him.

Navigating the audience of older teens who seemed to be regulars at The Voodoo returned Relic to a state of anxious dread. He felt all their eyes on him. Walking ahead with her guitar held upright by the neck, Bree seemed unaffected as usual, carving a path through the "alternative" folk who made up most of Laramie's thriving music scene.

They found Tyler alone in the corner, peering out the side window that overlooked Ferry Street. The palpable nervous energy that hung around their singer overpowered Relic's own, and he stepped around his drums to see what distressed Tyler.

"She's not here," Tyler said, sensing Relic's presence.

"Who? Miranda? I thought you guys broke up."

"We did," Tyler said, turning from the window, "but she still said she'd come."

"Something else wrong?" Relic asked, trying not to panic. He noticed Tyler's whole demeanor felt off, as if this concern for Miranda's presence was just a diversion or something.

Tyler shook his head and then cracked his neck. He wore a simple black t-shirt with the sleeves rolled up to reveal his muscled arms. As he loosened his shoulders and pushed the sides of his growing hair back, Relic realized the guy was really starting to look the part of a metal singer, and that managed to quell the concern before it blossomed into pure fright.

"Where the hell is Nick?"

Relic spun around to see Bree motioning to an unattended bass guitar sitting carelessly atop its case. But before Relic could even process that, he heard Tyler ask an even more unnerving question.

"Why the hell is my dad here?"

Not knowing which crisis to focus on, Relic's gaze was drawn to the figure that stood about a head taller than most of The Voodoo's occupants. Barry Richardson was built like a pregnant linebacker, and his bald head glistened under the venue's lights that had just kicked on to allow the bands to swap out the gear on stage. With eyes boring into his son, Barry carved his way through the crowd.

As Becca and Habitual Void finished clearing their stuff from the stage, Bree unslung her own guitar and set it on its stand. "I'll go look for Nick." She gave Relic a knowing glance—one that said, "I don't want to be here for this, but fill me in later."

Barry stood over them as Bree slipped away. "Your mother told me the show started at eight. Did I miss your performance?" The man's face was a mask, staring at his son as if he were a total stranger. Relic saw a package under Barry's arm, held like a running back might hold a football.

"No, we're on next," Tyler said, pushing his shaggy hair off his brow, which was now damp with sweat.

Barry gave a grunt in reply. He didn't even acknowledge Relic's presence. "Here." He presented the package to Tyler. It was wrapped simply in brown paper. "Thought you might need this." He turned around after Tyler took the package, uncaring if it fell to the floor after it left his own hands.

As Barry Richardson strode away from the teens, parting the crowd once more with his authoritative and sobering presence, Relic and Tyler shared a confused look, and then stared at the package. Tyler hesitated a moment, but shook his head and tore the paper from what appeared to be a nondescript shoebox.

Relic's stomach heaved as a flashback played through his mind from last year. He knew what was in that box before Tyler tossed the wrapping aside and slipped his fingers beneath the lid.

All at once, Relic was back in Crane & Co. Athletic Supply in the Roanoke Mall, spying on Barry ridiculing his youngest child.

"You sound like a whiny little faggot, son," the man said with absolute loathing.

From Relic's memory, Barry's voice adopted the same tone as the voices from Alternus that had haunted him all throughout freshman year. But gazing up at the man across the crowd, who now stood on the lower steps of the balcony access with his arms crossed like he owned the place, Relic felt fury where he would once have maybe felt fear.

"That asshole," Tyler breathed.

Relic saw what he expected.

"I can't believe they even make these in my size." Tyler sounded more detached about the situation than Relic expected. Altar Stone's singer eyed the Barbie-themed sneakers with as much interest as Relic might give a turd in the grass.

As he stared at the shoes, Relic's vision blurred ever so slightly, and on the faint edges of his hearing, a familiar voice demanded, "Release me."

Relic jolted, drawing Tyler's attention away from the cruel gift.

"What?"

Relic's eyes went from Tyler to Barry, who stood like a statue on the stairs. The man didn't look amused or at all bothered by the proceedings; he just observed. But something about his presence made Relic feel like Barry was somehow the source of that voice.

"Nothing," Relic answered, shaking his head and trying to calm his breathing. He hadn't heard that voice since his dad returned, and he was hoping it was just some sort of hallucination brought on by stress. Between the pre-show jitters and him worrying about his dad not making the set, Relic could convince himself that he imagined it. "Your dad is just a dick."

"Just figuring that out?" Tyler asked, closing the box.

Barry flinched then. Not much, but enough for Relic to notice. It was as if he were excited or relieved that his son was about to discard the shoes.

"Wait," Relic said, putting a hand out. "Let me wear 'em."

Tyler gave Relic a puzzled look.

Relic nodded toward Barry. "What do you think he expects you to do with those?"

Tyler looked back at the box thoughtfully. "He expects me to do what he would do, probably. Throw them across the room and yell about how they're for pussies."

"Yeah, he doesn't expect a metal drummer to strap them on and kick out some double bass, right?"

Tyler opened the box, and Relic once more noticed a reaction from Barry—a slight shift in his hand between his crossed arms.

"No," Tyler said. He grabbed the bright pink, jeweled sneakers and tossed the box against the wall with their gear. "I think I'm gonna wear 'em."

All the tension left Relic again when Barry's arms dropped to his sides as he watched his son lace up his new shoes.

"Found him," Bree said from the other side of the stage. The chatter from the crowd was thinning out as people filtered out to smoke or converse between bands. Relic saw Nick stumbling behind Bree, his long hair now falling over half his face these days.

"Dude, we need to set up," Relic said, almost as much to himself as to his bassist. He had been so distracted by Barry's arrival and gift that he had forgotten to start moving his drums to the stage. But one look at Nick's blood-shot eyes gave Relic pause. "Are you high?!"

The question was a slap in Nick's face, who straightened his posture and stepped toward his drummer. "Keep it down, man."

Relic was nearly knocked over by the stink of marijuana on Nick's breath. Overwhelmed by rage, he clenched his fists and tried not to scream, managing a harsh whisper. "This is our first real show, and you're out toking it up while we're supposed to be getting ready to play?!"

"I'm here, man," Nick said, having enough shame to at least look embarrassed about the situation. "Let's go play."

As he moved to get his bass, Relic noticed a strange hemp necklace poking out from the collar of Nick's NOFX shirt—the type of accessory that a Dave Matthews fan might wear. Something about it made Relic even more pissed, but Bree calmed him with a hand on his shoulder.

"Let's just focus on the show," she said softly. "We'll talk to him later."

Relic nodded and the band went about setting up their gear. There was something therapeutic about assembling his massive drum set. Even though he felt pressured to get everything situated quickly, the entire process felt like building a Lego set without the instructions to rely on, only his instincts.

The compounding crises of the last hour—the previous band's mockery, his dad running late, his singer's new shoes, his high bassist—felt more and more distant with each cymbal he arranged and each tom he tilted to the right angle. By the time his green monster was ready for the sound guy to mic it up, Relic's only real remaining concern was their setlist, so he joined the rest of the band in front of Bree's amp to finalize their choice of opening song; they settled on the HammerFall cover.

That was when Steven Meyers arrived.

Many concert goers were filtering back into The Voodoo, drawn in by the thunder of the sound guy testing Relic's drums through the PA. Steven stood about a head taller than most of the teens in the crowd, and Relic saw Gate come in behind him. Unknown Oath's rhythm section looked frantic, as if they had both just been chased into the place by something terrible.

Relic detached himself from the rest of Altar Stone and met his dad at the front of the stage. "You made it!"

Steven offered a very artificial smile, putting a stiff hand on Relic's shoulder. "Of course, man. I wouldn't miss an Altar Stone show!"

"You guys are going to slay," Gate added, but his eyes were fixed on something in the back of the venue. "I don't see him..."

"See who?" Relic asked.

"Nothing," Steven said, giving Gate a look that Relic couldn't see. His dad looked even more suspicious when he turned back to Relic. "I just, uh—just told a few people at work about the show. Was hoping they'd make it."

Before Relic could inquire further, Gate leveled his gaze on him and said, "Cut the shit, Stick." To Relic he said, "We need you guys to play the song."

Relic's stomach lurched and his dad recoiled slightly as if he were suddenly hit by a jolt of electricity.

Alternus. Just the thought of the song's title chilled Relic to the core. The memories of last year—the ones he had repressed all summer—rushed through him in a violent surge as he heard the echoes of his dad's drums in his head.

"It's fine, man," Gate was saying, waving a thick-fingered hand as if it could dispel the miasma rising within Relic, begging to be released through those ruinous rhythms. "You've detached her from the song." He clapped his hands together. "The door is closed."

"Wait," Relic began, but his dad held up a finger.

"Let me explain it to him," Steven hissed to Gate. "Just give me a min—"

"Relic?" Bree's voice shattered the suffocating bubble that was closing in on Relic and his older companions. "Oh, hey, Mr. Meyers!"

Steven offered a weak smile. "Hey, Bree. How many times I gotta tell you? Steve or Stick. I'm not one of your teachers."

"We gotta jam," Nick said, plucking his bass as the sound of more of The Voodoo's patrons returned from their informal intermission. Relic could tell they were eager for more music. "Sound guy is waving us on."

Looking from his dad to Gate then back to his dad, Relic suddenly felt like he was suffocating.

"Seriously," Gate said, leaning forward and holding out a fist for Relic to bump, "trust us. Just play it."

Relic slowly raised his fist to meet Gate's—the man who'd served as his mentor during his father's long absence. He felt like he could trust him with his life, but he still found his eyes wandering to his dad before touching the janitor's hairy knuckles.

"It's fine, Relic," Steven assured him, his eyes still wild but eerily comforting. "She can't come back. The song is yours now."

Swallowing anything he could possibly say in reply, Relic bumped Gate's fist and began to wonder how to even broach this subject to Bree after everything that had happened at the battle of the bands in the spring. He decided not to even try, instead making his way toward his drum throne while not meeting her gaze. The band would expect him to kick into HammerFall's "Child of the Damned," not the song that opened an interdimensional gateway in the basement of their high school.

As Relic took his seat, the venue lights lowered and the four members of Altar Stone were illuminated under two sets of stage lights. He picked up the sticks that rested on his snare, instinctively spinning them through his fingers, still avoiding the eyes that peered at him from the world beyond his drums.

"Let's see it, Stick Junior!" the singer for Habitual Void shouted from the back of the crowded room.

At that moment, Gate and Steven could not have asked for a better tonic to cure Relic of his reluctance. Becca Reynolds' goading voice was a tiny spark that "Alternus" needed, and before she even finished her taunt, Relic struck his high rack tom with the flam that signaled the song's opening fill.

The fire had been lit.

Time slowed. Relic finally allowed himself to look at Bree, her face peering over her bare shoulder like a small animal catching sight of a charging predator. In that brief moment as he rolled into the opening rhythm, it was as if Relic was truly noticing his girlfriend for the first time that evening.

Bree Thompkins stood frozen like a watchful soldier. Armed with her purple axe, she wore a black tank top that hugged her torso, reminding Relic of the time she returned from camp last summer. The excitement he felt that day had paled in comparison to how he felt during each glorious day of summer this year.

The flannel shirt tied around her waist covered her legs from this angle, but he could easily picture the frayed jean shorts she wore as he studied her body from that bushy red hair all the way down to her combat boots. The horror on her face didn't distract from that single moment of bliss he felt as he ended the drum fill and rolled into the swaying tom rhythm of "Alternus."

"Dude," Tyler hissed, leaning over Relic's drums. His voice was inaudible over the pattern Relic pounded out, but the face he made amplified each word he mouthed at his drummer. "We haven't practiced that!"

That didn't stop Nick from hitting the bassline appropriately, headbanging along to the beat—seemingly completely unbothered by the surprise choice of opening number.

Relic confidently spun a stick and landed the fill that preceded the opening vocal line, nodding for Tyler to attend to the mic. Shaking his head, Tyler spun around and tore the mic from its stand, planting his left Barbie sneaker on the stage monitor to assume an appropriate metal singer pose.

"The curse has come."

But it didn't come.

Relic had closed his eyes, slowly becoming entranced with the song that he thought he'd never hear again, but he whipped them open when he realized Tyler had missed his cue. On the front line, Bree seemed to still be too shocked to do anything, and Nick was still fingering his heavy strings as if nothing were out of the ordinary. But Tyler had once more turned to Relic, his mouth moving near the mic but nothing coming out.

It's the PA, Relic thought immediately. *They forgot to turn the mic up.* But that possibility was ruled out as Tyler tapped on the mic and ejected several clangy thumps out of The Voodoo's sound system.

Beyond the stage lights, Relic could see the faces of his father and Gate, watching the drummer intently and nervously. This caused Relic to miss a beat and both men cringed as if glass shattered.

"Fr-um fa-haaar be-yund," Tyler's voice whined and croaked like a dying animal, harsh and nearly unintelligible. He gave Relic a panicked look that said, "My voice is gone, man. We're screwed."

But Relic kept playing, landing another fill that led into Bree's guitar lead. Tyler kept motioning to his throat, the sleeves of the plain black tee straining against his flexed biceps. With the sides of his hair slicked back and the top left to curl like some 1950s greaser, Tyler looked like a gangster from an old black and white movie, threatening Relic to stop playing.

But the song wouldn't let go.

Relic felt warm tendrils creeping through his limbs, a sensation he hadn't felt all summer. It wasn't until now that he realized something had been missing from his life, and it was "Alternus," or the power that came with it.

With sudden horror, Relic saw his drumsticks illuminating with that familiar green luminescence. Faint at first, the gleam drew a gasp from the crowd and a roar of applause. But the fervor was short-lived.

As Bree held out the final note of her guitar solo—when Tyler was supposed to sing his next part—the stage lights flickered, and a shadow fell over The

Voodoo. Two shadows, actually, like the wings of some huge bird of prey. For the briefest of moments, Relic had the impression that they were dragon wings.

Whatever the shadow was, it swallowed the venue into total darkness as all electrical sounds from the stage fizzled out, leaving Relic to stumble out of the song by himself.

"Show's over," someone said in an amused tone, drawing a wave of groans from the crowd.

Relic wasn't sure how he knew, but it was the voice of a vampire.

CHAPTER 2

Two weeks before the disastrous show at The Voodoo, Relic stared down at Bree. Her face was flush, the freckles on her cheeks and the bridge of her nose almost disappeared in the sea of crimson that overtook her complexion. She had never been more beautiful to Relic.

"Are you ready?" she asked with a voice bearing the weight of anticipation.

Something about the vulnerable nature of their situation—him looking down on her as she steadied her breath from below—excited Relic, twisting his insides. It wasn't as if he weren't normally excited around his girlfriend, but there was a shared anxiety here that weakened them both, putting them each at the other's mercy.

He flexed his arms as he gripped the bar. "I've been ready for weeks now. Are you?!" His gaze wandered down her bare shoulders, and his body tensed even more as the anticipation built.

She managed a smile as she closed her eyes and drew in a ragged breath; Relic could see she was shaking. They'd been pushing themselves for the last few weeks, determined to take things to the next level.

And here they were.

When she exhaled, Relic could tell she was ready. "Let's do it." She clapped her hands then arched her back as she reached up and grabbed the bar. Her fingers brushed Relic's and he felt the familiar electricity whenever they touched. Suddenly, he didn't feel so ready.

But Bree thrust her hips and let out a bestial grunt as she lifted the barbell off the rack. Relic quickly loosened his grip as she began her set, taken aback by the sudden savagery that possessed his girlfriend. He only had to watch as she cranked one rep after the other, his hands having little to do as they trailed after the bar that Bree furiously raised and lowered.

Thunder boomed outside as rain continued to patter against the garage door in small, metallic plinks.

During the next several moments, Relic couldn't help but wonder what had driven his girlfriend to take such a strong interest in weightlifting. His own reason to exercise was merely to shed his remaining baby fat. However, puberty—late as it was—had been doing most of the work in that department, Dr. Weaver had told him.

Something beyond body image had set a fire in Bree, and as Relic watched her cute face contort into a mask of painful determination, he wondered if it all went back to last year. That thought shifted their positions in his mind, and Relic was no longer standing over Bree; they were in the Thompkinses' kitchen and Bree was burying a kitchen knife into the flank of a werewolf that was mauling Relic.

Was that it? Relic wondered. Bree wasn't one to wear her insecurities on her sleeve, so he had trouble believing that she suddenly wanted to get shredded like Schwarzenegger just because they had gotten attacked last fall—they had been through much worse since then.

Besides, they had both walked away from everything almost unscathed. Delilah was the one in a coma.

Bree hissed through clenched teeth as she pushed the ninety pounds up again. Relic nearly grabbed the bar when he saw it shake, but relaxed as she regained control and began another rep.

Thinking of Delilah Crane awoke a sleeping guilt within Relic. They hadn't been to visit her in the ICU at St. Regis in like a week, because even though the doctors said she was stable, Relic could hardly bear to see his friend like that—especially since he was the one who'd shoved an ensorcelled drumstick into her chest.

Relic, a distant voice said. *Relic...*

He was spacing out again. It had been happening all summer. Ever since the Widow stopped haunting his dreams, he had become afflicted with random bouts of drifting off while wide awake. And it had been getting worse.

Relic...

Something told him it was Delilah trying to speak to him. They were both of similar descendancy, and maybe she was reaching out from wherever she was trapped. Maybe stabbing her with powers drawn from Alternus had somehow trapped her there. Maybe—

"Relic!"

Blinking, Relic came back to the present and saw Bree struggling to get the bar up, her face twisted in fear, anger, and panic.

"Dude! Help!"

Relic regained control of his body and gripped the bar, helping her ease it into the rack.

"Bree, I'm sorry."

"Worst time for you to space out again, man." Bree let her arms fall back in exhaustion, and for the first time Relic could see just how swollen her biceps had gotten. His eyes wandered from her muscles to her yellow sports bra and he was reminded why he often didn't focus on her arms.

Bree snapped her fingers suddenly. "Hey, creep. My eyes are down here."

They shared a laugh as Relic stepped around the barbell and offered Bree a hand up. As she grasped it and pulled herself up in a move that Relic expected to turn into a kiss, Bree's smile melted and she gave him a stern look. "What was it this time?"

Not wanting to say, Relic merely shook his head and averted his gaze. "Nothing, I'm sorry. Was just thinking..."

She took his chin in her hand and turned him back to face her. As she stepped toward him, Relic expected a kiss again, but she stopped when their faces were about a foot apart and said, "Tell me."

Relic considered taking charge and kissing her then, just like the heroes do in the movies. He could escape this line of questioning by sweeping her off her feet and dragging her from the Thompkinses' garage into her bedroom before her parents got home. But images of Delilah comatose in her hospital bed crept into his mind, and Bree's lips seemed to slip further and further away until he had no choice but to relent.

He hung his head. "I think...this might sound crazy," Relic began.

Bree snorted a laugh. With everything they had been through since last year, he smiled as well, but continued.

"I feel like Delilah is trying to...I don't know, talk to me?"

Bree considered that for what felt like a long moment before asking, "You think she's there? Where your dad was?"

Relic shrugged, finding the idea strange considering Delilah's body was still here. Could her consciousness be trapped there? It wasn't something he had considered, but if she was reaching out to him like his dad and the Widow had, maybe it was possible. "I have no idea...I just keep getting this feeling. Last time we went to visit her, I didn't tell you, but I got this horrible, like, motion sickness or something...it's why I haven't been back there since."

"Maybe we should?"

Relic gave her a puzzled look.

"Go visit her. Like you said, we haven't been in a while. We should check in. Maybe see how you feel this time?"

Before he could respond, thunder boomed again outside, followed by a sharp car horn that startled Relic. Bree untangled herself from him and went to open the garage door, revealing Russ Thompkins' car in the driveway, headlights shining through the waning throes of the afternoon storm.

Relic waved as Bree's dad pulled the car into the other side of the garage. Strangely, Russ—who was typically cheerful to see Relic—didn't return the greeting as he put the car into park. Bree's dad looked deflated, getting out of his car without a trace of his chipper, usual self.

"Hey, Dad," Bree said, her voice hesitant. "Would you be able to drive us to the hospital to visit Delilah?"

Russ stared at the door leading to the kitchen, his eyes distant and confused. "Not tonight. I have some work to catch up on." After a brief pause, he finally looked at his daughter. "Has Mom called?"

Bree shook her head. "I don't think so. We've been out here." She motioned to Relic and the weights.

Russ didn't look at either, just lowered his gaze and walked inside.

After the door shut, Relic asked, "Was that...weird?"

Bree shrugged, as if unbothered. "They've been fighting. Mom keeps working late, and I think Dad is starting to get frustrated with her schedule." She moved over to Relic and pulled his face to hers for that kiss he had been wanting—but given the circumstances, it lacked the power of their usual kisses. "I'm sure after he has a couple drinks he'll be asking to watch you play some more *Resident Evil 2*."

"Hope so."

Bree patted his shoulder. "Well, I'm going to grab a quick shower. See if your mom can take us to the hospital."

The thought of Bree showering made it hard for Relic to walk, but eventually he trudged out onto the soaked pavement to make his way home.

If he hadn't been daydreaming about his girlfriend naked or admiring the sky as the storm clouds cleared, he might have heard the whispers that followed him through Greenbriar Heights.

Relic was surprised to find the driveway empty when he got home. Normally, his mom's Mazda would be there when she wasn't working, often right next to the Jeep belonging to Calvin Green, who had pretty much moved in with the Meyers at this point.

While Relic had evolved into a common form of teenager that found the idea of being left home alone exciting, he was slightly deflated as he opened the door to the quiet house. He had been hoping to pry some gossip out of his mom regarding the Thompkinses. Russ' behavior had unsettled him. If anyone in the neighborhood might know what was going on between the two, it would likely be his mom.

Unfortunately, he was left with an empty house that...smelled...musky?

He couldn't put his finger on it, but as he closed the front door, the air in the house felt somehow different. It was like stepping out into a bright sunny day only to be surprised by how cold the temperature was despite the warm and welcoming atmosphere.

His house felt spoiled somehow, and he couldn't think how else to describe it. Kicking his damp sneakers off, Relic cautiously moved toward the basement stairs. Following his nose, he breathed in the foreign presence like some sort of bloodhound.

The truth was, he didn't actually smell anything—not a scent he could identify at least—but something pulled him down the stairs regardless, and maybe the sniffing was just a way for him to normalize this confusing sensation.

There was a clear drop in temperature. Not that it was as hot as usual outside—the storm had cooled things off enough that it was currently a tolerable July day in Indiana, where it would usually have been sweltering—but stepping into the atmosphere of the basement chilled him more than usual.

As he reached the bottom of the stairs, he began to feel pretty foolish—like a five-year-old version of himself who was afraid of the dark basement. Relic forced himself to shake off the trepidation as he stepped into the familiar space. He was greeted by the calming view of his undisturbed drum set, its green finish lustrous even in the dark thanks to Bree recently dusting it for him.

His heart rate, which had been climbing as he descended into his lair, settled as he turned around, ripped off his sweaty Simpsons shirt, and pushed aside the curtains to the laundry room. The uneasiness continued to drain from him as Relic stepped in front of the tall mirror next to the washing machine.

He was still getting used to seeing himself without a shirt on and not being embarrassed or otherwise self-conscious. Patting his mostly flat stomach, Relic felt some of the chill leave his body, replaced by a warming reassurance that his sophomore year of high school might not be so bad. He had his band, his girlfriend, and a few less pounds, not to mention one less Widow haunting him.

"Relic..."

He spun around, the frozen fingers wrapping around his spine again. It was the same voice from before, the one he suspected to be Delilah's. However, it was still just him in the laundry room. He threw open the curtain and stepped back out into the basement's main room. This time, he looked past his drums and saw the broken window—the same one that the werewolf busted last year.

Shards of glass were scattered across the carpet, which was damp from the afternoon storm. Relic approached cautiously, beginning to wonder how he hadn't noticed the sounds from outside before. His neighbor Frank was shouting something to his half-deaf wife, Carol, next door. Kids laughed. An ice cream truck's crackly circus tunes played in the distance.

Summer continued out there without him.

Now, Relic was in some frozen hell that had begun to feel too much like his freshman year. As he reached the broken window, he looked around for anything that might have caused it: a fallen branch, a baseball, anything normal—*please be something normal!*

But there was nothing. Just broken glass, wet carpet, and...

Relic knelt down next to a familiar box that now looked somehow different. Had he closed it like that? The top flaps of the box were folded and tucked securely in that makeshift fashion that served its purpose when you didn't want to use tape.

He had no memory of ever doing that, and certainly didn't remember even seeing the box closed since it had found its home down here last year.

It had sat in this same corner for over three hundred days, undisturbed because Relic wasn't much of a reader. He opened the box now to reveal his dad's old collection of fantasy books. There were vibrant covers of heroes fighting monsters, something Relic could certainly appreciate, but apparently not enough to actually crack one of the old tomes open.

He did so now, picking up *The Withered Roots* and, just as he had last year, began flipping through its pages as if the answer to this strange puzzle could be found somewhere in all those archaic words. Relic came across the old notebook page that had inspired his band's name and smiled, setting the book aside near the box to show his dad.

He grabbed the next book that drew his attention, a beat-up copy of a 1980s pulp horror book called *Emerald Decay II: The Poisoned Well*. The cover showed a creepy green goblin crawling out of an old well, its eyes glowing red and its body covered in swampy, dangling growths. Next to the book's logo was an explosive call-out badge that read: "The official novelization of the Constrained Media film."

Relic remembered watching the first *Emerald Decay* film with Bree. They laughed through most of it, making light of all the 1970s campiness prevalent in early Constrained Media films. Nonetheless, Relic had more than one nightmare about the film's antagonist, the oddly named swamp goblin Shrubble Von Hellspawn.

Inexplicably, Relic became entranced by the book cover, wanting nothing more at that moment than to sit down and begin reading it. The compulsion to do something so torturous to himself—reading a book for enjoyment—was completely foreign to him, and his unease deepened.

Almost mindlessly, he set the copy of *Emerald Decay II: The Poisoned Well* on top of *The Withered Roots* next to his knee and shifted through the other old paperbacks in the box. What was he looking for? Did the answer to the question *Who broke the window?* lay deeper? He couldn't say. His curiosity had become a ravenous monstrosity, and his body was currently at its mercy.

Something caught his eye at the bottom of the box. It was a torn piece of old notebook paper with indecipherable doodles on it. The otherwise mundane discovery suddenly brought back a vision from when he was in the storage unit last year. Just like one of his "space-out" episodes, Relic's mind teleported him back in time. In an out-of-body experience, he watched his fourteen-year-old self discover the Altar Stone note in that grimy storage garage.

As he watched himself reach into the box of books again, Relic saw the small journal that was missing from the present-day box.

"It's gone," Relic From the Present gasped, causing Relic From the Past to jerk back and look over his shoulder. It took a moment for Relic to realize that he was looking at his mom and not himself, remembering that she had startled him, preventing him from actually touching the book then.

Shaking the vision away, Relic snapped out of it and began digging through his dad's box to find the journal in question.

But it was indeed gone.

Whatever had broken into his house had taken it.

Just like his past self, Relic nearly had a heart attack when Bree—who Relic wouldn't realize until later had been shouting his name from upstairs—asked, "What happened?"

CHAPTER 3

In the alley behind The Voodoo, Altar Stone despondently loaded their gear into Steven Meyers' van. It was a clunky old thing, which had once belonged to the parents of Unknown Oath's guitarist Jeff Horn before Steven bought it for only two hundred bucks last month.

It wasn't the most glamorous vehicle, but Relic much preferred his dad and Gate helping them get their gear to a show over Calvin. Nothing against his mom's fiancé, but a beat-up, road-weary utility van driven by rock legends was much more metal than a pristine Jeep Cherokee driven by a dweeb in a polo shirt.

"We'll take the gear to the school," Gate said when he slammed the van's back doors closed. "Renovations are done, so you can start practicing in the utility room again since school's about to start anyway."

Relic tried to ask his dad why he was so late getting back to the venue, or why he and Gate needed the band to play "Alternus" so desperately, but Steven was evasive.

"It's complicated," Steven said, his eyes heavy and half-lidded. He had pulled Relic aside while the rest of Altar Stone gathered near the sidewalk. "We'll talk about it tomorrow when you come over. Right now, me and Gate need to unload your stuff at the school, and then I have to get to work."

Relic had no choice but to join his bandmates as they walked toward the promise of a free meal at Rook's Home Plate Diner. They almost got past McCord's Candies before Nick started in.

"What the hell was that, dude?"

"Yeah," Bree added, addressing Relic, "I thought we were kicking off with 'Child of the Damned' tonight."

"No, I'm talking about Tyler. What was up with your voice? We just practiced yesterday." There was clear annoyance in Nick's tone, and Relic worried that a shouting match was about to break out—which wouldn't be the band's first.

However, Tyler just stared ahead as they turned the corner onto Main Street. The band had to split into pairs to let a couple in the middle of the sidewalk pass through them.

When Relic and Tyler rejoined Nick and Bree, Altar Stone's troubled singer just shook his head. "I don't know...I..." He looked at Relic, confused. "Listen...my voice is fine." He let out a low note: "Ahhhhhh. See? I don't get what happened."

Nick let out a sudden laugh. "You telling me you got stage fright at our first real show?!"

Relic glared at Nick, wondering why he was being such a dick. "Lay off, dude. The power went out anyway. It's not like we could have even played the song."

Shaking his head, Nick was not satisfied. "Still, man. I don't want to half-ass this. Either we all take this band seriously, or we shouldn't do it."

That seemed to snap Tyler out of his haze. He spun toward Nick and threw his arms out in an aggressive shrug. "Seriously?! Who was the one showing up at the last minute?! I seem to recall getting to the venue by five and unloading our gear with Relic and Bree while you were... Where the hell were you, Weber?! Smoking dope with your burnout girlfriend?"

Bree stepped between the two guys, pulling Tyler toward Relic as the three of them let another couple pass between them and their bassist. Nick kept walking, glaring side-eyed at Tyler as they crossed Ferry Street toward Rook's.

"Look," Bree said when they rejoined, her arm around Tyler's shoulder as she dragged him back toward Nick. Putting her other arm around Nick, she continued, saying, "We'll talk about how much tonight sucked *for all of us* over some burgers. Relic's treat."

Nick and Tyler offered her a weak chuckle as Relic's deep appreciation for Bree grew even stronger than he thought possible. But he still couldn't help being bothered as he watched Nick. The sense of relief that his band didn't break up right there on the downtown streets of Laramie was undercut by a strange sense of foreboding, which Relic associated with that damn hemp necklace Nick wore. Of all the mundane things to inflict such a feeling of dark despair within Relic, that simple accessory wrapped around Nick's neck managed to ruin what would have been a pleasant moment.

However, whatever power Nick's new trinket held soon paled to the awesome and terrible force that awaited Altar Stone within Rook's Home Plate Diner.

"There they are," a familiar and horrid voice called as Relic pulled open the diner's door. As he entered the mostly empty diner, Relic saw his favorite corner booth occupied by Habitual Void. Becca Reynolds was smiling wickedly at him as she held up her half-empty cup of soda. "The mighty Altar Stone!" Her band chuckled, and Relic felt a cold hatred that he reserved for ketchup and jazz rise within him. After their performance (or lack thereof), this was the last thing he needed tonight.

"Hey!" Dina came around the diner's counter clapping, clearly assuming that Becca was being genuine. "How'd it go?! I thought you guys would still be playing."

Bree calmly explained the situation to Relic's mom while the guys found a booth as far away from Habitual Void as the small restaurant would allow.

Relic's mom was quick to comfort. "I'm sorry, hon, that sucks! Tyler, how's your voice? Do you need some tea or something?"

Tyler gave her an awkward grin as he scooted into the booth, shaking his head. "It's fine, not really sure what happened. I'll just take a root beer float, thanks."

"Out of ice cream," a voice called from the kitchen window. Relic could see Rook's gruff face, offering an apologetic smile.

Dina waved him away. "I'll grab a pint next door, Rodney; these guys had a rough night. Besides, they keep bumming fries off us, they owe us. Same thing for the rest of you?"

They all agreed, and before Dina went off to get their order, she leaned over to Relic. "Please tell me that still counts as your dad's gig? I don't want to miss the next one!"

Offering her a little laugh, Relic shrugged. "Sure." He had kindly asked his mom to not come to the show at The Voodoo because he really wanted his dad to see them play, and secretly he thought it might be weird for Steven to be there with his mom and her new fiancé in the crowd. Maybe they could work up to that, but he really just wanted his dad there with zero possible complications.

That certainly hadn't worked out.

Once they were alone again, Relic decided he had to set the tone for dinner. "Okay, Bree's right: tonight just sucked. Dad asked me to play 'Alternus' on a whim, I think because he wasn't able to see us play it at the battle." The lie came quickly to Relic and he went with it full throttle. "I wanted to give him that, and I know that was selfish of me—springing it on everyone like that. I'm sorry."

He tapped the table near Tyler to get his attention. "I'm sure that's why something happened to your voice. You and I both know you didn't have stage fright like last time." He gave Nick a side eye at that, but his bassist didn't seem to be paying attention. Relic tried to bury his annoyance for now. "We were ready to go, and I screwed it up. I'm sorry."

While Bree gave him an encouraging smile, an awkward silence fell between them in which Tyler and Nick made no effort to even look across the table at each other. After a moment, Nick elbowed Relic and said, "Let's just add it to the practice setlist so we know Tyler can handle it."

Tyler bristled, but before he could respond, Bree leaned over the table and asked, "You mean 'Alternus'? Are we really going to be playing that one next time?" She voiced the question to the group, but her eyes were fixed on Relic.

Honestly, Relic didn't have an answer for that, and the question alone made him nervous. He wasn't sure where the uneasy feeling came from—he wasn't guilty of anything other than trusting his father. He had no clue what would happen if they played the song now that Cecily Moreau's wayward spirit was back in Alternus.

All he knew was that things had been quiet this summer. Hell, ever since the battle, he hadn't seen or heard about any tropes—the term Delilah and Marshall used to describe Alternians who had been able to take physical form in this world, usually as a result of possessing a person and turning them into some sort of monster.

Relic really didn't want to change that. He enjoyed just being a drummer who got to occasionally make out with his hot guitarist. But Bree's present question brought back a voice from the fateful battle of the bands.

"...he was the only thing holding Adratheon back from entering our world," Marshall had said cryptically. Those words had returned to Relic several times since then, but somehow they carried more weight now.

"I don't know," Relic replied, noticing that his bandmates were all staring at him for some sort of explanation. He saw his mom coming back from the kitchen holding a tray of root beer floats. "Let's talk about it later."

"All Scoopers had left tonight was that red velvet cake-flavored ice cream," Dina said, dropping off four glasses with a big basket of fires, "so I hope it doesn't taste too weird."

"Root beer cake, baby," Nick said, reaching eagerly for his drink and a handful of fries.

"Burgers up in five, boys," Rook shouted from the window, immediately leaning his broad face out to give Bree a grin. "And girl."

Dina began to take off her short apron, turning to face the only other guests. "How about you kids? Need anything else?"

Becca was getting up and shaking her head. "Nope, we're good. Money's on the table. Keep the change." Her voice sounded a little gravelly, Relic noted, wondering if all that screaming was tearing up her throat. He secretly (maybe a little guiltily) hoped that was the case.

Right behind Becca was her guitarist and Relic's new neighbor, Clayton McArthur. He stood about a head taller than Becca, who was about Relic's height, and his blond hair was long and swooped over to the side, nearly covering his eye. Their bassist looked like a polite kid who didn't quite fit in; Relic seemed to think his name was David or Daniel, but he went to a different school and mattered little to the Chambers High societal structure. And Habitual Void's drummer, Jay J. Lockwood ("Yes, with the first J spelled out, if you don't mind," Relic had heard the kid say before), a chubby incoming freshman with whom Relic felt a certain kinship, struggled to get his short, wide frame out of the booth to catch up with his crew.

"Should be enough for them too," Becca said as her band reached the front door. "I'll be damned if I let heavy metal royalty pay for a meal while I'm nearby." She gave Relic a sly wink before slipping out the door.

Dina beamed at Relic. "Well isn't that sweet!" She leaned over and gave her son an encouraging tap on the arm, completely oblivious to the seething look on his face. She clearly missed the condescending mockery.

"Hey, Weber," Clayton said, leaning over the back of the booth between Bree and Tyler. "Tell your girl thanks for spotting us before the show. I'll get you next time."

Nick gave a little wave. "No problem! Good show, man. See you at school next week."

Jay J. gave a nervous look as he followed the rest of his band, and Relic couldn't tell if the other drummer was scared of him or just super shy. Either way, Relic gave him a little wave and Jay J. nodded in return, smiling like a doofus.

"Seems like you guys are getting quite the reputation," Dina said, still not really reading the deflated mood that had settled in the rival band's wake. "I'm going to go change real quick, but Rook and I can give you all rides home when you're done eating."

Once Relic's mom was gone, Tyler slid his drink aside. In a low voice, he asked Nick, "What the hell was that about with the new kid? You and your burnout girlfriend scoring him weed? Is that why you were late to the show?"

Nick smiled as he dunked a few fries into ketchup, not even looking at Tyler. "It's called networking, man. Next time they play a show, who's the first band you think they're going to invite to open now?"

The thought of playing another show with Becca's band made Relic feel a little ill. But he was more focused on the revelation that Tammy and Nick were possibly dealing weed (in addition to smoking it), which didn't sit well with him. They could do whatever they wanted on their own time, but at a public venue at which his band was playing... Relic knew he would eventually have to address this.

Suddenly, a tightness gripped his chest, like the weight of everything that had happened tonight was pressing down on him—their ruined show, his dad's behavior, Nick's attitude, Tyler's voice, Becca's mockery—and he couldn't catch his breath.

That is, until he felt Bree's hand on his. He looked up into her eyes and saw both concern and comfort there; he latched onto both in equal measure.

A phone rang back in the kitchen.

"I'm going to use the restroom real quick," he told her, finally finding his breath. He squeezed her hand in gratitude as he scooted out of his seat. Dina smiled at him as she brought their burgers over, and Relic couldn't help but give her a huge grin in return—despite the night's tribulations, he was reminded again how happy his mom continued to look since getting engaged to Calvin.

The phone rang again.

Relic made his way back toward the restroom in a lighter mood, hearing his band's morale improve drastically behind him as they dug into their dinner. However, as he approached the kitchen doors, he was almost knocked over by one as it swung open.

"Oh, sorry, buddy," Rook said, using one of his huge hairy hands to catch the door before it smacked Relic in the face. He leaned around the door and shouted over Relic's head, "Dina, phone!" As Relic passed him, Rook added, "Jiggle the handle when you flush—thing's still all messed up."

Rook's Home Plate Diner was a decent establishment, except for its outdated restrooms. The men's room had one stall and one urinal, and neither worked properly. And while Relic didn't really have to go, he needed somewhere quiet, so he opened the rusty stall door and locked himself in.

Echoing a chilling moment at school during his freshman year, he dropped his shorts and sat on the toilet without the need to shit. He was relatively unsurprised to find himself hoping that one of the Luneral Dirge werewolves would creep into this bathroom as well—that kind of terror, at least, was familiar.

Whatever unknown foe was causing him to have a breakdown while he casually enjoyed a meal with his band was a foe that Relic had no desire to face off against.

As if the universe heard his plea, the restroom door opened and heavy boots stepped onto the dirty tile floor. Relic's heart froze as he heard what sounded like soft laughter. The footfalls stopped and Relic held his breath, convincing himself that he was hearing things.

"You feel it, don't you?"

"What?" Relic asked stupidly, out of instinct.

"The hexes," the voice replied, deep and smooth, like a lumbering beast in the mists that had the grace of a gazelle. "You feel them, just like I do. Crushing you...cursing you..."

Relic pulled his shorts up as quietly as possible, cringing as coins jingled in his pockets. Thoughts raced through his mind, but for some reason he couldn't yet fully understand—short of chalking it up to his own connection to Alternus—the name Adratheon surfaced and he spoke it.

"Adratheon?"

A deafening roar threw him against the wall. Relic grabbed his ears to hopefully dampen the agonizing power of that cry, to no avail. It was as if the painful noise were only in his head. When he fell to the floor, he managed to open his eyes enough to see that the boots he had heard entering the bathroom were not boots at all.

Standing a few feet from where he now lay, Relic saw two clawed feet, their black talons shining in the firelight—*Is the room on fire?!* Relic managed to wonder before he reminded himself he was staring at monster feet. He blinked his eyes to make sure he wasn't seeing things, and then it was all gone.

The pain in his head, the clawed feet, the laughter that sounded like what you'd hear while being buried alive by a maniac...it was all gone.

Relic finally sucked in a breath. "What the fu—"

"—ucky break!" Laughter poured into the bathroom as the door opened. "Best three out of five! Hold up your fingers and let me—"

The voices in the diner faded when Relic's mom's voice asked, "Relic, are you alright? Rook heard a bang or something."

"Fine, Mom." He got up, buttoning his pants and flushing the toilet (which didn't flush). "Stupidly slipped getting off the shitter."

"Don't be so vulgar, Relic."

CHAPTER 4

After they finished eating, Relic and Bree helped Rook close up the diner while Dina drove Nick and Tyler home.

"I need to swing by Calvin's to do some wedding planning," Dina had told Relic as she ushered his bandmates out the back door toward the employee parking lot. "I'll be home late." She called out over Relic's head, "Thanks again for giving them a lift, Rodney!"

"You bet," Rook called from the back.

Even though it was work, Relic enjoyed helping Rook close up the kitchen. There was something about working as a cook that always appealed to him; even though he didn't do much cooking at home, he secretly liked to watch cooking shows on TV, and it was definitely no secret that he liked to eat.

"You guys can come work nights here now that you're old enough," Rook said, wrapping up the last of the ingredients that needed to go in the walk-in. "Actually get paid for this labor, huh?"

"Yeah," Relic said, almost mindlessly. He hadn't given much thought to getting a part-time job, but he supposed he'd have to start earning a living eventually.

"I don't think you want us both here," Bree said jovially, wiping off the counter between the kitchen and the front, where food typically waited to be carried to guests. "Every time we had a show—or a big romantic date, right, Relic?—you'd have to cover two shifts."

Rook laughed. It was a booming, encouraging laugh that nearly made Relic forget about the incident in the bathroom just moments earlier. "Yeah, good point. Flip a coin or draw a straw—I'll take either of you."

They finished up and followed Rook out back to his car, which was a simple 1986 Toyota Corolla. Relic didn't imagine it was the type of car a major league baseball player would typically drive, but he knew Rook had a rough falling out since those days—so much so that he rarely even talked about it.

As they were about to get in the car, Relic thought he heard a rustle of leaves on the far side of the parking lot. When he turned to look, he didn't see anyone around. Strangely, it wasn't until then that he realized he didn't have his drumsticks.

Ever since he had discovered his abilities, he rarely went anywhere without his drumsticks. But after the show, he had just packed them up with the rest of his stuff, which was all now headed to the school basement. Shrugging off his discomfort, Relic got into the front passenger seat and Rook kicked on the rickety engine.

Not being much of a Doobie Brothers fan, Relic found the ride home uncomfortable. Bree and Rook chatted about mundane things—the latter seeming to take a strong interest in Bree's mom's work with Rothen—and Relic was left staring out the window as downtown Laramie slowly crept by.

At one time, he foolishly felt like the protector of this place, but after tonight's events he felt like he was being suffocated for his efforts. *Why do people stay here?* he wondered. *Is there really anything good in this place?*

His thoughts were dark and confused, and he wanted nothing more than an escape from them. He found his eyes wandering to the rearview mirror that gave him a perfect view of Bree. Her smiling face was a reminder that, whether he cared for Laramie or not, he and Bree found each other and started their dream band together here.

Maybe if protecting Laramie was his responsibility, then it was up to him to uncover whatever was plaguing it. Whether it was Adratheon (whoever he was), his hexes (whatever those were), or Habitual Void's terrible music (and good lord, was it terrible), he couldn't just hide from it and hope it all went away.

The car pulled to a stop at the edge of downtown marked by the Main Street and 9th Street intersection. The single red light kept Rook's car struggling to idle as no other cars passed in the other direction.

"This damn light needs to go," Rook groaned, cracking the knuckles on his massive hands. "This thing barely even deserves a four-way stop."

Relic returned his gaze to the window, his eyes catching a light on in the old Victorian-looking house near the intersection. The historic district always made him think about what Laramie was like during its earlier years, when all these huge houses were probably occupied by wealthy families holding bravely onto the fading styles of a dying age.

As he wondered that, a figure suddenly appeared in a third-floor window of that house, framed by the light of several burning candles. The silhouette was a person in a hooded robe, like a cultist off the cover of a pulp Lovecraft paperback. In that split-second, Relic imagined the figure wielding a ceremonial knife, holding it above the fresh corpse of a sacrificial lamb.

Rook's car heaved forward, jerking Relic's head. When he straightened and looked back, the figure was gone, and Relic was left wondering if he had yet again imagined something that wasn't really there.

Appropriately, the Doobie Brothers crooned about what a fool believes as the three made their way toward Greenbriar Heights.

"You want me to hang out a bit until your mom gets home?" Rook asked as Relic and Bree got out of his car. "And, Bree, I can swing you by your house."

"It's alright," Bree said. "I'll babysit Relic until his mommy gets home."

Rook released one of his infectious laughs while he started to get out of his car. "Oh, Relic, can I ask you something privately?"

"You girls gossip," Bree said, hopping up the porch steps. "I need to pee. Thanks for the lift, Rookie!"

"Brat," Rook called after her. "You know I hate that name."

"What's up?" Relic asked, sticking his hands in his pockets to fight the unease; he wasn't really accustomed to having one-on-ones with Rook. For some inexplicable reason, he was reminded of similar encounters with a man named Larry Belinsky, who would later be eviscerated.

Rook also put his huge hands into his ragged, baggy sweatpants, clearly uncomfortable himself. "So...weird question: now that your dad's back, have you seen—I don't know, either here or at his place—like, a little journal?"

Relic's heart stopped for the third or fourth time that evening. He fought to keep his eyes from straying over toward the side of his house where the replaced basement window told a long, winding story about the book in question.

"Journal?" Relic tried to sound completely oblivious, but he felt like he managed to achieve the opposite.

Rook shrugged, looking around the neighborhood as if the topic bored him. He gave a laugh that held no hint of his usual jovialness. "It's like a little notebook. I think it had a beat-up dark green cover. It's uh..." He rubbed the back of his balding head, shaking loose curls that retained their dark brown color.

He crossed his arms and looked directly into Relic's eyes. "Look, man, I'll level with you. My brother, Ricky, told me about this journal your dad had. And I think there might be some stuff in there that my family wouldn't want getting out." Rook smiled, probably trying to look kind, but it gave his face a sinister quality. "Maybe you could keep an eye out for it? And just maybe let me know before giving it to your pops?"

"Was it Ricky's?" Relic asked, not really sure what to ask. But this guy was basically expecting Relic to betray his father by stealing something of his.

Rook sighed. "It's a long story." He checked his watch. "But, hey, I'll let you go spend time with your girl—I know how rarely I could get a house to myself with my girl when I was your age." This time his laugh was genuine and lightened the very strange mood. "It'd just mean a lot to me if you could let me know if it turns up, man. And let me know when you'd like to start working in the kitchen."

Relic forced a smile and nodded. "Sure thing, Rook. Thanks again for the ride." He watched the car pull out of the driveway, his feet refusing to carry him inside until Rook's taillights were out of sight.

This night is really gunning for "weirdest night of my life."

Turning, he went inside to join Bree, hoping to find that precious escape he was craving. The basement light was on as he came into the house, so Relic took the stairs two at a time hoping to find his girlfriend waiting for him on the newly dubbed "make-out couch."

Unfortunately, Relic found her standing like a statue, her back to him, staring at the second new pane of glass the basement window had received in the last year.

"Bree?"

When she didn't answer, a strange kind of fear gripped him, one that he didn't quite understand. He was unaccustomed to feeling this kind of unknown terror while in the presence of Bree, as she almost always strengthened his resolve.

But it was almost like...she wasn't there.

"Hey, Bree?" He stepped toward her still unresponsive form. Something like frustration overcame him—not with Bree, but with the unrelenting unease the night kept dishing out for him—and he reached out for her shoulder more forcefully than he intended. Bree—

—could only stare at the broken window for a long silent moment, almost forgetting that Relic was in the basement with her. What she could only describe as déjà vu gripped her, locking her rational mind behind a foggy field of horrible memories.

Was it last year again? Had a giant wolfman just swung its paw through the clear protection Altar Stone had from the world above? Was it about to burst into her own house and try to gut her best friend on her kitchen floor while Bree groped desperately for anything that might fend off a fucking lycanthrope?

Bree stayed transfixed, the moment of discovery stretching out longer and longer as her mind continued to cave in on itself, crumbling under the weight of thoughts and emotions she had buried for the last few glorious months.

The jagged pieces of glass that remained in the Meyerses' basement window took on hideous shapes from Bree's worst dreams—mostly werewolves and vampires and other awful things that wanted her dead or worse. Each gleaming point of the fractured windowpane conjured a different fear within her.

One piece of glass came toward Bree's unblinking eye, the object in the deft hand of a doctor whose surgical mask was lowered enough for Bree to see that he had no lower jaw and certainly no normal medical license. His tongue flapped loosely from his lack of chin, slobbery and grotesque, as he warned Bree to, "Hole hill," which could have meant, "hold still." If so, the good doctor had no reason to worry—Bree was frozen in place.

The next piece of glass jutted out of Delilah Crane's gums like a fang. The dhampir appeared from behind, running a finger down Bree's exposed neck, sending unwelcome and unkind tingles all along her flesh, down to her clenched thighs. The glass tooth pierced Bree's tender neck, and blood spilled down her chest.

Why is that getting me so hot? Bree had time to wonder, before the traumatic fear once more overcame her. She felt Delilah's phantom teeth in her, draining her, and once more she was back in the basement of Chambers High, reliving one of the most terrifying moments of her life.

Bree had almost died at the hands of someone she had considered a friend—well, maybe once a romantic rival, but a friendly acquaintance nonetheless. The memory of it was like a sore in her mouth that wouldn't go away and hurt like a bitch, but she would keep tonguing it as if convinced that, after enough pain, it might heal.

But nothing was healing inside of Bree, and she wasn't sure how much longer she could keep tonguing it, trying to keep the pain to herself each time it intensified.

Finally, Bree managed to blink and regain her focus. "What happened?"

Relic, who had been kneeling over a box near the shattered glass, almost fell over in surprise. "Man, Bree! That's like the second time I just about had a heart attack looking at these damn books."

Bree repeated the question as she carefully stepped toward him.

"I don't know," Relic said, dropping whatever books he was holding back in the box and standing up. Bree thought he looked uneasy, the same way he had so many times last year. "I think Mom needs to put bars up on this thing."

"Did someone break in?"

Relic looked around, his demeanor too calm for Bree's liking. "I don't think so. I don't see anything missing." He looked back to her and shrugged. "I'll leave Mom a note—maybe she can get a frequent buyer discount or something from the window guys."

Bree offered a meager smile, reaching a hand out for Relic's shoulder. He caught it, though, and wrapped his fingers through hers. "Come on, let's catch the bus to the hospital."

The walk to the bus stop was filled with idle chatter—excitement about upcoming *Buffy* night, *Resident Evil 2*, and Altar Stone song ideas—but Bree couldn't shake the suspicion that Relic was hiding something from her again. Finally, as they took their seats on the nearly empty bus downtown, she asked, "What really happened, man? With the window."

Relic stared at the watch his dad had given him, nervously fiddling with his fingers. "I do actually think someone broke in."

In Bree's mind, she screamed as a werewolf broke through her front door. It dove toward the defenseless teens with its razor-claws slashing. Relic leapt in front of Bree and let himself get torn to shreds to save her. She cringed next to Relic on the bus as her own shrieking voice in her head threatened to break her psyche.

Bree pushed the half-true memory away before asking, "You said nothing was missing?"

Relic finally looked up into her eyes. "One of my dad's books—a notebook, I mean a journal, I think. I don't know what was in it, but I definitely remember seeing it when the box was in the storage unit." He looked at the passing trees out the window. "Now it's gone."

It always comes back to his dad, Bree thought miserably. She put her hand over his, knowing he had taken a step to share that with her. And while he squeezed her hand in return, his gaze continued to wander, so they rode to the hospital in silence.

The St. Regis Hospital dominated the entire block on the northwest side of Ferry & 7th, with its recently renovated four-story brick facade blocking out the eyesore that was the slums that sloped down toward the Wabash River. The bus dropped Bree and Relic off at the hospital's main entrance, and they held hands as they walked in, both nervous (for probably very different reasons).

Bree suspected that Relic wasn't quite sure why they hadn't been back in to visit Delilah in what felt like a month, but if he weren't a teenage boy with the memory of a slug, he might remember that his ex-girlfriend had tried to kill Bree at the battle of the bands.

It wasn't like Bree was still jealous of Delilah; the girl had her shot with Relic and it wasn't meant to be—not like her and Relic had always been meant to be. She squeezed his hand tighter as they boarded the elevator to the second floor.

No, Bree's reluctance to visit Delilah was rooted in the simple fact that the Crane girl represented a whole new aspect of Relic's life that she was afraid she'd never be able to keep up with. As hard as it was for her to come to grips with, Relic was a freaking supernatural monster hunter.

Who was she? His damsel in distress?

Fuck that, she thought, suddenly wanting to feel the cold reality of a dumbbell in her grip instead of her boyfriend's hand. But when she felt Relic's thumb rub against hers, the tenderness in his touch brought her back down to reality.

It wasn't his fault that he was what he was.

The elevator doors opened to the familiar sight of a sterile hallway leading toward the intensive care double doors.

Bree felt Relic's grip on her hand loosen and let go in return, putting her hands in her pockets as she followed him toward the nurses' station.

"Hi," Relic said. "We're here to see Delilah Crane."

The nurse—a middle-aged woman with chocolate skin and kind eyes—gave Relic a surprised look, then turned to give Bree a softer one before returning her gaze. "Oh, I'm sorry, you must not have heard. She's been discharged."

"Discharged?!" Relic put his hands on the counter. "What do you mean? When?"

"Last week," the nurse replied, checking a clipboard as if to confirm her information. She tapped a long nail on whatever she saw. "Yes, on Tuesday. She was released to a private facility."

Bree stepped forward. "What private facility?"

"I'm sorry, miss, we can't disclose that." She looked at both of them before adding, "You can speak to her father though; he's accepting visitors now."

Bree tried not to laugh. There's no way she'd want to see Guy Valentine, having spent the last several months hoping he'd never come out of his coma.

"Nurse Wilkins," a voice called from the window behind the counter, "you have a call on line two."

"I'm sorry," the nurse said to them, "I have to take this. If you want to visit with Mr. Valentine, just let me know."

"Meyers."

Bree spun around to face a familiar yet almost unrecognizable version of Officer Mindy Hayes standing near the entrance of the waiting room.

"Yeah?" Relic replied, stepping away from the nurses' station as Wilkins answered the phone.

"You looking for your girlfriend?"

Bree wished the question didn't piss her off, but it did. "I'm his girlfriend," she said before restraining herself. She cringed inwardly, feeling like such a tool.

"I meant the other one," Hayes said with a cruel smirk. She looked uneasy on her feet, leaning on the doorframe in her masculine street clothes. Bree had never seen the police officer out of uniform. "I saw her get wheeled out of here the other day. I think she got transferred over to Rothen."

"Rothen?!" Bree startled herself with her outburst, but she found the idea ridiculous. *Why would a comatose teenager get transferred to Mom's work?!* "Why would they take her there?"

Hayes nodded for them to follow her into the waiting room. She turned, walking sluggishly as she tried to dig something out of the pockets of her cargo pants. Bree thought the woman looked pretty haggard, dressed like a high school boy with her hair all disheveled. Something was certainly off with her.

However, Bree felt compelled to follow her and Relic into the waiting room. They took a seat across from Hayes, who was unfolding a piece of paper she'd produced from her pants.

"I've been keeping tabs on our young Miss Marshall," Hayes said before coughing into a fist. "I mean Miss Valentine, I guess. She came out of her coma the day before they moved her to the Rothen facility—"

"She's awake?!" Relic bolted up to his feet, startling Bree. "She came out of the coma?! Did they—I mean...does everyone know?"

"Everyone?" Hayes asked, looking up as if the question was ludicrous. "As in her adopted father?" She gave a harsh laugh. "You think he cares anymore now that her biological dad is down the hall?"

"What are you talking about?" Bree asked. "Is she, like, *not* adopted anymore now? Does Guy just get custody of her, even though—"

"Even though what?" Hayes asked, leaning forward with her elbows on her knees. "Even though her biological dad was apparently murdered? Or he just, I don't know, *reappeared* after being dead for the past three years?" She laughed again, leaning back and examining the paper, smoothing it out on her knee. "You think anything in this town works like it's supposed to?"

"Aren't you a cop?" Relic asked.

Bree saw that Mindy's mouth twitched at that, but remained a firm line, as if she were fighting the urge to show any emotion. Instead, the older woman showed the teens the creased page.

"This is a list of warrants out for Guy Anthony Valentine, age 44, residing at 1734 Ridgeway Lane, Apartment Six. Laramie, Indiana."

Bree just saw a bunch of boring legal text on the worn paper, wondering if she was supposed to be impressed or shocked and not just confused. Regardless, she could tell it was quite a long list and got the point that Guy Valentine wasn't just some petty criminal.

"I pulled these the minute I received word that Guy Valentine was admitted here," Mindy continued, still holding out the page as if it were some sort of smoking gun in a courtroom hearing. "I didn't even consult with my former partner before rushing down here to make the arrest." Mindy's arm relaxed then, letting the paper drop to her lap. "And that's why I'm not a cop anymore."

"What happened?" Bree asked, suddenly gripped by the woman's story. She grew up watching legal dramas with her mom (during the rare occasion the woman wasn't chained to her desk), and it was like she was suddenly in an episode of *L.A. Law.*

Mindy cast a glance toward the nurses' station, but the three of them were still alone in the waiting room and no one seemed interested in their discussion. She looked back at Bree and said, "Officially, I was negligent in handling the arrest...even though the suspect was in a coma and I never actually made the arrest." Her eyes became distant, staring low at something beyond Relic or Bree's feet. "It doesn't matter...they can do whatever they want around here. We're all just ants in some sick little glass case, forced to dig around mindlessly for their entertainment."

She's nuts, Bree thought, suddenly turning to Relic for any sign of an exit strategy. But her boyfriend was also staring distantly, only his gaze was toward the window that overlooked the Wabash Way slums. Bree felt bizarrely alone in the company of these two zombies.

"He's ready to see you now."

Bree snapped her head toward the voice and saw the nurse, Wilkins, motioning in their direction from behind her counter. Mindy Hayes stood up immediately and walked out of the waiting room, leaving Bree still confused but a little relieved. However, that relief withered quickly as Relic also got up to follow the woman.

Shit, Bree thought, dread gripping her as she got to her feet and followed the strange procession toward an awakened vampire. Moments later, the door to Guy Valentine's door opened and Bree—

—shrieked, turning and immediately lashing out with her arms. Relic barely dodged a wide elbow aimed for his face, and when he gave Bree an utterly perplexed look, the terror melted from her face and she reached out desperately for him. Her strong arms—*Wow, she's really getting strong!* Relic thought—were around him before he could say anything.

Feeling how powerfully she hugged him, Relic knew he shouldn't say anything. He just wrapped his own arms around her, glad this night was almost over.

Or so he thought.

Bree pulled away, a strange smile on her face. "Sorry, dude. I think your spacing out is contagious. I was just having a strange flashback to that day...you know, when," she motioned with a thumb over her shoulder, "this happened."

"The hospital?" Relic asked, and he saw her smile falter slightly at the question, but it was only a momentary thing. And yet...

She shook her head. "Don't worry about it." She put her hands on his waist and pulled their sexy parts together, as she often described the act. There was the briefest of moments before her lips found his in which Relic thought his girlfriend was hiding something from him. But as her tongue explored his mouth, the thought retreated down to the unthinking parts of his anatomy.

When she broke the kiss, Relic regained just enough sanity to voice his concern, asking, "Is everything alright, Bree?"

This time, there was no doubt in Relic's mind: the expression on Bree's face was one of pure guilt. Just the worst poker face of all time.

But as she pulled her shirt up over her head, Relic remembered that she had two extremely powerful weapons at her disposal that could demolish any rational thoughts his pitiful boy brain could conjure. By the time she got her bra off, Relic didn't care if his girlfriend was secretly a serial killer or some sort of shape-shifting alien superorganism looking to crossbreed with humans to take over the world.

Relic let Bree guide his hands to her nuclear warheads, which would soon lay waste to one of the worst nights of his life.

CHAPTER 5

The next morning, Relic awoke feeling relaxed, inspired, and relatively carefree. Given the aftermath of Altar Stone's awful debut show, there was no reason a Sunday morning should feel so...well, wonderful.

But as Relic stretched in his bed, rolling over to see the copy of *Emerald Decay II: The Poisoned Well*, he realized something that could only really be described as miraculous to him.

To understand this miracle, one must truly understand how much Relic Meyers detested the idea of reading—especially reading for pleasure. The advent of cinema and video games always made Relic feel that storytelling had evolved beyond written words on a page. I mean, you had to work to extract anything from those boring pieces of paper riddled with arcane markings known as the English language.

Seriously, Relic absolutely reviled having to read for school, and the thought of cracking a book open when he could just as easily visit Racoon City and blast some zombies in *Resident Evil 2* seemed like utter madness to him.

Understanding that deep revulsion, one might appreciate how miraculous it was that Relic had spent his final hour the previous night reading a book in his bed, for no reason other than pleasure.

Relic couldn't explain it, and as he was wiping the sleep from his eyes, looking at that eerie book cover, he couldn't even remember what had possessed him to pick the book up after Bree left.

He remembered seeing her tits for the first time last night (well, technically not the first time, but she had certainly grown since then), and he one hundred percent remembered her giving him his first handjob soon after that—something Bree had jokingly always said would have to wait until Altar Stone got signed. But he couldn't seem to remember consciously thinking, "Okay, it's time to read before bed."

Something just guided him to *The Emerald Decay II*. Maybe he was drawn to the name itself—it reminded him of the "Decade of Decay," the name commonly used for the period of time after his father's band had unleashed the Widow—or the fact that it was a Constrained Media film he hadn't yet seen.

Whatever drew him, it broke through a resistance within Relic that he thought would forever be impenetrable.

Staring at that book now, in well-rested good humor, Relic wondered if it might have been the semen. He laughed aloud. *Yes,* he thought, *that's it! The tyrannical semen holding sway over me hated reading and despised books, and Bree and I finally fought those belligerent hordes, driving them from the fortress of my brain for the sake of literacy!*

He closed his eyes and fell back into his soft pillow and—in the lunacy of being well rested and not being haunted by phantom voices—almost forgot that school started tomorrow.

"Relic?"

His mom's voice preceded three light taps on his closed door.

"Yeah?"

The door creaked open and Dina leaned in, smiling. "Hey, you want to head to your dad's early today? I need to go out with Calvin and pick out some stuff for the wedding." Her eyes fell to her son's bed. "Relic Willow Meyers!" She threw the door open and strode swiftly across his bedroom.

Relic instinctively pulled his sheets up—he only slept in his underwear and he suddenly feared she would start tearing his bed apart, knowing he hadn't washed his bed sheets in weeks.

"Where did you get this?!" She picked up *Emerald Decay II* and held it in his face as if it were illegal drugs.

Shocked, Relic could just stare. His mom knew that he had his dad's things—what was her deal?

Dropping the book, Dina locked eyes with him and leaned uncomfortably close. "I want you to tell me, Relic, and you better be honest... Who taught you how to read?"

A brief moment passed in which Relic recoiled from his mom's sudden rage, but when the joke finally landed, he relaxed and gave her a slight chuckle—she deserved more for that one, but he felt embarrassed falling for it.

"Seriously," Dina asked, taking a seat on the bed and looking at the old novel, "when did you start reading books?"

"Last night," Relic said, running a hand through his long hair, doing little to fix the bedhead. "Found it in that box of Dad's books we got from the storage unit last year."

A sudden pang of guilt dug into Relic's gut, thinking about how he hadn't told his mom about the possible robbery when he told her about the broken window. There'd been no real investigation or anything, Dina having assumed it was just some kids hitting baseballs or something.

Dina cringed back from the cover. "That little guy's gross. But, hey," she dropped the book again and gave his leg a pat, "whatever gets you away from those screens for a little bit. Now, get dressed and get whatever you need for your dad's. He wants to take you to school tomorrow for your first day."

A year ago, that would have melted Relic's heart, but now he groaned, not wanting to be escorted to high school by one of his parents. Dina left him alone to ponder how quickly life can change in a year, but as he was getting ready for his shower, she knocked again before cracking the door.

"Also," she said, presenting a thin square object in shiny green gift wrapping, "Calvin wanted me to give you that belated birthday present we were waiting on. He said the place he ordered it from had to ship it from Germany or something and it was backordered."

Curiosity piqued, Relic took the thing and shut the door so his mom wouldn't see him naked. Ripping it open, he revealed an album entitled *Nightfall in Middle-Earth* by the band Blind Guardian. The cover featured a dark lord on a throne with some spirit figure that made Relic uncomfortably think of the Widow. However, any bad memories were paled by the wonder that album

cover awoke in Relic, and before he knew it, he was scrambling to the shower so
he could properly explore the music inside.

"That's some crazy drumming on there," Steven commented as they listened to
the Blind Guardian album on the way to breakfast. "Last time I heard Thomen
the Omen play was in 1991 at this rinky-dink place in Berlin. It was a warm-up
show before some big concert they had that was recorded by this film crew."

Relic listened, captivated by both the music on the stereo and his father's
story about meeting the metal gods from some land far away.

"I mean, he was good then," Steven said, "but this sounds like he really found
his stride. Now if he'd just quit smoking cigarettes while playing." He chuckled
as he turned a corner, the van groaning under the strain of it.

"Did Unknown Oath play with them?" Relic asked, just imagining what it'd
be like to share the stage with a band that already seemed so legendary to him. He
wasn't sure if it was reading that book last night or discovering this new band,
but he was suddenly drowning in inspiration.

Steven shook his head. "We catered to a different crowd, unfortunately. Their
management had some other local act fill the only slot we might have got. But it
was fun hanging out with them. This Hansi guy can wail, right? What a singer!"

Joy swelled within Relic as he started banging his head along to "Mirror
Mirror" with his dad, living out some fantasy that just last year he couldn't even
conceive. Unfortunately, the fantasy was short-lived.

As the song ended, his dad reached over and turned the volume down, pulling
the van in to park near a small diner called Triple X that was famous for its
breakfast menu.

"Hey, man," he began, and Relic could tell something heavy was about to
drop on his pleasant morning, "I told you I'd talk to you about the show last
night."

"It's alright, Dad," Relic said, not even wanting to know what that had been all about. Aside from the most erotic moment of his young life with Bree in the basement, he didn't want to even think about last night. "We can just eat breakfast and talk about it later."

"Well," Steven said, insistent, "this is kind of important, because I don't want you hearing it from someone else." He tucked his hair behind his ears and nodded toward the diner, "And I can't really talk about it in there."

Reluctantly, Relic nodded.

"But first," Steven said, his voice suddenly straining. "Son, I'm going to need you to be honest with me…"

Uh oh, Relic thought, feeling something heavy indeed.

Steven looked back at him. "Have you been to see Guy Valentine?"

Relic looked down at his hands, thinking about how awesome this day had started out. *Why did we even go to the hospital?* Relic asked himself furiously, thinking back to that series of events that led him to having to hide something from his dad until now.

"Relic?"

"Yeah," he replied, looking up to his dad. He didn't want to start their new life together with a stupid lie that Relic didn't even think mattered anyway. "Bree and I went to see Delilah a couple weeks ago. I guess Guy had just recently woken up…"

As they entered Guy's room, Relic heard Bree gasp, but Mindy was blocking his view. When he could get around the woman, Relic saw an emaciated man casually sipping juice in the dark room. Heavy curtains were drawn over the windows, and several privacy screens were placed in front of them as if to make certain not a single shred of sunlight got through.

"You're not my daughter," Guy said casually, smiling at Bree as he licked his lips. "When they said a young woman was outside inquiring, I thought maybe she had finally come for me." He rolled his cup's straw between his fingers as he observed his guests. His black eyes narrowed on Mindy. "You don't give up, do you?"

"How would you know?" Mindy asked. "You've been under for a while now."

"Well," Guy said, setting his red drink down, which Relic suspected was filled with something other than juice. "They say comas don't necessarily stop a person from observing the world, even if it's in a dream-like haze. I seem to recall you lingering around here, sniffing through my things."

Mindy stiffened at that, and Relic thought maybe Guy really had been aware the whole time he'd been in the coma. Which meant Delilah could have been aware when he—

"I only told the nurse I'd see you out of curiosity," Guy said, reclining in his bed. Relic could see that the man didn't wear a normal patient's gown. Instead, his pale shoulders were exposed by a thin black tank top, his collar bones angular and pushing their way through his sallow skin. "If you start acting like a cop, I might get bored quickly."

Mindy held her tongue, just shifting her feet as if considering her approach.

Guy took the opportunity to turn his piercing gaze on Relic. "Meyers." The way he said Relic's name was chilling, sounding like both a threat and some sort of incantation. "I'm sorry about our last encounter." He pointed a crooked white finger at his head, pushing a strand of his long black hair out of his face. "My...condition got the better of me. But I'm told I'm cured." His smile was even more unsettling than his voice. "Thanks to you."

"You and Relic's father go back," Mindy interjected, "don't you?"

The vampire looked back at Hayes. "Is that a question, Officer?"

"I'm not an officer anymore," Mindy replied coldly. "Thanks to you."

Guy laughed. "Oh, I'm sure I've caused worse tragedies. But yes, Steven Meyers and I have had quite a few run-ins in the past. But I think we came to agreeable terms at our last meeting."

"Which was?" Mindy pressed.

Once more, Guy's smooth, hollow laugh seemed to make Relic's testicles seek higher ground. "I suppose you're referring to our little quarrel in April of '95. Rest assured, it's been settled. You can ask your partner—sorry, former partner—about the details. But my lawyers have cleared up the matter."

"*Your* lawyers?" Mindy inquired. "Or Marshall Crane's?"

Guy turned his attention back to the crimson fluid in his cup. He drew the straw up to his thin, spider-like lips (*Can lips be spider-like?* Relic wondered, because that's what they reminded him of) and declined to answer.

"Look," Mindy said, holding out the folded paper of Guy's warrants. "I know there's some sort of cover-up going on. These warrants were all removed from the system after you returned to Laramie—I know, because I pulled these before I came to arrest you. And when I was let go, I snuck back to the computer and saw they were all deleted. All gone, no records."

"Fascinating," Guy said between sips.

Folding up the paper, Mindy stepped closer to the bed. "This isn't about you, Valentine. Honestly, you're small potatoes. Sorry if that hurts your ego, but I know Rothen's involved in this somehow, and that's what I want. It's no secret that Crane's got beef with the company, and if moneybags is paying your legal fees, it seems like you might not be too hot on Rothen either."

Relic heard Bree exhale sharply at the mention of Rothen, but she said nothing.

"Just give me something, Valentine." Hayes had lost the aggression in her voice and now sounded almost pleading.

Guy set his cup down. "This is about your mother, isn't it?"

An icy silence sucked the air out of the dark room.

After a long moment of Guy and Mindy locking unflinching eyes, Relic began to wonder if they should take the opportunity to get out of there. Despite being in a dark room with a vampire that had tried to kill them a few months ago, things were starting to feel a little uncomfortable.

Finally, Guy raised a hand as if to wave the thought away. "Look, I'm sure the great Tanya Hayes is innocent of killing her entire unit—"

"Don't!" Mindy snapped, raising a finger toward Guy. "You keep her name out of your mouth. Besides, I don't even need your help. I came here to offer you *my* help since your buddy Crane will have his work cut out for him trying to close that deal with DeMono Tech before Rothen finds out what's going on."

Whatever all that meant—Relic felt so lost at this point—it struck a chord with Guy. The implacably calm undead creature looked uneasy at the mention of DeMono Tech, something Mindy Hayes apparently shouldn't have known about.

In the silence that followed, Relic heard Bree step forward to stand next to him. "What about Delilah?"

Guy's raptor eyes flicked over to Bree, the surprise melting from his ghoulish face. He looked incredibly bored as he said, "I don't know. They transferred her somewhere."

"...she's your daughter," Bree replied.

Guy only gave the weakest of shrugs. "She'll be fine. She's a Valentine now, and we," he cast his eyes on Mindy again, "aren't to be fucked with." He reached for his cup again before turning those cold, hollow eyes on Relic. "When a wayward child reconnects with their *true* father, they can finally become who they were meant to be."

Something about the way Guy said *true* made Relic legitimately shiver. He knew the asshole was just messing with him, but deep down, he couldn't help but remember all those speculations about his parentage when the Widow kept calling him her son.

Please don't let this dick be my real dad, Relic thought wildly, but stuffed the preposterous idea down before it took root.

Before any other words could break the tension settling between them, the door opened and a man in a well-tailored suit stepped into the dim room.

"Doctor Lavenza," Guy said, "I think I'm ready for my treatment. My guests were just leaving."

Dr. Lavenza just nodded and stepped around the teens and the disheveled Mindy Hayes. The man's name sounded familiar to Relic, but he couldn't put his finger on it.

"I'm sure you know where to find me if you end up wanting to talk," Mindy said, stepping swiftly toward the door. Relic and Bree had little choice but to follow.

Relic finished the story, leaving out the part about Guy trying to spook him with the *true* father talk, or mentioning the doctor—*Lavenza!* he thought suddenly, remembering that Adam Lavenza had been that stitched-together monster of a linebacker playing for Benton Central at the homecoming game last year, and his father, Frank, had been a well-known doctor.

"Why didn't you tell me you went to see him?" Steven looked at his son with a genuinely hurt expression. He didn't look angry as Relic had expected; this reaction was much, much worse.

"I don't know," Relic replied honestly. In truth, he hadn't even considered sharing the interaction with his father, since every time they hung out, Relic just wanted to be in the moment—he had dreamt so long of reconnecting with the man, he wasn't about to ruin it by talking about Guy fucking Valentine.

However, if Relic was being honest with himself, he'd realize that the actual reason he hadn't told his dad about this was because of what Guy had said about his *true* father. There was no reason for Relic to think that a vampire who had recently tried to kill him would be anyone to trust on such matters, but he didn't even want to speak the paranoid thoughts aloud.

His dad was Steven Meyers, end of story.

"I guess I didn't think it was that important," Relic added. "He looked pretty sick and didn't seem at all like he was before."

"Well, before he was controlled by Valaina," Steven said, matter-of-factly. "But he's still a prick."

"Yeah." Relic laughed, idly running a finger along the groove of the van's glovebox. "I'm sorry I didn't tell you about it. But what's Guy Valentine have to do with the show last night?"

Steven took a deep breath. "The reason Gate and I were late to the show last night is because we were trying to confront Guy about something. We think he may be involved in a cult."

The mention of a cult made Relic suddenly recall seeing the hooded person in that house downtown when Rook was driving him and Bree home from the show. "A cult? You mean the Cult of Alternus?"

Steven rubbed his forehead. "I wish, but I think this might be worse. The Cult of Alternus was mostly a club of hexers that extorted rich people...honestly, I think they did a lot of good." He gave a sardonic laugh. "Also, they kept Adra—well, they kept all the hexes in check."

"The hexes?"

Turning to his son, Steven leaned closer as if not wanting anyone outside of the van to hear. "I'm sure you've known for a while that Laramie isn't really normal. Even before," he motioned between them and then waved his hand as if to include the whole world, "all of this. But have you ever wondered why everyone seems to just, like, accept it?"

Relic didn't have an answer.

"It's the hexes," Steven said. "They're not, like, tangible things. Not like you see in movies—big stone altars with ancient carvings on them, marking some arcane barrier. But it's the same idea. There's some very old magic keeping all the bad shit in Laramie." He shrugged. "I wish I knew more about them, but all I know is that they suck, and I don't know what will happen if they break."

Two things were going haywire in Relic's brain. First off, the lyrics to the Unknown Oath song "The Remington Hex" made a little more sense to him now. Second, the dragon feet in Rook's Diner warning him about the hexes just got a whole lot more real to him.

Maybe he wasn't just completely hallucinating. The thought should have relieved him, but it instead made him feel suddenly claustrophobic.

Steven continued. "Anyway, Gate and I got to talking a few weeks ago, and we started looking into this whole hex thing. Now that I'm back, I don't want anything to screw this up." He motioned between them again. "So I just wanted to cover our tracks, right? Well, we asked around town and found out there were some rumors of Valentine being seen in strange places last week—country clubs, Lafayette University alumni dinners, the courthouse.

"We wanted to confront him," Steven said, making a fist, "but he's never at his place and we can't seem to pin him down. Gate found out that he'd been seen at a show last weekend, so we had hoped he would be at the Altar Stone show last night. I figured if you played 'Alternus,' he might react, you know?"

Relic raised an eyebrow. "So, does the song still have some kind of...power, or what?"

Steven looked out the windshield as a family made their way into Triple X. "Son, I think you'll soon realize...here," he looked at Relic, "hell, every-where—almost every song has power."

Relic held back his true thoughts—*Wow, that's corny, Dad*—and instead nodded as if he had just learned some life lesson.

Steven seemed to sense Relic's doubt. "You think that song alone is really what brought me back? You don't think there was another song you heard before 'Alternus' that made you want to get better on drums? A song you didn't fantasize about playing in front of thousands of screaming fans?"

Relic thought about the first time he heard HammerFall or Rhapsody. He thought about his shower this morning listening to his new Blind Guardian album. *Okay, corny but true.*

"A song doesn't have to open a gate to Alternus to have power. All that aside, I'm pretty sure whatever that Crane guy did at the school severed Valaina's connection to that song, if that's what you're asking."

"I guess that's what I meant—like, it's safe to play?" He certainly hoped it was, since he trusted his dad's prompting to play it last night.

Steven looked at him almost apologetically. "No, it's not safe. Alternians know that song—I played it for years there, it's like an anthem. And I'm pretty sure it'll draw them out of hiding."

Relic was struck dumb then, sitting up and motioning outside. "And you wanted us to play it last night?! Bringing a bunch of tropes down on a tiny club filled with kids?"

Steven shook his head, taking the keys out of the van's ignition. "You don't understand, man." He opened the door and got out before turning back to Relic. He exuded a sense of foreboding as he regarded his son.

"The safest place for any of those kids is wherever you are."

Tyler Richardson finished his last round of sit-ups and rocked flawlessly up to his feet. Beads of sweat trickled down his forehead and the back of his neck, his curling hair drenched along the sides. The feel of perspiration trickling its way down his toned body made him tingle, so he went to the tall mirror on his closet door.

Standing there in his underwear and pink Barbie shoes, Tyler couldn't help but smile. Last night was miserable, but today was a new day, and for once he was eager for school to start tomorrow.

Out of habit, he adjusted his package and flexed for himself, thinking that he'd have to make an effort to rip his shirt off at the next Altar Stone show and give the crowd something to see.

Thinking of the band instantly made his muscles deflate, and he instinctively reached up to his throat, hoping whatever happened at The Voodoo was an absolute fluke. He'd made a drastic decision to finally pursue singing—making a mortal enemy of his father—so he'd be damned if he would let one bad show screw things up.

A soft tap on the door made Tyler jerk away from the mirror.

"Hon," his mom said from out in the hall. "Your father and I were going to get some breakfast out this morning at Triple X. Did you want to come?"

Grinding his teeth at the thought of his dad, he went to the door and pulled it open. "Why don't you ask him if he wants me to come along—I wouldn't want to embarrass him," Tyler snapped.

Becky pulled away from the door, clearly not expecting such hostility. She was a plain woman, but her eyes were always kind and her voice meek. Tyler immediately felt guilty for taking his anger out on her.

But those kind eyes caught sight of his shoes and her expression of shock turned to one of disgust. "Take those silly things off, honey. You're not a girl."

He crossed his arms. "Apparently Dad thinks so. He got them for me."

His mom's lips tightened at that, and Tyler knew she wouldn't take the bait. Becky Richardson would never cross the great and powerful Barry Richardson. "Well, why don't you just go change and we can have a nice family breakfast. School starts tomorrow, hon."

Torn between craving some biscuits and gravy and wanting to stick it to his dad, Tyler sighed. The desperate tone in his mom's voice made it hard for him to stay angry. He turned around to kick his shoes off. "Fine, I'll be down in a minute."

The drive to Triple X was tense, with Tyler's dad going on and on about his campaign for the Indiana senate.

"Clinton getting his dick licked was probably the best thing to happen for Republicans in the last century."

"Barry!" Tyler's mom gasped, playfully slapping his arm across the car's console. "Not in front of Tyler."

Laughing, Barry eyed his son in the rearview mirror. "Oh, I'm sure our boy knows all about licking dicks."

"That's enough," Becky said.

The rest of the ride continued mostly in silence, for which Tyler was glad. He kept his eyes on the boring sidewalks of the east side. The lack of things to look at made his mind wander, curious if Relic remembered when they used to rollerblade all the way to this part of town. Back then, they always called it "midtown" because it was what they considered the middle point between their houses, where they'd meet up sometimes if their parents wouldn't give them rides.

Despite the atmosphere in the car, he smiled, suddenly even more eager for school. The thought of walking through the halls as a completely different person than he was freshman year was intoxicating and addicting. It had been on his mind all through summer.

When the Richardsons' car finally pulled into the Triple X parking lot, Tyler was surprised to see Relic's dad's van parked along the street.

What are the odds? Tyler thought humorously.

Of course, at that point, he didn't know that their dads were about to beat the shit out of each other.

CHAPTER 6

B ree spent her morning lifting weights. The guilt from last night had kept
her up way too late, and when she finally managed to go to sleep, the
familiar nightmares waited for her.

Now that she was wide awake, she spent about an hour doing free weights
before getting back on the bench press. The garage door was open to a gorgeous
August morning and she had Dream Theater blasting on her dad's stereo. She
should have been on cloud nine, but she couldn't shake the guilt no matter how
much she exercised.

Taking a deep breath as she found her grip on the bar, Bree replayed last
night again in her mind. Not the show—she could live with that—but in Relic's
basement, where she crossed a line with him that she swore to herself she'd never
do.

Bree unracked a respectable ninety pounds and angrily began her set.

One.

The broken window.

Two.

Those visions in the glass that seemed to hypnotize her.

Three. Her arms were aching, which shouldn't happen so soon with this
much weight.

Relic's face when she almost smacked him.

Uuuugh. F-f-four. *This should not be that hard,* Bree thought, slowly lowering
the bar again.

Her tits out, nipples stiff as pencil erasers, pulling Relic's hands toward them.

"Come on," Bree grunted, determined to get well past five reps for this set. Her teeth clenched as she finally fought through to the fourth. Still furious at her past self, she let the bar down again.

Relic groaned lightly as she reached into his shorts and began to do everything she could to deceive him, using such lowly—albeit, fairly enjoyable—methods to distract him from asking the questions she didn't want to answer.

"Fuuuuuuuck," Bree hissed through her clenched teeth, unable to even get the bar halfway up. "Come on, pussy! You can do this!" Her voice was strained and desperate, and she was embarrassed thinking that anyone in the neighborhood might hear her struggling like such a weakling. "Come on," she groaned quieter.

Suddenly, the bar shot up with unexpected ease as someone helped her rack the weights, and the tightness in her chest began to unwind.

"Shouldn't do that without a spotter."

Delilah looked down at Bree, giving her a coy smile. Feeling completely drained, Bree let her arms drop, breathing heavily. She felt even more ashamed now, knowing that Delilah had seen her struggling with such a pedestrian weight.

After a moment of catching her breath, Bree suddenly panicked. She spun around and sat up, looking past Delilah. "What are you doing here?" Bree got up and moved toward the driveway to make sure Relic wasn't out there for any reason.

"Relax," Delilah said calmly. Her voice sounded different to Bree, less shy and more arrogant. "He's out with his dad."

Bree turned back to her, narrowing her eyes. All the shame she felt for tricking Relic last night was now directed at the true source of all her issues. "Why are you here? I thought you were supposed to...I don't know, lay low?"

"Your mom," Delilah said flatly. "Remember?"

Bree's rage dissipated as quickly as it came. "Shit." She did remember.

After Relic and Bree had left Guy's room, they quickly detached themselves from Mindy Hayes' company. The woman made them both uncomfortable. They rode the bus back home, not really knowing what to say to each other beyond the normal, "Man, that was fucked," or, "Was he drinking blood?"

Eventually, Relic broached the subject Bree knew they were both reluctant to discuss. "Where the hell did they take Delilah?"

"I don't know," Bree said, feeling a twinge of guilt over the slight relief she felt not having to socialize with the girl who tried to drink all the blood from her neck. So she added, "I hope she's alright."

They made the best of the remainder of the afternoon, watching some *Mr. Bean* while they made out in Relic's basement. Bree fondly remembered Relic asking if he could feel her boobs and she jokingly said that he couldn't since he asked like a weirdo—but she eventually let him anyway.

Then, they had takeout with Dina and Calvin, and Bree walked home when Relic's dad picked him up.

As she took the short, familiar route from her boyfriend's house to hers, Bree felt a strange foreboding that seemed unfamiliar to her while on the boring streets of Greenbrier Heights. Well, maybe not completely unfamiliar...

Without warning, the memory of the intrusion last year froze her mid-step. The cool breeze that had been so pleasant now felt like a crypt chill, riddling her skin with goosebumps. She couldn't move; she just stared at the sidewalk in front of her.

And that's when the attack came.

Bree didn't hear it. One second she was a rigid statue, frozen in sudden and idiotic fear. And then there were claws digging into her back and what felt like several bowling balls knocking her to the ground.

There was a split second during her fall that Bree swore she saw a robed figure slip between two houses, its form barely caught by the glow of a porchlight. But then she was in the grass, struggling against more claws.

She wanted to scream, but she was too scared, and all she could do was roll over and try to get whatever dogs were attacking her to stop.

But they weren't dogs.

Bree had just enough time to think, *Skrimkins?!* and terror overcame her as she began to flail away from claws and fangs. The assailants—three, no, four skrimkins—scratched at her legs as they scrambled for her throat with chomping mouths full of crooked teeth.

Survival instinct kicking in, Bree wildly shook her limbs and rolled away, feeling herself break free of the little bastards' grip. But as she struggled to get to her feet, she looked over her shoulder and saw the crooked little hobbit-ghouls hopping after her with bloodlust in their eyes.

I'm in a fucking Constrained Media B-movie, Bree managed to think as she tripped and rolled away in the grass. She was just about to start shouting for help when she heard one of the horrid creatures give a pathetic little shriek.

Bree snuck a quick look behind her again and saw a dark figure land between her and the assailants. The faint streetlight nearby glinted off a blade in the figure's hand right before it slashed and cut a skrimkin in half. Only two more were left.

Just as she was about to take advantage of the distraction and flee for home, Bree saw a faint green glow in the form of a disc come spinning back toward the figure.

"Delilah?" Her voice was barely a whisper, but the mysterious figure threw her dark hair back to reveal the familiar pale face.

"Miss me?"

The last two skrimkins leapt for Delilah's throat, but she spun her wicked Alternian knife and turned the creatures into four pieces that fell noiselessly to the grass.

Before Bree could comprehend what had happened, let alone ask any questions, Delilah grabbed her hand and led her toward her house. "We need to get inside. Hurry."

Having no reason to refuse, Bree matched Delilah's pace and they nearly sprinted toward Bree's home. The automatic porch light came on, and Bree quietly opened the front door. Thankfully, the house was dark, meaning her dad was already in bed and her mom was probably still at work.

Bree let Delilah in and locked the door, putting her back to it and gasping for breath.

"You're bleeding," Delilah whispered, motioning to the door.

Bree moved away to see streaks of crimson on the cream-colored paint. Instinctively, she took her shirt off and began wiping it off.

"Your back is messed up," Delilah said. "We need to clean it."

Bree turned around, staring at Delilah in disbelief. "Is that...like, all you have to say?" She kept her voice low, but her shocked anger was barely disguised.

Delilah's eyes wandered down to Bree's bra, the hint of her smile touching her lips. "Get your first aid kit and bring it to your room."

Despite being annoyed with Delilah's demeanor after such a bizarre reunion, she obeyed. There was a small first aid kit below the sink in her bathroom. She grabbed it and tossed it on her bed—where Delilah had already helped herself to a seat—and closed the door.

When Bree turned around, Delilah had her legs crossed on the bed and was sorting through the first aid kit. The girl wore her typical dark clothes: tight black jeans with fashionable rips in them, revealing pale legs, and a short-sleeved black top cut low to show enough cleavage to catch Bree's eye.

Despite the stinging pain she was beginning to feel in her back, Bree was too curious about the girl's seemingly healthy appearance. "I thought you were in some private facility?"

"I was," she said, "until your mom pulled me out."

The words were a sudden blade in her back, unseen and unexpected. "My mom?!"

"Sit down," Delilah said, still sifting through the medical supplies. "You think those things have clean claws?" She unscrewed the cap on a tube of triple antibiotic ointment. "You're going to get an infection."

Bree obeyed, taking a seat near Delilah. Something about the act made her suddenly feel completely naked, and she turned her front away from the girl, making an attempt to casually cross her arms so she could cover her boobs.

"Why would my mom take you out of the hospital?"

Delilah began dabbing a cold, wet finger on Bree's wounds. "I was hoping you could tell me. That's why I waited until she was gone before coming to see you."

"How the hell would I know?" Bree heard the crinkle of bandages being opened after several scratches were dabbed with ointment. "She apparently doesn't tell me anything."

"Well," Delilah replied, as if expecting that response. "Maybe we can snoop around her office. Or at least I can so you don't have to be involved if you don't want."

Bree certainly didn't want to be involved, but she also felt weird about letting this girl root around her mom's stuff. However, she did just save Bree's life, so the reply came before Bree could give it any more thought. "Go for it."

After the bandages on her back were applied, Delilah said, "Turn around."

Hesitant, Bree did so, still keeping her arms over her bra. But when she faced Delilah, she saw the girl's dark eyes suddenly transfixed on what Bree was attempting to keep covered.

Looking down at her chest, Bree saw the subject of the fixation and her heart seemed to turn upside down. A thick drop of blood ran from a gash along her collar bone, and a trail of crimson traced the outline of her left breast, the blood now working its way down what Relic once jokingly called her "majestic canyon."

She felt almost as transfixed as Delilah watching the blood running down her sternum, remembering the horrible feel of the dhampir's fangs in her neck after the battle of the bands—horrible and shamefully exciting. Bree felt that embarrassing thrill now, half-naked and bleeding on her bed next to a creature of the night.

When Bree finally looked back to Delilah, she saw the girl's eyes still hypnotically fixed on Bree's chest. Her body was frozen and her eyes glimmered, and Bree thought she saw the girl's tongue poke out slightly between those parted, hungry lips.

While Bree contemplated ways in which she could defend herself if Delilah went all vampire-y again, Delilah's hands started to move toward a small pack at her waist that Bree hadn't noticed before. It was like a fanny pack, but more tactical-looking, as if it were supposed to be hanging from a soldier's belt.

Delilah drew out a vial of green fluid in plastic casing. Something about the feel of that thing must have snapped Delilah out of her trance, because her other hand dropped the ointment and she quickly stood up from the bed.

Before Bree could ask what the hell was happening, Delilah was fumbling with her pants and then pulling them down to reveal her pale white ass cheeks divided by a thin strip of black underwear—*A thong, dude?* Bree thought. *You're going monster hunting with that crammed up your crack?* Without saying a word, Delilah gently pressed the vial against the side of her butt and pressed a button on the end of it.

Bree saw the green fluid in the small vial get released into Delilah's—*mighty fine*—butt. In response, Delilah's body seemed to sigh, as if whatever that stuff was had cured her of some terrible condition.

Pulling her pants up, Delilah turned to give Bree a crooked grin. "Sorry about that. Didn't want to bite you again."

In the two weeks since that night, Delilah had only visited Bree two other times, and never at her house. Once Delilah had caught her at Marshall Crane's sporting goods store at the mall; the other time was when Relic had to go to some family reunion thing in the country and Bree had decided to take a bike ride down to Glen Acres Park.

Now, as Bree led Delilah back into her house, they passed a stack of CDs that Bree had left in the mudroom between the garage and kitchen. On top of that stack was Relic's HammerFall album that he had let her borrow, and the guilt from last night came crashing back once again.

That guilt presented as anger, which Bree gladly directed toward Delilah, who had caused all this in the first place. *Even though she saved your life,* Bree's more rational side told her. *Fuck off,* her dominating hormonal side kindly instructed.

"So, what about my mom?" Bree asked, getting herself a bottle of water from the kitchen fridge.

Delilah looked around the kitchen and peered toward the hall.

Bree shook her head. "My dad's out running errands. And you probably know more about where my mom is than I do."

Delilah smirked. "You sure she doesn't have this place bugged?"

After gulping down more water, Bree shrugged. "If she does, she knows all she needs to know already."

Nodding, Delilah crossed her arms and leaned against the counter with Bree. "Seems like your mom has the Rothen Corps running operations in some of the smaller towns outside of Laramie—Dayton, Frankfort, Romney, I forget the rest—I'm sure some sort of cover-up stuff. It seems the company isn't too focused around here, thankfully. So whatever she wants with me, it may be...off the books."

Bree didn't know what to make of that. Frankly, she didn't even want to know what her mom was involved with, so she didn't want to be part of this anymore. "So, you got what you needed when you checked her office last time, right? Why are you back?"

Delilah looked surprisingly hurt, but just casually replied, "Just two things. First, thanks again for not telling Relic. I don't think either of us wants him involved in anything Rothen has in store. The less he knows, the less anyone else has any reason to care *what* he really is."

Taking another drink, Bree felt some of her guilt wash away with that. She hadn't thought of the whole situation that way. While she wouldn't have deceived him at all unless she knew it was in his best interest, hearing Delilah confirm that they were protecting him made her feel better about the whole thing.

"And two," Delilah continued, pushing herself away from the counter, "can I use your shower? I had to take out a hag last night, I feel like some of her is still on me."

Snorting a laugh, Bree nodded. "You can use mine. I'll see if I have some spare clothes that are dark enough for you."

Delilah gave her a genuine smile. "Thank you, Bree." She walked past her toward Bree's bedroom before looking over her shoulder and adding, "For everything."

Bree finished her water while she waited to hear the shower running. Then, she went to her room to look for some clothes. The bathroom door was ajar, and Delilah's clothes were piled outside in Bree's bedroom.

"Oh, one more thing," Delilah called from the shower, as if able to hear Bree's presence over the running water. "You don't have to hide as much from Relic anymore. I'll be at school tomorrow, so he'll know I'm back at it anyway."

Bree felt her aching muscles loosen so much at that remark she almost collapsed on her bedroom floor. Despite the damage that had already been done—she couldn't take back that sexual manipulation used on him—nearly all of the guilt she was hanging onto that morning seemed to drift from her body like the steam now coming out of the cracked bathroom door.

Feeling much lighter, Bree moved toward her closet, but something caught her eye in Delilah's discarded clothes. The little belt pouch was open and Bree could see several vials of the green stuff Delilah had shot up into that ass of hers that haunted Bree's nightmares—and the occasional dream.

"They're some kind of steroids," Delilah had said the last night she had been in Bree's room. "Something Rothen developed using my dad's blood, I think. It's supposed to keep me from..." Delilah avoided Bree's gaze. "As long as I take it, I can control that side of myself."

Bree, hand trembling as she crouched down, picked up one of those vials.

"Besides," Delilah's playful voice echoed in her mind, the memory of her turning her head over her shoulder to admire her backside in the mirror, "it's doing wonders for my glutes. I think I can skip the gym as long as I keep taking this stuff."

Turning her back to the bathroom in case Delilah suddenly burst out of the shower, Bree inspected the vial. Her eyes became transfixed by the green fluid inside and the glass enclosing it suddenly shattered in her mind, taking her back to Relic's basement where the broken window triggered some deep trauma buried in her stubborn mind.

She closed her eyes, tightening her fist around the vampire blood cocktail. Her mind replayed that horrible night once again: Bree helpless while Relic was pinned to her kitchen floor by a werewolf, her boyfriend singing like a maniac to distract the creature.

The meekness she felt that night completely overtook her and she had almost no control over her body as she pulled her gym shorts down and injected her own ass with the mysterious substance.

What am I doing?! she thought in a panic, feeling something cold replace the sting of the needle in her butt. *I don't even know what this shit is!*

Whatever it was, though, it had to be better than just being a weak coward constantly in need of rescuing.

Bree withdrew the needle and looked at the empty vial, feeling something alien and powerful coursing through her.

Whatever it was, it made her smile. Rejuvenated, she went to the garage to finish her workout.

The Richardsons entered Triple X to a stream of, "Hey, Barry!" and, "There's the man!" Tyler stared down as the hostess took them toward their booth. The various greetings and praises his dad was getting made him almost completely forget that Relic was also here.

"Hey, man."

Tyler finally looked up and saw Relic and Steven Meyers in the booth across from theirs. Relic flashed him metal horns with one hand while the other hand was scooping up biscuits and gravy with a fork.

Smiling and nodding in return, Tyler remembered how they used to have homemade biscuits and gravy when he stayed over at Relic's house. His mom would use pancake mix to make clumpy biscuits while Tyler and Relic would make gravy that was so thick it was more like a paste.

"Well," Barry said, motioning for his wife to scoot into their side of the booth first. "If it isn't our little rock star—back to mingle around us small folk."

Tyler saw Relic's dad pop a skillet potato in his mouth as he cast Barry a cold look, his long hair framing a haggard face that reminded Tyler of some sort of Vietnam vet in an old 70s movie, just waiting to be pushed over the edge.

"There's never been much small about you, Barry," Steven said dryly through chewing teeth. He smiled warmly as he nodded toward Tyler's mom, "Nice to see you, Becky."

Becky regarded her menu instead of replying. Conversations in the diner had quieted or died completely now. Tyler felt heat rise to his face as he saw all the eyes turn in his dad's direction.

Barry didn't take his own seat, instead turning to face the Meyerses. "Looks like you've been quite the role model 'round here, Stevie. Got these boys trying to follow in your glamorous footsteps." He took a step toward their booth. "Tell me, was last night's little display the way you want your own son to spend his time? Because it's certainly not what I want for my boy."

The diner had grown quieter, but Tyler noted that many faces drawn to the encounter were more eager than disturbed, as if they were somehow in support of Barry Richardson's antagonistic presence.

"Go have a seat," Steven said calmly, straightening and putting his arms up on the back of his booth in a relaxed posture. "Maybe some breakfast will make you a little less cranky."

Barry leaned over and gripped the sides of their table with his big hands. Tyler couldn't see his face, but he was sure it was reddening. "I can show you cranky, Meyers," Barry said in a way that made it sound like he was warning both father and son.

"I think your wife's cranked me enough already," Steven said without pause.

Before Tyler could truly appreciate the jab—or get properly offended at what his friend's dad just implied about his mother—Barry's shoulder rotated and his arm shot out, slapping Steven across the face with a smack that sounded like a towel being whipped in the boys' locker room.

The whole diner seemed to gasp in unison, but before anyone could act, Steven Meyers was diving out the booth and tackling Barry Richardson to the ground. Chaos broke out almost immediately, with servers rushing to either get a manager, call the cops, or just avoid getting hit by one of the flailing appendages of the middle-aged men trying to tear each other apart.

Shrill shouts of "Barry!" from across the table snapped Tyler's attention from the scuffle, seeing his mom scooting out of the booth. Not sure what his tiny mother would do to diffuse the situation, Tyler quickly got to his feet. He saw Relic getting out of his booth as well, reaching for his dad.

Before Tyler could reach them, another man interceded and tried to wedge his leg between Steven and Barry. Both fathers had bloodied lips and noses and each got several good shots in before Tyler and Relic grabbed their respective parents to help the other man separate them.

In the chaos, Tyler saw Steven push his hair out of his face and shove his other hand into the pocket of his jeans, as if trying to hide something. However, Tyler didn't have time to give it much thought as his dad violently pulled his elbow out of his son's grasp. Barry Richardson turned a hateful gaze on Tyler, looking like some sort of maniac with burning eyes and blood smeared across his face.

"Get off me, pussy," Barry snarled, turning toward the man who had helped break up the fight as if the cutting words were meant for him and not his son—but Tyler knew better.

"You're such a nasty man," Becky snapped at Steven. Relic's dad was wiping blood from his nose with the back of his wrist, regarding Tyler's mom with a calm look of indifference.

"You haven't changed much either, Becks," Steven said before turning to a waitress. "We'll take our check." Motioning to the Richardsons, he added, "Put their tab on it as well."

"Don't you dare," Barry said, still puffing his chest out. "You're gonna need your money when I sue your ass off, Meyers."

Turning away, Steven Meyers pulled out his wallet, produced several bills, and dropped them on the table before putting a hand on his son's shoulder. "Come on, man. I don't know about you, but I'm full."

Tyler watched as Relic walked out with his father, suddenly insanely jealous of his drummer's life. When Relic gave him a quick smile over his shoulder, Tyler felt all that guilt come rushing back to him. He looked at his dad, seeing himself last year, some insecure jerk picking fights with people he felt threatened by.

For the first time in a long time, Tyler felt like crying, but he wouldn't let his dad see that. Instead, he turned back and sat down to endure the family breakfast in stubborn silence.

Later that night, Sebastian Ford heard the doorbell ring, which was odd considering how rarely anyone came by his family's house down in the Wabash slums. He paused his *X-Files* tape and went to the basement window where he could see the porch.

Even though it was dark, he would never mistake the figure who stood there. A strange mix of excitement and foreboding filled him. Regardless, he quickly went up the stairs, taking them two at a time.

"You got company, Sebby?" Laura's voice from the living room was raspy from years of smoking.

"Yeah," he answered, hurrying toward the door before his mom had a chance to even attempt getting off the couch—the huge woman had trouble even reaching for the remote when she forgot it on the end table. "We'll be in the basement."

"Okay, but not too late, sweetie. You have school tomorrow."

Opening the door just a crack, Sebastian gave Tyler Richardson a curious look. "Did you ride your bike all the way out here?"

Tyler put his strong hand on the door and slowly forced it open, not meeting Sebastian's eyes. He kicked his shoes off on the Halloween doormat that graced the entryway year-round and went to the basement stairs.

"Come on in," Sebastian said sarcastically, tucking his long hair behind his big ears. He closed the door and followed Tyler, thinking about how long it had been since his "friend" had visited. But the way Tyler was behaving, it was like they were in middle school all over again—the days when Tyler would act ashamed when visiting Sebastian in secret.

Presently, Sebastian struggled to walk as he reflected on those visits—hiding his growing erection in his pajama pants was nearly impossible. When he reached the bottom of the stairs, Tyler was already on his couch, staring at the TV screen that featured a frozen David Duchovny staring back at him.

Knowing the drill, Sebastian grabbed the remote and turned the show back on before finding a seat on Tyler's right side. The anticipation that roiled within Sebastian almost made him explode prematurely, but he played it cool and waited for Tyler to give some sort of indication of why he had come—or at least some feasible pretext for the visit.

After a moment of silently watching an episode that Sebastian had seen about twenty times, he decided to make the first move. "I heard about the show last night. I wanted to come, but I didn't want to make it weird for you. Is your throat alright?"

Tyler didn't reply. He just stared at the TV, the expression on his face completely foreign to Sebastian. His erection began to decline, giving way for Sebastian's empathy.

"Do you want me to get you some tea or something? It helps me whenever I throw my voice out."

Tyler blinked, a single tear rolling down his cheek.

It took incredible restraint for Sebastian not to gasp, but he tried to remain quiet and still. This was uncharted territory for them.

As they finished the *X-Files* episode, Tyler had cried for almost ten minutes before turning to look at Sebastian. "Sorry, I don't want to talk tonight."

"That's fine, man," Sebastian said. "Do whatever you need."

Tyler gently laid him back on the couch, pulled off Sebastian's pants, and used his mouth this time.

CHAPTER 7

Relic spent his last night of summer staying up late with his dad and watching movies, after having killed the entire afternoon listening to and talking about Blind Guardian. Steven Meyers had at one time owned most of the band's back catalog, but he said none of them really compared to their latest album.

"You know what this is based on?" Steven had asked, flipping through the *Nightfall in Middle-Earth* CD booklet.

"I thought it was *The Lord of the Rings* or something."

Steven looked at his son with a dorky grin, his lip a little swollen from the fight that morning. "Nope, that takes place much later than this. They based this on *The Silmarillion*."

The word was foreign to Relic. "Isn't that what you get when you eat raw eggs?"

Steven chuckled, looking back at the booklet. "Not salmonella. *The Silmarillion* was a Tolkien book that came out when I was in high school. Only the ubergeeks could really get into it. It was one of my favorite books back then. I read it like four times the first year I got it—three times to try to understand it, and a fourth just to appreciate it."

"Sounds like a lot of work," Relic said, thinking about the books he had brought over in his backpack—the copy of *The Withered Roots* and *Emerald Decay II*.

Oddly enough, it was just now that he thought there was an interesting theme between the two titles. They both sounded like the natural world crumbling.

There was probably some sort of intellectual correlation there, Relic speculated, but it was well beyond his grasp.

"I started reading one of your books last night."

Steven looked up again from the CD booklet, setting it aside and leaning forward in his junky recliner. The small barren apartment behind him was dimly lit by the late afternoon sun, and Relic thought his dad looked like some kind of junkie then, living in squalor with his bashed-up face and desperate eyes, as if begging for another hit of whatever sustained him. "Really? Which one?"

Relic went to his bag and got the books, only just now suspecting that his subconscious must have mentioned the books so he could finally talk to his dad about his missing (or stolen) journal. He brought the two paperbacks to the coffee table in the middle of the apartment's main room and set them in front of his dad.

"Two sequels?" Steven asked, picking them up with delicate hands. Relic was fascinated by the way his dad handled the books so reverently, like they were precious artifacts. Steven let out a little laugh. "Didn't I have the first ones in the series?"

"I don't know," Relic admitted. He pointed to *Emerald Decay II: The Poisoned Well*. "I just started reading this one because I remember seeing bits and pieces of the first movie." His finger shifted toward *The Withered Roots*, whose cover featured some sort of evil tree-mech fighting off a band of motley heroes. "This one—"

"Altar Stone," Steven finished with wonder in his voice. He didn't look up from the book, but Relic could *hear* the smile in his father's voice. "That's where you got the band name. Wow... I can't believe I didn't realize that until now."

There was a strange silence in which Relic just stood watching his father hold the two beat-up paperback books. His dad's thumbs slowly moved across the covers, as someone might do with a photo in some dramatic scene in a movie. Discomfort began to grip Relic, but before he could say anything to dispel the moment, his dad looked up.

"I'm sorry about breakfast, man." There was something in his father's eyes that Relic had never seen—not in photos of the man, or in the few appearances Steven Meyers made in Relic's memories of childhood.

It was a look of shame.

"It wasn't your fault," Relic said, not really sure how to comfort his dad over something like this. "Barry seemed to be looking for a fight. Honestly," Relic laughed, "it was kind of cool seeing you knock him down."

Steven didn't laugh, he only hung his head as he set the books down. "I provoked him. If I hadn't said that stuff about Becky—who honestly seems like a nice woman these days—he would have just done his little bully thing and left us alone." Steven pushed his long hair back. "He hasn't changed since high school, man."

Again, Relic didn't know what to say. He didn't like that his dad was taking this so hard. He was being honest—he genuinely enjoyed seeing his father stand up to someone Relic had hated throughout most of his childhood.

Steven rose then, reaching into his pocket. "I need you to know why I provoked him, because I don't want to hide things from you." He drew out a wallet—different than the one he had used to pay for breakfast, Relic noted—and held it with both hands as if afraid to open it. "I ruined my life by hiding things from your mother—and you, when you were little—and I'm not going to do it anymore.

"I mean, there *are* some things that I can't tell you yet," he continued, tapping the wallet against his fingers as he held Relic's gaze. "But I will soon, I promise." He held up the wallet now, showing his son. "For now, I can at least tell you about why I had to take Barry's wallet."

Later that night, while Tyler visited Sebastian, Relic lay awake in his bed, which at his dad's was just an old twin mattress on the floor. He didn't have as much stuff in his room here compared to at the house, but he managed to hang a few band flags (HammerFall, Iron Maiden, Metallica) as well as some posters from video game magazines. There was a small VCR/TV combo on a little nightstand at the foot of his bed playing *Walker, Texas Ranger* at a volume so low Relic couldn't even hear it. But he liked the light, just as he liked the spartan accommodations.

His mind wouldn't let him sleep. He wanted to call Bree again—they had only spoken briefly before she had to get another workout in before bed—but something about her voice made her sound distracted and antsy, so he didn't want to bother her with his problems.

Especially when he didn't even really know what those problems were.

Relic thought back to that afternoon.

"I did sneak a few twenties from it," Relic's dad had said when he revealed the wallet. His expression had all the guilt of a punk teen getting caught shoplifting. "But I figured he could at least pay for our breakfast after acting like such a dick."

Relic smiled and nodded in agreement, still watching the wallet, eager to know why his dad took it—and how his dad seemed to be a master pick-pocketer.

Steven Meyers sat back down in his old recliner as he opened the wallet. "Last month, Gate told me he saw Barry Richardson and Marshall Crane at the old Easton factory—you know that run-down place on Kossuth?" As he spoke, Steven inspected the wallet, handling it like it was a bomb. "Now, we weren't entirely surprised to see two guys like Barry and Marshall maybe working on something together, but Gate saw—or *thought* he saw—someone else with them that did surprise us. Which is the reason I asked you to play 'Alternus' last night."

Relic remembered feeling like he was in some kind of spy movie at that moment, about to uncover some sinister plot or find a piece to the puzzle. His heart had been racing.

Steven drew out a business card, which slowed Relic's heart a bit, until he actually saw what it was—it didn't seem very exciting to him, and certainly didn't deserve such a slow reveal. But his dad's face spoke differently.

Dropping the wallet on the coffee table, Steven slowly put the business card next to it, face-up so Relic could see. It was a plain white rectangle featuring some clean corporate text and a handsome man's photo. "Devon Andrews," it read, and then, "Vice President of Business Development, DeMono Tech."

The only thing that really stood out to Relic was the name Devon, who—

As realization hit him, he looked up to his dad. "Is that?"

Steven nodded. "That's the guy I paid to send your mom my money; Unknown Oath's band manager."

Relic rolled over in bed as he continued playing out the following discussion; his dad explaining Devon's role in handling the band's business affairs with their label, how he hadn't spoken to Devon for almost three months before returning to the States, and how Gate said he thought their manager had died in Madrid back in '96.

None of it really made sense to Relic, but he could tell it was a big deal to his dad. He supposed there could be no good coming from Marshall collaborating with Barry on anything, especially if it also involved his dad's estranged business partner.

Not really knowing what to think about any of it, he flipped on the lamp by his bed and pulled out *Emerald Decay II*. He was about eight chapters in and the main character, a girl named Jade, was lost in her town's woods looking for her missing friend who had snuck away to meet up with a boy. So far, Relic didn't care much for Jade, but he liked her other friend, the geeky kid named Luke who was obsessed with rocks.

As Jade searched through the woods, she kept having visions of the little goblin thing named Shrubble Von Hellspawn, who was depicted on the book's cover crawling out of the poisoned well. Something about the book really drew Relic in, but he couldn't put his finger on it. It wasn't particularly scary or exciting—if anything, it was slow and not much had really happened yet.

Whatever it was that kept Relic turning pages, he didn't really question it. He could almost hear music playing during certain scenes, and he wondered if this was how real musicians wrote songs. Maybe Bree would be able to help him put some actual notes to those ideas

It wasn't until his eyes were getting heavy that he realized he had forgotten to tell his dad about the journal that went missing from his box of books.

Oh well, Relic thought, replacing his bookmark and rubbing his eyes. He dropped *Emerald Decay II: The Poisoned Well* on the floor and flicked the light off.

I'll just tell him tomorrow.

While Relic was forgetting to tell his dad about the journal on Monday morning, Nick Weber was in front of his bathroom mirror, trying to flatten his bleach-tipped hair correctly across his brow like he had seen some modern bands do. His hair had been getting longer, but he didn't care to look like an old thrasher like Relic. Nick knew at least someone in the band had to try to look cool; if not cool, at least not stuck in the 80s.

His finger brushed the single bead that was encased in his hemp necklace resting above his shirt collar as he finished perfecting his first day of school look. He made a couple faces, turning his head to the left and then the right, making sure his hair covered just enough of an eye to make him look mysterious and unconcerned with the world.

"Nick," his dad called from the living room. "Need a hand."

Taking a deep breath, Nick left the bathroom and went down the hall to see what Doug Weber needed from him now.

Still in both his casts, Nick's dad looked like he had just survived a motorcycle wreck. But in reality, he had survived worse. About three weeks ago, Doug's contracting crew had been called in for an emergency renovation at the old

Easton plant, which had been pretty much abandoned since Nick was a little kid. Some foreign company had acquired the facility and needed to make adjustments before beginning operations at the end of the year.

The details were hazy for Nick, but apparently his dad had been carrying pipes across the factory floor when a crane malfunctioned and dropped a pallet from forty feet up where the ceiling was being repaired. Doug Weber managed to avoid getting killed, but he didn't manage to avoid losing his spot on the team—meaning the Weber household would have to get by on Doug's meager savings for the next three to six months while he recovered.

Nick reminded himself of all this when he reluctantly asked, "What's up, Pops?"

Doug didn't meet his eyes—he rarely did since the accident. He wasn't a man accustomed to asking for help. "Could you hand me the remote there? I forgot to grab it before sitting down and I am not going to try getting up again."

This was much better than trying to help his dad wipe his ass, so Nick made short work of the task with a pep in his step. Handing the TV remote out, Nick asked, "You going to be alright until Sasha gets off her shift?"

Doug gave him a confused look, glancing at the clock on the wall that read six in the morning. "You going somewhere this early? The bus doesn't come for another couple hours." His eyes narrowed. "Don't you think about skipping any classes on the first day of school, Nicky."

Shaking his head with a laugh, Nick said, "No, I just gotta meet a buddy down the street. I met him at the show on Saturday, he lives behind us in Harper Grove." Nick was impressed with how quickly the lie came to him. He had met that McArthur kid at the show, but he wasn't going to meet him now and he certainly didn't live in Harper Grove; he lived in Greenbriar with Relic and Bree.

But he *was* going to score some weed for him.

"Alright," Doug said, clicking on the TV. "Yeah, I'm good. Sasha said she'd bring breakfast if you wanted to hang out for any."

Nick headed for the door, grabbing his backpack off the nearby rocking chair. "I'll grab something at school." Really, Nick just wanted to be gone before his dad's stripper girlfriend got there. Since the accident, they'd been fighting a lot, and Nick had a feeling they were on the cusp of a breakup. His dad's girlfriends never lasted long. "Take it easy, Pops."

"You too, Nicky."

Stepping out of the house felt like some sort of spiritual experience for Nick. Their small, dimly lit home felt more and more like a retirement home or some sort of hospice facility—his dad stuck in a chair like an invalid waiting to die; meanwhile, Nick could barely eat a scrap of food in the house without feeling guilty that they might not be able to afford groceries the next day.

But the weather outside was glorious; only a few clouds in the sky, the sun hanging low over Laramie's east side, and the temperature was so perfect that he regretted having to pull the hoodie out of his bag to put over his t-shirt.

Once he had his head covered, he jogged over to the edge of Piper Lane and climbed the sloping hill that led into the trees separating his neighborhood from Harper Grove. He immediately saw his supplier in the shaded area near the playground that no one used anymore since the new one got built on the other side of the pond.

"Big day," the figure said.

"Yeah," Nick replied, removing his backpack and wondering what he meant by that—*Oh yeah,* he thought, *school, duh. He wants me to start selling to more Chambers students probably.* "I might be able to start moving some more." He drew out the envelope that held his supplier's cut.

The man stepped forward, his own hoodie pulled up over his long hair, framing a pair of aviator sunglasses and a five o'clock shadow around his jaw. He was looking around behind Nick, making sure no one was around.

Nick handed the crumpled envelope that contained just over two hundred dollars, leaving the Weber household only a hundred and fifty bucks for Nick's efforts. But he was determined to expand his clientele, starting today.

Removing his glasses, Ricky Warren took the envelope and used one finger to confirm its contents. "Not bad." He flicked his eyes up to Nick. "You ready to try for a couple more ounces?"

Trying to hide his eagerness, Nick nodded. "Yeah, I think so. I had to give some free samples at the show—like you said—but I think I got a few more customers lined up. Hoping to double that at the next show." *If we even have one,* Nick thought, remembering how bad Tyler had screwed them on Saturday.

"Use your girlfriend," Ricky said with a creepy grin. "I had a flock of girls giving out blowjobs to lure in customers. Gave them good practice for when they came to blow me—after paying me, of course." He gave a little cackle.

Nick felt compelled to chuckle with him, though he'd never subject Tammy to that. He could handle this himself—the selling weed, not the blowjobs. He felt pretty desperate to pull his weight at home, but he drew the line at taking shitty advice from washed-up rockers who thought they were still living in the glam scene.

Ricky's eyes fell on Nick's necklace. He raised a hand in a fingerless glove, pointing to the hemp band. "Good man, wearing the necklace. Keep it on, like I said—it'll mark you. We're putting the word out, so if you want to make real money," he held the envelope up, "make sure people can see it."

Instinctively touching the necklace, Nick nodded. "Yeah. Will do."

Ricky reached behind his back and produced a key dangling from a ring. He tossed it to Nick. "There's a row of lockers at the bus station off 18th Street—just a couple blocks from Chambers. That key will get you half a pound."

Half a pound?! Nick thought. Moving two ounces got him a hundred and fifty bucks. Maybe if he priced it better, he could be looking at almost five hundred. His heart was racing and his adrenaline was making it hard for him not to start shaking. But he held it together.

"Cool."

Ricky put his glasses back on. "How's your drummer?"

"Relic? He's fine, I guess. Got his dad back."

Ricky's smile faded then, but he nodded. "Yeah. That he does." The eyes behind his dark glasses were hidden, but Nick was certain they were distant and glazed over.

The weird silence that fell between them made Nick even more eager to get away from his supplier. Once upon a time, Nick thought guys like Ricky Warren were gods—touring the world, banging dozens of chicks, and making millions of dollars in the process. And while he still had a certain level of respect for the man whose withered shadow stood before him, he didn't really care to hang out with him.

Before Nick could think of anything to say that might let him casually exit this uncomfortable encounter, Ricky—still seemingly in a trance—said, "I used to think he was the dragon, man. This whole time, I thought it was him."

What the hell is he talking about? Nick actually took a step away then, unconcerned with any casualness about his exit. He just wanted to be gone.

Ricky straightened, tucking the money into the pocket of his tight, ragged jeans. His trademark smile locked onto Nick. "Same time next week, dude." He turned then and sauntered off.

"And like I said," Ricky sang out in some random melody, "let them see that necklace so we can both get riiiiiiiiiiich."

Nick cringed as the idiot's voice echoed through the trees, his epic pipes now sounding like nails on a chalkboard against the morning stillness.

Confused, annoyed, and eager to refine his salesmanship, Nick made his way toward the bus stop where he'd have to kill an hour and a half trying to decipher what the hell was wrong with Unknown Oath's former singer.

"I can wait here until after you go in," Steven Meyers said, turning the struggling van off. Giving Relic a grin, he added, "I'm sure you don't want *that* kind of attention on the first day of sophomore year."

In his mind, Relic heard Becca Reynolds saying something to the tune of, "Hey, it's Stick and Stick Junior. Can I get your autographs?" Plus, how many tenth-grade students walked into school with their daddy?

But before he spoke, Relic randomly thought of Tyler at The Voodoo show—before it went to shit—strapping those Barbie shoes on just to spite his father. Mockery loomed over his friend and he had leaned into it, owning it. That act inspired Relic.

"No, let's go," he finally said, nodding toward the school as he opened the creaking door. When Relic hopped out, he turned to face his dad. "When you were gone, people would make a lot of cracks about you, like you were some...thing that didn't exist." He smiled as he found the words to articulate his emotions. "I actually like the idea of them having to deal with us."

Father and son made their way toward the Chambers High School entrance.

"Some crazy memories here," Steven mumbled as teenagers rushed on either side of them, dodging faculty members who sipped their morning coffee on their way toward their scholastic duties.

"Tell me about it," Relic said morosely as they walked through the main doors and waded into the cacophony of sound.

The Little Chamber was close to bursting, with most of the bus students already mingling about. Relic saw many familiar faces, with plenty of new, younger ones. A sudden realization hit him that he really hadn't considered until now—he was no longer at the bottom of the food chain.

Either he had grown more than he realized over the summer, or the incoming freshman were worse off than he was last year. They all seemed short and soft-faced; just children.

Something rose in his chest then, and he was even more glad that he decided to have his dad accompany him. Pride felt pretty foreign to Relic—he thought he had a taste of it at the battle of the bands, or when Altar Stone had their first practices. But this was significantly more overwhelming.

"Stick?!"

Relic turned at the jovial, elated voice and wouldn't have been more surprised if it had come from a man-sized eggplant wearing a cowboy hat. Principal Lana Sinclair stood with a megaphone in one hand with her other hand over her mouth.

"Stick Meyers!"

What is happening?! Relic thought in a panic. Was he in trouble for bringing his dad in? Were parents not allowed in school?

"Lansy," his dad said, Steven's voice calmer but just as affectionate as Ms. Sinclair's.

The Chambers High School principal walked eagerly over, stepping lightly as if she were sneaking up on someone. She reached up with her free hand and hooked it around Steven's neck, his dad bending over so she could manage the embrace.

"What the heck brings you in today?" Releasing his dad, she turned to Relic. "Oh, of course! Dropping the sophomore off. You ready for tenth grade, mister?"

Something about the way she asked him made Relic feel like a little kid. It wasn't the tone of her voice, it was the way in which it seemed she was trying *not* to use a condescending tone. But Relic nodded regardless; this was—in fact—the head honcho of the Chambers universe.

"I was just coming to see Gate," Steven said. "I hope that's okay? I was just going to chat with him down in the utility room."

"Oh, of course," the principal said, patting Steven on the chest. "No one goes down there anyway, so you guys can have some privacy." She pointed a finger up to his face, her own face assuming a stern expression. "As long as you come to my office after, mister. We have some catching up to do!"

Before Steven could reply, Lana spun around and raised her megaphone. "Make a path over there, Miles! This isn't a zoo!" She marched off to resume her never-ending quest to establish order in the Little Chamber.

"She hasn't changed a bit," Steven said, watching her with a smile on his face.

"Do you know *everyone* in town?" Relic asked, giving his dad an annoyed look, even though he wasn't actually annoyed.

Steven shrugged. "Seems like nobody really left Laramie after high school." His eyes seemed to lose focus as he said that and, despite the shouting and laughter bouncing off the walls of the Little Chamber, Relic felt that annoying sensation that he was about to hear some whispering voices in his head, cutting through the surrounding merriment.

But instead, his dad merely focused his eyes on something and then smiled. Nodding in that direction, he said, "Holy shit, is that Altar Stone?"

Relic turned that way and was surprised to see Bree, Nick, and Tyler all standing together by the auditorium box office windows. They were so deep in discussion that they hadn't even noticed the Meyerses' loud encounter with the principal.

Seeing them all in such a good mood together relieved some of the tension Relic hadn't even realized he still carried in his gut. After Nick and Tyler almost went after each other's throats Saturday night, he was worried it'd be up to him to smooth things over.

"You better get going," his dad said, patting his shoulder. "I'll be down with Gate for a bit—if I don't see you before leaving, I'll definitely be at D&D on Wednesday."

With that, Steven cut through the crowd of kids toward the nearest stairwell while Relic made his way toward his band. He heard the discussion before they even noticed him approaching.

"I think it'd be perfect," Nick said, motioning to Tyler. "Give our singer a chance to get over his stage fright before we open for another band again."

"I don't have stage fright, dude," Tyler replied. Relic was shocked to hear that his singer wasn't angry at Nick again; his voice sounded almost unbothered by the accusation. "Whatever it was, it's gone. I was singing along to stuff all yesterday at Seb—I mean, in the shower—oh, 'sup, Relic."

Bree spun around. "Hey!" She kissed him.

On the mouth.

Relic felt his eyes go wide as she pulled back, his lips pulling apart in what must have been a dopey grin. Butterflies moshed in his stomach.

She had kissed him.

Putting her arm through his, Bree pulled him into the band's circle. But Relic felt in a daze. They had agreed last year that they wouldn't do any PDA at school, just to avoid any annoying "Awww, you guys are so cute" comments. But Relic was secretly saddened by the decision—having only really agreed at Bree's suggestion.

Maybe the summer had been enough to change Bree's mind on the topic. Or maybe Saturday night had deepened their relationship so they didn't have to worry about how outsiders viewed them.

Whatever it was, Relic was glad sophomore year was off to a better start than freshman year.

"What do you think, man?" Nick asked.

Relic was looking at Tyler, waiting for a response.

"Relic."

Turning to Nick, he realized the question was for him. "Think of what?"

Bree explained. "Tammy's parents are out of town on Halloween and she's planning a party at their huge house. She asked Nick if Altar Stone could play."

"Tammy?!" Relic asked, giving Nick a shocked look. "She wants a metal band to play her house party? How many of her friends are going to show up to listen to music they've probably never heard?"

Nick shrugged. "Who cares who shows up? It gives us a chance to practice our live show, right?"

"He's got a point," Tyler said. Relic couldn't help but give his singer another confused look. *Since when did these two start getting along so well?*

"Besides," Nick added, his hand adjusting that stupid necklace. "I think I could probably get quite a few people there."

"How's that?" Bree asked, running the fingers of one hand over her Altar Stone guitar pick necklace that Relic had gotten her for Christmas last year while the fingers of her other hand ran softly down Relic's arm in a way that made it hard for him not to pull her into a dark corner.

The morning bell rang, signaling it was time for all the students to migrate toward their lockers.

Nick spun on his heels before telling the band, "Let me worry about that." He turned back to them as he walked backward, leading them toward the main hall. "Can I tell her we'll do it?"

"I'm in," Tyler said. Relic just noticed then that he was actually wearing his Barbie sneakers. To school. *What is happening?* Relic thought, but Bree gripped his hand and he suddenly didn't really care.

"Sure," Bree said, "as long as Relic's cool with it."

Relic looked at each of them in turn, their faces reflecting his own eagerness to move past Saturday's debacle and get an actual show under their belts, regardless of the venue.

"Let's do it," Relic said unceremoniously, imagining them putting their fists together suddenly like the Power Rangers or something.

But instead, Nick just snapped his fingers and pointed toward them. "I'll let her know." He spun on his heels again, almost tripping this time, and they made their way to their second year of high school.

Thankfully, Relic reflected, it really was off to a much better start.

At least, until class started.

"Rick."

The name didn't mean much to Relic as he continued to sketch different versions of the Altar Stone logo in his otherwise empty notebook, annoyed that he had given up on art in middle school—it would have come in handy for needs like this.

"Rick Meyers," the teacher repeated, this time louder.

Relic looked up, confused. His English teacher, a short man with a balding head, bulging belly, and thick glasses, stared at him from behind the lectern.

"Are you ready to join us?"

Putting his mechanical pencil down, Relic felt the blood rush to his face. The morning was pleasant enough that he wasn't in the headspace to start crying over such embarrassment—something that would have almost been a certainty just a few months ago—but he felt like he might already hate Mr. Hackley.

"It's, uh, Relic," he managed to say meekly.

"Wonderful," Mr. Hackley said snidely, motioning to the screen at the front of the class that displayed the syllabus. "As I said, the first three weeks of class will be devoted to one of the greatest books you'll ever read: *To Kill a Mockingbird*."

Relic's mind already started wandering as Mr. Hackley laid out the next seventeen weeks of his life. Seeing the different books he'd have to read, he couldn't help but wish that he were back at his dad's apartment cracking open *Emerald Decay II*, seeing what Jade and Luke would do to avoid Shrubble in that secluded ranger station.

"...and you'll have assigned groups to complete the project," Mr. Hackley continued as he swapped out the transparent page projecting onto the overhead with another one containing blocks of names. "Your groups are listed here, so make sure you learn who you're working with."

Relic's eyes scanned the different names, finding his—Relic, not Rick—among two other names he didn't recognize and three he did. Derrick Shuck and Otis Whaley must be new kids this year, or just two guys who managed to avoid Relic's notice entirely last year. Janice Epstein was a teacher's pet that he really never interacted with before. But the other two names were...

Delilah Crane and Rebecca Reynolds?!

After reading the names, Relic scanned the room as casually as possible. But he really didn't need to bother with trying to be inconspicuous, since everyone's heads were snapping back and forth to see who they got stuck with. Relic had already seen Becca when he came into class, avoiding her gaze as much as he could. But Delilah...

There she was, at the back of the class behind Stacy Gomez. How he hadn't noticed her before was beyond him—but in all fairness, he hadn't expected her to be back at school since he thought she just got out of a freaking coma.

She smiled at him and gave a little wave, as if she hadn't been on death's door all summer. Seeing her now, healthy and looking almost more gorgeous than ever, Relic couldn't sort out his emotions. He wanted to attribute any impure thoughts he was having about her in that moment to just being excited and relieved that she was alive. He knew it wasn't because he was into her.

Besides, he was with Bree; he loved Bree and he was almost certain at this point that he, like Forrest Gump, knew what love was. Whatever Delilah was making him feel now was a fluke, not love. Plus, he really didn't even know whose side she was truly on anymore.

"You'll have time during the last ten minutes of class to meet with your group partners," Mr. Hackley said, flipping off the projector. "But for now, pull out your composition books and spend the next fifteen minutes filling up a single page describing—in painful and emotional detail—one thing that happened during your summer vacation."

A hand at the front of the class shot up.

"Yes, Miss Epstein?"

"Can we use more than one page?" The girl's voice was peppy and eager.

"No, Miss Epstein," the teacher said. "If I had meant more than one page I would have said 'one or more pages,' but I didn't say 'one or more pages,' I said *one* page. And that's what I meant. Time starts now."

Relic clicked his pencil and without even thinking began writing about the first night he and Bree started playing *Resident Evil 2* and he found the secret Brad Vickers zombie roaming beneath the courtyard of the Racoon City Police Station. He surprised himself with how much detail he went into, describing the elation and thrill he had felt, but leaving out the part where he and Bree made out afterward.

When he was satisfied, he sat up and looked around, realizing he was the first one done. Relic's eyes shot up toward Mr. Hackley's as if worried he'd get into trouble, but the teacher was just surveying the class, and only spared Relic one brief look that may have been surprise. Relic spent the remainder of the time peering over his shoulder at Delilah, but her head was down and she was focused on whatever she was writing.

Something made Relic desperate to read her page, as if it held some clue as to where she had been. If his mind had been functioning normally, he would have just planned to ask her, but panic was settling in once more and his mind told him only the most drastic measures would do.

"Pencils down," Mr. Hackley announced. "Put it down, Miss Epstein. Now, for the next ten minutes, I want you to exchange composition books with someone in your group—you remember who those individuals are, yes? Read your partner's work, and on the next page in their composition book write your notes. These notes can be general thoughts, suggestions, corrections, or any other form of responses." He jerked his head to the opposite side of class. "Understood? Alright, you have two minutes to exchange books. Starting now."

Relic spun around in his seat, hoping to catch Delilah's eye. She was already standing up, eyes fixed on him and moving between the desk rows to get to him. But just as Relic was standing up, Becca Reynolds appeared as if from nowhere. She held her book out to Relic. "Hope mine's not too boring for you, rock star. I don't have a famous dad or anything." Her smile was as vile as ever.

Looking over Becca's shoulder, he saw that Delilah had already been confronted with one of the other guys in their group. *Shit.* Relic seethed internally as he held out his book for Becca, taking hers and returning to his seat before she could say anything else.

He hadn't known they were going to trade in the middle of class; he might have tried to write something more profound than a session of playing a survival horror video game.

"Your ten-minute reviews start now," Mr. Hackley said.

Reluctantly, Relic flipped open Becca's book and as he read, true fear gripped him, twisting his insides in a way he didn't know was possible while sitting in a brightly lit classroom surrounded by peers.

Her handwriting was sloppy, but each instance of Adratheon's name was clear enough to make Relic's heart race faster and faster.

CHAPTER 8

By the time Relic met with his assigned group at the end of English class, he must have been visibly pale from reading Becca's composition book, because Janice Epstein asked if he was okay as they walked toward the rest of their group.

"Do you need to use my inhaler?" she asked, pulling it out of the pocket of her yellow overalls. "I have alcohol wipes so you won't get germs."

"I'm fine," Relic said, his eyes now fixed on Delilah as she gave him the slightest of smiles. She was still at her desk, and Relic tried to step away from Janice as he walked toward her, wanting at least a moment to talk to her before the whole group convened.

But Becca slid into view, pulling a chair up to Delilah's desk, upon which she placed Relic's composition book. She looked at him, as if she knew perfectly well how much her book had unsettled him. And suddenly he wanted Becca alone instead of Delilah so he could figure out what she knew about Adratheon.

Hope was lost as the other two members of the group joined the girls just as Relic and Janice got there.

"Good news, everyone!" Janice's voice was chipper and unrestrained by the moodiness most teens had developed by this time in their high school career. "I've read *To Kill a Mockingbird* four times—twice this summer—so whatever our assignment is, I think we'll be ready."

"Badass," one of the guys said—Derrick Shuck, Relic guessed, having no other clues to go off other than Otis seemed like a country name and the other guy wore work boots and a tucked-in flannel shirt—giving Janice a thumbs-up and a shy smile. *He likes her,* Relic thought, as if his mind craved some everyday teenage drama over the alternatives that Becca and Delilah had in store for him.

"I'm Otis, by the way," the other guy said, confirming Relic's suspicions with the introduction and a thick country accent. "My family just moved up here over the summer."

"Nice to meet you, Otis," Janice said, chipper as ever. "I'm Janice Epstein."

Relic gave a wave. "I'm Relic."

"Meyers," Becca finished for him. "As in Steven Meyers' son." She gestured toward Relic while giving Otis a wide-eyed smile. "Your first Laramie celebrity."

Otis nodded, raising his eyebrows and looking between Becca and Relic as if he were expected to say something to mark the occasion. "Neato."

Relic motioned back to Becca. "And this is Becca, your first Laramie smartass."

The group shared a chuckle, with Becca laughing the loudest, much to Relic's annoyance. He was hoping to finally cut her down a little, but she clearly enjoyed these weird teasing exchanges.

Derrick leaned toward Relic. "Your band was badass at the battle last year, man." He raised some metal horns and Relic felt some of the sting from Becca's sarcasm fade away. "Awesome drumming."

Feeling his face going a little red, Relic cocked a smile at him. "Thanks, man."

"I'm Delilah," the last group member said to Otis. "I moved here last year."

Becca spun Relic's composition book on Delilah's desk and asked, "Weren't you, like, in a coma for a month or something? After that big accident during the battle?"

Surprisingly, Relic appreciated Becca's blunt rudeness then. He spent the last two weeks since that hospital visit wondering if Delilah was even alive.

"Yeah," Delilah said, suddenly seeming every bit as shy as she had been throughout their freshman year. "A few months, actually. But apparently I came out of it fine."

"Really?" Relic asked, pointedly. "When was that?"

Delilah looked up at him, guilt heavy in her eyes.

"Oh, shit," Becca said, her voice dripping with cruel amusement, "you guys used to date, didn't you?"

Ignoring the question, Delilah told Relic, "A few weeks ago. I had to spend two weeks in physical therapy; they kept me under observation at this special facility." She lowered her gaze to her nails as she picked at them. "I couldn't have any visitors."

"They didn't have phones there?" Relic asked, not trying to hide his anger.

The class bell rang then.

"Awwww," Becca said, sliding Relic his composition book as she held her hand out for hers. "This was just getting good."

Relic angrily tossed Becca her book and grabbed his own, returning to his desk to grab his backpack.

"Relic," Delilah began from behind him, but he ignored her. His eyes were focused on Becca, wondering how he could confront her about what she wrote. He moved to follow, tempted to tail her through the hall until he could corner her somewhere. But Delilah pursued.

"Relic, can we talk?"

As they moved into the bustling hallway, Relic gave in and found a spot of empty wall before the bank of lockers next to Mr. Hackley's class.

"About what?" Relic actually felt real anger now. He had let himself feel genuine guilt for not visiting Delilah more in the hospital, and convinced himself that she was trying to communicate with him somehow from the beyond. But now that he was looking at her in the flesh, all he could see was her blood snarl as she pulled her fangs out of his girlfriend's neck.

"I think you know why I couldn't come see you," Delilah said quietly, warily eyeing students that passed.

"What are you talking about?" He didn't like how her demeanor made him feel like he was somehow in the wrong here—like he had done something deceitful.

She looked back at him with a surprised expression. "The cop—Hayes? You met her right, when you visited my dad?"

Relic was truly confused. "What about her? She seemed kind of nuts, and has some sort of problem with Rothen, but she didn't seem to care about me or Bree being there."

Delilah leaned closer to him. "She *is* nuts—she got fired from the force because she's trying to...I dunno, expose Rothen or something. And if she sees us hanging out or—who knows—even just talking on the phone, she'll probably start coming after you too."

"How do you know all this?" Relic felt like he walked into a theater in the middle of a spy thriller and had no idea what was happening.

"Algebra can suck my balls."

Relic turned just to meet Bree's lips as she gave him a kiss—again, pretty much in front of the entire school. He didn't have time to truly appreciate this new habit of hers, since he was more focused on her lack of surprise to see Delilah.

"How was English?" Bree's eyes looked from Relic to Delilah, back to Relic.

"Did you know she was here?" Relic asked Bree.

There was a sudden shift in Bree's eyes, as if the question had broken some sort of spell that had taken control of his girlfriend and made her eager to flaunt their relationship, as well as forget that Delilah had been essentially missing for the past two weeks.

"We bumped into each other in the bathroom already," Delilah said. "I explained everything to her before class."

Relic turned back to Delilah. "Care to explain everything to me then?" But even as he asked that, he caught a glimpse of Becca Reynolds down the hall. She was fixing her swooped-over hair in a mirror hanging from her locker door, and it didn't look like anyone else was nearby.

This might be his only chance.

"Never mind," Relic said, reaching out an arm for Bree as he told Delilah, "we'll talk about it at lunch. I need to get my chemistry book from my locker." He gripped Bree's shoulder and pulled her along.

"See you guys then," Delilah called after them.

"What's wrong?" Bree asked, noticing how he was focused on something down the hall.

"I need to ask Becca something."

Scoffing, Bree asked, "Becca Reynolds?! Ask her what, if she knows what a key is? My ears are still aching from her *singing* on Saturday."

Relic couldn't help but smile at that, liking that Bree seemed to detest the girl as much as he did. "I need you to do me a favor. Could you go down to the practice area and get my drumsticks?"

He felt her stop short and his arm suddenly seemed like it was wrapped around a tree, pulling him to a stop as well. *Man, she's strong*, he thought, not for the first time.

"What is it? Is something here?"

Relic smiled, shaking his head while sneaking another look at Becca to make sure he could still catch her. "No, it's just...I feel nervous without them. And Becca said something that just made me... Well, I'd just feel better if I had them, you know?"

"Well, class is about to start," she replied. "I don't know if I have time to get down there. You sure nothing's wrong? Can I just grab them after and get them to you at lunch?"

He kissed her. "That'd rule. Thanks, babe."

He had never called her "babe" before, but Bree smiled at it and said, "Tell Becca to stop hassling my man, alright?"

Relic chuckled. "See you at lunch."

They went in opposite directions and Relic saw Becca had turned away from her locker and began walking the opposite direction. The class bell rang and Relic cursed as he broke into a speedwalk to catch up to her.

Being late to his first day of chemistry wasn't on his docket, but he turned toward the stairwell and committed to catching Becca on the landing.

"Hey, Becca."

She turned, a smile splitting her obnoxious face. "Little Stick Meyers, wassup?"

Relic stepped closer to her than he was comfortable with, but he wanted her to step back away from the stairs. And she did, assuming a calm posture leaning against the railing.

"Your writing," he said, not sure how to begin. "Where'd you come up with that?"

She narrowed her eyes, the smile fading slightly. "What do you mean? It was just like a dream I had."

Relic noticed a change in Becca's voice, as if she were doubting herself. "A dream?"

Her eyes seemed to lose focus there, not looking at him but looking *through* him as she said, "Well, I guess not a dream. Maybe like a daydream?" She focused again on Relic's gaze, then shrugged. "I don't know. I mean, I know it's not as cool as playing *Resident Evil 2* in my basement, but it just kind of stuck with me."

Relic almost told her that he had nearly an identical experience in the restroom at Rook's Home Plate Diner just after Becca and her band had left. But he really didn't know what good that would do.

"We done then?"

Relic blinked, then stepped away as if to release her from his interrogation. He wasn't satisfied, but didn't think he should let her in on anything until he understood it more.

As she descended the stairs, she turned to give Relic one more smile. "If that Adratheon stuff gets you excited, wait until you hear the song we wrote about it at Tammy's party. I think you guys are supposed to open for us."

Something sank in Relic's stomach then, and he swore he heard that damn voice again.

"Relic...can you see?"

"No!"

Becca gave him a stunned look as she turned from the stairwell down the hall. Before her face completely disappeared, she called, "Fine, we'll open for you guys then."

After history class, Bree hurried downstairs toward the maintenance room. She still felt weird after yesterday's dose of Delilah's super serum. Her legs craved more stairs when she reached the bottom, and she momentarily considered bailing on this current task so she could go for a jog outside or sneak into the school weight room.

But no, she wouldn't screw Relic like that. Although, the thought of *screwing* Relic had been dominating her mind all freaking day, and now she worried that she might be getting turned on for the fifth time today—and it wasn't even noon yet. She shook her head of bushy red hair and tried to focus her thoughts on the task at hand.

First I get his drumsticks, then I figure out how to ravage him. Maybe after Buffy *night tomorrow...*

The downstairs halls were fairly vacant, with only a few students scrambling to either art or industrial tech. Bree was in such a hurry that she hadn't even thought about what happened down here at the end of freshman year, and as she rounded the corner toward the maintenance room her breath caught in her throat.

Immediately, she felt Delilah's teeth in her neck again, the feeling of inevitable death seeping into her body as if it were a poison released by the dhampir's venomous fangs. The world seemed to shatter like glass then—like the glass in Relic's basement window—the jagged lines splitting the hallway into different shapes that meant only to harm/rape/maim/kill her.

Her chest felt like it was caving in all of a sudden and she slipped her backpack from her shoulder and reached for the concrete wall nearby. She sucked in desperate, wheezing gasps of air.

Get it together, Bree, she told herself, gripping her left hand into a tight fist. *You're strong now. These fucking monsters don't know who they're messing with.* She continued to suck in air, but couldn't seem to catch her breath. *Come on!*

She turned, bracing her stiff body with her left hand on the wall and pulling back her right fist before slamming it into the concrete.

Snap out of it, you pussy! She punched the wall again. The feel of her fist hitting that concrete wasn't pain. It wasn't pleasure either, necessarily, but it was *real*, not some pretend thing to fear. It wasn't the past or the future. It was present.

After punching the wall a third time, Bree felt the pressure release from her chest and she sucked down a glorious, steady breath that eased the tension in her body. Closing her eyes and resting her forehead against the bumpy yellow stone, she felt a strange ecstasy, as if she had beaten the shit out of this...whatever it was. PTSD? Paranoia? Insecurity?

Bree wasn't a psychiatrist, but she knew whatever the feelings were, they were doing her no good and they deserved to have their collective ass kicked. After another few breaths, she pushed herself from the cool concrete and was stunned to see a splatter of blood on the yellow stripe that ran along the wall between the two green stripes.

Her right hand was covered in blood, front and back. *What the...?* She inspected her knuckles and saw that she had busted them open when punching the wall. *How did I not feel that?*

As if in response to her own question, she became dimly aware of the foreign substance flowing through her veins. It was as if she could literally *feel* the stuff working its way through her body. Looking down the hall either way, she was relieved to see that she was still alone, and even more relieved to realize she was right next to the girls' restroom.

Taking a few moments to clean up her hand as best she could—*Maybe Gate has a first aid kit in his office,* she wondered—Bree took a handful of damp paper towels to clean her blood off the wall. Then, as if the whole experience had been some normal daily occurrence, Bree went back about her task.

The door to the maintenance room was ajar and Bree approached holding her wounded hand in a wad of paper towels. However, before she could even reach for the door handle, she heard Steven Meyers inside, as if he was just now breaking a long silence.

"We have to try, right?" Relic's dad sounded tired and worried. "We can't just wait around and see what happens. You know how that played out last time."

"I'm not saying we don't try," replied Gate, but his voice had lost some of its commanding presence. She had noticed that about the man; he was quick to bend to Steven's leadership, as if he were the sidekick. She found that frustrating, since Gate had done so much to hold down the fort for Steven. "But why can't we just tell him—he can help, right?"

"No," Steven said. "This is my mess, and I'm cleaning it up. He's a sophomore in high school, man. He needs to drink a beer, get laid, fail some classes. Not go up against a fucking cult trying to control a demigod."

Marshall, Bree thought, remembering at the hospital when Mindy Hayes had said something about Marshall Crane paying for Guy Valentine's medical bills. *Are both of Delilah's dads in a cult?! And if so, does that mean Delilah is in the cult?*

Bree's head was spinning so much that she lost track of what the men in the other room were talking about.

"...I just think you could help him," Gate was saying. "Imagine if you told him, like, everything. Maybe he could do what you couldn't?"

There was a brief silence then before Steven replied, "I don't think I want to risk that yet. You know how this stuff works—knowing can lead to fear, and that's their domain. It's almost better if he doesn't know."

Bree almost scoffed aloud. *Sounds just like Delilah.* Everyone wanted to keep everyone in the freaking dark.

The silence that followed made Bree suddenly panic, as if one of them had heard something or would randomly walk out into the hall. She crept away from the door and then approached again, stepping loudly and humming so they would be aware of her just now showing up.

"There she is," Gate said with a smile as Bree slipped through the door's crack. The janitor was sitting behind his desk with his feet propped up and his hands laced together behind his head. "Shouldn't you be in class?"

"Don't start skipping now," Steven said, giving her a warm smile. "It's hard to stop."

"Nope," she grinned, "just grabbing Relic's sticks." She walked over toward Altar Stone's gear piled up near the back of the room. "It's actually time for lunch."

"Holy hell," Steven said, running both hands through his long hair. "I better go. Only meant to shoot the shit with you for a few minutes, Gate. Get back to work."

"I'm on call, buddy," Gate said, unbothered and not moving from his reclining position. "Unless some kid throws up or spills a Dr. Pepper in the hall, I do most of my work before or after school."

Bree made her way toward the door as the men continued their exchange.

"Sounds like my kind of job," Steven said. "Hey, Bree. Can I walk with you for a sec?"

Taken aback by the request, but feeling like she couldn't really refuse, she just shrugged. "Sure."

"Check you later, Gate." Steven slapped his friend's hand before jogging toward Bree. They left the room together. "I wanted to ask you something," he said when they were in the hall.

Bree cringed inwardly, knowing that whatever he asked, the way things had been going for her, she'd be forced to come up with another lie. "Yeah?"

Steven cleared his throat, and in a low voice asked, "Has Relic told you anything about—I mean, has he mentioned experiencing anything weird? Sort of like his dreams last year? Or hearing voices or anything?"

Immediately Bree thought of Relic's little "space out" moments that happened occasionally over the summer. And then her own traumatic visions that drove her to steal from Delilah. But not knowing how to articulate any of that, she just shook her head. "No. He hasn't mentioned anything."

Steven nodded, shoving his hands in his pockets. "Cool."

"Have you asked him about it?"

Biting his lower lip, Steven nodded his head with a sour expression on his face. "Yeah, but you know how he can be. I feel like he might not tell me if he thought something was wrong. He's a tough dude; likes to deal with stuff himself."

Bree smiled at that, but it wasn't a genuine smile. She was reminded of everything Relic had hidden from her last year, all the way up until the battle of the bands. Could he still be hiding stuff from her? *I'm certainly hiding things from him,* she thought miserably.

As they got to the stairwell, the trickle of students became a bustle, with rowdy teens heading for the glorious sanctuary from the rigors of learning—also known as the cafeteria.

"I need to head to my locker," Bree said as she stepped in the opposite direction Steven was walking.

He gave her a grin and a wave. "Have a good one. And do me a favor—just let me know if you get the sense he's not telling us something. Cool?"

Bree gave him a thumbs-up before spinning around, gripping Relic's drumsticks tightly as she speedwalked toward the cafeteria. She tried not to think about all the unspoken things between her and Relic, or the whole world-shattering-into-shards-of-predatorial-glass thing.

She drew on the strength that ran through her veins, the mysterious substance that made her crave pain and pleasure in equal measure.

Relief flooded her then, and she was so eager to be with her boyfriend that she didn't even realize his sticks had begun to glow faintly in her hand.

"Why are they even playing with us?" Relic asked Nick, too worked up to even enjoy his cheese fries. "When you said Tammy wanted us to play the party, I figured that meant it would just be us, not like an *actual* show with multiple bands."

Nick shrugged as he took a chug of his Dr. Pepper. "What's the problem, man? Habitual Void had a big pull at The Voodoo; they'll probably be able to help us pack the party."

"Then we have to listen to Becca scream," Tyler added.

Nick spun on him as if insulted. "Better than your croaking into the mic, dude."

Not again, Relic thought. The last thing he needed was them at each other's throats like Saturday night.

But Tyler seemed distracted, looking beyond Nick. Relic turned to see Miranda Cartwright coming their way, with Tammy Beck and Valerie Moore tagging along.

No no no, Relic mentally begged, *please don't sit here.*

"Tyler," Miranda snapped, stopping a few feet from the band's table, "I will only offer this once, so don't you dare come begging me for a second chance if you decide to blow this one." She flipped her hair. "Do you want to come sit with me?"

Tyler motioned to Nick and Relic. "We're having a band meeting, babe. Do you mind checking back later?"

Nick snorted, covering his nose to prevent Dr. Pepper from squirting out. Even Relic managed a smirk, thankful that Tyler both protected the sanctity of Altar Stone's lunch table and also lightened the mood that was shadowing Relic's thoughts.

"We're done this time," Miranda replied, raising her chin to indicate she was pleased with the rejection. Valerie nodded, as if the decision had been mutually agreed upon beforehand. "Enjoy your circle jerk." She stalked away with Valerie at her heels.

Tyler took a bite out of his apple before calling out, "Call you tonight, babe!"

Tammy snuck over to give Nick a kiss on the cheek. "Hey, Nicky," she whispered, as if not wanting to get caught downplaying Miranda's dramatic exit. "You guys going to play the party?"

Nick nodded.

"As long as you don't let Habitual Void play," Relic chimed in, finally taking a bite of his fries.

"Don't listen to him," Nick said with a wave of his hand. "He's just scared their drummer will start stalking him and asking for lessons after they see us actually play."

"Speaking of drummers," Tyler said, looking over Relic's shoulder.

Relic spun to see Bree approaching with his drumsticks in one hand, making it hard for her to balance her tray. He swung out of his seat and grabbed the sticks and the tray to help her.

"Thanks," she said brightly, kissing him for the third time in public. Relic thought he could really get used to this, almost forgetting all the crap that was piling up today. "Your dad said bye—he was still hanging out with Gate when I got those."

Relic felt a wave of normalcy wash over him as he set Bree's lunch tray down and spun his sticks in each hand. While he hadn't had to use them for anything other than drumming since the battle of the bands, it was reassuring to have them in case, oh, maybe a werewolf decided to ambush him on the toilet again.

"Hey, Tammy," Bree said, taking her seat.

"Tammy!" Miranda called.

Tammy whispered, "Bye, Bree," before returning to her domineering BFF.

"Guessing you're alright playing another show with Habitual Skroink?" Tyler asked Bree, taking another bite of his apple before nodding to where Tammy scampered off, adding, "At the party?"

Bree raised an eyebrow. "Oh, it's like a *show* show?" She shrugged as she tore open a carton of white milk. "Sure, as long as we get to play first this time."

"It's settled then," Nick said, grabbing his nearly empty lunch tray. "I'm going to find McArthur and talk specifics. You guys figure out what we're playing."

"That's kind of a band discussion, dude," Bree replied, motioning between them all. "Besides, Relic and I have been working on a few new songs, and I think it's past time you guys learned them."

"Sure," Nick said, not really taking the hint as he got up. "Let's knock it out at practice Wednesday." He turned and left before they could argue.

"Dude is becoming a flake," Tyler said, his mood still relatively morose. However, Relic seemed to prefer that over hot-tempered. Something had gotten into the guy, but Relic wasn't quite sure if it was comforting or worrisome. "Seems more into dealing weed than playing bass."

"Dealing weed?!" Relic tried to keep his voice down and leaned over the table. Lowering his voice more, he asked, "He's dealing weed?"

Tyler looked at Relic as if he had just asked the stupidest question he'd ever heard. "Obviously. You see who he hangs out with? That new McArthur kid in Becca's band is a total burnout, and all summer he's been hanging out at that skate park over by my neighborhood. All those pricks smoke weed out there."

"How do you know he's dealing though?" Bree asked, just as bothered as Relic.

Tyler shrugged. "Educated guess? He's always smelling like weed but I've never seen or heard of him using himself. And no way he's become that friendly without having some sort of angle—he's crossing social circles left and right."

Relic always considered Nick pretty sociable, though Tyler made a good point. Toward the tail end of freshman year, Nick had become chatty with the goths, gamers, some of the jocks, and even some upperclassmen. That had to be a boon for someone trying to deal in illegal substances.

What a dick, Relic thought, taking personal offense in Nick's reckless jeopardizing of the band over a thing as stupid as dealing drugs.

"As long as he keeps it out of band stuff," Bree said, as if reading Relic's mind. She took a bite of her own apple. Relic noticed she had swapped the usual cheese fries and pizza for a salad and yogurt. "And doesn't come to practice baked out of his skull."

"You guys mind if we sit?"

Relic looked over Bree's shoulder and saw the duo known as Autumnal Fall. Delilah and Sebastian were dressed so similarly they suddenly looked like twins (emphasized by the fact that Sebastian seemed to have grown a foot since the last time Relic saw him).

"Sure," Bree answered for the band.

"Here," Tyler said, scooting out of his chair and presenting it to them. "You can take my seat. I need to go take a shit."

Relic noticed something odd then. Tyler's dark mood seemed to be replaced with something like embarrassment, and he avoided eye contact with the newcomers.

Does he have a crush on my ex-girlfriend? Relic wondered, not sure if he should be relieved or jealous or just outright confused. They didn't seem like a good match to him, but he didn't give in to the speculation at the moment. His thoughts were too occupied by the anxiety of asking Delilah more about what she had mentioned before.

Unfortunately, Sebastian sat between them, and Relic wasn't sure he wanted the guy involved in those discussions. Instead, the four of them sat and talked about school, movies, music, and normal teenage stuff. All the while, Relic held Bree's hand under the table and forgot how complicated life could get for about fifteen minutes.

Unfortunately, trouble was waiting for him at home that afternoon.

CHAPTER 9

Walking home from the bus stop, Relic and Bree discussed the new Altar Stone songs they had been writing over the summer and whether or not they should try playing them live by Halloween.

"I honestly think it'd be better to try them out there," Bree offered, her hand still in his and Relic still not minding in the slightest. "We just need to finish the intro to 'Bane of the Worthy' and then it's pretty much done. I think I figured out a vocal melody for the creepy crawly song; would just need some lyrics."

The "creepy crawly" song was what they called a tom-heavy mid-tempo song that reminded Relic of some dark and spooky tunnel, with some gross worm-monster burrowing through on its thousands of legs. But thinking now of the riff Bree had written, he had a sudden idea.

"We should call it 'Emerald Decay,'" he told her. "You know, based on that old movie?"

Bree scrunched up her face and looked at him. "The one with the little goblin that attacks polluters? Didn't that movie really suck?"

Relic laughed. "I mean, yeah, sort of. But I remember some creepy parts. I think it might fit the vibe of the song. I've actually been reading the book the sequel was based on, it's called *The Poisoned Well*."

"Now *that's* a cool name," Bree said, pulling his arm so she could kiss him. But as they broke away, her fingers seemed to go limp in Relic's and her eyes were looking past him. "Who's that?"

Relic turned to see an unfamiliar car parked on the street outside his house. Then he saw a tall man in a very nice suit standing on the porch talking to his mom.

"No idea," Relic said. "Let's go find out."

They crossed the street and as they approached, Dina Meyers waved at them. "Hey, you two! How was the first day of school?"

The man turned around and Relic's stomach twisted into knots.

It was the man on the DeMono Tech business card that his dad had found in Barry Richardson's stolen wallet.

Devon Andrews.

The man smiled brightly, revealing the whitest teeth Relic had ever seen in person.

"You're way bigger than the pictures I've seen," Devon said to Relic. He had a British accent that sounded like it was desperate to be American. "And you must be Miss Thompkins. Dina tells me you've been almost like a sister to Relic."

"Ew, that's fuckin' gross," Bree replied, which made Relic turn abruptly toward her. While Bree could be blunt, she wasn't normally rude. *She's been acting so strange,* Relic thought, but he couldn't be sure if his judgement was off after such a bizarre day—which only seemed to be getting more bizarre.

Dina gave an awkward laugh. "I just meant they were inseparable. Still are! Especially now that they're in a band together."

"Oh!" Devon said, putting his hands in his pockets, giving him the look of some off-duty cop. "Like father, like son, huh?"

Relic didn't miss the flinch in his mom's eye. But she just motioned to the man. "Do you know who this is, Relic?"

Not wanting to say that he did, Relic shook his head.

"This is the man who kept our heads above water while your dad was away," she said, making Steven Meyers' abandonment of them seem like some noble soldier's dispatch to war. Although, in reality, it could have been viewed like that.

"Oh," Relic said with a nod, not really sure what to say other than, "Devon?"

"In the flesh," Devon said, holding up his hands as if to say he were guilty.

"Oh," Bree said, "Unknown Oath's manager? Are you here to get us signed?" She gave him a snarky smile.

Devon laughed. "I'm afraid I'm no longer in the business, young lass. But I'm sure you guys will have the chops." He turned back to Dina. "Anyway, do give me a ring if anything turns up. I'd like to surprise Steven if possible, so please don't mention I stopped by—I do like to get the jump on my wayward chums." He nodded to the teens as he made his way to his white luxury car. "A pleasure to finally meet you both! And you, lassie."

"I should go too," Bree said to Relic, pointing a thumb over her shoulder toward her house. "I need to pump some iron before dinner. Maybe go save Timmy from a well, apparently."

Relic laughed, but inwardly he was worried about whatever the actual reason for Devon's visit was.

"Why don't you come over after?" Dina called, eavesdropping from the porch. "Calvin's bringing burgers, I can have him pick up some extra."

"Definitely!" Bree called, then gave Relic a kiss that was difficult for him to enjoy in front of his mom, but he took it like a champ. "Then we'll work on that goofy goblin song."

"Creepy crawly," Relic called after her, smiling.

He ran up the porch and avoided his mom's gaze, but knew the observations were coming. "Well," she said, "you guys seemed to have a good first day."

"...and in other news," the TV said as he came into the living room, "a famous New York millionaire, real estate mogul, and aspiring socialite apparently choked to death on a Chicken McNugget. Stay tuned to find out just who did, in fact, have their break today..."

"It was fine," Relic lied, tossing his backpack on the couch. "What was Devon doing here?"

Dina sat down and turned the volume down on the news. "Oh, he was asking about some old notebook that had some stuff about your dad's band, like their early days. I think he's trying to write a book or something and wanted to check your dad's notes."

Relic thought of the stolen book—the journal of one Steven Meyers, whom Relic had yet to inform. His stomach twisted in knots like a pretzel. "He didn't say what was in it?"

She turned from the TV to Relic now, puzzled. "Just some notes about the band, it sounded like. Why? Something wrong?"

Relic tried to relax, turning toward the kitchen to grab an after-school snack. "No, I just thought it was weird he wanted to take something of Dad's without him knowing."

"Well," she said, "doesn't matter, I guess. I checked that old box of books in the basement and didn't see it. He probably took it with him to Europe and lost it."

Or someone broke into our house and stole it, Relic thought. *Someone who knew it was here and didn't want Dad to get it.* Would that *someone* be Devon? It seemed very strange to Relic that someone who stole something would come back later asking about it.

No, whoever took it beat this guy to the punch, Relic decided, grabbing the bag of Cheetos from the pantry. As he shoved a handful of cheese puffs into his mouth, he heard his mom turn up the volume on the news.

"Another mysterious murder has finally been solved," Monica Bridges was reporting, and Relic stepped around the kitchen corner to see the TV. "Holden Fey, the late singer of the popular band Gator Sponge, was killed last fall. The previous suspect, Ricky Warren, from the band Unknown Oath, has now been cleared of suspicion as recent evidence has tied the killing to 37-year-old Marcus Bell..."

Ricky's picture flashed on the screen and Dina gasped. "What the..."

Relic wondered if his mom had even heard about the killing last year; with so much going on, it seemed likely that she hadn't. A feeling that was a little like relief washed over Relic then, and he thought of Rook, who had given him a lift home on Saturday—Ricky's brother had to know what was going on.

Dina reached for the phone and dialed a number.

"Who are you calling?"

She held up a finger. "I want to make sure his brother knows—Hey, Kate, is Rook free? Well, tell him it's important."

Relic tossed the Cheetos onto the kitchen table and brushed off his hands as he stepped closer to the TV. Monica Bridges was finishing her report.

"...it has been uncovered by authorities that Bell, yet another vocalist for a different band—Grimstone—also originally from Laramie, had a long-standing feud with Fey. Both Gator Sponge and Grimstone toured in the past, in addition to playing festivals with Unknown Oath in both Germany and Spain. Police are still seeking a statement from Warren, who has not been seen publicly since the murder..."

Relic tuned the news out as he listened to his mom talking to Rook on the phone.

"...have you seen him?" she asked, sounding annoyed. "Well, if you do, tell him to go talk to the police. They're looking for him—the news said they wanted a statement from him." She paused, listening, giving Relic a little nod as if to say everything was fine. "Okay...well, let me know if you do... Right. Okay, see you tomorrow."

Dina hung up as a commercial break interrupted the news.

"Has he seen him?" Relic asked. Something about the whole situation made his spider sense tingle...but he couldn't put his finger on what it was—besides just being weird. Also, he had originally heard the news about Ricky right before one of the Luneral Dirge werewolves tried to kill him...so there was that.

Dina shook her head. "Hopefully it stays that way," she said softly, her eyes distant. "Ricky was a prick and kind of a nutcase."

Relic had no reply to that, only really associating Ricky as the voice of most of his past daddy issues.

"If you see him," his mom said, turning her face up to regard him sternly, "don't trust him. Just stay away from him."

Even though he didn't really want to, Relic couldn't help but ask, "Why?" Her look sharpened, so he motioned to the TV and added, "I just mean, they just said he didn't do it."

"I don't care about the murder," she snapped, startling Relic with her sudden anger. But it seemed to dissipate immediately when she spoke again. "Your dad would have never written that song if it wasn't for Ricky, maybe never would have left, and maybe..."

Her voice trailed off as her eyes went distant again.

"Mom? What do you mean he never would have written *that* song?" He knew precisely what song she meant, but wanted to hear her say it.

But when her eyes focused, she just gave her son a very fake smile, making her seem manic. She opened her mouth to say something, but the phone rang, startling them both. Dina reached for the diversion.

"Hello? Oh, hey, hon. Yes, we just saw…"

Relic turned to grab his backpack and head to his room. He dug *Emerald Decay II: The Poisoned Well* out of his bag, craving nothing more than getting lost in a book.

After dinner that night, Relic and Bree retreated into the basement as Calvin and Dina finished watching the *Field of Dreams* DVD. Relic was in a bad mood because Bree kept eating his fries like they were some shared commodity, but he tried to look past it as they focused on their exceptionally undisciplined songwriting process.

Sitting on the couch with her guitar, Bree repeatedly played the creepy crawly riff while Relic laid on the floor with his drumsticks, his notebook, and zero ideas for what part of the book the song should focus on.

In the background, the TV played *Match Night Mayhem*, pro wrestling at its absolute finest. The two combatants were the psychotic pilgrim heel Harrow Haley facing off against the babyface Jacky Theroux Jr., who was a boring legacy wrestler in simple white trunks. Harrow had been a favorite of Relic's since he was a kid, having several of the action figures that came with a bendable harrow-inspired weapon Haley would occasionally bring to the ring. Jacky was a new wrestler that Relic knew little about since he had stopped keeping up with the show.

"What if that was just an intro?" Bree said, plucking out the notes of the riff in a slow staccato. Something about the way she played it made Relic immediately visualize his own version of Jade Henry from *Emerald Decay II* creeping through the forest, Shrubble lurking in the shadows, the venom totem in his hand dripping glowing green foulness meant for the town's reservoir.

His hand began writing lyrics as if possessed.

Bree stopped playing. "You got something?"

Relic looked down at his hand, which had written "the poison is due for the one who must reap what was sown." It didn't read very well to Relic, and he really had no recollection of even thinking of those words.

"No," he said, dropping the pen and looking at the TV as the crowd went wild for Jacky dropkicking Harrow Haley over the ropes. "I feel super distracted today."

"Sounds like we need to clear the pipes," Bree said, setting her guitar aside. She unceremoniously pulled her shirt off to reveal an exquisite yellow bra that might have been completely see-through in better lighting.

Relic's eyes went wide, but the excitement of seeing his girlfriend almost topless again was mixed with sheer panic—his mom made a habit of wandering down the stairs at random intervals, and she could do so at any minute, probably resulting in stricter visitation rights. Relic whispered, "Dude, my mom..."

Bree slid off the couch, moving to straddle him. "We can be quick." She kissed him and he felt helpless to stop her. Yet, something about her lips felt slightly uncomfortable to Relic, who had enjoyed every kiss he and Bree ever shared up until that point. Why did this one feel so different? Was it the forcefulness?

Relic felt his usual biological reaction to her noticeably lessen at the thought. He was almost completely flaccid—which to him seemed like a scientific impossibility. A topless girl was throwing herself on him and he didn't feel aroused.

Something was definitely wrong with the world today.

"Bree," he tried to say between her eager, ravenous kisses. "Wait a second."

Her hands moved down to unbuckle his pants. "Come on. Hurry up."

"Why?" Relic asked, putting his hands on her bare shoulders. He tried to gently push her away from him so they could talk, but she wouldn't budge. *She's like a brick wall,* he thought. Something like fear overtook him and he panicked. "Bree!"

She pulled back then, her eyes wide. "What?"

He sat up, not really sure what to say now. She looked as if he were the one acting crazy. Had he just imagined what happened? He felt the need to suddenly apologize or make some excuse for his behavior.

But she had been the one that literally pounced on him.

"...and that might be the end for Harrow," the wrestling commentator, Randy Wreckage, announced in his typical hysterical fashion.

"Sorry," Relic finally said awkwardly, averting his eyes from the two things they wanted to fixate on, "it's been a weird day."

"...oh, the humanity!"

"So that's it?" Bree asked, her voice changing. Relic looked up to see anger replace shock in her eyes. Standing up, not bothering to cover herself, she motioned to Relic's crotch. "I jack you off and you can't be bothered to feed my beast?"

"What?!" Relic tried not to laugh in that completely surreal moment. *Feed my beast?!* "Bree, I—"

Randy Wreckage's voice screamed now from the TV as if someone had cranked the volume. "You can't unsee that, folks! Jacky is really giving it to the old Cornstalk Creeper!"

Bree turned and snatched her shirt. "No, I get it. I'll go take care of myself like last time." The phone began to ring then, adding more frantic energy to the room as Randy kept screaming out the play-by-play on *Match Night Mayhem*.

Relic tried to get up, but as Bree stepped around him, she stopped him with a firm hand on his shoulder, nodding to his notebook before adding, "Finish it yourself."

"Relic! Phone! It's your dad!"

Instinctively, Relic turned toward the phone on the table near the TV, giving Bree the chance she needed to escape. As he turned back, he saw her feet disappear up the stairs.

Dammit! What the hell just happened?!

Relic got up, torn between following his girlfriend or letting things calm down between them. He eventually decided to give Bree time to herself while he figured out why his dad was calling.

"Hello?"

His dad's breathing was heavy on the other line, as if he had been running. "Relic...are you alone?"

You could say that, he thought. "Yeah."

"Listen—I need you to check on something for me. You know the stuff you got out of storage? There was a box of books."

Relic looked down at it across the room, dreading what was coming next. "Yeah, it's right here."

"Okay...I need you to check it...check if there's a dark green notebook in there. Might have had some duct tape sealing it closed."

No, Dad, it's been stolen. I just didn't tell you. "I don't see it," he said, hoping he didn't have to elaborate. He technically wasn't lying...he certainly didn't see it.

There was a brief silence before Steven said, "Shit..."

The line went dead.

"Dad?" Nothing. Relic hung up the phone.

The crowd roared from the TV. "And that, folks, is what we call some real *Match Night Mayhem!*"

Relic leaned his head back. "Fuuuuu—"

"—uuuuuuck!" Bree growled, trying not to scream as she walked back home in the dark. As pissed as she was, she didn't want to draw attention. She wanted nothing more than complete solitude.

Well, actually she wanted to release whatever was building up inside of her. She had hoped Relic could help with that, but...

The moment played back through her head, but it had become twisted like some nightmare. Relic stared at her, blood pouring from his nose and mouth, begging for his girlfriend to leave him alone. Bree slammed her fist into the trunk of a tree as she passed it, not even feeling her scabbed knuckles bust open again. Her mind made her stare once more into her boyfriend's bewildered face as she guilted him for not putting out at her command.

What is happening to me? She felt hot tears in her eyes, but that only seemed to make her angrier.

"Everything alright?"

Bree spun around to see Delilah in a black hoodie, her hands in its pockets and its hood covering her long, dark hair.

"Is this what you do now?" Bree snapped. "Just follow us around and jump out at the worst possible times?!"

Delilah stepped closer, under the tree Bree had tried to knock over. She looked at the blood on the stump. She looked back at Bree, eyes narrowed and a slight smile on her black lips. "I knew it."

Bree stepped close to her, eager for a fight—verbal or physical, it didn't matter with the mood she was in—their faces only inches apart. "Knew what?"

Delilah nodded toward the Meyerses' house. "Something happen with Relic?"

Even hearing that name out of Delilah's mouth brought back the feeling of restrained jealousy that Bree had harbored during Relic's big crush on the pretty new rich girl. Those feelings flooded her now, and she leaned closer, almost touching her nose to Delilah's.

With an unflinching gaze, Delilah stared into Bree's eyes, searching for something. "You want to explode, right? Like, you feel it between your legs first," Delilah touched her down there when she said it.

Bree gasped, the rage expelling from her in a rush, but she grabbed Delilah by the shoulders and pushed her against the tree. She breathed heavily into the dhampir's face, doing everything in her power to hide her true thoughts behind a stoic mask.

But her legs quivered under Delilah's searching fingers.

"It's probably worse for you," the dhampir said, pulling Bree closer so their lips nearly brushed. Her other hand went down the back of Bree's pants, grabbing a handful of her ass. "I can't imagine what it's doing to you—I can barely deal when I start to come off it, and I'm made from this stuff."

Gritting her teeth, Bree fought every urge to throw the girl down in the grass and grind out every ounce of pent-up aggression that begged to be released, whatever it took—whoever it took.

Delilah kissed her then, pulling Bree's pants down more. The dhampir's lips were as cold as the grave and Bree was revolted—not just because of Delilah, but because of how she had acted with Relic. However, something would not let her break away. The thought of a neighbor maybe seeing her couldn't pierce the supernatural effects the drug was having on Bree's mind. She was lost in a primal lust.

She almost didn't feel the needle that Delilah jammed into her exposed backside.

Bree pulled away then, released suddenly from the grip of sexual desperation. Her eyes grew wide and a long moment passed before she even realized her pants were falling down to her knees.

With a grin, Delilah told her, "Sorry about that, but I need you lucid. Seems like coming down is different for you. Me? I crave junk food. You? Well..." She raised her eyebrows as her gaze shifted down to watch Bree pull up her pants.

"You kissed me," Bree said, ignoring the fact that she had *wanted* Delilah to do more than kiss her while her body came off the Rothen stuff.

Delilah waved a hand as if it were nothing. "Oh, relax. I won't tell your boyfriend. It's just us girls here—you don't think boys flick each other's peckers once in a while?" She moved away from the tree, suddenly urgent. "Like I said, I need your help, so I need you focused. All the horniness pass?"

Bree tried to fight against the blood rushing to her face. It was as if the injection had allowed her to reclaim control of her faculties, and now embarrassment replaced any lustful cravings. *I can't believe I let her kiss me!* But really, she couldn't believe how much she had liked it.

And that only made her feel more miserable.

Delilah took her sour face for confirmation. "Good. We need to move."

"Where?"

Delilah was already walking toward the distant woods that divided Greenbriar Heights from Sanctuary. "The ritual."

Exhausted from the day's events, Relic decided to lie in bed and read. He dodged his mom's questions about Bree's sudden exit and satisfied Calvin's brief questions about school until he could find sanctuary in his room.

He tossed the notebook—which still only contained one line for the song he and Bree were supposed to be finishing—on the bed and sighed.

For the briefest of moments, he considered calling Bree, but he had no clue what to even say to her after that episode in the basement. Besides, the memories of his recent interactions with Russ made him wary of even talking to a Thompkins at the moment.

Instead, he lost himself in *Emerald Decay II* again, absorbing the story while also reflecting on the surrealness of Relic Meyers reading for pleasure.

What a wild notion.

As he read about Jade and Luke escaping through the tunnels beneath the haunted Craven Woods outside of their town, Relic's mind started to wander, injecting random thoughts into the story, as if he were writing his own version. He mindlessly twirled the pen in his fingers as if about to jot something down on the notebook, but never actually doing so.

Not until, that is, he fell asleep in the middle of chapter seventeen.

The robed figures were gathered in the secluded ravine that ran between Greenbriar Heights and Sanctuary. Several times Delilah motioned for Bree to be quiet, the latter trying and failing to silently navigate through the random patches of dried leaves riddling the path.

Bree wanted to ask where they were going, but an undeniable thrill had settled within her—it could have been either the drug now pumping in her veins or just the aftereffect of the thrill that came with cheating on your boyfriend with his ex-girlfriend—and she wanted to get to the bottom of this strange and urgent request.

Delilah slowed her pace and knelt lower as they approached a flickering light in the distance: a campfire. Bree settled in behind her and whispered, "Why am I here?"

Without turning around, Delilah replied quietly, "Because I need you to watch and tell Relic what happens, just in case my plan doesn't work."

"What plan?"

Delilah scooted forward, staying low and quiet, motioning for Bree to follow. They rounded a copse and came upon a sunken part of the ravine. Flames burned near a steep incline below them, and Bree saw several figures wearing robes, hoods drawn, standing in a half-circle around the fire with their arms raised. There were low voices mumbling something.

Delilah motioned, leaning closer to Bree. "There's my dad."

Bree couldn't tell which figure she was pointing to—and really it didn't matter, because she could have meant Guy or Marshall for all Bree knew.

The voices grew louder and—Bree supposed she could have imagined it, the way the night was going—the fire seemed to grow higher in turn. The words seemed like gibberish, each individual's voice smashing into someone else's, becoming some muddy, discordant melody.

One word seemed to emerge from the verbal ooze.

"...Valaina..."

That cryptic name triggered the buried anxiety in Bree that she had kept hidden from the world under a summer's worth of shredding guitar, heavy metal, and weights. But just like the shattered glass in Relic's basement, the name Valaina brought back the stabbing pain of blood-sucking fangs in Bree's neck, along with the crippling insignificance she felt against supernatural threats emerging from every single corner of Laramie's unwashed butthole.

Delilah brushed Bree's arm suddenly, waking her from a trance. "Wait here," Delilah whispered, as if Bree were eager to jump in the middle of whatever this was.

Crouching lower near a thorny bush, Bree watched through jagged branches to see what the hell this crazy girl was doing.

"Valaina," the voices continued chanting, their words becoming clearer as the fire seemed to shrink against some haze settling over the convened cultists, "heed us and guide us toward your Chosen..."

Snoring into a drool stain on his pillow, Relic still held the pen as if he had fallen asleep with the intent of writing in his notebook, but never quite got around to it.

"Relic..." the elusive voice that had been haunting him all summer whispered, billowing the curtains lightly against his closed window. "...It's time..."

The pen began glowing in Relic's hands, a dull green aura that drew it upright. Relic's fingers tightened in response, then he began writing.

"Hey," Delilah called, breaking the uneven chanting. One of the figures threw their hood back—Guy Valentine, Bree saw—and broke away from the other five members of the convened.

"Girl," Guy snarled. "What are you doing out? I told you to make sure to tape *King of Queens* for me!"

The other figures began to turn toward the intrusion, some still trying to continue their chanting.

Bree saw Marshall Crane step forward to grab Guy by the shoulder. "Don't break the circle—the rest of you, keep chanting. The girl knows what this is about—Delilah, get back! You know how dangerous this can be!"

Delilah gracefully slid down the rocky incline, presenting herself to her adopted father. "I figured you might want to see that your daughter was alright—wide awake now!"

The chanting was ragged and uncommitted, the other figures seeming to struggle to keep their attention from the intrusion.

"Come off it, Delilah," Marshall scoffed. "You know you're no longer my daughter. You're a Valentine again—act like it and go back to the shadows."

Guy laughed at that and the fire seemed to react to his breaking the chanting again, shrinking.

"Valaina!" Marshall bellowed, putting his hood back on and returning to his place. "Heed us and guide us—Leave, Delilah! Or we cannot protect you!—toward your Chosen..."

The flames grew higher again. Bree's heart seemed to skip a beat, racing to regain its normal rhythm and making her feel like she were about to freeze up again. But Delilah's injection did its work and channeled all that anxiety into a strange sort of calm.

"Something's wrong," someone said.

The chanting began weakening again, but Marshall's voice bellowed once more. "With conviction! Valaina! Daughter of Adratheon!" The name Adratheon seemed to be a splash of gasoline thrown into the fire. The flames burst outward, knocking the cultists down.

Bree saw Delilah scramble back up the hill. "Run!" But before Bree could even rise from her knees, the ground rumbled (or her legs quivered, she couldn't tell) and she fell onto her left side.

One of the cultists shrieked. "Not again!"

Then came the familiar, wretched sounds of the skrimkins, as if from every direction. Chaos erupted, with several voices barking warnings or commands. But Marshall's voice bellowed over it all.

"The circle is broken! The girl has ruined our connection to the chosen one! Reconvene at the sanctum!"

The cultists scrambled away from the dying fire, even Guy, leaving his daughter to fend for herself against the incoming monsters.

"I think it worked," Delilah said with a laugh—actually laughing!—as she helped Bree to her feet. The dhampir had a knife out; where she had gotten it, Bree had no idea, but it glowed with the arcane power that seemed to react to—or did it attract?—Alternians.

A scrambling skrimkin dove for Bree, and she pulled her leg away just before its claws would have nabbed her. She was reminded of the movie these things had somehow emerged from; *Skrimkins* was always more comedic to her than scary, but there was nothing funny about these ravenous little creatures that began melting from the shadows like dozens of ghoulish monkeys.

Delilah slashed her knife and cut the head off the one that groped for Bree's legs, and then Bree felt a small pair of arms wrap around her neck, little claws trying to pierce the tender flesh around her throat. Enraged, she grabbed the sucker's limbs and wrenched it free. She pulled the snarling thing around in front of her, gripped both hands around its flailing arms, and ripped the pathetic creature in two.

Unnatural yellow blood sprayed across Bree's face and she smiled, feeling a primal rage carry the Rothen compound through her muscled limbs. Turning to face the oncoming horde, Bree cracked her bloody knuckles before going to work.

As the cult fled the sudden skrimkin invasion, Nick was meeting with Clayton McArthur right outside Greenbriar Heights, having snuck out of the house and then ridden his bike all the way down Creasy Lane with three ounces in his bag.

He didn't notice his necklace start to glow as Clayton handed him the most money he'd ever made in a single deal, and he didn't sense the skrimkin eyes peering at him from the trees as he counted that money after Clayton departed.

But Nick did notice that he hadn't been attacked or killed by the creatures, who seemed to keep their distance from the artifact around his neck, which seemed to captivate their little lantern eyes; eyes that shared the same pale yellow glow as Nick's necklace.

Across town in his room, Tyler didn't see his pink hi-tops begin to cast a similar yellowish hue across his bedroom carpet. He was up to a hundred and thirty-two crunches, and by the time he got to two hundred, those shoes would be back to their normal pink color—no supernatural aura coming off them.

Unlike Nick, however, Tyler did sense the skrimkin eyes that peered at him from the corners of his second-story bedroom window. However, Tyler's mind associated that feeling of being watched with the same sense of displacement that had been haunting him most of his life.

As he continued his crunches, a smile tugged at the corners of his mouth. It wasn't a smile of young love (though his thoughts had been lingering on Sebastian throughout the day) or athletic glories he used to settle for. Nor was it the smile that Valaina's Chosen might wear, knowing they would play a role in the usurpation of Adratheon's hidden power.

Tyler's smile was finally just for himself.

Relic dreamed of violence. These were not prophetic or omniscient dreams of his girlfriend doing battle alongside his ex-girlfriend against the forces of Valiana and/or Adratheon. No, these were *new* dreams of his own making. And his hand scribbled furiously in his sleep, transforming those violent images into first a cohesive story and then a condensed set of rhythmic sentences that would serve nicely as song lyrics.

Somewhere deep in his slumbering consciousness was laughter, wicked and knowing. A chilling part of Relic's muddled mind questioned whether or not that laughter was his own.

CHAPTER 10

Relic read the lyrics again, wondering if he was going nuts. He remembered reading his book before bed, assuming he had fallen asleep in the middle of a chapter like the night before. But he had no recollection of writing anything before passing out.

The lyrics for "Night of the Harrow" weren't all that bad, but he couldn't put a melody to them—at least not based on what Bree had been writing.

Bree, he thought, lowering the notebook, just then remembering their fight last night. *Was it a fight?* he wondered. He honestly didn't know what to consider it. All he knew was that he felt the desperate need to apologize to her, feeling like a dick now for not running after her last night, or at least calling her before falling asleep.

He got ready quickly and hurried toward the kitchen. Before he could get there, the doorbell rang. Curious who would be visiting this early in the morning on a Tuesday, he rushed to answer it.

"Bree?"

Holding a cardboard drink carrier containing two coffees in one hand and a paper McDonald's sack in the other, Bree stood like some special guest on a sitcom bursting into the scene to a wave of applause. Her wide smile seemed comical, and not at all normal for Bree, Relic thought.

"Allow me to present: the perfect apology meal!"

Relic snorted a laugh, taking the bag as he let Bree in.

She kicked her shoes off before dropping her backpack on the couch and moving toward the kitchen. "Dad took me early, since he had to head to the airport for Boston this morning. Where's your mom?"

Relic followed. "Working. Hey, listen, Bree...about last night..."

Setting the drink carrier down on the table, Bree spun around, holding out a coffee to Relic. "Totally my fault, sorry." She pointed to her head and stuck out her tongue before adding, "That time of the month, you know? I talked to my mom about maybe getting some medication for it."

Holding the coffee, Relic listened to Bree talk about as fast as that guy in the Micro Machines commercials. Also...

"Is this coffee?"

Bree took a big drink of hers. "Yeah."

"I don't drink coffee." *And you know that*, Relic thought, wondering if Bree was putting on some act or something because of their fight last night.

"You should," she said sharply, before taking another drink and grabbing the bag of food back out of his hands. "Wakes you right up. You want your mom's sandwich? I already had some eggs before my workout." Regardless, she tore into the bag as she took a seat at the table.

As Bree unwrapped a bacon, egg, and cheese biscuit and nearly ate half of it in a single bite, Relic slowly pulled a chair out and asked, "You sure everything's cool?"

She looked at him as she chewed, shifting all the food into her cheek so she could reply, "Yeah." She reached out and took his hand in a noticeably strong grip. "Like I said, I'm sorry—what happened last night: I'll never do that again, I promise. We don't owe each other things, you know?" She chewed some more before adding, "Saturday was my idea, and that was nasty for me to make you feel guilty for it."

Relic smiled, squeezing her hand in return (maybe just not as powerfully). And while everything she was saying comforted him, it was *how* she was saying it that made him feel... How did he feel? What was bothering him?

As if that curiosity triggered his memory, he stood up. "Almost forgot." He hurried to his bedroom and got the notebook off his bed, bringing it back to show Bree. After reading it, she shoved the rest of her sandwich in her mouth and ran down to the basement to get her guitar.

They spent the next thirty minutes before heading to the bus writing the entirety of "Night of the Harrow."

Later that day, between history and home economics, Relic went to talk to Gate in the maintenance room.

The janitor sighed. "Why don't you just ask him, man? I mean...he's here in the flesh now, right? Take advantage of it."

Relic ran a hand through the back of his hair while rolling a rubber band between his sneaker and the floor, not sure how to articulate his hesitance. "He sounded weird last night when he called. And then he hung up on me." Looking up at Gate, he thought maybe he did secretly know why he had kept the robbery from his dad. "Do you ever think, like...maybe when Dad came back..."

Gate raised an eyebrow, waiting for the question.

Relic stepped away from the wall he had been leaning on, motioning to the center of the room. "Like, you know how Mr. Crane said that he was like holding Adratheon back? What if... You don't think Dad is, like, I don't know..."

His face still passive, Gate finished for him. "Adratheon's disciple?"

Relic shrugged, waiting for Gate's answer.

The janitor leaned forward over his desk. "Kid, there's a lot your dad can't share with you, because like I told you back with the werewolves...there *is* a price that comes with knowing the enormity of some of this stuff. You and your friends have already paid a little, but not nearly as much as your pops. Adratheon cost him everything." Gate leaned back. "No, there's no chance he's in league with Adratheon. Not anymore."

Silence fell between them and finally Gate motioned for Relic to say more. "Alright, if you feel like you can't ask your dad about when he left, ask me. I was there with him. I won't lie."

"Did you know about some journal my dad kept?"

Gate bit his lip, looking off to the side as if accessing old, dusty thoughts in the back of his mind. "I mean, your dad wrote lyrics all the time, so there were notebooks around." He looked back at Relic. "Anything more specific?"

Relic described it as best he could, mentioning that both Rook and Devon Andrews were also looking for it.

Gate snarled at the mention of Unknown Oath's former manager, but seemed more fixated on—and surprised by—Rook's interest in the thing. "I remember Ricky had brought some old book one time, something he and his brother got in a fight over—Wait," he said, standing up suddenly. He was looking at the ground as if seeing it opening wide and releasing a terrifying entity from the depths of the earth. With his eyes fixed there, he said, "Before we wrote the song, Ricky brought a book that he said his brother found in his grandma's library…"

Confused, Relic asked if it was the journal.

Gate just shook his head. "This was a tome, man, like the kind you see in movies about old cults and shit. Your pops was fascinated with it, wouldn't even let me—hell, anyone—look at it until he finished reading it."

Finally, his eyes settled on Relic. "He burned that thing, man. I remember now, Rodney made some big deal about not wanting whatever was in it—about the Warrens—getting out; dude seemed super secretive about their family's past. So whatever was in it—if Stick wanted to retain any of it—he would have taken notes…"

Overwhelmed by a myriad of conflicting emotions, Relic could only take comfort at that moment in one single thought: he felt a whole lot less guilty about keeping secrets from his dad now.

Howard Sloan approached Relic's locker at the end of the school day. "I saw your dad last night."

"Where?" Relic asked, shutting his locker door and shouldering his backpack, his thoughts already drifting toward *Buffy* night, and he was only half-interested in hearing what Howie had to say.

Bree had told him over lunch earlier that with her dad in Boston and her mom visiting her sister in Michigan, they'd have the house to themselves for their Tuesday night ritual of watching *Buffy the Vampire Slayer*. And that meant make-out city.

"At Esposito's, out on the patio," Howard said. "I was in Alvin's car—we were going to check out the new 40K armies at The Game Warden. You know the Tau Empire have a new—"

"Howie," Relic said. "My dad?"

Howard blinked and continued. "I figured he was on a date...only, he wasn't really dressed up. And I think..." His robotic-like voice trailed off then, his face twisting slightly.

"What?"

Cocking his head slightly, Howard continued. "It looked like he was with Mrs. Thomkins."

Confused, Relic just blinked at him. "Bree's mom?!"

He shrugged. "It looked like her, but I don't know for sure. I guess you'll have to ask him."

Yeah, sure, Relic thought, *add it to the fucking list.*

Making his way to the bus, Relic considered the implications of his girlfriend's mom cheating on his girlfriend's dad with his own dad...

He wasn't sure how they were going to get through D&D tomorrow night without some sort of argument breaking out.

"Hey, was your mom home last night?"

Bree pulled back from Relic, perplexed. "Weird question to ask me while you're copping a feel."

His arm was around her shoulder as they sat next to each other on Bree's living room couch, his hand ungracefully grabbing a handful of her left boob. Releasing it, he shifted and turned to her. "Howard said he might have seen her at Esposito's...with my dad."

Bree had been taking a drink of Dr. Pepper and almost sprayed it all over the coffee table. Looking at Relic with her hand over her mouth, soda dripping down her chin, she was doing all she could to contain her laughter.

"What?"

Shaking her head, she wiped her hand on her pajama pants. "Just thinking about my mom and your dad boning... How weird would that be?" She waved the thought away. "No, she left yesterday afternoon for Michigan—said she would be working on the road this week."

Pulling Relic's hand back to her chest, she leaned toward him with a grin. "Now, where were we?"

They only started kissing again when the White Castle commercial ended and a commercial for the network started.

"Our *Skrimkin* marathon continues tomorrow night with another triple feature," the announcer said.

Bree pulled away from Relic, looking at the TV.

The commercial was playing clips from the old Constrained Media horror comedy franchise. Relic remembered watching the *Skrimkins* movies when he was a kid, because they were just scary enough to make him feel edgy watching them, but not scary enough to cause too many nightmares.

Seeing the clips of the movies again, Relic thought they kind of held up—those little bastards still looked kind of creepy. But they didn't creep Relic out as much as they did his girlfriend apparently. She looked like she was witnessing someone get flayed as she watched the light-hearted commercial.

"What's wrong?"

She was still glued to the ad, zoned out.

He touched her shoulder. "Bree?"

Jerking back at first, she blinked and then smiled at him. "Sorry, was just... Why are they playing those movies again?"

She leaned back to kiss him, but Relic put a hand on her cheek, looking into her eyes. "Are you alright?"

"Yeah, why?"

He didn't know how to say it. "You've just been...I don't know. Acting...different."

"News flash," she teased, making a face. "I'm a girl. Remember?"

He wanted to ask more, but when she kissed him, it felt right this time. Relic let her climb on top of him as she guided him to lay back on the couch. When they were like this, there was no weirdness between them and the confusion of his life melted away at the touch of Bree's lips.

Relic wanted more of this—only this.

And when Bree whispered the question huskily into his ear, "Can we have sex tonight?"

He thought—but his penis knew—they were ready.

Ding dong.

But the world wasn't.

"Someone better be dead," Bree growled through clenched teeth, so fiercely that Relic actually felt himself shrink back from her. He got up as she went to the door, suddenly feeling some dark premonition.

"Bree, wait—"

But she had already yanked the door open. "What the hell do you want?!"

Relic saw Delilah push her way into the house. "Close it," she warned. The dhampir fell back against the door, breathless and panting. It was then that she saw Relic and her eyes whipped back to Bree. "Did you tell him?"

Bree looked at Relic, panicked, then back to Delilah.

"Tell me what?"

There was a sudden slam against the door, making Delilah slip to the floor. She sat against it, putting her feet against the nearby stairs for leverage. "I lost both my knives, and that son of bitch is...weakening me or something. I can't fight it."

The door banged again, something scraping and hissing against the wood.

"What's out there?" Relic asked.

Delilah looked up to Relic, and he realized he had never seen her scared like this before.

Licking her dry lips and swallowing, she said, "Shrubble Von Hellspawn."

Interlude 1

Gustave's Refrain

C arl Sinclair looked almost nothing like his sister Lana. While the principal of Chambers High School had poise, grace, and abundant charm, Carl had all the physical qualities of a batshit crazy hermit that people avoided at all costs.

Fortunately for most people in the unincorporated community of Romney, Indiana, Carl kept to himself throughout most of his adult life, which made avoiding him a fairly easy task. It was only on days when Carl—in his mom's rickety old Cadillac—ventured from his haunted home built right on the southernmost edge of Laramie that folks needed to worry.

On such a day, the afternoon before the Cult of Valaina's first ritual of the 1998 - 1999 school year, Carl pulled into the parking lot of the only grocery store in town, the Romney Food Mart. He took a moment to observe his reflection in the car's grimy window. His hair was combed neatly (for a change) and he wore his short-sleeved, button-up shirt with the navy clip-on tie.

His eyes had heavy bags under them from sleepless nights during which he cried, calling out for his momma who had been dead for eight years to the day. Carl pulled his sallow cheeks down to combat his elderly appearance, to no avail. While he was nearly six years younger than his sister, he in fact looked like he could have been her father.

Forcing a smile, Carl's addled mind convinced itself that he looked quite dapper, and he turned to stride into the store for supplies. Trying to remember the feeling the muscles in his face made when he showed his teeth to the car window, Carl replicated the act several times as he walked through the market's aisles. Each time he did, a shopper would quickly avert their eyes and pretend they had found a killer deal on a distant shelf.

Unbothered, Carl went about getting the necessary items for the occasion. By the time he reached the check-out line, his basket contained a carton of whole milk, eggs, several bags of Hostess Donettes, three rolls of duct tape, a coil of rope, four straight razors, a large bottle of rubbing alcohol, and one of every candy bar on display near the cashier.

When his turn came, Carl neatly unpacked his items on the counter, pulling back his lips in that way people did on TV when they wanted to pretend the world made sense. The cashier—Rachel, according to the nametag—seemed different than the other folks that shrunk away from him.

She returned the look of pleasantry. "Find everything okay?"

Carl's face didn't change, but after a long moment of silence he loudly said, "Oh sure." He liked how big his voice sounded in the store. It didn't echo like it did in his house, but against the quiet sounds of the place, he sounded like he was the daddy of it all. "Just getting supplies for the big night."

Rachel's smile seemed to falter, but she held it as best a girl of maybe sixteen or seventeen could in this abysmal place where people shuffled along without the guidance of their dead mommas. "Got a big get-together?"

Carl laughed, loudly and jaggedly. In his defense, he didn't get the chance to laugh a lot at home, so he wasn't quite practiced in the act. "Oh, nothing too fancy. Just me and my momma watching movies. The TV is playing my favorite pictures back-to-back tonight. Do you like *Skrimkins*?"

Rachel shook her head, still trying to hold her smile as she rang up the groceries. "Oh no, I don't watch scary movies."

Carl felt his face slacken, his lips sagging as his brow furrowed. "They're not scary. They're funny. Momma doesn't let me watch scary movies."

Rachel averted her eyes, her hands moving faster now to complete the transaction. "That'll be thirty-five seventy."

Carl's eyes remained fixed on her, trying to imagine what the girl would look like in his bath. She was very small—it looked like she didn't have boobies—and wouldn't work for his needs, but he felt that he liked her. His hand started tapping his thigh in frustration when she wouldn't return his gaze.

"Hey, Rachel, let me bag those," a man's voice said. "How you doing, Mr. Sinclair?"

Carl turned to see a familiar face. He didn't recall the name, but the man wore a short-sleeved work shirt and a tie, and his name tag read *Albert Tolle - Store Manager.*

Carl showed his teeth again. "Super duper."

After paying, Carl took both bags of groceries and whistled the theme song to the first *Skrimkins* movie as he walked back to his momma's car.

"Sorry, I didn't know," Rachel was saying.

Al shook his head, trying to keep his face calm. He really wanted to bang Rachel and needed to look like the protective hero here. "Oh, it's fine. I know you just moved out here—you probably haven't heard about him. Just try to say as little as possible when he comes in."

Turning from the departing Cadillac, Rachel observed the mostly empty store. She stepped around the counter closer to Al and he could smell that seductive body spray the girl favored. He sucked in his gut as best he could when she leaned closer.

"What's his deal?"

Assuming the look of a streetwise older man, Al gave a little laugh. "Where to start, right? He lives in that haunted Crane place—you've heard of Eli Crane, right? No? Oh, sorry, I keep forgetting how young you are." Al laughed again. "Well, I'm sure you've heard of Marshall Crane—just moved back up in Laramie. His family has always been big real estate people, and Eli Crane was the first around here.

"He built this huge farm on the edge of Laramie, like, 200 years ago. Anyway, weird stuff started happening there; people say it's cursed. There's a well on the property that people say *things* crawled out of and ate all the livestock nearby. Farms dried up, and soon the Crane place was pretty much left to rot."

Rachel's wide eyes were fixed on every word Al said and he didn't want to lose the girl's attention.

"I actually went to school with Carl's sister, Lana," he continued. "Apparently, their mom—Suzanne, I think...yeah, Suzy the Slut Sinclair—started sleeping around and their dad divorced her, taking Lana to Laramie and leaving old Carl there with his whore *momma*."

Rachel snickered at that, and he smiled, sensing that his newest cashier was a dirty girl. He felt his odds increasing. "Old Suzy Sinclair died a while ago, but people say because she died in that house—where Eli Crane was brutally murdered by his sons—she haunts the place, driving her son nuts."

"Wow," Rachel said with wonder in her eyes. "Sounds like a Stephen King book or something."

Al straightened then, leaning against the counter and crossing his arms. "I thought you didn't like scary stuff." He smiled at her coyly.

Rachel blushed. "I just said that—I actually read a lot of horror books, especially close to Halloween."

Al filed that away in his lonely, desperate brain. If he was going to score with this chick, he needed to find out more stuff she liked; he also needed to figure out just how dirty this broad was. "You want to hear about the time Carl got caught jacking off by the doctor's office?"

The look on Rachel's face told Al that she certainly did not care to hear that story, nor did she seem in the least bit as dirty as he had hoped.

Carl set the groceries down on the row of stacked magazines and catalogs in the foyer that served as a table. Most of the magazines were *National Geographic* or maternity-focused, and almost all the catalogs were women's clothing—basically any periodical that contained pictures of boobies.

Piles of toys and old board games lined the other side of the foyer, spilling out in a chaotic mess that comforted someone like Carl—someone who didn't like to see things change or die or age or become anything other than a means to soothe.

And the house did soothe him, despite the heavy, musty smell sometimes making Carl feel sick when he returned home from a more sanitized environment. However, soon the memories would return or the muffled, restrained murmurs from the other room would remind him he was well and truly home.

Now those murmurs were accompanied by a soft thumping on the floor, which certainly did not soothe him. Carl shook his head, smiling—not the fake Hollywood smile he had assumed outside the Romney Food Mart; this smile was genuine.

"Hungry, Momma?" Carl dug the Hostess Donettes out of the paper sack. "I got your favorite." He walked around a massive pile of bras and panties that were pushed up against a beaten-up couch in the living room.

Heavy curtains shielded that room from the afternoon sunlight, preventing any glare from reaching the eight different TVs stacked against the wall on the other side of the room—one of those TVs was on, playing *Geraldo* on mute.

The muffled, struggling voice got louder, but the thumping stopped. Carl smiled at his momma as he showed her the sweets she had asked for. When she didn't react, he frowned.

"These are the right ones, aren't they?"

His "momma" was actually Brenda Phillips, a resident of Indianapolis that had gone missing last week while driving up to Chicago. Brenda had taken a detour in order to avoid construction, and wound up getting kidnapped while at a truck stop not far from where she now sat naked, bound to an old recliner.

Brenda had the great misfortune of being around the same size as the late Suzy Sinclair when the woman had died, and Brenda's breasts just happened to be of the same fullness and roundness that wasn't always exactly common on women with her (or Suzy's) frame.

Now, Brenda didn't care so much about being naked at the moment, she just wanted to get off this damn chair. She urged the psycho toward her by making a face that said, "I need this tape off my mouth! Hurry! There's something I need to tell you that cannot wait any longer!"

Carl didn't seem to get the message. He lowered the Donettes and walked toward her lazily and sullenly. His nose twitched as the smell of the woman's refuse became more pungent. Setting the bag of treats down, he reached his horrid, skeletal fingers toward the tape on her mouth, stopping just before he reached it.

"Remember," he said with a dopey smile, "no one can hear you out here, right? I just don't like hearing you sound so upset, that's why I put the tape on. Can you just be nice, Momma?"

Brenda nodded, her red-rimmed eyes not leaking tears for a change. She had cried the first few days of captivity, but after she learned that this nutjob didn't seem interested in killing or raping her, she regained her faculties and tried to start reasoning ways she could maybe manipulate him into releasing her.

Carl carefully removed the tape, letting Brenda flex her cramped jaw and air out her rancid mouth. "Can I please get out of this chair, honey?" Brenda asked, as much as it pained her to play this sick game. It seemed the only thing that worked on him. "I want to use the potty."

Looking affronted, Carl pointed at the base of the chair. "I cut a hole, Momma. Just go." He went around to the back of the chair, pushing aside huge stacks of toilet paper. "I'll change the bowl."

"I can't...wipe, sweetie."

He grabbed a roll. "I'll wipe you like last time, when you were asleep."

"No!"

Carl came back around to the front of the chair, his hand reaching out desperately for her breast, grabbing it and squeezing tightly as if it were some sort of child's comfort toy. "Are you being mean again, Momma?"

Brenda steadied her breath, trying to ignore the pathetic man's groping. But his grip was strong enough to remind her that, despite her size advantage, she probably wouldn't be able to overpower the man unless he was somehow calm or otherwise subdued.

She needed him to retreat into that infantile calmness that would overtake him when he was suckling on her in front of the TV. Only, she needed her hands free, not chained to this disgusting toilet chair.

"Tonight is important," she said, trying to sound motherly, but she only felt ridiculous and scared. "We should be together on the couch there, so I can hold you while you suck. So we can watch your pictures."

Carl's eyes widened at that. Whether it was her voice or the change in routine that seemed to ignite a curiosity in this creature of habit, Brenda just knew she might be onto something.

She risked it further. "Maybe I can help you with your pee pee, too, so you don't have to do it yourself."

His hand stopped the rhythmic pawing of her breast then, but his mouth fell open slightly before he said, "Momma doesn't touch it."

Brenda swallowed. "Momma can touch it. She can show you how to do it right, sweetie. Please?"

Carl nodded and began feeding her the Donettes.

As the afternoon wore on, Brenda was left alone with her thoughts while Carl took his bath. Earlier, she hadn't felt like pressing her luck by asking if momma could bathe him, but now that she had time to consider it, she wished she had been brave enough to try.

While it was a massive victory alone that she got him to consider letting her go that evening, it would have been even better to have Carl acting like a little boy, naked in the bath, instead of sucking her tit while she tugged him.

If that's what it takes to get out of this, Brenda thought, trying to hold back the vomit.

The house groaned as Carl filled the bathtub with water upstairs. The pipes squealed. The place sounded like it was going to fall apart at any moment. Brenda couldn't help but struggle against the bindings again, but the cuffs were tight and the chains were unyielding. She couldn't help but imagine—yet again—how many women had been bound to this chair.

That thought led to: What eventually happened to those women after either Carl sucked them dry or they refused to play the role of his dead momma?

For some reason, Brenda struggled to imagine that wretched little hoarder killing or butchering people—he just seemed so pathetic. But maybe that was exactly what killers were: just pathetic sickos. She had never known or met a killer, so why would his patheticness exclude him from being among the ranks of psychos?

Then again...

The house groaned once more and Brenda's head snapped toward the dining room, swearing she felt a...presence there. But all she saw was that long table, buckling under the weight of heaping piles of garbage. Flies buzzed and rats were surely scurrying through the rotting food, but there was no one with her.

No one she could see, at least.

Brenda had not been a believer in the supernatural—ghosts made for great movies and books, but she was a grounded person that believed in what she could regard with her senses. Yet, this place made her feel even more naked and exposed than she already was. The goosebumps on her flesh were not from being cold—it was actually quite hot (and stinky) in the house.

Her beliefs were changing after having to spend several nights in this place. And as Carl turned off the water upstairs, the house seemed to sigh and laugh at Brenda's circumstances, getting off on it. The house wanted her here—it wanted Carl to keep her here. It didn't want to let either of them go.

A disgusting thought came to Brenda Philips as she heard the man-child upstairs whistling a tune as he splashed in the tub.

Carl Sinclair was a prisoner as well, bound to this house because the spirits that lived here wanted to watch—it was those spirits that were truly latched onto her, curled up naked in her lap, dry-sucking and masturbating for hours on end.

But whether it was sympathy that she felt for Carl Sinclair in that moment of strange revelation or just a different sort of revulsion, Brenda just knew she had to be gone from this place and she needed to kill this man; as much for herself as for him.

Carl Sinclair was not chained naked to a chair, but he was just as helpless against whatever lived in this house as she was.

Evening came and Carl used a small key to unlock Brenda's cuffs. Her first instinct was to bowl over him, using her weight to hopefully break some of his bones as she crashed atop him. But she was a smart woman and knew that this was not her chance. She could barely even get up out of the chair without his help.

As repulsed as she was with his touch, she let the man take her hand and pull her to her feet. He wore those nasty pajamas of his, stained with splatters of lord-knows-what, and the baby lotion smell of his shampoo made her want to gag. But this would be her only opportunity, and she played the doting mother as best she could, keeping her touch light and caring.

"The first movie is about to start," Carl said, his pajama bottoms sticking up absurdly as he escorted her to the couch—which looked just as disgusting as the toilet chair.

Brenda's legs wobbled, and she definitely needed Carl's help to get across the living room. Her eyes kept darting to the door, but feeling how strong the man's grip was on her, she restrained herself from trying to hobble out into the middle of nowhere, weak, naked, and directionless.

She needed to kill him—or at the very least, incapacitate him somehow—in order to get her bearings.

"You sit here, Momma," Carl said excitedly, motioning to the edge of the couch where all the bras and panties were piled up. "Best seat in the house."

And closest to the door, she thought. Easing herself down, Brenda heard the couch groan under their combined weight. Carl casually took his pants off and lay down, putting his head in her lap. For a moment he watched the TV as the opening credits to *Skrimkins* played, but he quickly turned to grab her left breast. "I don't like the beginning," he said before starting his demented nursing ritual.

Brenda could feel his eyes on her and knew what was expected. She swallowed as she kept her eyes on the movie, reaching over with her right hand and doing what was promised. Carl quivered under her touch, but her disgust was replaced with an odd sense of relief.

This might be easier than I thought, Brenda thought as Carl buckled under her strokes. On the screen, she watched a young woman walking through a park, looking for her lost dog. But in her mind, she imagined grabbing this sick bastard by his balls and twisting, pulling them off if she could.

Brenda almost smiled then, watching the little creature on the TV scamper through dead leaves, frightening the girl it pursued. She pulled faster, feeling like her window might be closing. Carl's body contorted and he sucked harder. The movie's soundtrack seemed to become discordant then, and the scampering footsteps seemed to be coming from within the house. Brenda felt the need to finish him off quicker. Quicker.

"Come on, baby," she whispered in her best motherly voice. And that seemed to do it. Carl almost folded in on himself. The girl on the TV screamed as the skrimkin pursuing her leapt out. And more skittering little feet seemed to close in on her as Carl squirted on her hand, repulsing her.

Suddenly enraged, Brenda shifted and grabbed Carl's testicles with all of her might, twisting, pulling, crushing. The shriek that emerged from Carl was satisfying and empowering. Brenda bolted to her feet, still holding Carl's balls, feeling strength she never imagined her lumpy body producing. Flailing his legs while in an awkward handstand, her kidnapper tried to break her grip.

"Momma!!!" His voice was shrill, terrified, and angry.

Brenda gathered up all that alien strength in her other arm then and wrapped a hand around Carl's throat, lifting with all her might. Whether it was the adrenaline or the man was even more emaciated than he looked, Brenda felt like she was holding a toddler. In a mad frenzy, she swung the flailing, crying middle-aged man toward the corner of the wall behind the couch.

Carl Sinclair's spine hit the sharp end of a solid two by four that somehow managed to avoid centuries of decay beneath the crumbling plaster. Something in the man's back cracked loudly, and his head was thrown against another stud in the wall. He fell onto the couch in a lifeless heap.

Brenda had no time to celebrate the grotesque victory. Something else was in the house with her—many somethings—and their skittering claws were coming for her, she knew it. Grabbing a handful of undergarments from the pile, hoping something might fit, Brenda ran out the door.

As the naked woman streaked across the front lawn toward the nearest road, she didn't even notice the well near the side of the house—the subject of many legends regarding the home.

She also didn't notice the goblin-like creature that emerged from it then, eager to be free from the cradle that he had been banished to for so long, and eager to kill the only one who could stop him.

Al Tolle whistled a tune in his car, one that he hadn't thought of since high school orchestra. It was an old Moreau piece that he couldn't remember the name of. Odd that it had come to him so randomly.

As he turned onto a side road, he was shocked to see a woman running alongside the pavement.

Holy shit! Is she naked? Al thought, slowing his car down so he could see better. He saw a big lovely woman struggling to get her big lovely breasts into a much too small bra while also trying to wave his car down for a ride.

After striking out with Rachel, Al felt renewed hope as he rolled his window down. Maybe he wouldn't have to spend the night with his right hand yet again.

"Need a ride, ma'am?"

CHAPTER 11

Bree couldn't follow what Delilah and Relic bickered about. The name Shuckle Von Hickorydock—or whatever they had said—was completely foreign to her at that panicked moment. The scraping sound against her family's door was the center of Bree's entire universe now, and it froze her limbs in place. A basement window conjured in her mind, cracking.

The glass shattered more with each slam, scrape, or snarl from the other side of that door, and *snap*, just like that, Bree was back in the fall of 1997 when a werewolf busted into the house and almost killed Relic in front of her.

Her: the powerless, weak, terrified girl...

Bree's fists clenched at that thought. *No,* a voice inside her said, *you stabbed that mangy bastard with a knife!* She might have attributed this voice to the VANDAL serum taking effect inside of her; that is, if she had the luxury of conscious thought in that brief moment before whatever monster on the other side of that door got in and massacred them.

"Open the door," Bree said, stepping toward Delilah.

"Wait," Relic said, panicked. "Bree, I don't have my sticks!"

"Go get them," she replied, not turning from the door that seemed to shake on its hinges. "Take the back door. We'll hold it off. Open the door, D."

Bree felt the others exchange a look, hesitating, so she reached for the door-knob. "Now! Go!"

She barely heard Relic's light steps as he scrambled into the kitchen and across the tile.

"Wait," Delilah called after him. "Bree, there are more skrimkins out there!"

"Then go help him." She turned the doorknob. "Whatever this thing is, it's not getting into my house. Not this time."

When Delilah scrambled after Relic, Bree pulled the door open just as another slam shook it. The Alternian would have fallen into the entryway from the forward motion of its banging on the door, but instead its face made contact with Bree's bare foot as she kicked upward, sending the pale green figure flying into the air. It landed in a clumsy heap in the Thompkinses' front yard.

Bree barely felt the kick, but the noise of her skin slapping against the creature's coarse flesh sounded like the worst belly flop she could imagine. Even though there was a monster standing up not fifteen feet from her, she took a moment to inspect her family's front door, which displayed several scuffs and dents.

She turned rage-filled eyes on the thing that now stood in her yard. Despite being short, the creature was probably twice the height of a skrimkin and shared some traits with those little critters. This guy had pale green skin that seemed to hang off its muscled limbs. Bree thought he looked like an oversized goblin from her *Dungeons & Dragons Monster Manual*, but he had tufts of mossy growths where humans might have hair. He wore the tattered remains of clothing, hanging off him like damp, rotting shrouds.

"You're not the one," the thing said, scowling at Bree with his lantern yellow eyes. "Where is he?! The one who summoned me?!" He lifted a gnarled staff that stood as tall as him, a strange collection of bone talismans hanging from its crook. "He must bleed to free the cradle!"

Bree cracked her knuckles, wondering why she wasn't more afraid of this horrifying thing. "You first, Yoda." She charged at him, not giving herself time to question this whole action hero thing.

The thing raised its staff defensively, a sickly green glow brightening from the bones that rattled from it. But whatever spell it tried to work took too long, and Bree knocked the staff aside with one hand before rocking the thing's ugly head with a satisfying haymaker.

Once more, the creature soared away from Bree. But this time it rolled to its feet, the rotting rags it wore swaying with the motion. He seemed entirely unfazed by the punch even though Bree thought she had certainly knocked its head off. She was eager to try again, but before she could fully turn toward him, he was holding his glowing staff out and chanting in some animalistic, growly tongue.

The earth lurched beneath Bree's feet and a creaking sound came from behind her. As she turned to see what it was, a rope wrapped around her neck. She reached up to prevent it from strangling her and realized it wasn't a rope—it was like one of those long weeds she would help her dad pull out of the garden, with the nasty little roots growing from it like thick and ratty hairs.

"It is your turn to be plucked," the creature mocked from behind Bree. Its croaking voice was like a hag with lung cancer, and it managed to shake her bowels now as true fear replaced the effects of the VANDAL serum. Suddenly she was a fifteen-year-old girl again and not Xena the Warrior Princess.

The creature laughed as if he sensed her growing terror. "How does it feel to be a weed? Tossed aside for the chosen one to take root?"

What the hell is he talking about? Bree managed to wonder as she struggled against being choked to death. The creaking sound came again, and then something snapped around her left wrist, pulling her hand away from her neck. Flexing her right arm with all her might, Bree could barely keep the root around her neck from crushing her throat. Her heart thundered as she realized this could be her final moments, the panic making it harder and harder to breathe.

When the creaking came again and her right wrist became bound, she accepted that she was about to die, but was overcome with guilt for not having been able to tell Relic the truth about everything.

The sense of ultimate failure in that moment made her surrender, and she let go.

Relic grabbed his drumsticks from his room, thankful that his mom wasn't home to try to stop him from going to help Bree. As he spun them in his fingers, they came to life with the familiar Alternus magic, bathing the dark house in an arcane green glow.

Knowing Bree needed him, he barely hesitated when one of those skrimkins from the movies appeared in the front doorway he had left open. It let out a feral hiss and spread its little claws. Relic kept running through the living room and booted the thing up into the air, slashing it in half with his stick. Dark blood sprayed over him. He heard Delilah struggling and saw her on her back in his front yard, four or five of the skrimkins on her.

Just as Relic was about to move to help her, he hesitated. He could see Shrubble Von Hellspawn's glowing staff illuminating the Thompkinses' front yard. The poisonous green aura extended to the clear image of Bree struggling against writhing appendages coming out of the ground.

"Bree!" Relic screamed, breaking into a run, forgetting about Delilah altogether. It wasn't until he passed by her that he heard her struggles, calling for his help; but he had no time. *She's strong*, he thought as blood pounded in his ears, *she can hold those things off*. Delilah screamed again and Relic was afraid to even look behind him, not wanting to see her die.

When he got close enough, Relic spun the stick in his right hand, igniting it in a brilliant emerald fire that made Shrubble's own corruptive magic look even sicker by comparison. He hurled the stick, not even aiming, knowing it would strike true.

And it did.

Shrubble's vile spell faded and Relic heard Bree suck in a desperate, papery breath. Seeing the vines that held her go limp, he returned his attention to Shrubble, who had been thrown backward by the power of Relic's stick. The primary antagonist of *Emerald Decay* lithely got to his feet, pulling the burning drumstick out of his shoulder and dropping it as if it scalded the palm of his hand.

"You wretched polluters," Shrubble said, calmer than Relic expected. It was as if the creature was reading from a script. "You will reap what you sow. I am the bastard son of Mother Nature, and my wrath is that of the leaf, bough, and rain, visiting upon you the poison you hath visited upon them."

Confused, Relic turned to Bree, but as she got to her feet, she just gave Relic the same expression that he imagined his own face wore. He turned back to Shrubble. "Dude, this isn't *Emerald Decay*."

Shrubble held up a finger. "Ah, but it is!" That finger then pointed to Relic. "Your own adaptation. You wrote the words, and here I am, bound by Adratheon's will—just as you. And to fulfill the hex," Shrubble bent to grab his staff, "one of us dies."

"Fine by me," Relic said, sick of listening to this ugly little bitch. He flipped his other stick into the air, caught it, and pulled it back in his right hand to throw.

Delilah's desperate voice split the night. "Relic!"

Spinning, Relic saw the dhampir scrambling away from nearly a dozen skrimkins. She crawled over the forms of several of their small bodies, as if for each one she incapacitated, three more scrambled out of the shadows.

"Come on," Relic said to Bree, breaking into another sprint toward his ex, already forgetting about the wounded Shrubble. As he got closer, Relic saw Delilah was covered in scratches, her clothes torn to shreds. He only had the one stick, so he couldn't throw it, feeling too winded by the time he finally got close enough to be at all accurate.

"Get down!" Relic turned his remaining stick downward and rammed it like a dagger into the little skull of the first foe. He rotated the stick and used the limp body stuck to it as a flail, smacking the next skrimkin aside. Now able to put himself between Delilah and the monsters, he began kicking at them as he tried to dislodge his stick from the first one's skull.

Freezing pain shot through Relic's leg as a tiny hand jammed its claw into his leg. Immediately he could feel a gush of blood pour down his calf and into his shoe. Another skrimkin launched itself into his face and it felt like a boxer just caught him with a right hook, knocking him backward. More pain as those nasty little claws began poking, scratching, and raking him.

But then Bree was there. Relic was almost delirious from the mixture of adrenaline, fear, and pain that roiled within him, so he couldn't be sure if he was hallucinating, but it looked like Bree had turned into the Incredible Hulk. His girlfriend roared as she began picking up skrimkins by the pair and slamming their heads together in a wash of dark, chunky gore.

Pieces of bones and brains began to rain down on Relic as he kept trying to pull his drumstick free. When he finally managed to loosen it and get to his feet, he saw that Bree had single-handedly ripped, smashed, and otherwise mutilated every single one of the wretches.

"Shit," Relic said, breathing heavily, looking at the aftermath with wide, unblinking eyes. "That's a lot to clean up."

"No," Delilah said, her voice faint from the ground where she lay. Relic turned and saw her eyes fixed on the dead bodies, staring in disbelief. She raised a finger. "Look."

Relic did. The sick green glow of Shrubble's magic gathered around the dead skrimkin at their feet—blood, guts, brains, everything began to pulsate with eldritch energy.

Relic looked at Delilah and saw the recognition in her eyes. They had seen this thing happen after hunting down the wendigo, when the Widow seemed to...absorb the monster, gaining its power. The mucousy green mists swirled around the teens, disintegrating the skrimkin and peeling the creatures' blood off Bree's fists, Relic's legs, and Delilah's everywhere.

They heard a wicked, hag-like cackle from where Shrubble had been, but there was no sign of him now...just a trail of the essence he stole from the slaughtered Alternians.

Without discussion, Relic ran back toward Bree's yard. Gasping for breath—it felt like he hadn't run this much in his entire life—he reached his discarded drumstick in the grass.

But Shrubble Von Hellspawn was nowhere to be seen.

Tyler awoke with a start. His brow was sweaty even though all he wore was his underwear and...his shoes? *Weird,* he thought, kicking the pink things off so he could flex his toes and air out his damp socks. Turning to the clock, he saw that it was only 9:25 at night.

"What..." he said groggily.

He didn't even remember falling asleep. All he remembered was the dream.

Reaching for the phone next to his bed, he dialed Nick's number. It rang twice before Nick's dad answered.

"Hello?"

"Hey, Mr. Weber. It's Tyler. Is Nick there?"

Doug shouted for his son, seeming to make an effort to cover the phone, though it didn't do much. Tyler had to pull his own phone away from his ear.

After a moment, Doug said, "I think he's still out. Y'all didn't have practice tonight?"

"No, usually only on Wednesday," Tyler said, his mind drifting back to his dream in which Nick was also playing bass, but not with Altar Stone. "I'll just catch him at school tomorrow," Tyler said, wondering if he had just busted Nick on a night he was sneaking out with Tammy or something.

Hanging up the phone, Tyler kept his hand on it. He considered calling Relic, but remembered that it was Tuesday and he was probably over at Bree's watching that stupid vampire show. Instead, he picked up and called the only person he could really talk to.

"Tyler?"

"Hey, man. You busy?"

"No, just doing some reading for English class. What's up?"

Tyler didn't really know what was up. "I guess I fell asleep after taking a run. I honestly don't even remember getting in bed, but just now woke up. I had..." Why was he telling Sebastian this? *Because he's the only one that listens,* Tyler reminded himself. "I had a pretty fucked up dream."

Something rustled on the other end of the line, followed by the sound of a door shutting. Sebastian's voice was lower when he asked, "Fucked up good, or fucked up bad?"

Tyler scoffed. "Just...fucked up. It was, like, very real feeling...almost like I was watching something happen—like... I don't know."

"Well, what was it about?"

Tyler told him how he had dreamed of Nick playing bass in this empty room. There was nothing around him but darkness and swirling mists, and Tyler couldn't tell what song Nick was playing. It wasn't any of the covers Altar Stone had been practicing, and it didn't sound like any of the new stuff Bree had been writing.

"But it was a real song," Tyler said. "Almost like...almost like I was writing it in my dream."

"That's happened to me," Sebastian said.

"Yeah, but you write music, man." Tyler sat up, getting frustrated that he couldn't explain how weird the whole thing was. "It's just—Nick and I have been getting into these arguments—a lot recently. It felt like when we were on the football team together, he was jealous of me or something. And now it's almost like he's just coming down on me all the time as some sort of payback. Especially after Saturday night."

Sebastian inhaled then, as if about to ask a question.

Tyler felt like he knew what was coming, but wanted to hear Sebastian ask it. "What?"

"Is that why you...came over on Saturday?"

Sighing, Tyler said, "This isn't about that. I came over because I wanted to, not because Nick is an asshole. Anyway, it was just a weird dream and it felt too real. I didn't tell you on Saturday, but when I couldn't sing at the show, I...heard something. In my head."

"Like voices?" Sebastian asked eagerly. He loved freaky stuff, which may have been what truly drove Tyler to call him.

"Yeah," Tyler replied, standing up so he could pace around his room. He was getting antsy even saying this aloud. "It was like this...laughter. Said something like 'a draggy on' or some shit...it was the laughter that really stuck with me though."

"A dragon?"

Tyler sighed again. "Never mind what he said, man. The thing is, I heard the same thing in the dream. It was like something was laughing and taunting Nick from the darkness. And the reason it freaked me out so much..."

Sebastian waited a few seconds before asking why.

"It felt like it was me, dude. It felt like I was threatening Nick before—"

Tyler looked in the mirror, almost relieved to see that he was still himself. "Before I killed him."

Nick could have sworn he heard laughter over the distorted guitars and Dustin's sloppy drumming. Looking around the maintenance room, he didn't see anything out of the ordinary.

Shaking his head, he focused on the simple bassline for Bag of Sax's newest song that sounded like the last four songs of theirs he had learned. As he locked in with Wesley Brown's guitar riff, Nick let his eyes wander to Dustin Hodges behind Relic's drum kit. A pang of guilt crept into his gut as he watched a drummer commit the ultimate heresy—playing another drummer's kit without permission.

Relic didn't deserve this kind of betrayal, but as Nick watched the puff of smoke coming out of the joint in Dustin's wormy lips, he knew this would be the best way for him to get more customers. The band's singer and former bassist, Shannon Cooper, sat atop Gate's desk as she roasted her own bone.

Nick closed his eyes against all that and just focused on his playing.

The more shows he could play with whatever bands he could, the more weed he could move. Nick still didn't know how he would get the money to his dad without questions being asked, but he'd worry about that part later. Now was the time to wheel and deal.

The echoing, villainous laughter came again, and Nick jerked his head in either direction, convinced he was being watched by spectral eyes from somewhere in the shadowed room. But no; Bag of Sax was alone in the school. Gate had left at five o'clock and Nick used the key Relic entrusted with him to give the four of them access to the only place they could practice.

Dustin fell off-beat again, clumsily trying to play it off like he was doing some complicated fill, laughing and puffing the free sample Nick had given him. Nick forced himself to smile, thinking of all the advice Ricky Warren had given him about using his charm to manipulate buyers.

That's all Dustin, Shannon, and Wes were to Nick, he realized at that moment—buyers. The epiphany only comforted him a little; he doubted Relic would care if he let a friend, a buyer, or Brad Pitt play his drums, he'd still be pissed. And honestly, Nick couldn't blame him.

So, he would have to do everything he could to make sure nobody found out about his new nocturnal activities. Fortunately, it seemed like Relic himself had plenty of his own nocturnal habits. Nick remembered last Halloween when he was trying to score with Tammy in the cemetery and Relic and his ex-girlfriend had been—*What had they been doing?*

Strangely, Nick couldn't remember why Relic and Delilah had been there that night, only that they were in a hurry and seemed to really freak Tammy out. But everything freaked Tammy out, especially back then, when she was so concerned about being in Miranda's little gang that she wouldn't let Nick touch or talk to her in front of anyone.

Realizing he was losing focus, Nick turned to face Wes, who was mouthing the lyrics to Bag of Sax's latest musical odyssey called "Wendy Hole Stuffer," which was, as Nick understood it, about shoving a junior bacon cheeseburger up your rectum. Or having sex with a girl named Wendy. Really, there was no way to know with Wesley's lyrics combined with Shannon's singing.

As he continued riding an open E, Nick tried as best he could to shake the feeling that someone—or something—was spying on them. But it wouldn't go away. His neck itched and his increasing paranoia made him imagine someone pulling the hemp necklace Ricky had given him and strangling him.

Tyler's angry face flashed in his mind for some reason then, a mental photo Nick kept from their confrontation after the show—or lack thereof—on Saturday. But this wasn't as shocking to Nick. The expression on his singer's face visited him frequently, asking Nick, "What's your problem with me, man?!"

Nick never had a good answer. He didn't know where the animosity he had toward Tyler came from, besides not really liking his attitude when they were on the team. However, thinking of football just compiled the guilt, having not yet told his dad he'd quit.

Dustin missed another fill, but the glazy red look in his eyes made Nick just smile and nod his head to the untrained rhythm the drummer produced. *It doesn't matter*, Nick thought, ignoring the laughter in his mind. *They're just buyers, man, and Dad needs the money.*

Later that night, Relic sat by his living room window, anxiously tapping his thighs with his sticks. Bree was in his bed, having passed out almost immediately after the adrenaline of the encounter had worn off.

"I'm going to have a chat with my dad," Delilah had said angrily at Bree earlier, while the teens patched themselves up with the Thompkinses' limited medical supplies. "He keeps dodging me, and I've been staying out of the apartment while he feeds on those junkies—it's just gross." She wrapped her left bicep with a bandage. "But I'm going to have to interrupt his meal, I think. This has to be tied to the cult and that ceremony."

The girls had told Relic about the ritual they interrupted, and he was angry they had kept it from him. But there were too many other things to worry about at the moment. It sounded like this version of Shrubble might be the result of the cult summoning "Valaina's Chosen." Relic didn't exactly know what that meant, other than he should probably find and kill the thing as quickly as possible.

Now, as he kept his eyes fixed on the pools of streetlight outside, snapping his head at any sign of movement—usually just a blowing branch—he tried to make sense of what they had all experienced. If the Widow had been the demi-god-like entity Valaina inhabiting the ghost of psycho-murderer Cecily Moreau, did that mean Shrubble Von Hellspawn was some other powerful Alternian overlord, able to absorb the energy of lesser Alternians?

There was literal magic going down in Laramie, so it was unlikely he could find any rational comprehension of what was actually going on, but there were always rules, right? Last semester, they had found out the rules to how the Widow could be returned to Alternus, so it only seemed likely they could figure out exactly what Shrubble was and where he came from.

Headlights came down the street and Relic was relieved to see his mom's Mazda turn onto their road, then into the driveway. Normally, he would probably panic seeing his mom come home while he had a girl in his bed, but making out with Bree like a couple normal teenagers had felt like some distant memory after everything that happened between then and now.

Relic just kept tapping out mindless rhythms as his mom came in.

"Hey, hon. What are you still doing up?"

He tried to give her a normal grin, still tapping his sticks. "Couldn't sleep. Just kind of antsy." Looking toward his room, he asked, "Is it alright if Bree stays over? I can sleep downstairs, she's just already crashed in my bed."

Looking that way herself, Dina turned back to Relic. "Is everything alright?"

"Yeah, her parents are both out of town. I think she just got freaked out a little." *Understatement of 1998,* Relic thought. But he regretted phrasing it like that when he saw the look on his mom's face.

"Relic." She set her purse on the couch and came closer to him. "Did something happen? Did you guys...*see* something again?"

Shaking his head, Relic looked down at his sticks as casually as he could, afraid if he looked in her eyes she would see the lie. "No, we were just watching *Buffy* and she didn't feel like sleeping in a house by herself." Hoping to divert her suspicions, he quickly asked with feigned interest, "How was work?"

Dina sighed, taking the bait. "Oh, fine... That is, until Calvin showed up."

"Huh?" Since when did Calvin showing up negatively affect his mom's mood?

She flopped down on the loveseat near the kitchen, sighing even louder as she leaned her head back, exhausted. "He wanted to tell me in person—we lost the wedding venue...back to square one."

"What venue?"

She looked up, her face scrunched up in annoyance. "I told you last month, Relic. We booked that Mansfield Orchards place, out past West Laramie? Do you not listen to anything I say?"

Relic gave a coy smile, glad to not have her asking too many questions about the night. "Sorry, Mom. It's been a very busy summer for me, trying to clear the undead from the streets of Raccoon City and all."

Dina scoffed, leaning her head back again. "Don't let my little old wedding plans interfere with your video game schedule or anything. Oh!" She got up suddenly, moving to her purse. "Almost forgot." She pulled out a folded-up sheet and handed it to Relic. "Fill that out. Rook said you were going to help out in the kitchen now that you're old enough."

Relic unfolded the job application, a weird mix of dread and excitement churning within him. He held very tangible proof in his hands that he was growing up, which meant new responsibilities—outside of the life-and-death battles with Alternians—were creeping up on him.

Once upon a time, Relic might have groaned and tossed the paper away, finding any excuse he could to not face the reality that he would one day have to set out on his own and make a living. But now, he just nodded, strangely emboldened by Shrubble's sudden attack.

Despite the confusion, shock, and panic from a few hours ago weighing down his thoughts, Relic also felt strength and purpose, keeping him stable. Where that strength came from, he couldn't say, but he supposed the girl sleeping in his bed was mostly responsible.

Relic looked at all the blank lines on the job description, reminding him so much of the blank lines in his notebook before he wrote "Night of the Harrow." Thinking of that song now lit a sudden urgency in him, which he didn't understand. So instead of connecting it to Shrubble's sudden appearance, he associated it with the need to fill out the application and just grow up already.

He set his drumsticks aside and got up to look for a pen.

CHAPTER 12

The next day, Relic awoke with a purpose: to tell his dad about the stolen journal and Shrubble Von Hellspawn. But by the time he had gotten to school with Bree, so many things had diverted his thoughts that when third period rolled around, he was only concerned with inviting Nick and Tyler to D&D night so they could go over the new song he and Bree had written.

"You wrote a song about *Emerald Decay*?" Nick asked as the three of them changed into their gym clothes. The sour smell of the boys' locker room somehow seemed to complement Nick's tone, Relic thought. "That old tree-hugger horror movie with the goblin?"

Tyler took his jeans off and seemed to make a show of adjusting himself through his underwear, as if making sure his bandmates knew what he was packing (at least, that was how Relic interpreted it, always feeling nervous and insecure in that department). "Did you already write lyrics?"

Nodding, Relic said, "Some, but sort of just a draft. Don't really know the melody yet." He left out the part about writing them in his sleep. But the sense of urgency from last night persisted and he felt like Altar Stone *needed* to perform some original stuff at the party. "Mostly just wanted to lock the structure down."

As Relic took his shirt off, he noticed all the bruises from last night had healed even more since he checked them in the morning. *Super healing,* he thought—not the super power he would have chosen, but he'd take it.

"Cool," Tyler said, putting on his gym shorts.

"Hey."

The three of them turned in unison to see Sebastian Ford, already in his gym clothes. Relic was taken aback, not used to Delilah's fellow keyboardist acting chummy with them.

"Hey," Relic replied. "What's up?"

"Did you guys hear about the old Crane place? There was a murder there last night."

Nick scoffed, pulling his gym shirt on. "Can't start off a school year around here without a good murder."

Relic noticed Sebastian's eyes shuffling between Nick and Relic, avoiding Tyler. But Relic supposed that shouldn't surprise him, with Tyler's prolific history of homophobia. *Maybe that's why he keeps wearing those Barbie shoes,* Relic thought, *like some sort of ironic joke?*

"I heard it was the principal's brother," Sebastian added. "He was some kind of hermit."

Tyler shut his locker. "A bum living in a haunted house—doesn't seem like a huge loss." He stepped between Relic and Nick then, giving Sebastian a weak, almost playful shove. "Step aside, cocksucker."

"Dude," Relic said, offering at least a slight defense. But he noticed Sebastian oddly smiling as he turned away to also head toward class.

"Told you last year," Nick said, closing his own locker, "dude's such an asshole. Which I guess makes him a perfect singer, right?"

Relic snorted a laugh and joined the rest of the guys making their way toward the gym for a thirty-five-minute exercise in avoiding exercise.

In the other locker room, Bree was securing herself in a yellow sports bra with some difficulty. It wasn't the injuries from the battle with Shrubble—those had already begun healing, which she supposed was another side effect of the VANDAL stuff—it was her boobs already outgrowing her clothes again.

She felt both Delilah and Becca's wandering eyes, but it didn't bother her. Having developed before so many other girls her age, Bree was used to looks like that, and whether it was jealousy, disgust, or something else, there was nothing really to be done about it.

"So, are you and Sebastian boinking yet?" Becca asked Delilah.

"Why would we?" Delilah asked, completely unbothered by the snarky question. "He's gay and my friend and a bandmate."

Becca snorted a laugh. "Doesn't stop Bree."

Spinning around and puffing her chest out while she put her hair in a ponytail, Bree replied with raised eyebrows, "Oh, trust me. Relic's certainly not gay."

Delilah laughed this time, pulling on her gym shoes.

"So, you *are* tapping that then?" Becca asked, her vile smirk untarnished as she pulled her own shirt down over her bare chest, not needing the additional support.

Bree was about to tell Becca where she could shove all her nosey questions, but Janice Epstein had just joined them then, dropping her huge backpack onto the bench between the rows of lockers. The smell of medicine assaulted Bree's nostrils.

"You alright?" Delilah asked, standing up to check on her, apparently not liking the look on Janice's face.

The girl turned her ghastly expression so Bree could see then. "You didn't hear? The principal's brother got chopped up in the old Crane place." Her eyes darted to Delilah. "The one out in the country, near Romney. Harper told me some gang of bikers came to rob him, cutting up his body or something."

Bree heard the pounding on her front door then, shattering glass. Her gaze shifted from Janice to Delilah, their eyes locking; Bree knew the dhampir was thinking the same thing.

Janice continued sharing shocked details from the gossip, but Bree barely heard any of them. Her pulse was rising and she felt jagged roots tickling her neck, poised to bring their strangling embrace.

Some distant voice asked, "What's her problem?"

The laughter from other girls in the locker room took on a twisted, sinister quality, mocking Bree like that wretched little shaman who almost killed her. And then Bree sensed herself being dragged away, her feet clumsily trying to keep pace with whoever had her by the arm.

It's pulling me under, Bree thought, feeling that animated weed tighten around her neck, restricting her breath. *It never actually let me go...I just dreamed that Relic saved me.* The world started blackening.

But then she felt a slight chill below her waist, and then a pinch on her ass, snapping her out of the dark episode. She was in a stall and Delilah was shaking her head.

"You're taking all my doses," she said with annoyance, tucking the empty vial back into her bag. She fixed her eyes on Bree. "You good now? Can you get through gym class?"

In a daze, Bree nodded, wanting to kiss the girl for providing the sweet relief from the aftereffects of Shrubble Von Hellspawn.

"Good," Delilah said. "Because we're skipping school and going out to that house."

"Do we actually have to play?" Tyler asked, dribbling a basketball between his legs.

Relic scowled. "What do you mean *have to* play?! It's awesome, man. Gate's a badass dungeon master."

Lining up a shot, Tyler shrugged. "It's bad enough we have to play songs about dragons and stuff. People are going to start thinking I'm a nerd."

Nick gave a mocking laugh, nodding toward Tyler's choice of footwear. "Yeah, that seems like a huge concern of yours, twinkle toes."

"Don't be jealous of my style," Tyler said before sinking a three-pointer.

"Guys."

Relic turned to see Bree approaching, her face white and eyes wide. Next to her, Delilah looked less spooked, but the calm and detached facade she kept up at Chambers had fallen away.

"Yeah," Nick said, dribbling a ball between his legs, "we heard. Someone gutted the principal's brother."

Relic kept his attention on the girls, taking a step toward Bree and grabbing her hand. "You okay?" She squeezed his hand in response, once again reminding Relic how damn strong she was. But despite her grip, her hand trembled.

"It's connected," Bree whispered.

"Did you know the guy or something?" Tyler asked, stepping toward them.

"My dad went to school with the principal," Relic replied, covering for Bree. "We were just all talking the other day, so the timing is just...wild."

"Hm," Tyler said dismissively, turning back around to take another shot.

"We should go check the place out," Delilah said, not as quietly as Bree.

"Why the hell would you want to go out to that place?" Nick asked, coming over to join the discussion. "Some sort of family reunion thing? Is Crane even your dad anymore?"

Delilah shook her head, keeping her gaze on Relic. "We might find some answers."

"You know that *song* we wrote?" Bree said, eyebrows raised pointedly. "Delilah says there's a well out there. Might be cool to check it out—maybe get some more ideas for the lyrics."

"Dude," Nick said, putting a hand on Relic's shoulder to turn him around. "We need to get a band photo. Wasn't there like a well in *Emerald Decay* that the little dude kept crawling out of?" Nick touched his head and then held his arms wide as if presenting the vast scope of his brilliance. "That's perfect!"

"Yeah," Tyler said, tossing the basketball over his head, wildly missing the goal. "Beats gym class. How do we get out there?"

Relic could tell when he looked at Bree that she hadn't intended to make this a band trip, but neither of them could deny...it was a badass idea.

"This is a terrible idea," Gate groaned, his eyes nervously darting in every direction as if someone from the school were tailing them down 231. "Better not tell your dad about this." He slowed down as they turned right down a side access with no signs indicating it was actually a road.

Relic looked in the back of the van. Bree and Delilah rode in the middle seat, with Nick and Tyler in the back. The guys were talking about the upcoming show at Tammy's party, but both girls kept their eyes forward, looking as eager as Relic to get to this house and hopefully find something that explained this whole Shrubble situation.

Delilah fidgeted with the digital camera in her hands; the fact that her former adopted father had gotten her one for Christmas at least added an element of sanity to this whole expedition. They'd be able to get some Altar Stone band pictures that they could use to make fliers for the show.

Turning back to Gate, Relic spoke softly, explaining everything that happened last night in more detail. In order to get the janitor to risk his job and go against every adult instinct he had, Relic had to only briefly explain that this trip had to do with his dad's return. Now, Relic felt like he owed him the whole truth, so he gave as much of it as he could in a low voice without drawing the attention of Nick or Tyler.

"I don't know what you're hoping to find out there," Gate said. "Your dad and I last went there back in '81 and it was a dump even back then. That house has always been nothing but trouble."

That's probably why we'll find something there, Relic thought, but he kept it to himself. It seemed almost miraculous they randomly put this little field trip together, so he wouldn't jinx it by opening his mouth if he didn't have to.

"Speak of the devil and she appears," Gate said, nodding up the road as he began slowing down.

The legendary Crane Estate looked like it was about to fall apart. There were a few farm fixtures around the land, but the main structure was a great white crumbling eyesore that ruined an otherwise peaceful horizon. Even at this distance, Relic felt like he could smell the decay of the place.

Yellow police tape lined the perimeter, blocking off the drive with a giant X of yellow *Do Not Cross* bands stretching between the property's old rusty archway. Gate pulled the van to a stop along the road.

"Wicked," Tyler said, already scooting out of his seat to open the van's sliding door. "This place looks perfect."

"Yeah, there's the well," Nick said, tapping the window before following Tyler out of the van. "This'll look badass."

Relic took a moment to appreciate the fact that his bassist and vocalist seemed to still be getting along. Morbidly, he found himself almost *appreciating* this murder, as it might hold some answers to what happened last night while also keeping his band unified in macabre curiosity. Unfortunately, that feeling brought intense guilt, and he shook the thoughts away as he got out of the van.

Delilah caught his wrist once they were outside. Turning to her, he saw her eyes focused on something behind him, in the vast empty farmland surrounding the Crane Estate. "Do you feel that?" Her voice was just barely a whisper.

Relic focused, his eyes shifting between her and the decrepit house. *Dread?* he wondered. *Yeah, plenty of it.* But he just waited for her to explain.

Finally her eyes found his. "I felt it during that ritual. That...thickness?"

"Don't touch the tape!" Gate shouted, slamming the driver's side door. "Better yet, Nick, don't touch anything! No one can know we were here."

"I don't think I feel anything," Relic said, not sure he understood the sensation she described.

She let go of his arm and tucked her camera back into her bag as she followed the others toward the house. "This place is evil," she told Relic and Bree as they joined her. "Marshall said he only came here once when he was a teenager, but said it was a stain on the family or something. He wanted to have it torn down, or that name taken off the sign, but the Sinclairs wouldn't let it go."

Relic found that odd. It seemed like real estate moguls like Marshall Crane wouldn't have a problem forcing people off properties. There had to have been more to it, but he filed that away as they carefully stepped through the police tape.

The act of crossing that makeshift barrier triggered something in Relic, as if he had just passed through a physical boundary—a forcefield or something. While the look of the world was unchanged, the *feel* of it certainly did change, and he opened his mouth to tell Delilah that he was pretty sure he felt what she felt now. But before he could, Nick was shouting something and laughing.

Relic joined Bree and Delilah as they jogged up the drive to see what the commotion was. Gate was standing near Nick and Tyler to the side of the house. The well. Seeing that structure actually did change the way the world looked to Relic. His vision flashed between the present and some alternate world where an identical version of that well appeared in grainy artwork, complete with faded colors, streaks, and flakes of the scene falling away—creating the weathered cover of *Emerald Decay II: The Poisoned Well.*

It was the same exact well, from the shape of every stone to the rotted wooden posts that supported the sides. The background was slightly different, but even the angle he currently stood at.... it was all the same. Relic had stared at that book cover long enough to memorize it, and the exactitude of it all stole his breath.

"What is this thing?" Nick asked, standing over a metal device on wheels.

"A harrow," Gate said. "Used for tearing up the soil so it'll take seed better."

Night of the Harrow, Relic thought. It was all too surreal, too freaking weird.

Tyler was crouched near the thing. "Yeah, that looks like blood all over those spiky wheels. Wonder if this was used for the murder." He turned toward the well. "Maybe they found the body down there."

They didn't, Relic thought, not sure how he knew—but he did. He knew there was nothing down that well anymore. Being this close to it, there was no doubt in his mind, that is where Shrubble Von Hellspawn emerged.

The cradle. The word came to him unbidden.

Now, to figure out why.

"Relic?"

He turned to Bree, who looked at him with that mom-like expression of concern. He stepped toward her, whispering, "It's the same as the book. And that harrow—"

Recognition was clear on her face immediately. "The song..."

"Bree." Relic swallowed, looking at the house as a horrifying realization finally pieced all these cryptic clues together. He looked at her, seeing all the panic in his guts displayed on Bree's face now. "Did I do this?"

The sound of a sharp slap jolted Relic, making him gasp. But he turned to see Nick had just stood up and clapped his hands together. "Let's act like a metal band and get some super serious photos taken in front of this freaky murder hole."

Relic had no problem keeping a morose, heavy metal expression on his face during the photo shoot. His mind was beset by guilt, confusion, and paranoia. While posing with his band in front of the bloody harrow, he tried to make probable connections between the song he sleep-wrote, the cult's ritual, and Shrubble stepping out of the pages of *Emerald Decay II*.

Afterward, they all made their way toward the house, which also had police tape surrounding the wrap-around porch, blocking the front door.

"We shouldn't go in there," Gate said, sounding more eager than ever to leave the place. "You guys got your photos—let's not push our luck."

"I bet we could get in through there," Tyler said, pointing toward several pieces of siding that had been propped up in front of a broken window. "They didn't tape that all up."

"We can just put the tape back," Nick said, pointing to the front door. "They'll never know we were here."

"Suit yourself," Gate said, pulling out a pack of cigarettes. "Can't say I didn't warn you."

Nick turned to him curiously. "Scared of the principal's old dump, Mr. Murphy?"

Gate snapped his lighter on and shielded the flame from the wind as he drew it to his cigarette. "Yep. You should be too."

"You been in there?" Tyler asked now, stepping toward the janitor. "Seen inside?"

Gate nodded, exhaling a cloud of smoke. "Unknown Oath played our third show in there, back before Lana's parents split up."

Relic thought back to his dad and Principal Sinclair hugging.

"Nice," Nick said, impressed. "Haunted house show." He turned and carefully weaved his body through the police tape. "Now I gotta go in—see where Unknown Oath cut their teeth. It's like a pilgrimage now."

Tyler followed. Relic was once more struck by how this whole thing seemed to really bring his band together—maybe that was why he grabbed Bree's hand and followed them up the porch steps. Nick carefully pulled aside enough of the police tape that they could open the door, immediately replacing the crime scene marker after Altar Stone and their dhampir companion crossed the threshold.

The smell was the first thing to hit Relic as he entered the cursed place, but then the sight of all the garbage was enough to make him almost throw up.

"Whoa," Tyler said, drawing everyone's attention to the cracked wall between the foyer and what might have served as the living room. There was dried blood pooled around the floor and the piles of clothes and magazines.

"Are those all bras?" Bree asked, revolted.

Tyler used his pink shoe to poke one of the open magazines, which showed a smiling woman from the 1970s in not-so-modest lingerie, her pubic hair and nipples visible. "Dude sure loved his knockers."

Relic felt an odd blush creep up his cheeks when Bree lightly smacked his stomach with the back of her hand for gawking at the creepy collection.

Footsteps on the ratty rug leading down the foyer drew Relic's attention. "Hey. Where you going?"

Delilah didn't turn around when she replied in a detached voice. "Checking something."

Making to follow her, Relic was stopped short by Bree's hand. He turned to see her motioning toward the row of TVs. Not sure what she was indicating, he followed her, lightly stepping over the bras and magazines. There were numbered tags all over the room, which Relic suspected were points of interest for the police investigation.

"Ugh, smells like a toilet in here," Nick groaned, walking toward the dining room while Bree and Relic inspected a stack of VHS tapes on top of one of the TVs. "What kind of undead morons would want to haunt this place? Crapper the Flatulent Ghost?"

Relic's eyes widened as he followed Bree's pointing finger. There were dozens of copies of all five of the *Skrimkins* movies: at least twenty copies of *Skrimkins*, maybe half that number of *Skrimkins 2*, only a few copies of *Skrimkins 3: The Last Hatch*, and then one copy each of *Skrimkins 4: We're Back* and *Skrimkins 5: One More Swarm*.

"This can't be a coincidence," Bree whispered. Relic felt the terror in her voice and was compelled to reach for her hand again. She grasped it eagerly.

He swallowed. "Yeah...but I still don't know what it means. Was the principal's brother the one responsible? Or did I somehow get him killed?"

"Yes!" Tyler shouted.

Bree and Relic turned to see him holding a small card up.

"What is it?" Nick asked from the other side of the dining room table, unable to even see Tyler over the mountain of garbage.

"It's a 1984 Donruss Don Mattingly rookie card!" Tyler said, sounding like an excited little boy. "It's in a case—you can get like a few hundred bucks for this thing."

"Dude, dibs on the finder's fee," Nick said, moving to join Tyler. "You pussies wouldn't have even come in here if it weren't for me."

Before Relic could tell them they couldn't take anything, Delilah appeared in the foyer. "We should go," she said, her voice much calmer than her appearance. Relic rarely saw Delilah unsettled, but she certainly looked that way now. He was reminded of how scared she looked when Shrubble had chased her to Bree's house.

Neither Tyler nor Nick needed convincing, both admiring the baseball card that Relic knew he'd never convince them to leave behind. But he had more important things on his mind.

"What's wrong?" Relic asked Delilah once they were outside and far enough away from Nick and Tyler. "Did you see something?"

After checking to see that the other two members of Altar Stone were distracted enough, she pulled out her digital camera. Relic and Bree looked over either of Delilah's shoulders as she scrolled through the band's photos on her camera's display.

Finally, she got to the photos from inside the house. The first few were of a study, just as messy as the rest of the house, but still retaining shelves of old books that the previous occupant probably never touched.

Delilah clicked through these quickly, then stopped on a picture of an old leather album. "I found this tucked behind some books, hidden behind a row of encyclopedias—where someone maybe wanted it to stay hidden because no one actually reads those things."

The next photo was a shot of the open book, featuring random color photos from someone's high school days. Relic noticed a familiar face among the pictures. "That's the principal," Relic said, pointing to the camera's display.

Delilah didn't respond, she just pushed the arrow on the camera to skip to the next shot.

Relic's dad looked so much like Relic's own reflection in that photo. Steven Meyers was sticking his tongue out and flashing two metal horns next to Lana Sinclair, who made a similar face. Both of them were wearing what looked like cult robes with their hoods lowered.

The permanent marker below the picture made Relic so light-headed he thought he would pass out.

"What does that say?" Bree asked, leaning forward.

Relic looked toward Gate, who waited in the driver's seat of the van. The look on the man's face told Relic that they had found what he didn't want them to find.

"Adratheon's Chosen," Relic said.

He heard that mocking laughter once more.

CHAPTER 13

The ride back to town was somber, with Relic not even able to talk to Gate in front of the others out of fear that he might begin shouting at the man. He clearly knew something he wasn't saying, and Relic felt betrayed by one of the only men he had been able to trust before his father had returned.

And now that his father seemed to be some sort of disciple of Adratheon, Relic didn't even know who he could trust. *Maybe Adratheon's a cool guy,* Relic thought to himself in an odd moment of sarcastic malaise. *Maybe Dad didn't say he worshiped some interdimensional hexer because, in reality, it wasn't a big deal, right?*

Sighing, Relic sunk into himself as he watched the trees pass by outside, waiting to be out of the van.

They had convinced Gate just to take them to Relic's house, since D&D was after dinner and Nick didn't have a ride until his dad got his cast off.

"We can work on that song until then," Tyler suggested.

Should we? Relic wondered. If writing that damn song had caused all this to happen, what would happen if the band put music to it, like they had with "Alternus" at the battle of the bands last semester?

Then again, maybe this was all because of the cult's ritual, and the song was the only thing that could counteract Shrubble's power? Relic realized he could run over the possibilities for the rest of the semester and still probably be no closer to any real solution. He needed to confront his dad...about everything.

"I'll go grab my guitar," Bree said, hopping out of the van as Gate pulled to a stop in front of Relic's house. "Go call you guys' parents so we don't get the cops called on us or something—I don't want anything ruining the game tonight."

She gave Relic a quick look over her shoulder before adding, "I freaking need it."

She was right, Relic knew. All this heavy stuff going on...they needed a break from it. He remembered what his dad had told him so many times since returning from Alternus:

"The world's always trying to end itself, dude. Can't let that stop you from being a teenager."

It seemed like those words hadn't resonated with him until Bree spoke the sentiment aloud. Relic missed being excited for *Resident Evil 2* marathons, or D&D night, or going to the theater to watch action movies. Laramie might be dead-set on sucking itself into a vortex, but it wasn't going to happen tonight.

Tonight he was going to play *Dungeons & Dragons* with his band.

"Here," Delilah said.

Relic spun around to see her holding the camera out to him as Nick slipped around her to escape the van.

"You hold onto this." She nodded at him knowingly. "Maybe your dad will want to see it."

"Yeah. You not hanging out?"

She shook her head. "I need to talk to my dad too. But I think it'll go better if it's just me."

"Need a ride?" Gate asked. "I need to go grab my stuff anyway."

Relic pocketed the camera as Gate drove Delilah to Guy's apartment. Relic led Nick and Tyler into his house where they found Relic's mom sweeping the floor.

"Hey," she said, flipping the vacuum off. "You guys mind kicking your shoes off over there? I have the wedding planner coming over with some cake samples and I just finished cleaning this gross carpet." Giving Tyler a strange look, Dina added, "Quite the pair you got on there."

Tyler kicked off his pink shoes and followed Nick to the basement to call their parents and wait for Bree. Relic went to his room to grab his notebook with the lyrics. But when he pushed his door open and began stepping through the threshold, a vision struck him again like it had at the well.

His room...shifted; the colorful images of the heavy metal and fantasy posters adorning his wall seemed to bleed and go sepia tone, giving Relic a strange sensation like he was stepping into a cold fire.

In that chilling moment, Relic realized the room was changing into how it had looked during his childhood. The posters were replaced by striped wallpaper, and the discarded clothing on the floor became action figures and random toys. He even saw himself in the bed, bundled up in the *Masters of the Universe* comforter that he used in the basement nowadays.

Most shocking was the robed figure standing at the foot of his bed. Adratheon's cruel laughter began echoing in the distance as Relic watched the cultist sway, their arms raised over Relic's bed, casting some incantation—the words were lost to Relic, his mind beset by wicked mockery from beyond.

The way everything looked—almost like an image wrapped in plastic—made Relic think of the photo Delilah had shown him. That was why he wasn't even surprised when the cultist lowered their hood to reveal it was Steven Meyers. His dad gave the sleeping Relic a macabre smile as the vision started to fade.

When the world returned to how it should be, Relic stared at the notebook on his bed. Blinking several times, making sure the room was indeed how it should have been, he realized that it was a different notebook in place of the one he had left there before school.

It was his dad's journal, the one that had been stolen from the basement two weeks ago. He rushed over to it, touching it only slightly to ensure that it was physical and not some sort of hallucination. He moved it to reveal his own notebook beneath it, as if someone had intentionally placed his dad's here, knowing he was going to be needing his lyrics.

He stuck his head out of the bedroom. "Mom!"

Dina peered around the corner of the living room down the hall. "Yeah?"

What am I going to ask her? he thought. If he asked about the journal, she would immediately start asking all sorts of questions: "Where did you get this? What's the big deal? What's in it? You didn't tell me someone broke into the house and stole your things!"

"Did you... Were you home all day?"

She gave him a puzzled look. "Yeah, I told you I was off today. I have wedding planning stuff."

"And no one's been here?"

Her face remained unchanged, perplexed. "Calvin came by and took me to lunch."

So you weren't here all day, Relic thought, annoyed. He gave her a nod and retreated to his room. It was pointless to ask her if she had locked the front door; part of him knew she hadn't.

"Something wrong, Relic?"

Relic wanted to laugh, but just said, "No," and sat on his bed, opening the small journal. The first half of the thing was filled with sketches of various band logos for what Relic assumed were his dad's original names for Unknown Oath; some that stuck out to him were Dragon's Child, Majestra, and, Relic's favorite, Broodle Broth.

But his father's real writing began in the middle of the book, starting with scattered lines that looked like song lyrics and then evolving into chunks of almost illegible notes. Relic's frantic eyes glossed over most of the words, but he stopped at a random page and read:

Maybe I should take the book to someone—I don't think Ricky truly realized what it was when he loaned it to me. But what if some other band got their hands on it and beat us to the punch?

The rest of the paragraph was illegible, and Relic kept flipping, hoping that maybe his dad's penmanship might improve. However, it seemed to only get worse the further he flipped through the notes.

Finally, he landed on a page with a word he absolutely recognized, but something about seeing it written in his father's hand confirmed the dreadful reality he hoped was just his paranoid delusions.

Adratheon's Chosen was written across the top of the page, and in squished, rushed letters Relic could make out words like *hexlords* and *bargain* and several occurrences of *The Dominion Hexes* (which was always underlined at least twice). Then he turned to a page that was pristine compared to the others, as if his father had taken care to record the passage legibly; it was titled "Dealing with the Dragon."

As Relic began steadying his darting eyes to focus on the writing below that title, he heard the front door slam and then footsteps coming down the hall. Tucking his dad's journal under his bedsheets, Relic grabbed his own notebook and stood up to greet Bree, who had her axe in hand.

She must have seen the worry on his face. "What's up?"

Relic shook his head, wanting to tell her what he had just found but knowing they wouldn't have time to properly discuss it right now. Thinking of a good cover, he simply raised the notebook and said, "Just these lyrics...it's freaking me out having written this and then...at the Crane place..."

Bree stepped forward to put her hand on the back of his neck. She meant to do it gently, he knew, but it felt like she was grabbing a dog by the collar. The kiss she gave him made the forceful embrace more bearable.

"Let's go put some music to it—maybe that will help." She smiled. "That's what bands do, right? Make sense of crazy shit by writing songs about it?"

Relic smiled. "Good point."

Altar Stone wrote until it was time for the pre-game pizza at Bree's house. By the time six o'clock rolled around, they pretty much had a new song ready to rehearse—so much so that they were all groaning about not having their gear in Relic's basement, each of them wanting to hear the song they had crafted.

During their writing session, Relic was relieved to hear Tyler's voice back in working order. It had only been a few days since The Voodoo disaster, so whatever had affected his throat must have been psychological or something. He sounded great now.

While Relic scribbled down structure notes while Bree played all her parts unplugged, Nick plucked invisible bass strings against his leg while Tyler looked over Relic's shoulder and put the lyrics to different melodies. The process felt natural, and Relic felt immense relief that playing the song didn't have some arcane repercussions—like opening a portal to a different dimension.

But he supposed if it were anything like "Alternus," they would have to play this song in front of a live crowd to truly see its power. Relic couldn't help but wonder then if they were actually going to play this song at Tammy's party. There was a sensation in the pit of his stomach, which he supposed might be the "gut feeling" that detectives liked to talk about when it came to trusting their hunches in old movies.

Relic's gut told him that they had to play this song live as soon as possible.

The doorbell signaled the end of their creative efforts and Altar Stone went upstairs to meet Unknown Oath's rhythm section.

"Hey, man," Steven said, looking at his son with a forced expression. Though, his face was still showing the damage it had taken during breakfast on Sunday, so Relic didn't think much of it—he was probably just still in pain. Steven gave Bree a similar smile and nodded to the other guys. "I heard we'll have a couple new party members tonight."

"Hey, Mr. Meyers," Tyler said. "Sorry my dad's such a dick."

"Not really news to us," Gate said, his thick arm wrapped around a stack of D&D books. He nodded toward the Thompkinses' house. "Let's do this."

The group walked to Bree's, Relic slowing his pace hoping his dad would take the hint and hang back from the others so they could talk. Fortunately, he did just before they had to cross the street to get to Bree's.

Before Relic could even say anything, his dad just said, "Gate told me where you guys went."

Not wanting to draw attention, Relic just kept his eyes forward as he asked, "Now can you tell me what the heck is going on then?"

Steven put his hands into the pockets of his jeans, kicking a pebble across the street as if he were a child that had just been scolded. "Gate will take care of it. Then we can talk after the game if you still have questions."

Still have questions? Relic thought, finally turning toward his dad to hopefully make his confusion clear. But his dad didn't seem to want to meet his eyes, so they just followed the rest of the game group into the Thompkinses' house.

As they crammed in through the door, a frenzied voice from the kitchen called out, "There you are!"

A robed and hooded figure leapt into view, standing in the kitchen doorway like some sort of cult warden. Relic gasped loudly and nearly stumbled back. Tyler and Nick gave him flabbergasted looks.

"Dad," Bree groaned, dodging around the other band members as she carried her guitar back to her room, "you're such a geek."

Russ Thompkins lowered his hood. "Sorry, I don't have much use for the wizard costume anymore, so," he flourished his hands in the wide sleeves of the robe, "tonight I'm going all in on Salvorin Crawthorn, the Last Conjurer of Belatham."

Gate moved toward the kitchen with his gaming supplies. "As long as you got enough pizza, you can dress up as whoever you want. Just not Maganaut—that bitch is dead from last game."

Tyler looked back at Relic, pointing to Russ and whispering, "Is he for real?"

Relic could only smile. He hadn't seen Russ this happy in a while. Suddenly, the evening felt like it might be a normal break from all the dire shit that had been piling up this week—which was still just the first week of school.

As the teens dug into the pizza, Relic overheard the adults talking near the head of the table. His dad asked Russ something that Relic couldn't hear, and Russ motioned with his hands like something had exploded. He wore a bright smile that meant whatever had blown up was a good thing.

"...she said it totally fell through," Russ said. Relic tried to hear bits and pieces of the conversation through his band's chatter about the Crane Estate, but he only caught maybe half of what was said. "I thought...fight after fight...but she's like a new woman, man...fine now. Yeah. DeMono Tech...Crane blew it...had a chance, but now Rothen can..."

"What's wrong?"

Startled, Relic turned to Bree. She was handing him a paper plate with a piece of sausage pizza, which he took gratefully and smiled. "Nothing. Just glad to see your dad back to normal."

Bree smiled back. "Yeah. I think whatever him and Mom were fighting about got resolved. Probably something at her work—she always lets job stuff affect her way too much."

After everyone had some pizza, Gate called the game to a start and they all found their chairs.

"Okay," Gate began in his dungeon master voice, "for the new guys." He sat behind his DM screen with his fingers steepled. "This game takes place in the world of Aetha, specifically on the continent of Noveth and the region known as Westerra."

Nick breathed out loudly. "Is this all going to be on the test?"

"The recent events are as follows: Salvorin Crawthorn," Gate continued, ignoring Nick and motioning to Russ, who had his hood drawn again, "is the only human resident in the halfling town of Belatham, and he has been charged by the Arcania to clear out the old tower in the nearby woods.

"The halfling scoundrel, Rake Stallow," Gate motioned to Steven Meyers, "was offered an introduction to the syndicate of thieves known as the Guild in return for helping Salvorin." He then nodded toward Bree and Relic, "And the elven N'vresk siblings, Lethanna the druid and Kraves the ranger, were sent by the Eldercrowns to assist with the task.

"You two," Gate said, standing up to lean over the DM screen and hand Tyler and Nick their respective character sheets, "are playing as Vandrik Burl the dwarven Oather—which is a paladin—and his reluctant travel companion, the half-orc fighter Lash, who happens to be in the Guild."

"Dibs on Lash," Nick said, snatching his sheet.

"Aren't dwarves fat and ugly?" Tyler asked, looking at his sheet as if it were some repulsive image. "Also," Tyler looked at Relic and Bree, "you two are siblings? Gross, dude."

Relic chuckled.

"So, are we still at the temple?" Bree asked Gate, ignoring Tyler's comment. "Like, fully healed after that last encounter?"

Gate nodded. "It's the next day, and the halfling cleric, Shayne, wanders in as you all are waking up." He cleared his throat to get into Shayne's character and looked at Steven. "Rake, the Guild has sent someone—they arrived last night."

Steven cracked open a beer Russ had given him. "How would you know? Guild agents don't announce their arrivals this far south of Andelor."

Gate was checking his notes behind the screen. "You don't often see half-orcs down here in the Acerage. If he's not with the Guild, feel free to pull my ears and call me a gnome."

"Rude," Russ said with a laugh, holding his hood away from his mouth so he could take a bite of pizza.

"Alright," Steven said, setting his can down. "I'm going to make sure the others are aware before I go meet this big shot."

Bree made a motion above the table like she were nudging something with both hands. "I'm going to wake up my dire badger—come on, Trunks, time to work—and follow, dragging my brother with me."

Relic mimed himself getting pulled by the arm.

Gate looked at Nick. "Alright, Lash, you're waiting impatiently out in the vestibule. You've had a rough trek down to the Acreage—which is the halfling country—and the only reason you came in with Vandrik is because you stumbled across his wrecked caravan and decided to help fend off the goblins ambushing it, mostly because you were hoping for loot."

Nick smiled. "Sounds about right."

"Why didn't I kill him?" Tyler asked.

Gate waved the question away. "You're an Oather. You only really care about killing witches. You were coming to Belatham because the Arcania sent you to help with taking back the tower. So, you two see this strange group of miscreants, and Lash, you have a letter with you that you were instructed to only open in the presence of Rake—the Guild would have your head if you let it fall into the wrong hands or opened it prematurely."

"So much responsibility," Nick groaned.

Russ tapped the table. "Salvorin steps forward, noticing the Oather with the Arcanian mark on his neck and says, 'Good Sir, have you come to reclaim the Warwick Academy?'"

"Uh," Tyler said, looking to Gate for guidance, "I think so?"

Gate nodded. "You have other motives, but yeah, you'd likely let him assume he knows exactly why you're here—Oathers typically keep their true motives hidden."

"I have a note!" Nick declared in a deep voice, holding up a fake scroll.

Steven pointed at the invisible message, an excited look on his bruised face. "From the Guild? Open it! Read it"

"Can I?" Nick asked Gate, but Gate just motioned for him to make the call himself. "Alright, I open it and read it aloud."

Gate sat up straighter in his seat, casting a quick glance at Steven—Relic felt something tangible and foreboding passing between them—and then began:

"The letter explains that there is a Hexlord that has been freed."

At the mention of a "hexlord," Relic realized this was what his dad had meant earlier—this was how he planned to explain things to Relic. So he leaned forward and gave Gate his full attention.

"The letter is brief, and says that the Guild and the Arcania must work together to fight against the threat of the Hexlords. But when Shayne overhears, she gasps and begins breathing heavily."

Bree raised a finger. "I'm going to check on her to see if she's alright."

Gate assumed Shayne's voice to say, "The Hexlords are the elite minions of Avaxian, a demi-god of ruthless ambition that tried to take over all of Westerra. A powerful cult managed to lock Avaxian away in an abyssal prison, and they siphoned Avaxian's trapped power to fulfill their ambitions through hexcraft and deceit."

Relic looked at his dad, who gave him knowing looks during Gate's roleplaying.

"But Avaxian was more cunning than the cult," Shayne continued through Gate, "and he managed to siphon his power through a bard named Graythan Morgrave."

Gustave Moreau, Relic thought, finding his dad's method of explaining things both clever and obnoxious at the same time.

"The bard carried out Avaxian's ploy," Gate had Shayne say, "using his smuggled power to create hidden gateways to his prison that only his most elusive thralls could use—the ones we call the Hexlords. These devious creatures guard Avaxian's divided power, awaiting the time when their weakened lord is strong enough to piece himself back together and take over all of Westerra as he originally devised."

There was a brief silence as Gate finished Shayne's speech, and then Tyler commented, "Dude, I just want to kill something."

The table shared a laugh, even Relic who, despite the weight of everything that was laid before him, found comfort in his dad sharing that with him—even if it was in a super complicated way. He found a level of trust restored between them, and was grateful when the "real" game began.

"Dude," Nick laughed, "that was badass, Mr. Murphy!"

"Thanks, kid. But like I tell you every time—call me Gate."

Nick didn't seem to hear him as they made their way back to Relic's house. "But that gnoll leader being all like, 'Get the half-orc first!' And I just cleaved through all four of them..."

Tyler laughed loudly as he walked with Nick and Gate, replaying the highlights of the three-hour session. It warmed Relic's heart.

"I hope that made sense," Steven said, low enough that only Relic could hear.

Nodding, Relic looked at his dad, wanting to push for more. But tonight was a lot. "Yeah, I think. I just still don't know what it all has to do with—I mean, that song we wrote before the game. What if we play it, and—"

Holding up a hand, Steven stopped his son, his eyes focusing on the distant black trees on the horizon. "There's so much you can't control, man. Trust me, I went through so much of what you're dealing with—maybe more, but I won't say that for sure." He looked back at Relic. "I think you know enough about how this stuff works...knowing too much about all that happens in this town can be a bad thing. The last thing we can afford to do...is be afraid."

When Relic and his dad reached the van, Tyler was waiting for them. "Thanks for inviting us, man. Was really fun." His smile somehow looked both artificial and genuine, and it took a moment for Relic to realize that it was a *real* Tyler smile—not the cruel, mocking grins that he had gotten from Tyler for the past few years or the restrained ones he still offered the world on occasion.

His childhood friend was reawakened, and it was probably that revelation that kept Relic from asking his father any burning questions that still bothered him. Standing on the curb, waving as the van drove away, Relic cursed himself for not confronting his dad about the vision in his room, the vision of Adratheon at Rook's, or the photo of him and their principal possibly at some cult party.

It was a lot for the third day of sophomore year of high school, so he allowed himself to let it go for now as he turned to head inside, unaware that Cecily Moreau was waiting for him in his dreams.

CHAPTER 14

B ree tossed and turned in her bed Wednesday night, feeling like sleep was a futile pursuit. The VANDAL serum was leaving her system again, its euphoric presence replaced by uncomfortable cravings that only seemed to worsen with each dose she took. She tried to tend to those cravings herself, but every time she thought release would come, Relic's face would appear in her mind, that expression of horror he had given her when she had desperately thrown herself at him.

It was no use.

For Bree, shame was the antithesis to that kind of release. And now it felt like any sort of intimacy or sexual urges were intricately woven into the threads of that memory. It would take time and careful effort to undo that stitching.

Sitting up in bed, she decided she may as well make use of these unplanned waking hours. She wanted to lift heavy things, maybe go for a run. Looking at the clock, she saw it was almost midnight—she wouldn't be able to put on any music. Bree grabbed her old Walkman with the Rush mixtape her dad had made her a few years ago and got some junky workout clothes on.

As she navigated the dark living room, she saw headlights coming up the drive. Realizing she'd finally get a chance to see her mom on a weeknight, she eagerly went to the kitchen, quickly filled up a water bottle, and turned toward the mudroom.

However, her mom didn't come in from the garage. Bree heard the car door slam and her mom's muffled voice, but she never came into the house. Walking toward the door, Bree could hear Lydia Thomkins clearer now; she was on her mobile phone, talking angrily.

"...I don't care what you have to tell them, Devon," she was saying, "I'm not going to present this to the board until I have a firm agreement from Fabian. I heard what happened with Crane—on the off chance we don't meet the required specifications, I don't want him having the option of pulling out."

There was a long pause before Lydia added, "Well make it happen, because I need to find out how to get funding for the labs to reopen." There were footsteps, and Bree slipped away from the door, around the kitchen table, and back into the living room. She put her headphones on and began to casually walk into the kitchen so she could properly act surprised by her mom's presence.

"...we can discuss it tomorrow—oh, you're up late, Bree—I'll call you tomorrow. I have to go." Lydia clicked off her phone as Bree pretended to be completely shocked to see her mom.

Lowering her headphones, Bree motioned to the garage. "I was going to go work out. Couldn't sleep."

"It's almost midnight," her mom said with a wave of her hand. "Here, I have some melatonin in the cabinet. We can chill out—as the kids say— and watch a brainless movie until you pass out." Without waiting for an answer, Lydia went to change out of her plum-colored suit.

Honestly, Bree was totally content to hang out with her mom a little. They rarely saw each other anymore, and conking out on the couch sounded preferable to sweating her ass off in the garage for the third night in a row.

Once Bree was properly medicated and Lydia poured herself some wine, mother and daughter sat on the living room couch under the muted glow of their TV. As Lydia cruised the channels, looking for something to watch, she asked, "So, what's new with you, dear?"

Bree looked at her mom, thinking she had never looked so beautiful to her. She had ditched her gaudy Rothen garb for an old Fleetwood Mac shirt that hung off her chest in a way that reminded Bree how similarly they were built. Lydia's auburn hair was tousled up in a lazy bun and all her makeup had been washed off. Bree wished her mom didn't have to get so spruced up for her job—and while she was wishing, she wished that her mom didn't want to chit chat at the moment.

Well, Mom, Bree thought, *I'm taking the drugs that you gave the dhampir that happens to be my boyfriend's ex, I'm hornier than Bowser's spiked shell, and today my band and I snuck onto a crime scene and discovered that we might have accidentally released a goblin-like shaman that is running around eating up the other monsters in town.*

Bree settled on, "Not much."

"Oh, come on," Lydia urged. "I'm stuck in an office all day. You're in a rock band, dating your drummer, and just starting sophomore year of high school. Give me something so I can live vicariously through you." She settled on TBS, which tended to play late night movies; tonight it was *Baby Boom,* which made Bree think of Relic. She smiled.

"Relic and I wrote a new song," Bree offered, yawning. She couldn't believe how well the melatonin was already helping; or it could have been the idle chit chat that usually put Bree to sleep. "And we have another show on Halloween."

"That's exciting!" Lydia gasped, taking a sip of her wine. Bree was pleased to see that her mom was being genuine—she could tell when she faked stuff, having heard her on the phone for work and, on some unfortunate occasions, overheard her parents going to town on each other in the bedroom. "Are you two...advancing things at all?" She raised her eyebrows.

Bree normally wouldn't be shy to tell her mom about sex stuff, but she couldn't stop seeing Relic's terrified face, or shake the guilt she felt for tugging him off as a means of distraction. Not being a good liar, Bree latched onto some diversionary truth that just came back to her. "Speaking of Relic; did you hear that his mom lost her wedding venue?"

Gasping again, with more stunned shock than pleasant surprise, Lydia set her wine down on the coffee table. "She didn't?! Oh my god, I have to call her—that's terrible. I—" Lydia stopped then, her eyes going distant.

"Mom?"

She blinked, focusing again on Bree. "Sorry, I just had an idea that might help her."

A question came to Bree then so suddenly, she couldn't stop it from falling out of her weary lips—sleep was coming hard and fast. "Are you having an affair with Relic's dad?"

Lydia tilted her head, her brow furrowing only slightly.

"Someone I know...said they saw you, like, on a date with him."

The smile that spread across her mom's lips was unsettling. It was the smile of a comic book villain about to unveil their nefarious plot.

"Steven and I are old friends, Bree. I had to meet with him secretly—when I was supposed to be heading up to Michigan—because there are strict laws against the things we were discussing." She calmly reached for her wine, keeping her shrewd eyes on her daughter. "Which I can trust you will keep quiet about, right?"

Bree blinked, curling up now on the couch and fighting to keep her eyes open, wanting to embrace the tiredness that finally sought to overtake her. "Keep quiet about what?"

Lydia waved a hand as she sat back, pulled her legs up onto the couch, and returned to watching the movie. "Oh, boring work stuff. His old band manager actually works for a company we want to partner with. Corporate espionage is not as thrilling as a James Bond movie, hon."

Before Lydia had even finished the thought, Bree was already descending into sleep.

Just down the street, Relic had already been sleeping for a while. For the first couple hours, he was granted peaceful slumber, a reprieve from the spiraling vortex of unanswered questions, potential threats emerging from every corner of Laramie, and a sinking suspicion that something was up with his girlfriend.

However, just as Bree had finally managed to drift off, Relic found himself in a familiar dreamworld, where a thin veil of greenish mist was the only thing separating him from oblivion. That was where he heard the whispers again.

"Relic..."

The dreary, light voice that carried his name could only be associated with one thing in his memory, and that was the face of the Widow. What he once believed was a comatose Delilah calling out to him from her mental prison, he now recognized as the cursed muse that had haunted him throughout freshman year.

"What do you want?!" Relic shouted. His voice boomed in that surreal world, pushing the mist away in a gust. *Whoa*, his sleeping mind thought, *that's new*. He looked down and saw his own hands for a change. *Very new.*

He had been accustomed to being a formless specter when he experienced these dreams—just an immaterial vessel, forced to witness whatever portents the powers that be decreed he must see.

The realization that he was actually *here* suddenly changed the landscape. The mist took on shapes and thickened, until a Tim Burton version of his neighborhood materialized, passing by him as if he were on a conveyor belt. The sudden motion made him consider moving his legs—but he was already walking, on his way back home from Bree's.

It was the night of the robbery.

Yellow eyes began to glow all around him, lurking in the tall, living trees that didn't actually border his street in the real world. Relic began to run, wanting to be free of those watching eyes (which reminded him of the skrimkins) and hoping to see if the intruder was still in his house.

Checking the side of his house, he saw the window was already broken. So he leaped up the porch that was not really his porch (but close enough), pushed open the door, and hurried down the basement stairs.

Cecily Moreau sat by his father's box of books, her back turned. The shattered glass from the window formed a sharp, icy pattern around her—if Relic had been in a video game, he would have known she was the NPC he had to talk to for this particular quest.

At the sound of his gasp, Cecily turned her head. It wasn't the Widow's torn and tortured face that looked at him; it was how Cecily Moreau must have truly looked before Valaina ruined her.

"You heard me," Cecily said, turning back to the box. Her pale skin was draped in a sheer, bloody nightgown, and she looked every bit the ghost that she was. "I've been calling for a while."

"Why?" was all Relic could think to ask. He stepped toward her, cautiously.

"I wanted to show you," she said.

As Relic stepped even closer, he could see the contents of the box over her shoulder and he felt like he was about to get so sick that he might choke on nocturnal vomit in the real world.

He forgot exactly how many of her children she had killed, but Cecily Moreau regarded the bloody box full of their body parts like it were a treasure chest she had been seeking all her life. Relic kept his gaze averted, but whatever power he held over this dream world made him smell unpleasant things wafting from that gruesome package.

"Thanks for showing me," Relic said, wanting to wake up.

"What do you see?"

Relic looked around the room, noticing how similar the place looked to how it had his freshman year—his drums still dominating almost half the room. This was certainly not the night of the robbery. He turned back toward Cecily and the box now just had books.

"Books," he said.

"Because you want to see books," Cecily said. "This is a cursed place, Relic, but I needed you to see—nobody showed me until it was too late. My husband came here to treat with Adratheon. He called it the Between, and I think it's where I'll remain now."

"This is a dream," Relic said, as if convincing himself of the fact.

Cecily just nodded. "I think that's how Adratheon reached Gustave...the man loved to dream. Here in the Between, the mind can hide, and I'd rather hide now and forever—from our world and theirs. But this place will fall if Adratheon awakens the hexes."

The hexes, Relic thought, remembering what his dad had told him. After the game earlier that night, Relic thought he now had a general sense of what these hexes were, but he didn't fully understand the extent of what they had to do with him or his dad.

"It's Adratheon, isn't it?" Relic asked, knowing the answer. "The hexes."

Cecily nodded slowly. "Gustave could have killed him... Adratheon broke himself apart, allowing my husband to hide his essence in each of his seven symphonies. The eighth was supposed to be the final piece of the ritual, but..." She began sobbing.

Not knowing what compelled him to—he was still terrified of this woman—Relic moved to console her. It must have been the raw emotion he heard in her cries, the sorrow and guilt—somehow it resonated within him and pulled him to offer whatever comfort he could.

But as Relic neared her, the basement spun, twisting in a blur to become something else. The mist swirled and turned from pale green in color to a soft, heavenly blue. Cecily stood before him as if she had just stepped out of some classical painting.

"Oh, Gustave," she said in a sophisticated accent, much different than the one she used with Relic. "It was wonderful! I believe it is just your best piece yet." She was speaking to someone beyond the mist, and a voice boomed in response, sounding just like Adratheon's from the restroom at Rook's.

"You will have a special seat during the performance, my dear. As my ninth symphony is devoted specifically to you."

Cecily beamed. "Oh—"

The serene blue mist changed to a hateful, bruised purple, and Cecily was stripped of her high society attire. Her face was bruised and beaten to match the surrounding, swirling mist, and she lay on a table with her arms and legs tied. Arcane symbols were painted all over her naked body.

"—Gustave! What have I done?!" She wailed, struggling against the bindings as a man in a fine, long-tailed coat secured her wrists tighter. "Please, my love! Tell me how I—Why are you doing this?!"

Gustave Moreau looked at her with something Relic thought was pure admiration in his eyes, but there was a hateful smile on his lips—Adratheon's smile. "The bargain has been made, my dear, sweet Cecily. We both must fulfill our parts now." He ran a hand down her trembling face, stroking her cheek sweetly. "I do apologize for my temper, sweetling. It has been a difficult process, but—"

He twirled dramatically, raising a hand upward. "—tonight is the culmination! He shall have his reward and we shall have ours. He has promised! And if his disciples attest to his power, so shall we trust in its deliverance!"

"Gustave, please!"

Slamming a fist down, Gustave turned a furious face on his wife. "*Don't* ruin this now, you craven whore! I'll hold you down while he tears your slit to ribbons if you deprive the world of my masterpiece!" He spun on his heels, chipper once more, waving a finger in the air as he departed. "The ninth symphony shall ring throughout the Chambers tonight, dear Cecily! I've made sure you'll hear it down here. As long as you cease your pointless, slutty blathering!"

The vision faded.

Cecily knelt by Relic as she had before in the basement, the mist soft and pink, only blackness beyond.

"She came to me during that symphony," Cecily said, her voice raw and quavering. "She promised me the revenge I wanted. She said her father and Gustave had become one, and she and I must become one to stand against such a terrible power."

Relic could piece together the rest from what Marshall Crane had told them of the Moreaus. Valaina had tricked Cecily to surrender Adratheon's intended vessel to her, usurping Adratheon's plans while keeping the hexes intact.

Amazingly, he didn't question any of it. The tangible weight of the visions made Relic feel as if he had just re-lived history—glimpsed into the private happenings of people who had lived and died so long before his time. The thrill of it all made Relic actually *hope* this was all real; otherwise he might need to check himself into an asylum.

Kneeling down, Relic put a hand on Cecily's shoulder. It was ice-cold, but he held it. "I'm sorry that happened to you."

She looked at him, the tears in her eyes looking much less sad to him now. "Why? Relic, you freed me. Valaina had no use for me. Her cruel presence kept me alive past the grave, but when you banished us, you...defeated the Widow."

Drawing in a ragged breath as she looked away, she added, "My husband's music gave birth to evil in our world, and yours..." The dream started to fade away, and Relic felt his hand pass through her dissipating shoulder. "...your music can undo it, Relic."

Waking up with tears in his eyes, Relic saw that it was way too early to actually get up, but he didn't dare sleep again.

He clicked the light on and read *Emerald Decay II* until drowsiness claimed him again anyway.

Mercifully, Relic did not return to the Between for the brief slumber he fell into Thursday morning. He awoke feeling rested, but his senses dulled. It took a few blinks for his vision to stop blurring, and the sounds of laughter and chatter drifting in through his slightly ajar bedroom door were not immediately heard.

Confused, Relic got up to see who his mom was talking to on speaker phone in the kitchen. Despite feeling refreshed, he also felt a little grumpy after that emotional encounter with Cecily—which he recalled in vivid detail.

Pulling his underwear out of his ass, Relic thumped toward the kitchen. If he had actually *listened* to those voices instead of just hearing them as bothersome sounds, he would have recognized the familiar tones.

But he rounded the corner, rubbing his eyes as he asked, "Mom, can you keep it down?"

A snorting laughter that was certainly familiar asked, "Can you?"

Relic lowered his hand from his eyes and saw his mom, Bree, and Mrs. Thompkins sitting at the kitchen table, staring at him—well, part of him. Relic looked down, horrified to see not only was he just in his underwear, but his compromised faculties had failed to notice his prominent erection.

Mortified, Relic spun around, trying not to look any of the women in the eye. He caught brief glimpses of his mom averting her wide-eyed gaze to the floor, Bree raising her eyebrows and giving him a devilish grin, and Lydia discreetly covering her mouth.

"Sorry," he stammered, as he walked back to his bedroom.

Bree must have said something salacious in his wake that earned a gasping "Breanne!" from her mother. Relic couldn't help but let some of his embarrassment melt away into humor as he imagined what she might have said.

After getting dressed and brushing his teeth, trying to figure out the *perfect* opening line when he went back to the kitchen, he returned to the gathering with—what Relic considered—a masterfully delivered, "Man, I sure woke up stiff this morning."

"Relic!" Dina gasped. "So inappropriate!"

Bree tried to restrain her laugh, at least to respectable levels, and added, "It's alright—like they say, early to bed, early to rise."

Lydia covered her mouth, but Dina had trouble not laughing at that.

Relic—who probably would have dropped dead over a situation like this just a few months ago—smiled easily and genuinely as he grabbed a box of Cinnamon Toast Crunch from the pantry. "Yeah, the sun wasn't the only thing that came up early this morning."

By the time Relic got to the table with a bowl and some milk, everyone was having a welcome chuckle.

Looking at Bree after the laughter waned enough, Relic asked, "Why are you here so early? Aren't you usually pumping iron at this time?"

Bree motioned to her mom, who took a sip of coffee. "We wanted to come tell your mom."

He looked at Dina, then back at Bree. "What?"

Dina dropped her hands to the table in a show of not being able to contain it any longer. "They got us a venue!"

"Dude," Bree said, "it's the Wane Street Manor!"

Relic paused mid-bite and he was immediately plucked out of his kitchen with the three excited, happy ladies and plopped back into the Between with a sobbing, sorrowful ghost of a woman. The Widow of Wane Street meant something completely different to Relic now, and the mention of her old home sent an icy tingle through his veins.

"Oh," Relic managed through a mouthful of cereal.

"And it's all paid for," Lydia said, holding out a flat hand tipped in exquisitely polished and filed purple nails. "Consider it a Rothen-sponsored affair."

"No!" Dina gasped. "Lydia, I can't—"

"You most certainly can!" Lyda interjected. "I know how much weddings can cost, and most of these places try to gut you, nickel and dime-ing you every step of the way. You absolutely need to take advantage of breaks when you can." She set her coffee mug down. "Besides, you're actually doing me a favor. If you let me help with the planning a little, you could help me with a little work project."

"Oh, for sure," Dina said, almost gasping with excitement. "I would welcome the help! Calvin is so busy trying to keep his folks out of things—they want to use this whole wedding for an extended family reunion. Just let me know what you need."

Lydia smiled brightly. "You bet. Oh!" She turned to Relic. "And Bree left out the best part. There's a stage in the ballroom, with a full sound system and everything. Maybe you can talk your mom into letting Altar Stone be the wedding band."

Dina slapped her hands together, jerking Relic's attention toward her. She looked like a little girl—he had never seen her so genuinely excited. "Hon! Can you guys learn some Rod Stewart?!"

Bree laughed even harder than she had over the boner jokes.

CHAPTER 15

The wedding was planned for March, giving Altar Stone—at the very least—a second show lined up for their big Laramie, Indiana, tour. Relic and Bree were initially not sold on the idea of their metal band playing a wedding, but one trip to the Wane Street Manor was enough to change their minds.

"This stage is ripe for thrashing," Bree said when they were touring the place with Calvin and Dina toward the end of August. To prove the point, she played air guitar and swung her hair in wide circles.

Relic chuckled, instinctively pulling his sticks out of his back pocket and spinning them through his fingers as he paced the big empty stage. He had taken to carrying them around again since Shrubble's appearance.

Fortunately, the last couple weeks had been fairly quiet in terms of tropes or errant hexlords running amok in Laramie—he and Delilah only had to dust a few straggling skrimkins and some sort of fish guy like the one from *Creature from the Black Lagoon*.

Standing on the stage in Wane Street Manor felt thrilling and dangerous, but in a much safer way than patrolling with Delilah. He pictured his drums set up there, playing Altar Stone songs in front of a packed ballroom.

This could be pretty awesome, he thought.

"You guys think you can pack this place?"

Relic, whose back had been toward the ballroom's entrance, turned to see Calvin walking in. His mom's fiancé wore one of his trademark collared shirts—this one a dark forest green—and straight-legged jeans that made him look every bit his age.

"Isn't that you guys' job?" Bree asked, sitting on the edge of the stage so she could slide off. "It's your wedding guests, right?"

Calvin gave her a knowing smile as he adjusted his glasses. "Well, we were actually just talking to the events manager upstairs, and it turns out Lydia pulled some strings at her work and got the place rented out for two separate events in March—the Calvin Green & Dina Meyers wedding in the parlor followed by a special concert here in the ballroom."

"What?" Bree asked, turning a beaming face to Relic and then back to Calvin. "You mean we get to, like, headline our own show here? Not just be, like, a wedding band?"

Relic wasn't exactly sure what that meant. Why would his mom want his band to distract from her big day by holding a concert in the same venue as her wedding reception?

Calvin must have sensed Relic's confusion and he motioned over his shoulder. "Since Rothen technically owns this place, Lydia made it so not only can we get this venue pretty much for free," he raised his eyebrows to emphasize the point, as if the teens couldn't appreciate how huge that was, "but if you guys put on a concert separately instead of just playing the reception, we can actually charge admission and offset some of the other wedding costs—which tend to add up."

While that sounded great to Relic, now he was wondering if they'd even be able to find anyone to pay to see Altar Stone. The band wasn't necessarily a big deal yet, aside from the notoriety they had gotten from the battle last school year. But seeing the gleam in Bree's eyes as she looked at him over her shoulder, Relic let hope take root.

He felt up to the challenge.

"Relic..."

His guts tightened. That was Cecily's voice again. Bree and Calvin were talking about something he couldn't hear anymore—all Relic knew was the echo of the Widow and the blood thundering in his ears. He turned back toward the stage curtains and saw them sway slightly, as if something had just brushed past them. But he, Calvin, and Bree were still alone in the ballroom.

As if in a trance, Relic walked toward the back of the stage, drawn by the faint sense that he knew where the voice had come from. While that didn't seem possible, it didn't stop him from pushing aside the curtains and investigating backstage.

"This is where...he found me," Cecily said, her voice guiding Relic past the speakers and boxes of lights that were stacked behind the curtains.

He moved toward a dark hallway that branched off from the loading bay. Around that corner, he saw a fluorescent light blinking, barely illuminating a rickety staircase leading down toward a much newer-looking door—the dichotomy was striking. There was a card reader near that door's handle, and immediately Relic remembered all the things Russ had told him and Bree about the labs Rothen used to operate in this place.

Just as Relic was about to take an apprehensive step onto those stairs to get closer to the sterile door below, he heard his name again.

"Relic?"

Cecily's voice once again conjured in his mind the image of her children's body parts stuffed into that old box. Suddenly, the realization overcame him that he had felt sympathy last night for a woman—possessed or not—who had ruthlessly butchered her children.

"Relic..."

He wanted to scream for her to shut up, but something kept him frozen in place, considering whether he should shut this woman's presence from his mind as best he could or continue to listen, heeding her warnings.

"Relic!"

Jolted, he turned and the Widow's face was mere inches from his, her expression a grim copy of her enraged husband's from Relic's dreams. Cecily's rotting lips were pulled back in a vicious snarl, and she unlatched her jaw impossibly wide before thrusting her face at his.

Relic threw himself backward, barely avoiding falling down the stairs. His heart thundered as he felt his sticks slip out of his hands, leaving him defenseless. Closing his eyes, he prepared himself to be eviscerated by the Widow of Wane Street, leaving him a shredded corpse like those victims last year.

But when he heard Bree's voice, he opened his eyes to see her looking down at him trying not to laugh her ass off.

"Dude, you were spaced again." She reached a hand down for him, and Relic wasn't too shaken to notice the bicep that strained against her shirtsleeve. "Sorry if I scared you."

Brushing himself off, he just shook his head and looked down the stairs. "This place is just freaky."

"Yeah," Bree said, scooping up his drumsticks and handing them to Relic. "Perfect place for an Altar Stone show."

Throughout most of September, Relic fell into a sense of welcomed normalcy. Bree had begun acting more like herself, which Relic attributed to the lack of any home invasions or noticeable cult activity. Their focus was on the band, and after they managed to solidify "Night of the Harrow," Relic had experienced his first real writer's block moment.

Bree had no shortage of riffs, and she assured Relic that they could just bring those to Nick and Tyler during a rehearsal and put something together as a whole band. But something made Relic reluctant to open that door—it was as if writing music was an intimate thing between himself and Bree, and even though the other two guys seemed just as devoted to Altar Stone as the founders were, Relic felt the need for him and Bree to bring the full skeleton of a song to practice rather than just a few bones.

Unfortunately, he had written most of "Night of the Harrow" in his sleep—maybe possessed by Valaina, Adratheon, Cecily, or some strange combination of their fell powers—so he wasn't even sure yet if he *could* write songs.

It was just four weeks before the show at Tammy's basement that Relic finally decided to seek some professional advice about his creative blockage.

Since his dad had an entire weekend off work the first weekend of October, Relic managed to also get those days off work at Rook's so he could stay over at his dad's apartment. The thing about his dad's place: there wasn't really anything to do, so Relic figured he should have plenty of time to pick his dad's brain and maybe get a start on another Altar Stone tune for the show.

Whatever Steven Meyers did while he wasn't working, he certainly didn't do it at home.

His meager apartment was a prime example of spartan living, with the only forms of entertainment being a cheap DVD player, a stereo (mostly for his growing collection of vinyl records), and stacks of fantasy books—and although these were all fine forms of entertainment as far as Relic was concerned, the place was just too barren for him to fully appreciate any of them.

"Maybe we should grab some movies," Steven said as they walked to the van in the parking lot of Chambers High on Friday afternoon. "We can run by the house to get your stuff, then pick up some movies and a pizza."

"Buying!" Relic said, pointing to his dad. "Not renting. Your DVD collection is weak. Also, how do you not have a PlayStation or something yet?"

"Hey," Steven said, sliding into the driver's seat, "you're the big man with a job now. Why don't you buy one and keep it at my place. I need to learn how to use one of those things."

Relic snorted, closing his door. "Yeah, five-fifty an hour for a couple night-shifts a week...I'm rolling in it."

"Gotta start somewhere, bud." Steven flashed him a grin as he started the van. "Stick!"

Both of the Meyers boys turned to see Principal Sinclair waving from the curb in front of the school's entrance, walking swiftly to the vehicle.

"Hang tight," Steven said, letting the van run as he got back out of it.

Relic watched as the two adults convened near the long line of cars waiting to get out of the crowded parking lot. His dad's back was to him, mostly screening Lana, but Relic could tell she was distressed, talking animatedly about something urgent.

After just a minute or two, Relic's dad gave the principal a comforting hug, his hand gently going to the back of her head. They stayed that way for a long moment before Lana broke away and patted Steven's chest. His dad came jogging back to the van, and Relic could tell his expression was feigned.

"Alright," he said as he got back in. "Let's go buy some flicks."

Relic waited until they were moving before he asked, "What was that about? With the principal?"

Steven shook his head slowly. "Some details about her brother—I still wish you hadn't gone there, man." He held up one hand while he turned the steering wheel with the other. "I get why you did—trust me. You just do not need to be anywhere that Carl Sinclair has been."

The questions that Relic had about the principal's brother, the Crane Estate, and the aftermath of the killing were so numerous that he never even knew where to begin anytime he got the nerve to broach the subject with his dad. He understood the logic of keeping certain things secret in this town, but Relic was starting to suspect Steven Meyers was doing far more harm than good by trying to keep his son safe.

During the drive to Greenbriar Heights, they mostly discussed school and band stuff, with Relic finally bringing up the subject of his creative block.

"Yeah, that can be rough," his dad said. "I remember when we were writing *Lead Her Astray*, I struggled a lot with the lyrics—Ricky could barely even write his own name, let alone a coherent sentence—so a lot of it came down to me."

"How'd you deal with it?" Relic asked, knowing there was unlikely a silver bullet that could help him, but he'd take any advice.

"Well, it's different for everyone," Steven said, pulling to a stop in front of Relic's house. "For me, it was books. Reading is where I could clear my thoughts. That's actually..." Steven looked at the house, his voice drifting. "...that's kind of what started this mess—reading so much that I didn't know when to stop."

"What do you mean?"

Steven looked at him, giving a weak smile. "Let's talk about it later tonight. After we watch at least one brainless action movie, yeah?"

Relic conceded, and went inside to get his stuff.

About ten minutes later they were walking into The CD Palace. "Man, it always weirds me out how much this place hasn't changed—aside from the name." Steven followed Relic into the shop, the pungent aroma of patchouli enveloping them. "I just remember more trippy tie-dye posters."

"Whoa, I'm not sure this place can handle this much talent."

No way, Relic thought, recognizing Becca's voice. He looked out across the aisles of CDs, but didn't see her. *What the hell is she doing here?*

"I think you guys exceed the legal limit of bass drums allowed in here," she added, pulling Relic's attention to the counter. Leaning with her elbows on the glass display case, Becca Reynolds regarded them with eyes lined in heavy black makeup. She had shaved the sides of her head and left the hair up top hanging over to one side, dyed violet.

"Hey," Steven said, pointing at her while cocking his head. "The singer, right? For Artificial Void?"

Her face soured slightly, as if she could dish it out but not take it—even though Relic didn't think his dad was being mean, just forgetful. "Habitual Void," she corrected.

Steven snapped his fingers. "That's it. Cool name. I heard you guys had a big pull at The Voodoo back in July. Sorry I missed your set—but I'm sure I'm not the target audience. Still learning what this whole 'hardcore' thing is," he said, making air quotes around the genre. "Seems to me it's just death metal with lazy drumming."

Relic snickered at that—he couldn't help himself.

"Well," Becca said, "not everyone is Steven fuckin' Meyers, right?"

Laughing, Steven put up his hands. "I'm as lazy as it gets, man. I keep my double bass slow and wouldn't touch a blast beat with a ten-foot pole."

Becca did something then that Relic found odd; she smiled. Not in a cruel, sarcastic way, as if she had some inside joke you were the target of. She looked happy and—Relic was almost revolted to even consider—pretty.

"Where's your DVD section?" Steven asked.

Becca pointed toward the back wall and Steven snapped his fingers again, pointed that way, and began walking. Relic turned to follow.

"Hey, Meyers."

Looking back at her while his dad went to find movies, Relic saw Becca motioning for him to come closer to the counter. He did, curious to know what she wanted.

She leaned toward him conspiratorially. "You hear about the principal's brother?"

Relic thought back to Lana's secret discussion with his father. "You mean that he got murdered? Yeah, I think everyone heard about that."

Becca shook her head. "No, his body. It's gone."

Relic narrowed his eyes, not sure what she meant. "You mean, like, rotted away?" He imagined the dead man buried in his coffin—he wasn't sure how long it took someone to fully decompose, but he guessed it might take longer than a month or two.

Pulling back with a look of confusion, she shook her head. "No, like, it's just gone. He was buried out in Romney and someone found his grave all dug up, his coffin opened, and the body gone."

"What..." Relic didn't even know what to ask. Despite the strange things that he had already witnessed in Laramie, this news managed to both shock and confuse him. Was Carl, like, a zombie now? Was it grave robbers? He thought grave robbers just took valuables, not entire bodies.

As if in response to all these thoughts, a vision of Shrubble Von Hellspawn came to him—a flashback from the encounter outside of Bree's house. The well, the bloody harrow, the *Skrimkins* tapes in Carl Sinclair's house... Relic didn't need to be a detective to know there was a connection.

"You think it's Adratheon, right?"

Relic, whose gaze had been locked on some glittering diamond ring in the display case while his mind wandered, jerked his gaze back to Becca. His heart stopped beating and his mouth went dry. "What'd you say?"

"You dig stuff with dragons, right?"

Having no clue what she was talking about, and recovering from what he had thought she said, he nodded.

She bent down behind the counter. "I hear your band talking about your D&D games all the time at lunch, and you're always reading some dweeby book at school with a dragon on the cover." She reappeared and placed a wrapped jewel case on the display.

Everything about Adratheon, Shrubble Von Hellspawn, his father's secrets, and pretty much anything else about his present life fell away as Relic regarded that album cover.

Featuring an armored, dragon-mounted warrior wielding a glimmering sword in the moonlight, the album cover bore the familiar band's name in epic, stone-carved letters: Rhapsody. Relic had nearly played his *Legendary Tales* album to death since Bree had gotten it for him last Christmas. He had no idea his new all-time favorite band had a new one out.

At the bottom of the majestic scene of swirling, foreboding mists enshrouding a blackened castle in the distance that was being struck by lightning, the title of the album read in the most testicle-tingling letters Relic had ever seen: *Symphony of Enchanted Lands.*

His hand shaking, Relic reached out to pick the album up.

"I think they call it 'Symphonic Epic Hollywood Metal' or something," Becca said, mirth in her voice. But Relic's sense of wonder could not be dispelled by anything she did or said at this point.

"Is this new?"

"Yeah," she replied. "I think it just came out this week. Was surprised I could get it in on release—I think it really only hit mainstream shelves in Europe on the fifth."

Breaking his hypnotic focus on the CD in his hand, he looked up at her, confused. "What do you mean? Like, you imported it?" He knew that was not cheap or easy; she must have gone out of her way to make it happen.

She nodded, once again the genuine smile she had given his dad returned to her face and Relic thought she was beyond just pretty in that moment—she was beautiful.

"Why?"

She shrugged. "Like I said, I figured you'd like it. You like dorky shit."

Yeah, but you're a bitch, he wanted to say, *you make fun of me all the time. You gloated when my band blew our first real show.* But he didn't say any of that. He just blinked and said, "Thanks," before returning his gaze to the album. Flipping it over, he saw the track listing and only one of the ten tracks seemed to matter to his subconscious; the rest of the songs were just blurry, arcane symbols to him.

The song entitled "Emerald Sword" triggered something in him. Without even hearing the music, he knew how powerful it was, how important it would be to him. He pictured his shiny green drums, his sticks aglow with the hazy green magic of Alternus, and the wretched, perverted green shade of Shrubble's flesh, each of those hues swirling and combining to form a mythical weapon of unknowable power: the Emerald Sword.

For a moment, The CD Palace fell away and he was in the same indigo atmosphere of the album's cover, swirling mists and lightning striking. But Relic saw himself from the lens of an out-of-body camera, which circled him as he donned a suit of gleaming emerald armor, and from his waist he grasped the silver hilt of that mystical sword. When he drew the weapon, its blade was made entirely of the green precious stone, a razor-sharp jewel ready to cleave a hexlord in two.

He didn't hear his dad until the fourth or fifth time his name summoned him back to reality.

"Relic!"

Turning, he saw his dad holding up a copy of *Killer Klowns from Outer Space* on VHS. "Told you I should keep that VCR."

"He caused the hexes."

Relic jerked his head back to Becca, knowing he had misheard her again. He tried to play it cool, steadying his breath before asking, "Huh?"

She shook her head. "Those drums are killing your hearing, man. I was talking about your dad—he caused the hexes."

"Come check out these DVDs, man," Steven called, not hearing Becca.

"Be right there," Relic replied, his face still frozen on Becca's. Lowering his voice as he stepped toward her, he didn't even know what to say. "What did—how...I mean..."

She looked at him as if he had disappointed her. "Doesn't mean anything, does it? Man, I was hoping you might have known. It's been bugging me all week."

Lost, Relic set the album on the display and asked what she was talking about.

Making sure Steven was still busy looking at movies, she leaned over the counter closer to Relic. Their faces were so close that he could smell her breath; it was fresh, as if she had just sucked on a mint or chewed gum.

"I was getting baked with Clayton and Jay J.—on some stuff your bassist sold us actually—and I had one of those weird...I don't know, whatever they are—you read my thing in English class."

Adratheon, Relic thought, his pulse rising.

She continued, her gaze drifting from him. "I think we were listening to your dad's band or something—or maybe Clayton just mentioned you guys, I forget. But anyway, I had this weird image of your dad in my head, playing drums in some smoky place. Did they have a music video with, like, green smoke and stuff? Well, anyway, wherever the vision was from, that same voice started saying he caused the hexes."

Refocusing on Relic, she pumped her eyebrows up as if it would impress Relic and not horrify him. "Wicked, huh?"

Not knowing what else to say, Relic said, "Yeah."

"That is wicked," Steven said, startling Relic as he approached behind him. But Steven was focused on the Rhapsody CD. "Aside from those shitty programmed drums, I thought that first album you have of theirs was pretty badass. Hope they got a human on the skins this time."

"Did you cause the hexes?"

The way Becca asked the question point-blank almost made Relic faint. His skin crawled as he turned to see his father's reaction. But Steven just wore that casual, amused expression that seemed to say, "Nothing shocks me, man, I'm here just being all ready for anything."

"The hexes?" he asked, setting two VHS tapes and four DVDs on the glass display case. "What are those?"

Becca shrugged, grabbing the stacks of movies and turning them so she could inspect them. "Was hoping you might be able to tell us. I keep hearing weird shit, especially when partaking of known substances."

Steven laughed. "Ah, yeah, that'll do it. I'd check with your dealer then. You getting that, man? I want to hear it."

Struggling to keep up, Relic nodded, sliding the album toward the movies. Becca chatted with his dad while Relic tried to calmly process everything, but it wasn't until he was back in his dad's van that he could properly articulate his thoughts.

"She's hearing Adratheon, Dad."

Setting their bag of purchases between their seats, Steven withdrew the Rhapsody album and handed it to Relic. "Crack it open, man. I think better with some tunes in the background." As Relic did just that, beyond eager to hear the thing anyway, Steven started the van. "We gotta find out who her dealer is."

Without even thinking, Relic told him.

Steven turned to him wide-eyed. "Nick?! As in, your bassist Nick?! Dude, I don't mind you getting high occasionally, but you can't let your bandmates get caught dealing drugs around here. Christ, man, at least go out to Dayton to score weed, don't shit where you eat."

"I don't touch that stuff," Relic said, slipping the CD in. He never cared to try marijuana, as his only exposure to it had been the smell, and he cared little for it. "But what would weed have to do with her knowing about Adratheon?"

Steven shook his head, turning the volume on the stereo up as the opening track, "Epicus Furor," sped up Relic's already racing heart. "I honestly don't know, man. But it's worth looking into."

Before Relic could reply to that, the intro track transitioned into "Emerald Sword." The first cymbal hit and opening riff caused father and son to look at each other wide-eyed.

The next four and half minutes were lost to headbanging and fist raising. During that time, Relic felt every concern once again fade away, and he wanted nothing more than to have his dad take him back to school so he could play his drums and work on a new Altar Stone song.

With Relic spending the weekend at his dad's, Bree thought it was the best time for her and Delilah to look into the cult. Not wanting to explain to Relic her own involvement with Rothen, or Delilah's undercover work, Bree had kept her distance from anything related to the Cult of Valaina while in her boyfriend's presence.

She continued to promise herself that she would tell Relic everything once she could get clean from the VANDAL serum. Bree knew it was a lie, but the lie seemed to get easier and easier to tell herself with each dose she shot into her ass.

Flexing in front of the mirror presently, Bree was more focused on how much her biceps grew with each of those shots. She had never felt as strong and capable, nearly immune to the earth-shattering fear that plagued her before that fateful night she took her first dose. Not wanting to cover her guns up despite the October chill settling in, Bree pulled a sleeveless flannel shirt over her tank top just in time to answer the doorbell.

"You ready?" Delilah asked, raising an eyebrow.

"That's a loaded question," Bree said, stepping onto the porch and closing the door. "But if you mean am I ready to figure out what your dad's up to, sure."

They made their way out of Greenbriar Heights in silence, not even speaking to each other until they reached the neighborhood's entrance. Something had been bothering Bree recently, and this had been the first time she had Delilah alone to ask about it.

"So, the VANDAL serum has kept you from, like, needing blood. But what about your dad?"

Delilah gave a chuckle. "You'd be surprised how many people want their blood sucked around here. Why do you think I stay out patrolling so much? My dad has a new donor almost every other night, and I can't stand the sound of him sucking them off."

"Ew," Bree said with a laugh. They walked along Greenbush Street for a while before Bree decided to press the matter again. "So, has my mom asked why you need so much extra serum?"

"As long as I give routine updates," Delilah said, stretching her arms above her head, "she gives me anything I need. She's desperate for this whole DeMono Tech deal to go through. But it sounds like it depends on how the wedding goes now."

"Wedding?"

Delilah looked at Bree. "You didn't know? She's using Relic's mom's wedding as cover for the DeMono Tech merger—hoping to show the place has value. She said if that goes smoothly, she can open the old labs and finalize the buyout, blocking Marshall from trying to outbid her."

Bree wasn't really sure what all that meant, but she was worried about the whole "using Relic's mom's wedding as a cover" part—that didn't sit well with her. Not only did she want Dina to have her special day, she also wanted Altar Stone to have their concert.

"But tonight is about Carl Sinclair," Delilah reminded her. "Whoever took his body has to be somehow involved with Marshall's cult—I haven't seen any signs of a corpse wandering around town, and I'm pretty sure if Rothen had something to do with it, your mom would have told me." Delilah motioned for them to cross the street. "Which means, my old pops has to be involved."

Bree didn't really understand why it mattered if someone stole the body of a murder victim, but she had slowly become addicted to joining Delilah on her patrols, so she allowed the girl to lead her along on another one of her hunches.

"So, where exactly are we going then?" Bree asked once they reached the other side of Greenbush.

Delilah motioned forward. "It seems like the cult has really only been holding rituals around Sanctuary, so there must be some latent power around here that Marshall is tapping into. My dad—as in, my vampire dad—is like an iron trap when it comes to what he does with the cult. And even if I go asking him about stuff, he might start wondering why—and we don't want him knowing I've been talking to your mom about any of this. So, we snoop."

Just snooping around didn't sound particularly exciting to Bree. She kept clenching and unclenching her firsts, the VANDAL serum making her itch for a fight, and the thought of just sitting around hoping to find a clue made her dread whatever the night held for them.

But the sudden scream told her that things might not be so simple.

Delilah broke into a sprint down the sidewalk, leaping up onto the wall marking Sanctuary's borders. Bree hurried after her, grabbing hold of the brick barrier and pulling herself over.

Another blood-curdling cry came from the distance, and Bree felt her pulse quicken as she looked for any sign of danger. Aside from the shriek, it was a peaceful evening in the luxurious neighborhood.

"It's starting," Delilah called as she sprinted into the thick trees that ran between the massive houses in the neighborhood. "Sounds like it's coming from Crane's place. Come on."

Bree hurried after, not sure what was starting, but knowing she needed to be there for it. Her legs were eager and her heart felt ready for some pumping, so she broke into a full sprint to catch up with Delilah.

The shouting ceased as they neared Crane's house, but there were clear signs of activity. Several cars were parked along the drive and the gentle, pulsing glow of a fire lit the trees that surrounded the property. Bree followed Delilah as the dhampir hurried around the back of the house toward the orange glow.

Bree could hear shouts when she lost sight of Delilah around the corner of the house and pushed herself to close the gap so she could tell what was being said.

"...none of your concern!"

Bree turned the corner to see Marshall Crane waving a finger in Delilah's face, several hooded and cloaked figures tending to something near the fire.

"What's wrong with her?" Delilah was asking, trying to see around Marshall where the rest of the cultists were attending to what looked like a crumpled figure at the base of a stone brazier, which held the raging fire.

"You're a spy," Marshall shouted, his eyes snapping to Bree and then back to his former adopted daughter. "Don't act like I don't know all about your association with this one's mother."

Delilah looked at Bree and then turned back to Marshall. "Where's my dad? Dad! You over there?"

All the cultists kept their backs to Delilah, huddled around what Bree could tell now was a body on the ground, covered in a dark sheet.

Once more, Marshall moved to screen the rest of the cultists from Delilah. "This is private property, young lady. Don't make me call the police. Officer Barnes would surely appreciate any reason I gave him to take you into custody."

Bree thought she saw the body on the ground move, but as she reached toward Delilah's arm to keep the girl from pushing their luck, she noticed the autumn breeze shake loose leaves from overhead. *It was just the wind,* Bree said to herself, unable to pull her eyes from that dark sheet.

Delilah didn't resist Bree's touch, the dhampir stepping back away from the glowering face of her one-time father figure.

"I think it was you," Delilah said to him. "Whatever happened at your family's old estate—you did it, didn't you?"

Marshall stepped forward. "You did! With your incessant meddling! I took you in, I cared for you, paid your medical expenses—and how do you repay me? Becoming a leashed rat for Rothen and ruining the deal I spent the last six months brokering!"

Both girls shrank back from that sudden fury. Behind Marshall, the cultists were now completely screening whatever was under the black sheet and lifting it, carrying it toward Crane's mansion. The fire seemed to be dying unnaturally fast.

Marshall raised a hateful finger at Delilah. "Interloper. The ritual would have worked—we would have summoned the Chosen—would have had Adratheon contained once more had you not broken our concentration!"

The fire was out now, and Bree felt sudden terror being alone in the dark with this man. "Come on," she whispered to Delilah, pulling her arm. Marshall's words were like a fist to her gut—had she helped cause all this? Did they really interfere with something *good* that Marshall was doing? She only heard mentions of this Adratheon person, but in her mind he was essentially the god of Alternus and needed to be locked away where he belonged.

Once again, Delilah didn't resist, not turning away from Marshall, but not eager to stand her ground against his icy glare. Yet it seemed she couldn't resist one more jab. "Was that Carl Sinclair's body? Can you at least tell us if you know how to stop this thing—whatever killed him? It came for us before, and it'll probably come again."

The words seemed to slap the anger from Marshall's face, leaving him with a look of worried disbelief. "You saw him? The hexlord?"

Delilah regained her ground, pulling her arm from Bree's grasp. "If by *hexlord* you mean that little sphincter from the *Emerald Decay* movies, yeah, we saw him. Him and his little critters tried to kill us—seemed to need Relic for something."

Marshall stepped forward, his pointing finger turning into an outreached, pleading hand. "And you killed it?"

Bree stepped forward now. "No. Relic hurt it, but it sucked off the dead critters and bailed."

Cocking his head at her, Marshall looked completely perplexed. "...sucked off?"

Delilah reminded him of what the Widow had done with the wendigo last year, and toward the tail end of the explanation, Marshall's hand began to go to his head like Doc Brown in *Back to the Future*. Despite the circumstances, Bree was desperately hoping for a "Great Scott!"

"It knows..." Marshall turned from them, his other hand going to his temple as if to help him sort through his emotions and thoughts. "The Widow figured out that Adratheon was still a threat and began consuming Alternians to absorb his latent power still coursing through this place..."

He seemed to be talking to himself, but Bree thought this explained every-thing—the song she wrote with Relic somehow drawing Shrubble to them just as a swarm of skrimkins had invaded the neighborhood. They pretty much rang the dinner bell for him. *And he needs Relic,* Bree thought, *just like the Widow did.*

Bree had heard dating teenage boys could be challenging, but this was ridicu-lous.

"So you know what he wants?" Delilah asked.

Marshall turned on her, his hair disheveled and his moustache twitching. "He wants what they all want," he said with a mix of fear and dark knowledge. "They all want Adratheon."

Bree looked to Delilah for an explanation, but she looked just as puzzled. Turning back to Marshall, she asked, "Do you know where to find him then? Adratheon?"

He looked at her with an unreadable expression. "We've found him." He motioned to his back yard. "We're *in* him. Laramie *is* Adratheon—he claimed this place when he laid the hexes, trapping his essence in the very borders of the city." Turning toward his house, he added, "My family's old estate was just the first hexlord's domain. I hoped Valaina's Chosen might have meant an answer to Adratheon's cunning plan for ascension, but it seems I have misread the signs."

"So you did free the hexlord?" Delilah asked, referring to Shrubble (if Bree was keeping up with all of this nonsense).

Marshall hung his head slightly. "The hexlords guard Adratheon's power, not Valaina's. I *meant* to return that power to Alternus, where it belongs—in Valaina's control, who is under *our* control." He turned to face the girls again. "There, it is where it belongs. There, it will be safe."

Bree almost laughed. She didn't pretend to know all the inner work-ings of this Cult of Valaina, but she hardly imagined they planned on using Adratheon's power to end world hunger or cure cancer. Marshall Crane just wanted that power for himself.

Still, she couldn't help but feel like he was their ally in this now—which was a miserable thought.

"Sounds like we both screwed the pooch then," Delilah said. "How do we fix it?"

Marshall observed the dark grass, as if it held some cryptic clues to solve their predicament. "I don't know. But I will consult the texts and see what I can piece together." He looked back up at Bree and Delilah in turn. "In the meantime, avoid tropes—they will be both Shrubble's prey and his minions. You know as well as I that tropes are at the mercy of their basest instincts."

"Yeah," Delilah said, turning. "Try living with one."

CHAPTER 16

B ack at Steven's apartment, Relic and his dad ended up spending the rest
of the afternoon and early evening sprawled on the living room floor
listening to *Symphony of Enchanted Lands* together. They excitedly passed the
CD booklet back and forth, learning about the band's fantasy saga their music
was based on.

"I used to dream of doing this," Steven said after their third listen of "Wisdom
of the Kings." "Writing a huge fantasy story—but like a full novel—and putting
out a power metal album based on it. *But* I'd actually have a live drummer. Not
this weak-ass programmed shit."

Honestly, Relic had a hard time telling the drums were programmed, but he
trusted his dad. They did sound far too syncopated for his taste, and the fills
felt very rigid. However, playing double bass for a whole song like that sounded
so daunting to him that he was almost relieved to hear that it wasn't a human
being; no one deserved that type of percussive punishment.

At the same time, it made him eager to push himself to that level.

The phone rang then and Steven paused the music—he always seemed to
hate listening to quiet music, a quality that Relic associated with his own "all or
nothing" mentality—and went to grab the cordless phone from the kitchen.

"Gate, you're supposed to be on your way already with the pizzas... Oh."
Steven laughed, looking at Relic. "Sorry, Bree. Yeah, he's here—we're listening
to the new direction Altar Stone is doomed to take if your boyfriend has any say
in the matter. One sec," he said, holding the phone out for Relic.

"Hey, Bree."

Nothing could have prepared Relic for the flood that followed. Bree told him about her encounter with Marshall, which also led to her explaining why she had been helping Delilah with looking into the cult, which also meant she had to explain how she had been attacked by skrimkins weeks before Relic even knew about the threat.

Relic was saying, "Okay..." so many times in different inflections that his dad kept looking at him worriedly from the living room as he sorted through their unwatched movie purchases.

As Bree was apologizing to Relic for not telling him any of this sooner, the apartment door opened and Gate carried in a stack of three pizza boxes with two smaller boxes of breadsticks on top.

"Why's it so quiet in here?" the man asked.

Relic turned his back to Gate so he could focus, not entirely sure how to react. He honestly didn't remember Bree ever lying to him before, and with each new thing she revealed, it felt like he wasn't even talking to Bree. The Bree he grew up with—the Bree he had fallen in love with—did not hide things. It was like an inside joke between them; she was incapable of lying.

One time in fifth grade, Relic was invited over to the Thompkinses' house on Easter because his mom had to work. They both loved Reese's Peanut Butter Cups to a frightening degree—so much that the only real altercation they had growing up was over those glorious confections. Relic had gone to the bathroom and left his easter eggs on the floor, and when he returned two were broken open and empty. Within minutes, Bree had confessed to her devious theft and given Relic two of her own peanut butter-filled eggs as recompense.

That memory came to him as Bree continued trying to explain her reasoning.

"I wanted to handle it this time." Her voice now was oddly stubborn, which seemed to anger Relic more—as if she were somehow *blaming* him for handling things on his own in the past.

"So Delilah can help you but I can't?" Relic heard his voice break when he asked that, emotion boiling to the surface.

"She...she told me to wait to tell you, until we found out more. And besides, don't act like you didn't keep things from me all through last year."

That knocked the wind out of him. How could she throw that back at him? He hadn't known what the fuck was happening! He had no reason to believe that any of it even concerned Bree at the time. But all of this concerned him now, and she certainly knew that. The phone felt hot against his ear, as if it were burning his flesh.

He was suddenly glad to be at his dad's—he was afraid if Bree had told him all this in person, he would have to associate all of these emotions with her physical presence, and he did not want that. There was a buffer of space between them right now, and he needed to use it.

"Look," he said, "we'll talk about it later. Maybe jog your memory over the weekend and see if you forgot to tell me anything else."

The silence that followed spoke volumes, and Relic could picture the scowl on his girlfriend's face—still beautiful, but now in a creepy, femme fatale way.

Maybe she didn't deserve that jab, but he couldn't shake the feeling that she was still not telling him something. And that suspicion, combined with her admissions, made it hard for him to feel as sympathetic as he wanted to.

"I said I was sorry, Relic."

Once again, her voice sounded more stubborn than remorseful, so Relic just replied with, "Yeah, I know. I have to go—my dad wants to start a movie."

Bree hung up without saying goodbye, which seemed to pull the rug out from under Relic. *Wait,* he thought, *I'm supposed to be the one pissed off. I'm supposed to be the one that hangs up angrily.*

Everything felt wrong as he slowly placed the phone back on its base.

"Everything alright, dude?"

Relic turned to see his dad sitting with his legs crossed on the living room floor, a half-eaten slice of pizza in his hand. Gate was sitting on the couch, pulling his second slice from the box on the small coffee table.

Walking over in a daze, Relic sat down and grabbed his own slice before telling them what he had just learned.

Neither of them seemed that shocked about the cult, but when he got to part about Shrubble Von Hellspawn, it was now Relic's turn to apologize.

"I was just trying to handle it like you do, Dad," Relic tried to explain between bites—even monsters and hexlords from other dimensions couldn't ruin his appetite for sausage pizza. "Like you said—the more people who know, the more fear for these things to feast on."

"He's got you there, Stick," Gate said with a nod of his head. "Also, I'm not sure why you think he needs to tell us everything—he managed to get you out of that shithole without us getting in his way."

"Yeah, but he's my kid, dude." Steven reached for another piece, shaking his head in annoyance. "Now that I'm back, I want to help."

"Do you?!" Relic blurted out, surprising himself with the intensity of the question. But after the phone call with Bree, he needed to blow off all this steam before it melted his brain. "You won't even tell me about Adratheon—how do you know so much about him? What the hell is he?! How do you know about all his hexlords?!"

Frustrated, Relic tossed his crust into the box and threw himself back into the couch. The brief silence that followed made Gate's chewing sound both comical and intentionally loud.

"Didn't you read my journal?"

Relic looked at his dad, the memory of finding that stolen notebook on his bed replaying in his head. He had only flipped through the thing when he found it, tucking it away to return to later. But things had gotten so hectic that he had forgotten all about it.

Steven stood up, wiping his hands on his jeans. "I just figured you had read it and understood it, 'cause you never said anything about it. I gave it to your mom to put in your room."

Sitting back up, Relic thought again of the shattered glass in the basement. "Where did you get it?! I never told you it was stolen."

Steven recoiled, turning to Gate and then back to Relic. "Stolen? What are you talking about? I got it from Ricky. He said he found it when he was cleaning out his parents' old house."

Relic also looked at Gate, who was watching them while eating his next slice, then back to his dad. "It was in the basement until the end of the summer when someone broke the window and stole it."

Gate and Steven exchanged looks.

"Why would Ricky steal your journal and then give it back to you?" Gate asked.

"Also," Relic followed up, trying to make sense of all this information, "what did you want me to read in there? It was mostly like a bunch of scribbles—I could barely make anything out."

"I can explain that," Steven said, getting up to grab the phone. "But first I think we need to find out why that son of a bitch broke into the house."

Relic and Gate watched as Steven dialed a number and listened to several rings.

"Damn," Steven hung up. "Gate, where else would he be? The diner?"

The mention of the diner made Relic remember how oddly Rook had behaved the night he gave him a ride home. Did he know about his brother trying to get the book? He had to have known he was back in town.

"How about we put the pizza in the fridge? I'm suddenly craving burgers."

"He's acting like we can't take care of ourselves," Bree said, pacing around her room, still wired from their brief encounter with the cult. Her last dose of VANDAL was two days ago, and she felt herself coming down again. She tried to keep her attention away from Delilah sprawled on her bed.

"You guys fight like a married couple," the dhampir said. "Just let him stew a bit—he'll realize he's being ridiculous. Like you said, he's kept way more stuff from you. Besides, you can't really tell him about your mom, right?"

Bree stopped pacing. "What do you mean?"

Sitting up, Delilah tilted her head in a way that looked a little too seductive for Bree's tastes. "I mean, your mom's kind of like the super villain here, right? A regular sexy Lex Luthor. That's why you didn't tell him about the serum you've been taking. Or why you were even helping me look into the cult in the first place."

Rage twisted in Bree's stomach, mixing with the normal yearning the VANDAL junk left her with. She clenched her fists, but didn't have anything to say.

Apparently sensing her anger, Delilah stood up pointing to the tall mirror near the bathroom. "Look, Bree." Standing behind her, Delilah gently touched Bree's bare arm, lifting it as her dark eyes studied their reflections. Instinctively, Bree flexed her arm as Delilah positioned it.

Bree breathed in softly and raggedly as Delilah traced a black-nailed finger along the definition in her arm. She couldn't help but think about the way the dhampir had kissed her the night of the first skrimkin attack—the way she forcefully took a handful of her ass.

Given the circumstances, Bree had assumed the girl was just using the situation to get what she wanted—Bree's help. But was there a chance that Delilah was attracted to Bree? And did she have the same feelings?

That question made Bree pull her arm away suddenly. The same feelings?! She didn't have any feelings toward Delilah.

...Did she?

The dhampir seemed unbothered by Bree's reaction. "You earned those yourself. The serum can't do that, it just blocks out anything that distracts you from getting what you want." As Bree turned to face the girl, Delilah just smiled that annoyingly playful smile she often wore—the one that said she knew it all and only told you what you needed to know at the moment. "Don't let your boyfriend get in the way."

"I'm not," Bree said, not entirely sure what Delilah was getting at. "I'm just pissed right now, that's all. But Relic and I are fine—like you said, he just needs some time to process it all."

Delilah tightened her lips and nodded before pulling her shirt over her head. "Whatever you say. You know him better than me." She began taking her bra off.

Bree averted her eyes, about to ask what she was doing.

"I need to borrow your shower again," Delilah said, sensing the question. "That's cool, right?"

Without speaking, Bree just motioned for her to go ahead.

"Oh, and Bree," Delilah said, looking over her shoulder as she stood naked now in the bathroom doorway. "If you *want* to join me, I can give you a hand. I know the effect that stuff has on you." She turned around so Bree could see everything as she slowly began closing the door. "If that's what you want..."

Bree, not really knowing or trusting what she wanted at the moment, went to lift weights instead.

"Are you freaking kidding me?" Dina asked them, hands planted on the counter where the three of them sat down on three empty stools. She pointed to Relic, a mocking smile on her lips. "You ask for the weekend off and then come in anyway?"

Relic tried to feign a casual chuckle before asking, "Is Rook busy?" The diner's rush hour wasn't what it had been over summer, but there were still enough tables that they might have to wait awhile to talk to the cook.

She shrugged, looking at Steven (shaking her head in a "you should be ashamed of yourself" way) and then Gate (to whom she gave a kind smile). "I'll tell him you're here. Want some burgers?"

Only a minute or two after Dina went in the back, Rook came around wiping his hands on his apron. "I thought you'd be out partying, dude." He motioned to Relic as he turned to Steven. "Kid asks for the weekend off and then comes in to spend his hard-earned money."

"That's our fault," Steven said with a smile.

"What do you know, Rodney?" Gate said, holding out a hand to shake. "Been too long."

Rook reached his muscled arm out to take Gate's hand in a solid grip. "Sure has, Murphy. Should come down more often—I bet I can beat that cafeteria food at the school. What brings you guys in tonight?"

Steven leaned forward in the barstool, speaking so low that Relic struggled to hear him over the din from behind them. "You seen Ricky lately? He came to see me a couple weeks back, but never told me where he was staying."

Rook shot Relic a worried look before leaning closer to Steven to ask, "He didn't mess with you or anything, did he?"

Steven laughed at that. "Ricky? No, man, he just wanted to drop something off. Said he'd like to get together, but didn't leave me a number or anything. I guess I expected him to stop by again, but..." Steven shrugged and held out his empty hands to show what came of that.

Rook considered that a moment before asking. "What'd he drop off?"

"A journal he stole from my basement," Relic said, surprising himself as much as it had the other three men. "A couple weeks before that time you dropped me off at my house, asking about something of my dad's."

Letting his face fall, Rook rubbed the back of his thick neck. "Yeah, I was afraid of that." He looked over his shoulder to make sure no one was coming out of the kitchen behind him before leaning over the counter with his huge arms crossed atop it. "Look, kid, I should have told you. But I didn't want to freak anyone out..."

The kitchen door swung open and Dina came out with a tray of food. "Kenny's getting backed up in there, Rook." She went around the counter to deliver the food.

"Yeah, one minute."

"Freak anyone out about what?" Steven asked, leaning closer.

Rook gave Relic's dad a somber look. "He was saying some crazy shit when he came back to town, man. Sounded like he wanted to hurt someone."

"Someone, being me," Steven said, not asking.

Nodding, Rook hung his head again. "I should have gone to the cops or something—but this was before the news came out about that guy from Crater Splooge, or whatever their name was, so I didn't know if I'd be putting the guy in prison for the rest of his life by giving away his location... He's my brother, ya know?"

Steven nodded. "I get it, man. Honestly, I can't imagine taking threats of violence seriously from Ricky, so I don't really hold it against you. Did he say why he wanted to hurt me though?"

Rook gave a soft, disbelieving laugh. "He was out of it, man. Said you were a dragon or something."

Adratheon. Relic pictured those huge, clawed feet in the diner's restroom, almost jerking himself away from his dad; in that moment of frightful revelation, he had the sudden feeling that Steven Meyers might be that horrid figure.

"Despite the nutty stuff he was saying," Rook continued, "he seemed sane enough after I sat him down and got him to eat something—he looked emaciated. He told me he wanted to prove something to me, but he'd need to find your journal."

From the edges of his vision, Relic saw his dad run a hand through his hair, his face puzzled. "Why would he want my journal? That makes no sense... I don't even think he would have understood any of what I wrote in there." He looked at his son knowingly when he added, "It was mostly just random stories and lyrics."

Rook pushed himself away from the counter. "I don't know, man. He said something about that Rothen stuff—you know, Nexaphane? But the rest just seemed like gibberish to me."

Relic didn't fail to notice his dad's posture stiffening at the mention of Nexaphane, which was a name that sounded familiar to Relic. He was pretty sure that was one of the drugs that Bree's mom worked on, but what it had to do with any of this was beyond him.

"Is he staying with you?" Gate asked.

Shaking his head, Rook motioned toward the front of the diner. "He's got a shitty little place above that head shop on Ferry Street. I think the chick who owns it used to be one of his groupies, gives him a deal—lord knows the guy wouldn't dream of actually getting a job."

"Rook! Can I get a hand?"

Knocking on the counter, Rook added, "Don't tell him I told you where he was. I think he was trying to lay low. But I think I've already fulfilled my brotherly duties for this lifetime. Just keep him out of trouble if you can, guys."

"Absolutely," Steven said.

After Rook returned to work and Dina dropped off their second dinner, the three of them ate in silence for a few minutes. Relic was sure each of them were trying to sort through all of this.

Finally, Steven Meyers spun around on his stool and leaned over to Relic's ear. "I'm pretty sure I know where your bassist is getting his supply."

Chapter 17

On Monday, Relic returned to Chambers High in a much better mood. He and his dad spent the rest of the weekend listening to *Symphony of Enchanted Lands,* watching movies, and generally not talking about Adratheon or the Nexaphane or Shrubble Von Hellspawn. It was like an unspoken agreement between the two of them: just enjoy the weekend and deal with it all next week.

"You should talk to the band," Steven said presently, shifting the van into park outside the school. "Especially Nick. I'm not entirely sure what Ricky's up to, but your friends shouldn't be involved in whatever it is."

"Are you going to talk to Ricky then?" Relic asked, giving his dad a sidelong look as he reached for the door handle. "You know, I hear dads are supposed to, like, set a good example..."

Steven chuckled. "Yeah, man, I'm going to talk to him. Figure out what he needed to read in my journal—and what made him give it back. Stay out of trouble today, my man. See you Thursday for D&D!"

Relic flashed his dad metal horns as he shut the van's door.

"Oh, Relic!"

He turned to see his dad holding up the Rhapsody album through the open window. "Don't want to forget this! I'll grab my own copy at the mall if they have it."

Just seeing that album cover again reinvigorated Relic with the same inspiration he felt upon first hearing "Emerald Sword." He grabbed it and gave his dad one last smile before jogging toward the school.

The Little Chamber was already emptying when Relic got inside, but he saw his band hanging near the rear of the crowd—Tyler's shoes were always hard to miss, even though the bright pink color was fading after so much wear.

Whether it was not seeing her for almost three full days, the fact that they just had what he considered their first real fight as a couple, or he was still supercharged with symphonic metal majesty at the moment, something happened to Relic when Bree looked over to him.

There wasn't exactly vulnerability in her eyes, but seeing her face then—which displayed some strange mix of stubborn strength and desperate yearning—made him want to run over there, drop to his knees, and declare how absolutely in love with her he was.

But before he could even take a step toward her, a familiar voice said, "So, you dig the album then?"

He turned to his right and saw Becca and Jay J. from Habitual Void approaching. "Hey, Relic," Jay J. said shyly.

"Hey," Relic replied and, turning to Becca, he asked, "Huh?"

She nodded down to his hand. "That Rrrrrrrhapsody band." She rolled her Rs like some snooty aristocrat, seemingly mocking him again.

As much as he wanted to gush about how wild he was for the stuff, he just nodded and opted to put on a show of drumming knowledge for Jay's sake. "Yeah, it's great. Just wish they didn't program the drums. Would have loved to hear an actual drummer play that much double bass."

"Well, you guys should cover it then at the party," Becca said. And then she looked at him in a noticeably different way—a way that suddenly made Relic question whether this girl was hot for him or completely detested him. She held his gaze with that confusing look as she led Jay J. into the departing crowd. "I'd love to watch your legs kick some dragon ass."

What is happening? Relic wondered, feeling like he had no clue how to read people anymore. And as he turned back to find Bree, he realized his band had deserted him. *Shit.* He was suddenly worried that Bree might have misinterpreted his brief conversation with Becca.

As if he didn't have enough to worry about.

Tyler sat in third period algebra staring at the back of Miranda Cartwright's head. Her gentle curls reminded him of the time she tried giving him head at the start of freshman year. She said she had read an article about the act and wanted to see what it was like. He had thought it would be easy enough to stay hard during such an activity, because he wouldn't really have any eyes on him.

Naturally, it was an utter failure, and Miranda was convinced she just didn't understand the whole operation. Tyler, needing to keep the charade up so he wouldn't have to deal with his dad's constant bullshit, let the poor girl blame herself. He didn't let on that he just wasn't into girls.

There was something else to it though. Even if it had been, say, Sebastian Ford gobbling down his manhood, Tyler wasn't sure he would have been able to lay back and enjoy it—not like Sebastian could when the roles were reversed. The truth was, living a lie was a full-time job, and there was no time for that kind of recreation.

When the bell rang, Miranda turned around, giving him *that* look. "Can we talk?"

Not wanting to, but knowing a refusal now would just mean he'd have to dread a future encounter, he said, "Sure."

The class dispersed and Tyler followed Miranda from the room. She led him through the hall toward the stairwell. Relic Meyers barreled around the corner, nearly bumping into Miranda.

"Watch it!" She stepped away from Relic as if he were radioactive.

Relic ignored her. "Hey, Tyler. You good to practice after school? Gate can give us all rides home."

Nodding, Tyler said, "Sure, man. We still on for D&D this week?"

"Hell yeah," Relic said, flashing metal horns. His eyes went wide then. "Oh." He pulled his backpack around and produced a CD with a dragon-riding warrior. "Be ready to learn some of this, man. I want to cover it for the party."

Something triggered in Tyler then, a subtle shift in his whole identity—or the identity that he had nurtured for himself throughout middle school and his first year of high school. He felt the early tremors of this shift during their first session of *Dungeons & Dragons*, but he was resistant to it, digging his pink-clad heels in to avoid relearning who he thought the world wanted him to be.

But something about that fucking album cover was a rallying cry, begging him to join in a revolution of self-discovery that allowed him to embrace the child-like voice within him that cried, "Holy shit, that dude's riding a dragon and wielding a freaking sword and I want to be part of this epic saga unfolding on this perilous landscape of high fantasy adventure."

But Tyler settled for a simple, "Sweet, man. Looks badass."

Relic flashed his trademark metal horns again and hurried off to his next destination.

"Ugh," Miranda groaned, "I don't know why you hang out with these freaking nerds."

That didn't have the effect Miranda was hoping for. If anything, Miranda had just shoved Tyler with both hands further down a path that had beckoned him since Homecoming last year. But he continued to follow her. She led him down to the basement, and then down the art wing.

"Where are we going?" Tyler asked. "I have history on the second floor next period."

Miranda didn't answer, just tossed her hair over her shoulder as she turned a corner. No other students were down here in the dark hallway with spare desks stacked along the walls.

Finally, she led him into an unused room that only had a single flickering fluorescent light. There, she turned and dropped her backpack so she could make a show of crossing her arms under those perky tits she liked to show off.

"I need you to take me to Tammy's party," she said, her eyes looking to the ceiling as if it pained her to admit this.

"We're playing the party," Tyler said, confused by her meaning. "How can I *take* you to a party that my band is playing?"

She threw her head back in a dramatic display of annoyance. "Ty, we just have to go together, okay? Everyone is saying that I turned you gay, and it's becoming a whole thing. This is good for both of us."

"Turned me gay?"

She looked at him now. "Come on, Ty. The shoes! You're always talking about *Dungeons & Dragons* and flirting with Sebastian Ford at lunch. I don't care if you're gay, it's fine. I'm just sick of people cracking jokes, like, I did something to turn you gay."

Tyler supposed none of this should have shocked him. Part of him knew he had spent the last several weeks *daring* the world to pose the question to him.

Tyler, are you gay?

What's with the pink shoes, man?

Are you a butt pirate?

But the only thing that came to Tyler's lips in that moment was, "What if you did turn me gay, Miranda?"

As expected, Miranda's face went white.

Tyler leaned into it, encouraged by the reaction "What if something you did made me want to suck another guy's dick, or made me want to take it up the ass? What if you were the cause of me becoming a total faggot?"

She looked at him as if he had slapped her in the face. And then something happened that he would have never predicted.

Miranda Cartwright began crying.

Something snapped within Tyler. Here was a girl that got everything she wanted, and she was exactly what she wanted to be. Nobody questioned what she was. That luxury that she existed in suddenly infuriated Tyler, and he couldn't stop himself from asking, "You're great at this, aren't you?"

She looked at him with desperation in her red-rimmed eyes.

"Making this all about yourself," Tyler continued, unable to back down now. "People are talking about me being gay, and how you somehow turned me gay, but it's all about you, right? Like, the problem is with you being the cause of it all?"

Miranda's eyes were wide and confused, as if there were no other alternative. Of course it was about her, who else would be the subject of it all?

Knowing that he really wasn't ready to come out and had nothing to gain by making Miranda see the fallacy of her ways, Tyler just sighed. "Yeah, let's go to the party, Miranda. Say whatever you need to say—that we banged before coming to Tammy's, or you sucked me off...I don't care. Make up whatever you want—whatever's best for your image."

The look she gave him was not of relief, but of hurt—a look that Tyler was not accustomed to seeing from Miranda Cartwright before this confrontation—and it made him feel guilty for some odd reason.

"What happened to you, Tyler?"

He laughed lightly then, as if the question were just absolutely ridiculous. "Clean yourself up, Miranda," he said, "people will think I just dumped you or something."

Tyler turned and left her there, making every effort to not care what she—or anyone else—might think of him.

At lunch, Relic found Nick and Tyler sitting at their table alone. Relic set his tray down and dropped his backpack on the empty seat next to the one he claimed.

"Where's Bree?"

Nick pushed his hair out of his eye. He had dyed it black and swooped it to the side, which looked to Relic like an unsettling combination of heavy metal and punk rock aesthetics—he didn't care for the new look much, but to each their own. "Her and Delilah went to get sodas or something."

Eager to talk to her after missing her this morning, Relic left his stuff and went toward the doors leading to the Little Chamber. The vending machines were usually crowded at the tail end of lunch, when everyone wanted some junk food to cap off their meals, but at the moment there were only a few groups of students hanging around drinking their sodas.

Relic saw Delilah and Bree back near the restrooms, secluded in a shadowed corner as if dealing drugs. *Weird,* he thought, immediately wondering if that was how Nick conducted his business—he just hoped his bassist wasn't dealing at school; that would be idiotic.

Something possessed Relic to wait and watch the two girls, curious what they were talking about in such privacy. He hadn't really known they talked at all outside of when they were all hanging out. It made him uncomfortable thinking about his ex-girlfriend sharing too much with his current girlfriend. What if they were talking about him?

Annoyed that he didn't have some sort of listening device, Relic assumed a casual posture on the wall near the soft drink machine, hoping to blend in with the spattering of other students.

Bree motioned toward the cafeteria as if to say, "I need to go eat, hurry up."

Delilah responded with a drawn-out look, which Relic interpreted as, "Don't rush me, this is serious." But it could have just as easily been Bree saying, "Relic is such a dick," and Delilah saying, "Oh, don't I know it."

Then, Delilah unzipped the pack she wore around her waist, which looked like a fanny pack only cooler, all tactical looking; something an action hero would wear.

Relic's pulse quickened when he saw Delilah draw out two small vials of green liquid. Bree's hand shot out to take them, her head snapping around to make sure no one saw. Instinctively, Relic slipped back around the corner of the wall to ensure she wouldn't see him.

He waited there, heart thundering in his chest, trying to work out what he had just witnessed. It turned out he was indeed watching a drug deal of some sort, but he just couldn't imagine either Delilah or Bree using any sort of drug that they would have to hide like that.

As he waited for Bree to come around the corner, Relic considered what he would say to her. Should he confront her? "Hey, Bree. I was spying on you and I didn't really like what I saw." He was ready to reconcile with her this morning and he didn't want to add another fight on top of their current one.

But his rapid thoughts came to a screeching halt when Bree stepped into view. Her eyes widened when she saw him and an enormous smile split her face as she said, "Hey, babe!" She had never called him "babe" and it had a mysterious effect on Relic; he felt his bowels unknot and his heart flutter.

She bounced over to him, put a tender hand on his neck and her other hand on his slimming waist as she leaned up and gave him a kiss that somehow put his spiraling life into crystal-clear focus.

In that moment, he didn't care what Delilah had given her, or what they had talked about in private. He didn't care that she had lied to him and gotten herself into danger without asking for his help.

He really only cared about one thing.

"I love you, Bree."

The smile seemed to melt off her face then and Relic almost despaired. But before he could say, "Sorry, I didn't mean it, Bree! Let's go back to two seconds ago! I don't want to blow this by rushing it; I just wanted you to know how much I care, I'm sorry," Bree brought her other hand up to Relic's neck, cradling his head in both of her strong hands.

"I love you too, Relic."

They made out in front of their peers, which Relic thought would have been an epic scene in a movie. But it turned out to be sort of embarrassing when a teacher came by and told them to break it up.

Laughing, they returned to their band's lunch table.

Relic was the first one to get to the maintenance room at the end of the school day, which was fine by him. He wanted to talk with Gate before the rest of the band arrived.

"You think my dad is going to actually talk to Ricky?" Relic asked him.

Gate shrugged, seemingly uninterested in the prospect. "Honestly, don't know how much good it would do. The guy was a burnout—not sure if you know what that means, but he barely knew what was going on during the Unknown Oath days... He just showed up to gigs and sometimes managed to make it to a practice or two."

Relic had a hard time accepting that. Both Gate and his dad made it sound like Ricky was completely removed from the Unknown Oath operation, but if that were true, why was he back in town and seemingly interested in the state of things?

"What about Jeff?" The question was out of Relic's mouth before he even knew why he asked it, but saying the name out loud reminded him that Gate had told him Jeff was the one that had originally given his dad the book about the Cult of Altnerus—the book that crumbled to dust after the Widow was released.

Gate looked up from his thumbnail that he had been picking at. "What about him? I think he's still touring with random German metal bands. He was also kind of a burnout, just not as bad as Ricky."

Relic paced toward his drums, his mind creating links between what happened with his dad's band and what was happening to his own band now. There had to be some connection between the Widow and this Shrubble Von Hellspawn situation. Was the Widow one of these hexlords? If so, did his dad know about it, or did he really write "Alternus" in his sleep like Relic had written "Night of the Harrow?"

As if he somehow read Relic's thoughts, Gate said, "I think the book Jeff brought to your dad was just a catalyst to it all—like a lit match tossed onto a bunch of kindling that your dad already doused in kerosene. I've tried every which way to get your dad to talk about what was going on in his mind back then, but he's tight-lipped on the subject."

Tell me about it, Relic thought.

Nick and Tyler came in then, shortly followed by Bree. Relic moved toward Gate so he could gather everyone for a quick band meeting. He asked Tyler for the Rhapsody album and then set it on the desk so they could all see it.

"Whoa," Bree gasped, stepping over to pick it up, "you didn't tell me Rhapsody had a new album out!"

Relic was so pleased to see her excitement that he blurted out, "I didn't even know it was coming out. Becca just randomly got it for me."

The excitement left Bree's face as she gave him a puzzled look. Holding up the album next to her confused expression, she asked, "Becca Reynolds got you this?"

"No," Relic said, annoyed that he didn't even stop to realize Bree had gotten him the first Rhapsody album as a gift last Christmas—the best Christmas gift he had ever gotten. "She didn't, like, *get* it for me. My dad bought it, she just ordered it for the shop because she knew that I—we liked them."

Bree turned her attention back to the album and Relic felt like he had hurt her somehow.

"You said we're covering some of this stuff for the house party?" Tyler asked, looking over Bree's shoulder. Even though he had that doubtful look on his face and his arms were defiantly crossed, he seemed genuinely interested.

"Yeah," Relic said, confident now. Originally he had just wanted to show the band what he had in mind for the next song he wanted to write, but he'd have to convene with Bree for that. Part of him was worried he wouldn't be able to handle the double bass, but he felt like he needed to.

"Looks like something from a D&D campaign," Nick added, looking over Bree's other shoulder. "Let's pop it in."

Gate snatched the case out of Bree's hand and took it toward the small stereo he had on the shelf. Relic instructed him to play the second track.

Bree could barely contain her glee when she heard the opening riff. Nick laughed as he shook his head from side to side on beat when the drums and bass came in with that speedy downbeat.

Tyler joined in the delighted commentary as the vocals kicked in. "Do I have to sing with that Italian accent? Don't tempt me—I will."

After the big anthem of a chorus, Bree stepped over toward Relic. "Dude, there's a lot of keyboards on this stuff. I'm sure I could figure the parts out, but we don't have a great keyboard setup...plus," she held up both hands, wiggling all her fingers, "I only have two hands."

Gate laughed. "And those hands will be pulling double duty—this Luca Turilli guy shreds."

"What if we got Sebastian?" Tyler asked, still banging his head. "Maybe he could fill in for us?"

Relic made a face as if to consider that, but he was actually waiting to see if Bree would suggest Delilah; he hadn't so easily forgotten about their little clandestine meeting at lunch. But Bree was looking at him with a similar face, maybe also waiting for him to suggest Delilah?

"I say we ask him," Nick said, visibly getting more into the song, playing air bass to it. "I've never heard anything like this around here. We break this out live...that's gonna turn some heads, my dear lords and ladies."

Relic laughed, elated that they were all on board. However, his legs were already cramping as he imagined trying to play the song. He had his work cut out for him, but he refused to be the band's weak link.

"Alright," Nick said when the song ended. "I'm ready to play." He moved to retrieve his bass. "Are we learning this first or playing through our current set?"

Bree joined him. "Let's go through what we got first. Maybe try 'Alternus' again, Tyler?"

Kicking his shoes off, Tyler went to turn on their PA. "Works for me. I probably need some more time listening to that Rhapsody stuff before I get my head around the dude's vocal style."

"Just make it your own," Relic said, moving toward his drums. "I like your voice better than Fabio's, personally." Something stopped Relic then as he neared his drums. A cold stillness settled in his chest, similar to the feeling he got when he found his basement broken into.

A sense of unholy desecration fell over him.

His bandmates were still talking, but they may as well have been speaking in Mandarin or some other foreign tongue. All Relic heard was an abyssal ringing that rose to a crescendo.

"Who was on my drums?"

Silence fell over the room. Relic turned toward them. Tyler's face was perplexed, Nick's was skeptical, and Bree's was merely surprised.

"Did any of you see anyone playing my drums?"

Gate sat back at his desk. "I make sure no one touches them while I'm here, man."

Bree shook her head. "I'm only ever here with you."

Tyler shrugged. "Same. You know I couldn't play them even if I wanted to. Remember the last time I tried?"

Nick inspected the drums. "What's wrong with them?"

Relic looked back at the kit, unable to pinpoint what exactly made him suspect they might have been messed with. He went around to his drum throne and sat down. Everything looked...different. Picking up his sticks, he went around the toms, mimicking hits to make sure everything lined up.

"Feels like something's been moved," he said. As he went around the rest of his drums, he saw the first blinding clue. "My crash is fucking cracked!" He bolted up from his throne and grabbed the cymbal. "Who the hell did this?!"

Bree came over. "Are you sure it wasn't already chipped? You cracked two cymbals last year, man. I keep telling you not to crash so hard."

"That wasn't there," Relic said, more angrily than he intended. He knew Bree was only trying to help. But as he got up, he saw the next, most damning evidence that something was going on.

"Is that a fucking joint?!"

Gate moaned. "Ugh...not surprised. Ricky used to get stoned down here with Valentine. I'm sorry, Relic. I should be better about locking that door."

But Relic's eyes were narrowed on Nick. "Customers of yours, man?" He tried to hold his bassist's gaze, but his eyes kept falling to that stupid goddamn necklace Nick wore.

"Come on, man," Nick said. "I don't know who it could have been."

Relic tried to think of a likely culprit and it slapped him in the face. Becca had admitted to him that she got stoned with her drummer all the time.

"That little piece of shit," Relic seethed between his teeth.

His bandmates all exchanged looks, not following.

"Jay J. fucking Lockwood."

CHAPTER 18

The broken cymbal rarely left Relic's mind that evening, but he managed to get through practice. Each time he went to crash it, he had to be mindful to not hit too hard. He wasn't sure how soon he could replace the cymbal, so all he could do for now was mitigate how big the crack became.

That little scumbag, Relic thought while Altar Stone rehearsed "Bane of the Worthy." The anger he felt toward the other drummer made it harder and harder for him to check his hits. He pounded the tom buildup into the last chorus harder than ever, thinking about each of those times Jay J. would look at Relic with those worshipping eyes, only to bang his skins behind his back.

Relic never thought much about the life of a celebrity, dealing with stalkers or nutjobs who would steal your socks or underwear so they could sniff them while whacking off. But at the moment, he felt like he was some big-time rock star and Habitual Void's drummer was a little fanboy that would break into Altar Stone's practice space and doodle around on his drums as some form of hero worship.

All those thoughts just made him angrier, wanting nothing more than to pound Jay J.'s pudgy little face.

"Not bad," Nick said when the final notes of "Bane of the Worthy" faded out. "What's that...like, our fourth or fifth time even playing that one all the way through? Sounds show-ready if you ask me."

Tyler was slipping his shoes on—he only ever practiced in bare feet or socks. "Yeah, felt good. You guys want me to talk to Sebastian about maybe playing keys for us or what?"

Bree clicked her guitar case closed. "You hang out with Sebastian Ford? Didn't you and the other jocks used to put *Playgirls* in his gym locker?"

Tyler chuckled. "Yeah, but he thought it was funny. We talk a lot." Relic noticed that there wasn't a lot of mockery in that laugh—it sounded...kind.

"Where'd you get *Playgirls*?" Nick asked with a fine example of a mocking laugh. "That's what I want to know."

Tyler straightened, pink shoes back on. "From under my bed. Because I'm gay."

The other three teens were struck dumb then, not really sure how to follow that up. Relic himself felt a strange veil yanked away from his face, the obviousness of the whole situation so clear to him now.

"Did you just come out, Ty?" Bree asked, breaking the silence.

Tyler gave a crooked smile. "I guess so."

Without skipping a beat, Bree went and wrapped her arms around his neck. Relic noticed his singer's eyes widen in shock, but he lifted his arms and returned the embrace, smiling. Relic felt himself grinning like a dope, and when Tyler looked toward him, Relic felt a magnetic pull that carried him toward the pair, adding his own hug to theirs.

"Thanks for telling us, man." Relic felt his eyes burning, but for a change he didn't have to fight against the tears.

"Don't leave me hanging here!" Nick said with a goofy voice, stomping his way over to wrap his long arms around the three of them.

There was the sound of a lighter snapping open behind them. "I'd come give you a hug, kid," Gate said, "but I think I'd get arrested or something."

Altar Stone laughed, not knowing that their band was about to fall apart.

Gate drove Bree and Nick home, since the former needed to lift before it was too late and the latter needed to check on his dad. Relic and Tyler decided to go crash Autumnal Fall's practice at Delilah's place. Tyler was insistent on Sebastian playing keys for them, and Relic felt like he should be there for the discussion.

Relic pulled his jacket tighter against the October breeze blowing down Teal Road. "So, are you and Sebastian...sort of...?"

Tyler gave Relic a sidelong look, grinning sheepishly. "Haven't I shared enough with you all today?"

Relic laughed. "Just curious, man. You don't have to say. Just wondering if that might be why you wanted him playing for us."

"It's not that. I mean, we mess around sometimes. He was the first guy who really knew about me, you know? And it was because I was hassling him in the locker room—because I used to be a total dick—"

"Yep," Relic said, holding back a smirk as he kept his eyes forward.

Tyler just grunted at that. "Anyway, I just think he's a badass keyboardist. And I think he's kind of in a rut with Delilah. She doesn't seem that interested in doing music—he says it's almost like she just uses the whole 'being in a band' thing as a social status or something."

Or as a cover, Relic wanted to say. It pained him how much Tyler shared with him (all of them) and how much he felt he couldn't share with Tyler in return. Maybe someday soon, he hoped, but not until he knew it wouldn't make things worse.

"So, you're thinking more like him being a permanent member of Altar Stone?" Relic asked. "Not just, like, a one-time thing? You think we should add a full-time keyboardist?"

Tyler shrugged. "Why not? If you want to play more of that symphonic stuff, we'll need one eventually, right? I bet he could help a lot with writing music too. He's way more eclectic than you might think; he doesn't just play or listen to all that electronic goth stuff."

Relic was getting on board with this concept. But... "Okay. Just...what if you guys do end up...you know? Getting together? For real? Wouldn't being a band together complicate things?"

Turning to look at Relic directly now, Tyler smiled. "Like you and Bree?"

Embarrassingly, Relic hadn't even made that connection. He chuckled and said, "Good point. I guess I have no room to talk."

Tyler waved a hand as if it didn't matter anyway. "I've known Sebastian probably as long as you've known Bree, so regardless of what happens between us, it's not like we're going to be all dramatic about it." He shrugged then, cocking his head slightly. "And if it does become a problem, we just fire him and have Delilah play keys."

Relic laughed again, feeling as if he had reunited with an old, comfortable friend.

Cutting through the Tecumseh Bluffs neighborhood, they spent the rest of the walk discussing more trivial things, like recent movies, other power metal bands that Relic had discovered through his dad, and a device Tyler's cousin had shown him called an MP3 player.

"It's like a little thing with a digital screen," Tyler explained, "and you can store a bunch of music on it."

"Weird," Relic said, thinking it sounded like a stupid gimmick. How would people listen to their CDs? Would they have to, like, put them on a computer somehow just to listen to them on a little gadget instead of just sticking it into a CD player?

Sounded dumb. He doubted it would catch on.

They reached the Concord Village apartments and Relic decided it was a much longer walk than he cared for. Next time he would opt for the bus. As they approached Guy Valentine's building, Relic felt a pang of sadness for his ex-girlfriend.

Despite all the other circumstances, Delilah had lived in a literal mansion last year (even if it was under the care of a possibly maniacal cult leader). Now, she lived in one of the crappiest-looking apartment complexes in town with her potentially evil vampire of a dad that may or may not be some sort of minion of this Adratheon guy.

Overall, it was quite the downgrade.

"You been here before?" Tyler asked, apparently noticing the way Relic regarded the dump.

Relic shook his head, realizing that he hadn't really made an effort to hang out with Delilah outside of school, aside from the random times they would patrol Laramie together to make sure nothing sinister was taking root. But they typically stuck to his side of town, where trouble seemed to be drawn.

"Guessing you have?" Relic said, since he had known where it was and all.

"Just outside. Skipped class with Sebastian once and walked with him, but didn't go in—he was meeting up to write songs with Delilah."

Relic still had trouble picturing Delilah playing music. She had a good voice and knew her way around a keyboard for sure, but to Relic, she just didn't seem all too interested in the whole thing.

They took the stairs down to the lower-level apartments, which were partially underground like a walk-out basement. Tyler rapped his fist on the door numbered eight.

Guy Valentine answered. The vampire looked very little like the classic Hollywood takes on Dracula or the more recent versions of Lestat. Delilah's biological father was more like The Dude from *The Big Lebowski* trying to pose as a member of Type O Negative. His long dark hair framed an emaciated face, and he wore a dirty flannel shirt open to reveal a scrawny midsection hugged by a tight black waffle tank top.

He gave Tyler a confused look, but when he saw Relic he jerked back slightly. "Whoa," he said. "Thought I just woke up back in 1973 suddenly." He turned and left the door open. "You look way too much like your old man, buddy."

Tyler stepped through the doorway and Relic apprehensively followed. The place was as dark as Relic would have imagined a vampire den to be, with heavy curtains pulled over all the windows and only dim light provided by a few small lamps. He could hear voices from one of the bedrooms.

"Got a couple more handsome boys to entertain, oh dear daughter," Guy called, plopping down on the couch. "And add a key change to the second chorus, it's sounding way too repetitive." He clicked the remote at the TV, which was muted, surfing through silent channels.

"Tyler? Relic?"

Turning, Relic hardly even noticed Delilah. Without makeup or the goth fashions she favored, the girl that stood before them was almost a stranger to him. She had her hair tied back in a lazy ponytail and wore a baggy t-shirt hanging halfway past her thighs with one bare shoulder protruding from its collar and shorts (he suspected, at least) that were too short to be seen.

He was bothered by how hot she looked.

"Hey, can I talk to Sebastian for a minute?" Tyler asked.

Delilah motioned down the hall. "Yeah, he's in my room." When Tyler moved past her, she watched until he disappeared into her room. "Relic," she whispered, motioning for him to join her in the living room, "come here. Dad, turn the TV off."

Guy groaned, glaring at her as if to say, "Not now." But after only a brief glance at his daughter's face, he complied.

"Tell him what you told me," she said, motioning to Relic who now sat on the opposite end of the couch. "About the body."

"Why don't you just tear those curtains down, girl?" he snarled. "If you want me killed, that's much quicker."

She waved that way. "Come on, you can trust Relic. Besides, I could tell him anyway. I'm just letting you disclose it so you know I'm not spreading it around behind your back."

"As if that's any better," Guy said, straightening as he turned to Relic. "Alright, your dad usually finds out about this shit anyway, so I guess it's better you hear it from me. Sounds like you already knew about the whole Carl Sinclair thing—that degenerate tit licker? Well—and I ain't telling you who—but one of the members of the cult had this notion to dig up his body so Marshall could do his little witchery to see what actually happened."

Relic had plenty of questions at that point, but he let the man continue.

"Well, my loving daughter here interrupted our ritual to find out who Valaina's Chosen was, which would have allowed us to deal with the hexlords—you know what those are right? Considering who your daddy is and all.

"Anyway, one of our members objected to the whole thing—said it wasn't right to disturb Carl's grave and all that. Wouldn't take part in the ritual." Guy looked at his pale hands, considering what he said next. "But Marshall's not a man to take no for an answer, so he used more...drastic measures to complete the necessary rites. I don't know if he killed the woman, but if a dead body is fresh enough to stand in for a live one...well, certain powers don't ask too many questions."

Relic had trouble following. He leaned in closer. "Are you saying Marshall...killed someone so he could, what...talk to a dead body?" Guy didn't meet his gaze, but when he looked at Delilah, she gave him a dark confirmation. "Why?"

Guy put a hand on his brow, as if this tale were taking a toll on him. "The energy that haunts the old Sinclair place latches itself to its victims, piece by piece. It's in his bones now, and Marshall is one of the few people who knows how to speak its language."

"Relic," Delilah said, "Marshall killed one of his own followers so he could understand how Carl Sinclair died." She looked at her dad almost sympathetically. "I mean, it sounds like the principal's brother was a sick and twisted monster, but the way he died..."

Guy stood up suddenly. "None of this would have happened if you hadn't stuck your nose in this, girl!"

There was a sudden rap on the door.

"Finally," Guy said, striding to answer it. "I'm starving."

Expecting to see a pizza delivery guy when Valentine opened the door, Relic was surprised by a beautiful young woman's smiling face.

"There's my dark prince," she purred. But her posture and demeanor changed when she saw the teens. "Oh, sorry, I didn't know it was family time."

"Nah," Guy said, waving a dismissive hand toward his daughter and Relic. "They're just hanging out. Go back to my room and get yourself hydrated. I'll be there in a second."

The woman gave Relic a little wink as she stepped into the dark. Despite the low light, he could see she wore revealing clothing, her tube top letting her tanned shoulders breathe. He also noticed the two puncture wounds on her neck just below her jawline.

Relic felt a queasy sensation in his bowels then, understanding what Guy had meant by being starving. He had wondered how he had kept his bloodlust under control—now he knew.

Something came over him then; a need to get straight answers from people, making him more bold than he would normally dare to be. "Is that why you're not evil anymore? As long as you get enough to eat, you can play nice?"

Guy gave him a devilish grin. "Don't go thinking they've declawed me. But no, the Widow was the one that had her way with me—making me her bitch. I suppose I have you to thank for being rid of that shrew." He crossed his arms near the hall before heading back for a snack. "And don't think I'm going to make a habit of shitting where I eat. Crane's done right by me, and I owe him a lot. But I think he overstepped, which is why I decided to rat on him...just this once."

He looked at his daughter. "You can tell him the rest. I need to eat...feeling lightheaded." Turning, he left them alone.

"Tell me what?" Relic asked.

Delilah gave him a worried look and then took a deep breath. "Relic, you know that song you wrote? Bree told me about it, the one you wrote in your sleep?"

Even though he was slightly annoyed that Bree had shared that, he nodded.

She looked at him apologetically. "That was what released the hexlord—the Shrubble thing that attacked us."

Confused, Relic pointed toward the hall. "He said that was Valaina's Chosen. Wasn't it the ritual that summoned him?"

She shook her head, as if it pained her to do so. "The ritual was for Valaina's Chosen to show them the way to return Adratheon's power to Alternus. The Chosen was intended to defeat the hexlords before Adratheon could reclaim his power from them, and the Chosen would take that power back to Valaina in Alternus where the cult could then use it to fuel their rituals like before."

Relic swallowed. "So, you're saying that I'm Valaina's Chosen? She chose me? The one who sealed her away?"

Delilah scooted off her chair and knelt by him in a position that Relic thought looked apologetic. "We don't know...but she couldn't choose anyone else, right? Of all the Alternians here—me, my dad, all those skrimkins running around—none of them are powerful enough. She could only choose someone that could stand against Adratheon."

"Because I helped release him, right?" Relic shook his head. "Because when I freed my dad, I also released Adratheon. My dad had it under control and I blew it."

"No," Delilah said, her voice soft and hesitant. "Because you are Adratheon's spawn."

"Oh, Guy! Yes! YES! Suck me dry!"

Footsteps pounded down the hall toward the living room and Tyler and Sebastian appeared, both of them regarding Delilah and Relic with wide-eyed panic.

"Is your dad killing someone?!" Tyler asked.

Relic laughed, softly at first and then progressively more maniacal. He didn't know how else to react to any of this.

When he got home that evening, Relic immediately retreated to his room, not even replying to his mom, who was in the kitchen making dinner. He pulled his dad's journal out from its hiding place under his bedsheets and flipped back to the page about "Dealing with the Dragon."

The words there watered those awful seeds Delilah had planted.

"Hey, mister! I was calling your name like twenty times. Why are you so late getting home?"

Relic looked up, tears in his eyes. His mom's annoyed face melted into one of compassion. She wiped her hands on her jeans as she moved to kneel down next to his bed.

"Relic, what's wrong?"

He wanted to tell her that he was sorry he never truly appreciated how good things had been before he messed it all up by obsessing about bringing his dad back. He wanted to thank her for doing her best to keep all this from him.

At the same time, he also wanted to scream at her for not doing more, as if it were completely her responsibility to keep her idiotic son from meddling with all the vile things of the world. He wanted to accuse her of letting this all happen to him, knowing full well she had no real hand in it.

So instead, he wiped his eyes and said, "Just a bad day."

When she hugged him, Relic tucked his Steven Meyers journal back under his bedsheets and embraced her with everything he had.

CHAPTER 19

Sebastian's audition for Altar Stone the next afternoon was uplifting. There was an energy the keyboards brought to the band's sound that allowed Relic to better cope with the fact that his real dad might very well be an interdimensional tyrant. He hadn't yet truly accepted the fact that Steven Meyers might not be his biological father, since the primary source of that information came from a vampire who had publicly feuded with Steven Meyers on several documented occasions, but it was certainly on his mind.

Relic had no reason to doubt Delilah's belief in her father's claims, but he would need more proof than what he currently had to accept that his own family tree was truly that skewed. Also, even if he were Adratheon's son, why would that automatically make him Valaina's Chosen? Wouldn't she choose someone or something not so closely related?

Too many unanswered questions.

Delilah had accompanied Sebastian to the tryout, ostensibly for moral support, but Relic had the feeling that she also didn't want to let Adratheon's child too far out of her sight. She sat behind Gate's desk while the janitor tended to a few projects elsewhere in the school.

They played through a couple warm-up songs with plenty of synth, including Dio's "Rainbow in the Dark" and Bon Jovi's "Runaway" before Bree proposed they show Sebastian the Rhapsody album. During each of those covers, Relic, Tyler, Nick, and Bree continually exchanged excited glances while Sebastian nailed all his parts as if he had studied the songs much longer than a single evening.

"Alright," Bree said after finishing Bon Jovi, "I'm sold, Sebastian. Any objections to adding a fifth member to the band?"

Relic did an exaggerated drum fill before standing up and saying, "Nope!"

"Yeah, that was sick, Bash," Nick remarked. "That's your name now. Because we're going to bash some heads at that party."

Sebastian smiled shyly at that.

"Told you, guys," Tyler said. "He's a perfect fit."

Relic didn't miss the look that passed between Altar Stone's singer and keyboardist.

The band took a break to show Sebastian the Rhapsody song they wanted to cover. After blowing their new keyboardist's mind, Relic agreed to loan the CD to Sebastian so he could learn it.

"Thanks," Sebastian said, "I can burn it at home tonight and give it back tomorrow."

Relic's shock must have shown. His facial expression shouted, *Don't burn my stuff, dude!*

Sebastian explained. "My uncle works for Mitsubishi. He got me this new CD drive for my computer that can copy CDs—they call it burning."

That sounded complicated to Relic, who didn't mess much with computers aside from playing *Baldur's Gate* and *Doom* on Bree's sometimes. He just nodded. "Cool, I still need to practice along with it—make sure I can actually play double bass for that long."

"You should start jogging with weights on your ankles," Bree instructed as she put her guitar away. "I read online that lots of metal drummers do it to build up endurance." She stood up and hooked a thumb over her shoulder. "I'm going to drop a few sinkers real quick before we head out."

"Lovely," Nick said, already making his own way toward the door, stepping aside to let Gate enter. "See you guys tomorrow for D&D, right?"

"I'll give you a lift, Nick," Gate offered, dropping his bag of tools on the desk. "Kill the lights when you leave, Relic. Door will lock when you shut it."

Sebastian looked up from the Rhapsody album, giving a coy grin that Relic had never seen on the guy's face. "So, Relic, if I'm in the band now...does that mean I get to join your D&D night?"

"It's required," Tyler replied, slipping his shoes back on. "If you can't fend off a gnoll invasion while an incarnate unleashes an arcane storm above a secluded hamlet, how the hell you going to play in a power metal band?"

The three of them laughed. Tyler offered to have his mom drop Sebastian off on the way home, leaving Relic and Delilah alone.

"You guys are sounding pretty tight these days," she remarked, crossing one arm over her stomach to hold the elbow of her other arm. She looked like a normal teenager then, which somehow managed to annoy Relic. He wanted to be angry with her, as if his life was actually going pretty well before she dropped that bomb on him yesterday.

But he knew that wasn't fair. Spinning the crash cymbal on his set so the crack was farther away from him, he quietly asked Delilah a question that had been shoved down by other matters, but now resurfaced unexpectedly.

"What did you give Bree yesterday at lunch?" He slowly shifted his vision from the cymbal to the dhampir.

Delilah didn't change her posture, but she did give a sheepish smile as if she were the villain in an episode of *Scooby-Doo, Where are You!* that just had her identity revealed. "I told her to wait—I said someone would probably see, but the bathroom was crowded and she wouldn't wait until after school."

"Wait for what?"

Now Delilah's grin faded and she pushed herself from Gate's desk where she had been leaning. "Maybe you should ask Bree about it."

"I will. But I'm asking you now. And I know one of you will probably lie about it, so..."

She stepped toward him, her hands raised as if they could calm the tension that was rising between them. Softly she said, "Just understand that I was trying to help her. She's been dealing with some major PTSD that she won't really talk about, but the stuff I've been giving her is helping her cope—it's making her stronger. Like, *literally* stronger. Have you seen her guns lately?"

"What, so you're supplying her steroids or something?"

Lowering her hands, she shrugged her shoulders in a sign of defeat. "I've been working for her mom. The stuff is from Rothen, Lydia gives it to me for gathering intel on the cult. It's a serum created from mine and my dad's blood as a way to prevent our—well, our bloodlust; to prevent what happened at the battle of the bands from happening again."

Relic's head was spinning. On top of all this hexlord bullshit, he just found out he may be the son of—not the Widow this time, but her father—Adratheon, and now it seemed his girlfriend was getting loaded on a vampire blood cocktail.

Before Relic could even speak in reply, they heard Bree's footsteps coming from the hallway.

"It won't hurt her," Delilah whispered quickly. "Her mom knows—I wouldn't have let her keep taking it if it did. You know I wouldn't do that."

The footsteps were right outside the door now.

"Just cut her some slack," Delilah whispered even softer, "she's had it rough."

Bree appeared. "Whew! That was a three-flusher. Where'd everyone go?"

Gate's little Camry pulled into Nick's neighborhood, blaring Skid Row as the two occupants nodded along to the beat of "Youth Gone Wild."

As the car came to a stop in front of the Webers' small house, Gate put the car in park, clicked off the stereo, and motioned for Nick to wait. "I wanted to ask you something..."

"Yeah?"

"I used to have a decent supplier around here, but someone's been making moves and now I'm getting iced out. Massive inflation going on."

Nick nodded, scratching his neck. Gate noticed a strange gleam coming from the stone encased in hemp that rested atop the kid's shirt collar. "How much you need?"

Gate snorted. "I'd settle for a dimebag at this point. I do my best dungeon master planning when I'm at least a little lit."

"Tell you what, man." Nick looked over his shoulder as he reached into his pocket. "I've been giving some free samples to potential customers—no obligations here though." He pulled a small plastic bag clutched between two fingers, subtly holding it out to Gate near the car's gear shift.

"Thanks, kid," Gate said with a grin. "I'll owe you anyway."

Nick opened the door and got out. "Don't mention it, man! Thanks for the ride! Hope that stuff helps with your game writing. Looking forward to killing a dragon soon!"

Inspecting the weed, Gate quietly added, "Me too, kid. Me too."

Relic and Bree had expected just Russ Thompkins to pick them up from practice, but were surprised to see Lydia with him.

"What are you doing out of the office, Mom?" Bree asked as they got in. "Doesn't that place, like, shut down if you take a night off?"

"Your dad already made that joke, dear. Relic, you're ours tonight. I told your mother that we'd feed you two before this dashing man takes me out for drinks to celebrate."

"What's the occasion?" Relic asked.

Russ looked over his shoulder as he put the car in drive. "The deal is done! Thanks to your dad—oh, and of course my lovely wife's shrewd business acumen."

Lydia laughed. "No, I think most of the credit goes to Steven. His old manager is a shark—but the deal isn't *done*, Russ, I told you."

Mr. Thompkins waved a hand as he steered the car out of the school parking lot. "I know, I know. There's always the fine print. But I can feel it." He put the hand on his wife's thigh with a meaty smack. "You've got it."

Relic remembered Devon Andrews, who had been at his house at the beginning of the school year, also asking about his dad's journal. He wanted to ask what his dad had done to help with whatever deal she was talking about, but with everything else swirling around in his mind, he really didn't have enough mental energy to care.

"So, where to?" Russ asked. "Want to pick something up and take it home so you don't miss your show?"

Relic seemed to always have enough mental energy to care about food. They opted for Long John Silver's because sometimes Relic just needed to eat some greasy, fried onion-y bread balls.

"Alright," Lydia said as Relic and Bree unloaded their stuff at the Thompkinses' house. "You kids behave yourselves. We'll be back in a couple hours."

"And don't tell me what happens in *Buffy*!" Russ warned.

"It's still reruns, Dad!"

Relic's mood had been lightened so much that he didn't realize he had left his drumsticks in the Thompkinses' car. He also was so distracted talking to Bree like a pirate as they lugged their Long John Silver's inside that he failed to notice the glowing yellow eyes regarding the teens from the neighbor's bushes.

"So, it's our fault then?" Bree asked once they were seated at the kitchen table and digging into their fried dinners. "Like, we released him? Got Carl Sinclair killed?"

Relic shook his head, sucking down some Diet Coke to better swallow his hushpuppies. "It's my fault apparently, I wrote the song. Like my dad wrote 'Alternus' and set the Widow free."

"Yeah, but you wrote the lyrics in your sleep," she said, shoving some fries in her mouth and chewing them loudly as she added, "like, how's that your fault? What if you're still hearing the Widow's voice and it was all her somehow?"

Relic thought about the dream he had of Cecily. Fortunately, he hadn't experienced any further dreams as vivid as that one, but he did have that vision at Wane Street Manor. Bree was right, in a way—the Widow (even if she truly was gone) wasn't done with him.

"Delilah also said that Adratheon is my dad."

Bree scoffed at that. "Didn't she also say the Widow was your mom? How's that work then? She saying that Adratheon banged his daughter and that's where you came from? Bullshit, look how much you look like your dad, man!"

Relic hadn't even considered that. She was right again. He bore traits from both his parents, so he didn't buy that either of these theories had much credibility. He smiled at her then, realizing how just talking to her about his worries lessened the grip they had on him.

That realization made him want to discuss the serum Delilah had told him about, but before he could, Bree brought up another topic that he had almost forgotten about.

"What about this whole Ricky situation? With your dad's journal?"

Relic snapped his fingers. "Man, I keep forgetting about that thing. I still need to figure out what's in it. I kept getting distracted reading that damn *Emerald Decay* book."

Bree brushed her hands off. "Well, let's go check it out now. You said you couldn't read your dad's handwriting, but you know how bad mine is. Maybe I can interpret it."

Suddenly Relic felt like he was in a buddy cop movie, finally having someone to bounce ideas off of and put their heads together to solve tough problems. He smashed his cardboard platter shut, not even interested in food anymore. "Let's do it."

He grabbed his backpack as they headed for the door, once more not noticing that his drumsticks weren't in his back pocket where he tended to keep them.

The temperature had seemed to drop twenty degrees since they first got home, and the full moon was high in the sky, only partially obscured by clouds.

"Yeesh," Bree said. "Should have worn a jacket." She rubbed her swollen upper arms with her hands.

Relic put his arm around her to help.

Bree turned her face to smile at him and in a mock lady-like voice said, "Oh, my sweet prince. How shall I ever repay you?"

Relic dropped his gaze down to her chest and said deeply, "Oh, I can think of a couple things."

Their laughter covered up the sound of the slapping footsteps behind them. It wasn't until the unseen pursuer was a mere ten feet away that Bree turned to see a monstrous form charging wildly. A four-legged thing leapt into the air toward them, claws gleaming in the moonlight.

"Look out!" Bree called, pushing Relic away while diving in the opposite direction. The thing landed in a heap, rolling in the grass as it scrambled back to its feet.

Relic reached for his sticks, only now realizing the possibly fatal mistake he had made. Panic gripping him, he tried to discern exactly what their assailant was. It wasn't Shrubble, unless that little goblin could get down on all fours like a canine. This wasn't a werewolf either, or a regular wolf for that matter.

Under the faint glow of the streetlight, Relic could see that this creature had gray scaly flesh that collected in wrinkled humps near its neck and limbs. It had large ears like a fox but a lizard-like snout with a row of spikes trailing its back like a mohawk. It regarded Relic with hungry yellow eyes.

"The fucking chupacabra!" Bree shouted from behind him. "From that shitty movie *Suck Farm!*"

Visions of the 1986 Constrained Media horror comedy flashed in Relic's mind, distracting him from the fact that the livestock vampire creature from that film was leaping toward him now. Its mass hit Relic's flesh, and he felt one of its hooked claws rip into his shirt, somehow missing his shoulder. He rolled with its momentum, falling into the grass again, while the creature landed on its feet this time.

Relic spun, preparing to dodge it again. But just as the thing was getting its footing, it turned its head like a dog that just heard someone whistle for it. That's when Relic saw Bree soaring impossibly high in the air, both of her fists together and raised over her head in a double-axe handle like Harrow Haley during *Match Night Mayhem.*

The chupacabra readied to leap away, but it was too late. Bree's feet landed on the thing's back in a sickening crunch and her fists swung down, completely obliterating the cryptid's head in a spray of putrid yellow blood that looked like watered-down mustard.

Dumbstruck, Relic just stared at his girlfriend, almost expecting her skin to start turning green as she morphed into She-Hulk—or maybe he just wished she would. Bree looked at her hands in either amazement or horror, still standing in an awkward crouch from her landing when she looked up to Relic.

"Holy shit," was all Relic could think to say as he got to his feet. A car drove by down the street, but neither of them even cared; they both just stared at the acrid, unnatural blood dripping from Bree's hands.

"I don't know what happened," Bree said, her eyes wide in an expression of fear—but Relic wasn't really sure if she was truly afraid of what she did or just afraid of how Relic would react to it. After hearing Delilah's explanation of what Bree had been taking, he supposed Bree might be more concerned with what it was doing to her rather than what she had done to the creature.

Thinking back now, Relic remembered she had bravely confronted Shrubble, and he imagined the more of that stuff she had taken since then had only made her more powerful.

While Relic struggled with what to say next, he felt a strange tingling, reminding him of the time he first fought the ghouls with his drumsticks in the cemetery—the first time he tapped into his Alternian heritage.

"What do we do with this?" Bree asked, standing up now and shaking her hands off. "We can't just leave it here, right?"

Relic looked down at the dead chupacabra. Whatever sensation was brewing in him strengthened as he looked at it. "Delilah used to handle disposal," Relic said, scratching his head. "I guess we could, like, bury it or something?"

"You see that?" Bree asked.

Relic did see that, but he wasn't sure what to make of it. He jerked his head in every direction, making sure Shrubble Von Hellspawn wasn't lurking in the shadows. But there was no sign.

This can't be, Relic thought as he looked back down to see that familiar green energy swirling off the dead creature. It was coalescing toward him, as if he were siphoning the thing's energy. *I don't want to do this,* Relic thought, panicked, *I'm not a hexlord, I'm not the Widow's child or Valaina's Chosen, I'm not the son of Adratheon, I don't want this!*

But none of his thoughts kept him from consuming the thing.

Bree said something, but he couldn't hear it over the power he was absorbing from the dead Alternian. It was deafening and amazing, terrible and all-encompassing. A menacing laugh echoed in his mind and he knew it was Adratheon.

For a brief moment, Relic knew absolute serenity, a feeling as if everything were resolved and he had no more burning questions. The world made sense.

Bree's touch snapped Relic back to reality. He blinked away the momentary ecstasy and saw a ghoulish yellow stain on the grass where Constrained Media's version of the chupacabra had been moments before. Now, it was apparently part of Relic Meyers: the son of Adratheon, Douchebag Lord of All that Blows Chunks.

"What'd you do?" Bree asked.

"Nothing. Whatever that was...I tried to stop it, but couldn't."

Bree ran her hands over his shoulders, neck, and face. "Are you alright? Did it do anything to you?"

Relic shook his head, still in shock. "No. I...I mean, I feel..." He looked at her and smiled out of pure stupefaction. "I feel freaking awesome."

After examining his eyes for a long moment, she nodded behind him. "Let's get inside. Maybe your dad's doodle book can explain this."

Relic was doubtful, but he was completely clueless at this point—he was just grateful Bree had witnessed and accepted this thing, because he couldn't deal with any more secrets.

"Alright," Steven told Gate, "do *not* tell Relic about this."

Inspecting the crudely rolled cigarette with a frown, Gate nodded. "Trust me, I'm not about to tell your son how terribly you roll joints." He checked his lighter, giving Steven a raised eyebrow. "You sure you wanna do this, man? Apparently Valentine and the Dirge guys were toking in the boiler room when the Widow got them."

Steven shook his head. "I definitely don't want to do this. But I don't want to rely on Ricky's word. He claimed he's just looking to score a few bucks before he moves out to the West Coast." Looking over his shoulder as if someone were in the apartment with them, he added, "He's up to something, man."

"Alright," Gate said, lifting the joint to his lips, "bottoms up." He snapped the lighter and began to blaze the potentially cursed fatty. After taking a practice drag of the joint, Gate leaned over and passed it to Steven to take a much less elegant drag, coughing more than once before exhaling.

"Seems pretty skunky," Gate said, cocking an eyebrow as he focused on any potential side effects beyond a typical high. "Definitely seems laced with something. Call it paranoia, but seems like a...I dunno, a chemical taste to it."

Passing the joint back to Gate, Steven shrugged. "You'd know better than me, man. I haven't touched this stuff since that party in seventh grade that we weren't invited to."

Gate laughed, taking another deep drag. As he exhaled, he said, "Brings back memories, dude. Guessing you couldn't get him to talk about the book at all?"

Steven heard a distant laugh then, jerking his head toward the door and then the curtained window, as if expecting to see someone in his apartment with them. "No, he... Did you hear something?"

Handing the joint back to Steven, Gate frowned. "Don't tell me you wig out on this stuff, Stick."

Hesitantly taking the joint, Steven just held it, listening to the stillness in his living room. "But no, Ricky wouldn't talk about the book. He acted all embarrassed when I brought it up, apologizing for stealing it." Frowning at the joint, his gaze blurred. "Said he thought I was Adratheon..."

Gate laughed softly at that; Steven did not.

"Did you know that was what he was doing in Boston?" Steven continued, still staring at—no, *through*—the burning roach between his calloused fingers. "He thought that new Gator Sponge record was about the Widow, and he offered to sing for the band to prevent them from doing what we did."

The laugher in Steven's head was louder now, and certainly familiar. He handed the weed back to Gate, who asked, "So, you think he did try to kill Holden? Thinking he was Adratheon?"

Steven didn't answer, his gaze becoming even more distant as the laughter grew louder in his head. *He knows,* Adratheon told him. *He knows what you did...*

"Now that I think about it," Steven said, "I have a feeling I know what he wanted with my journal..."

Relic paced around his room, inspecting his hands as if they would suddenly start glowing with that green Alternian magic. But they remained the same calloused palms that he used to grab drumsticks, junk food, and the occasional erection that would interrupt his showers.

Bree flipped through his dad's old journal. She seemed to not be having any more luck than Relic trying to decipher Steven Meyers' ramblings.

"There's some pages missing," Bree said.

Relic stopped staring at his mundane hands and took a seat next to her on his bed. Immediately, he saw what she meant: there were several torn edges near the notebook's spine where three, maybe four pages had been torn out.

"The rest of this book just seems to talk about the hexlords and the Widow," Bree said, flipping through the other pages of jumbled, frantic blocks of text.

"It's almost like your dad was trying to write down fragments of things when he heard them—like, it's not really organized." She flipped to a page in the middle. "Here he's writing about Cecily's crimes, and then," she turned toward the back of the book, "here he's writing about Cecily being the Widow. But they look like they were written years apart." She turned to several different pages, pointing to the same name on each. "Lots of mentions of Adratheon."

"The missing pages," Relic said, clenching and unclenching his fists. "Those have to be about..."

"...what I did," Steven mumbled.

"Huh?" Gate asked, exhaling another big cloud, looking like he had never been more relaxed in his entire life. He didn't offer the joint back to Steven this time.

"He knows what I did," Steven said, refocusing his vision on his friend.

"You mean the song?"

Steven shook his head. "Before that."

Gate met his eyes. "Do you mean the stuff with Lana? When you guys found Gustave Moreau's little room?"

"After that."

Gate's serenity fled from his eyes then. He looked at his best friend since middle school as if he were suddenly a stranger.

Steven felt deep shame looking into Gate's eyes, despite the sense of relaxation the weed provided. He had kept the truth to himself, hoping that if he never spoke it aloud it would remain some sort of speculation that he couldn't necessarily prove. Steven had buried it so deep that he even forgot that he had most likely written about it in his journal, and surely that was why Ricky refrained from murdering him.

I gave the journal to Relic, Steven thought, *without even reading it myself. He would have learned what I did, with no context to why it happened or how I had no idea what the effects would be...*

Steven put his hand out, silently asking for the joint. After Gate handed it to him, he said, "I heard Adratheon's voice long before I knew what the Cult of Alternus even was. I hear him now actually—he's laughing at me. Because he knows you're about to find out what I did..."

Gate just regarded him with those distant eyes, the look of a stranger deciding if another stranger posed any sort of threat. That look broke Steven's heart, but he supposed it was less than he deserved.

Steven told him his secret, and the look on Gate's face remained unchanged until the end—that was when Gerald Murphy got up and left the apartment.

Steven Meyers wept alone.

CHAPTER 20

The next few weeks leading up to Tammy's show kept Relic too busy to worry much about his dark lineage or the slumbering threat of Shrubble Von Hellspawn. He spent nearly every day after school—when he wasn't frying burgers at Rook's—working on his double bass so he could get through "Emerald Sword." Whether it was the random jogs he had been taking with ankle weights (at Bree's suggestion) or the mystical energy he sapped from a chupacabra, Relic was impressed with his progress.

His first time getting through the song's entirety was with just himself and Bree providing guitar accompaniment. They had made out for nearly an hour afterward as a means of celebration. The first time playing the whole song as a band was euphoric, and Relic was almost ashamed of how much he relished the shocked looks on Nick, Tyler, and Sebastian's faces when they watched his legs machine-gun through Rhapsody's masterpiece.

Relic should have known things were going too well.

Not only was his own playing reaching new heights, Altar Stone was completely elevated by the addition of Sebastian. On top of that, lunches were even more enjoyable with Sebastian around—the band discussed their new song ideas as well as regaled Delilah or Howard Sloan with the exploits of their D&D heroes on Wednesday nights.

By the time Halloween rolled around, Relic almost forgot all about the troubles his sophomore year had dealt him—with the exception of the broken cymbal.

All he could think about was his cymbal as he helped the band unload their gear from Steven's van that afternoon. The McArthurs had pulled their much cleaner minivan alongside Altar Stone to unload Habitual Void's instruments.

"Hey, Meyers," Becca said, giving him a much kinder smile than he was used to. But Relic hardly noticed the singer as she pulled Jay J.'s bass drum—which didn't even have a case—out of the van; Relic's eyes were locked on the pudgy drummer, who was carelessly dislodging his stack of cymbals from between an amp and the van's interior.

Jay J. looked at Relic as he turned around to carry the cymbals inside. Whatever he saw in Relic's eyes seemed to startle him and he quickly followed Becca up the hill to Tammy's garage.

"We're setting up the stage in the basement," Tammy called from the garage, where she sipped on a can of Sprite. "Hey, baby! Can you help me move the furniture?"

Nick ran to help his girlfriend without carrying any of Altar Stone's stuff in the process (which annoyed Relic) while Bree was single-handedly lugging her half stack slowly up the driveway behind him.

"Every band's got one."

Relic turned toward his dad, who was unloading both of Relic's bass drum cases with the deft hands of someone who had done it hundreds of times.

"Slackers?" Relic asked.

"Bassists," Gate replied, grabbing Nick's amp. "But usually it's the singers who don't bother carrying anything—they don't even need to bring their own mic, those bums."

Tyler and Sebastian both waited to grab what they could. "I resent that," Tyler said. "Besides, Bree said she'd teach me guitar, so I may actually have to lug an instrument around like the rest of you peasants."

Once all the gear was unloaded, Steven and Gate—not wanting to cramp the band's style by having a couple adults crash the party—went to a nearby bar while Altar Stone drank soda and ate chips. People started arriving as Habitual Void got their gear all set up.

"You okay, man?"

Blinking, Relic turned to Bree. She was setting her can of red cream soda down on the counter of the Becks' wet bar, concern in her eyes.

Relic gave a pitiful excuse for a smile before nodding toward the stage, which was really just a two-foot vertical platform that barely held Lockwood's drums. "Yeah, just tempted to ask Jay J. if I can borrow his crash cymbal."

Bree snorted. "You should, man."

Relic pushed himself away from the bar, but stopped short of approaching the other band as he felt Bree's hand on his arm. Turning to her, he saw that she had only been joking.

"Let's just worry about our own set," Bree said, pulling him closer so could kiss him. But for some reason, not even her lips could truly settle the wrath rising within him. He reclaimed his spot next to her and continued to nurse his Diet Coke.

The immense rage he felt toward the Lockwood kid surprised Relic—sure, the fact that a drummer could disrespect another drummer by not only playing his kit without permission, but break a piece of that kit that costs at least a hundred bucks to replace was more than infuriating. However, the severity of the hatred was something Relic hadn't experienced.

Seething in anger is not the ideal condition in which to self-reflect, but Relic did try to suss out what could be causing this. He wondered if his intense focus on the band and not the myriad of problems that plagued his personal life had made the whole broken cymbal thing that much more of a crisis to him.

That revelation went away as soon as Jay J. began tuning his single rack tom (which sounded disgustingly wobbly, like a wet fish). Relic just glared at him, wondering how to make the kid feel as small as possible for what he had done.

"Hey, Meyers."

Relic blinked away what loathing he could and turned to face Habitual Void's guitarist, Clayton McArthur. "Where's your bassist? He said he'd have some herbal refreshments for the party."

Relic was almost relieved to discover that his anger was not only reserved for Jay J. Lockwood. *That dick is not going to sell his shit at our first real show,* Relic swore internally. He set down his Diet Coke and pushed himself away from Bree.

"I'll go find him." Sensing Bree was about to follow him, he turned and pointed toward their gear to the side of the stage. "Can you make sure no one messes with my cymbals?"

She raised her drink in a confirming salute, giving Relic an understanding smile.

Not even remotely sure where Nick would be, Relic went upstairs, dodging the small groups of preppy teens that didn't seem to want to slum it in the basement with the weird kids. He saw Tammy in the kitchen filling a huge punch bowl with purple and red juices.

"Hey, have you seen Nick?"

Tammy nodded toward the sliding door leading to the deck. "That old guy was out back smoking on the deck. I told Nick to get rid of him."

Old guy? Relic immediately thought of his father, but his dad didn't smoke. *Did she mean Gate?* They were both supposedly at a nearby bar playing pool, unless something was wrong. Relic strode toward the back yard and slipped out the sliding door. A few partygoers were loitering on the deck, but no sign of Nick or an old dude.

Moving toward the balcony that overlooked the steep hill leading into the woods, Relic saw them—two figures partially obscured by the sporadic autumn leaves still remaining on the trees. He hurried down the stairs to see who Nick was talking to.

Ricky Warren looked remarkably unchanged to Relic from the Unknown Oath posters adorning his bedroom walls. With Nick's back toward Relic, Ricky was the first to notice him.

The singer gave a boyish laugh. "Holy flashback, Batman! You look just like your dad when I first met him."

Nick spun, a guilty look on his face. "Oh, hey, Relic."

"Getting ready to deal some drugs at our first show, Nick? Or are you just looking to break into another basement, Ricky?"

His mouth moving to form the right words, Nick clearly had no good defense. But Ricky stepped forward.

"No worries, my man. I specifically told him no selling!" He spun to make a show of waving a finger at Nick. "No *selling* at the party, right?" Turning back to Relic, he flashed his signature smile. "And I'm done with the crank myself. Smashing your window—look, I thought your dad still lived there. I was super messed up when I got back to town.

"But it's cool now." He dug into the back pocket of his tight jeans and drew out some folded-up notebook paper, handing it to Relic. "Your dad's not the dragon—I get it now, dude. Also, there's money in there to give to your mom—for the window." Ricky laughed. "Or just keep the money; I won't tell, man."

"What do you mean my dad's not the dragon?" Relic asked, partially unfolding the paper to see several twenty-dollar bills tucked into the makeshift envelope.

Ricky motioned with his hands to indicate previous events. "Well, he was...sorta. But that was before you were born." Waving those hands now to disregard it all, he added, "But it's fine, dude. He came to see me, and we're cool. We're on the same side now, and we're gonna find Adratheon before he can get these hexlords."

"What the hell are you guys talking about?" Nick said, stepping out from behind Ricky. "You got another D&D group, Relic?"

Ricky's face got serious for a moment, motioning to the paper in Relic's hands. "It's all in there, man. I don't think your dad even remembers writing it, but I feel like you should know—everything he did to you and your mom... I dunno, man. I just think everyone deserves to know where they came from."

With that, Ricky turned and patted Nick on the shoulder. "Remember, no selling, kid. No *selling* that stuff, right?"

Nick nodded and Ricky disappeared back into the woods. Turning back to Relic, Nick adjusted that stupid hemp necklace he wore and gave his drummer a nod. "I'm gonna go warm up my fingers, man. See you inside."

Alone, Relic opened the missing journal pages and read about how his father and Lana Sinclair performed a ritual that awakened a half-dead, slumbering Adratheon. Steven Meyers, wanting the power that this eldritch lord promised, allowed the "dragon" to possess him so it could regain its strength through a willing human vessel. Relic's eyes began to water—from rage, not just sadness—as he read the details about how his father did indeed allow the Widow to possess the love of his life, Dina Monroe, just before their first and only child was conceived.

Which meant Relic Meyers was some profane product of the incestuous relationship between an evil father screwing—through a willing human vessel—his just-as-evil daughter—through an unwilling human vessel—to give birth to... What? *What the fuck am I? What did my father do?*

Relic's fist tightened, crushing the journal entries and the money they contained.

In the distance he heard a rhythm being ruined by Jay J. Lockwood. The rest of Habitual Void provided chaotic accompaniment, marking the death throes of their soundcheck.

After isolating in the woods for almost an hour, contemplating what to do with the knowledge he had gained, Relic finally decided to return to the party. Navigating the chatting groups of pretty people upstairs, he noticed several of them trying to inconspicuously take hits off poorly concealed joints. The stench was overwhelming.

Relic supposed he should be furious with Nick, but in light of what he had just learned, dealing pot at a high school party seemed like an awfully low-stakes concern. The sound of Habitual Void getting ready to play echoed up the basement stairs, and Relic cringed as he heard a rattly crash cymbal. When he reached the basement landing, he saw Jay J. finishing another fill, and the wobbling lone crash spun clockwise around as if to display its damaged rim just for Relic.

Of course his own cymbals are cracked, Relic thought furiously. *Dude hits like a freaking idiot.*

Working his way back to Bree, Relic made a puking face as Habitual Void finished their "soundcheck."

"Let's hear it for Tammy Beck," Becca shouted into the mic, straining the small PA system that flooded the clean, finished basement with her angry voice, "for letting us crash this little Halloween party. Why isn't anyone wearing costumes, anyway?"

Someone shouted from the corner of the room, "I am!"

"Oh, it's the killer from *Scream*?" Becca snarled. "Very original." Jay J. did a little rimshot which made Relic reluctantly smirk, despite how much he hated the kid. "Alright, our first one is dedicated to my favorite drummer out there—make sure you all stick around for Altar Stone and hear what his legs can do." Relic felt his face go hot, and out of the corner of his eye noticed Bree glaring at Becca. "This one's called 'Adratheon's Lair!'"

Relic shot Bree a nervous look; her eyes told him she was just as concerned. Clayton kicked into a simple riff that Jay J. tried to syncopate with while Becca growled into the mic like a nasally congested dragon. She then started singing nonsense that Relic couldn't understand.

Something within him reacted to that song—and it wasn't just his revulsion over the genre of music. His vision faded and mist-like green magic that came off the chupacabra enveloped him. Suddenly his lungs wouldn't work and it felt like his heart was being squeezed and pulled into his churning guts as the realization sunk in:

Altar Stone might not be the only band that can summon Alternians, because he heard the leathery sound of dragon wings descending from above.

"Thank you!" Becca shouted over scattered applause and random cheers. "You're too kind."

Relic jerked his head to Bree, who clapped unenthusiastically.

"It's over already?" Relic asked, wondering how much time had passed.

"Already?" Bree replied with a stunned look. "You should be glad hardcore songs only last a couple minutes."

Relic didn't tell her that it felt more like fifteen seconds to him. Instead he just laughed and gave his own weak applause. The rest of Habitual Void's set was much less shocking or interesting, but throughout each song Relic became increasingly bothered by the one about Adratheon. He wished he had been able to hear what Becca had been singing, but then again, it was probably better that neither he nor anyone else could make out the words. He would have to ask her about it later.

"Alright, this is our last one," Becca called out, wiping sweat from her brow. "Stick around for the power metal warriors of Altar Stone who will regale us with exploits from their D&D campaign, no doubt. Thanks again, Tammy Beck! Sorry I spit in your chocolate milk in sixth grade. This one's for you, it's called 'Scabby Crack!'"

Bree laughed. "Gross, dude." She motioned toward their gear. "We should probably get our stuff ready."

Relic was pleasantly surprised to see both Tyler and Sebastian already tending to the band's gear. He was almost even more shocked to see them both in costume. Sebastian was wearing a black cloak with a hood, along with white face paint and black pits around his eyes. Tyler was shirtless, a weird bandolier around his exposed, muscled chest.

After Habitual Void's final notes rang out, Altar Stone was able to chat a little while waiting to load their stuff on stage.

"Who are you?" Relic asked, but he immediately felt embarrassed for not recognizing before asking.

Tyler looked affronted. "He-Man, dude. We used to play with those action figures all the time—figured you'd be the one person to get it."

"I thought he was going for some Marvel character," Sebastian said with a shy grin. "You need a blond pageboy haircut to pull off He-Man."

"Screw that," Tyler said, laughing and adjusting his own hair. "Not going to cover up this do."

"I didn't know we were doing costumes," Nick groaned, stepping over Sebastian's keyboard case to get to his own instrument.

Relic looked at his own green gym shorts, HammerFall tee, and black wrestling shoes (which his dad told him made it much easier to play long bouts of double bass—he was not wrong). Then to Bree's sleeveless flannel shirt exposing her toned arms. "We're not," Relic replied, "which you may have noticed if you weren't so busy dealing drugs."

Nick gave him a wide-eyed stare, looking to make sure no one heard. "I'm not, man. You heard Ricky—I'm not selling. He just wanted me to pass out some samples."

Relic scoffed, spinning his sticks. "Same thing. Just stop doing it at our shows."

"Yeah," Tyler echoed, "I don't want to be around that shit. If you're going to do it, do it on your own time, got it?"

Sullenly, Nick nodded.

"Okay, okay, okay," Bree said, "let's focus on the set. We still opening with 'Alternus' then?"

The band had agreed that they wanted to do "Alternus" justice after what happened at The Voodoo. Tyler assured them that his voice was top notch, and whatever happened there wouldn't be an issue again.

"Yeah," Relic said, picking up his first bass drum as the stage was cleared, "but then we go *right* into 'Emerald Sword,' just in case my legs start giving out after we try 'Night of the Harrow' out." Their new song didn't have anywhere near Rhapsody-level double bass, but it had a pretty fast breakdown that tended to cramp the muscles along Relic's shins.

"Oh shit," hissed Sebastian.

Relic looked over his shoulder to see Sebastian whispering to Tyler and pointing to a huge figure that just came down the stairs. Relic thought he recognized the guy, but he couldn't put his finger on it...

Before he could give it much thought, Bree urged him to get his drums set up, reminding him that they needed to set up around him since his kit took up so much space. Relic forgot about the weird giant and focused on assembling his drums, the nervous pre-show energy driving all other thoughts from his mind.

Before long they were all arranged on the small stage and Relic was behind his kit making sure each drum was correctly positioned. The crack in his cymbal seemed to have gotten even bigger just by moving the drums from the practice space to the show. He glared out into the crowd looking for Jay J., who he saw right up front staring at him over Sebastian's keyboard.

When Relic scowled, the kid seemed to shrink away, ducking behind the white and black keys. Some of the more eager members of the crowd consisted of Tammy, Miranda (who kept reaching up to touch Tyler while simultaneously looking over her shoulder to make sure people saw her doing so), and the spattering of metalheads that were anxious to see another Altar Stone show—their battle of the bands performance was still talked about with reverence by these social outcasts.

"Check," Tyler said into the mic, as Relic tapped out a few beats on his toms and Bree finished tuning her guitar. "We are Altar Stone."

There were perhaps fifteen to twenty teens in that basement, but when they cheered, Relic felt like the band was in an arena. His heart soared. It was because of this elation that his reaction was so delayed when he absently noticed glowing yellow eyes in the woods through the basement's glass doors; and why he didn't give much thought to the fact that the large stranger loomed over the crowd from the back the of the room, glaring at Tyler with those same glowing yellow eyes.

Relic was almost in a trance, seeing the world through that misty green haze that had enveloped him when he sucked down that chupacabra. He did a flam on his high tom and began the fill that would roll into the intro of "Alternus." It was second nature at this point, and he barely even heard Tyler introduce the song:

"This one is about a place where music dies and murder thrives..."

Nick came in with the bassline and Relic snapped out of the pocket to do a sporadic fill across his toms—not something he had practiced—and crashed snare and cymbal perfectly on time.

The tragedy began when Tyler sang; or at least, tried to sing.

"Thuuuugh," he croaked, way off key, "curse...haaaas cuuuugghh."

"Come on!" Nick shouted, turning his back to the crowd and glaring at Tyler.

Relic instinctively did a fill to cover up the mistake. His trance must have been fading because he certainly noticed the yellow glow coming off Tyler's pink shoes now. *Could everyone see that?* he wondered. Certainly they couldn't...or they were just too distracted by his groaning.

Bree had moved over to Tyler, but when she reached an arm out to him, he shouldered it away, moving to get off the stage.

A couple boos came from the crowd and Relic did another fill, angrier this time.

"Not again, man," he could hear Nick say, unslinging his bass. Relic was nearly blinded by the yellow glare from his necklace; it was like a flare fired up into a night sky, making him cringe away.

"Richardson!" a voice bellowed from the crowd. It was that large fig-ure—*Trent!* Relic realized finally, Sebastian's date to homecoming last year. "Come here!"

Sensing something dire was happening, but almost unable to stop drum-ming, Relic did another massive fill, this one spanning several bars, as if he were kicking into a drum solo. Relic saw Sebastian moving to intervene as Tyler stalked toward the threatening figure; the crowd parted for them to meet.

Bree had taken off her guitar and was motioning for Relic to cut it out, but he couldn't seem to stop himself from playing stuff that he hadn't even known he could play. His feet were blazing, and it felt as if the same sensation of consuming the chupacabra was overcoming him, fueling him.

Time slowed as he reached the tail end of the fill, Tyler and his monstrous challenger almost within reaching distance. Those yellow eyes outside were like dozens of tiny suns threatening to blind Relic, Bree's own eyes burning yellow as well. Relic did a sextuplet between toms and kick drums, and time almost stopped before he could smash his snare and damaged crash; in that moment he could see the drugs coursing through Bree's system like a green river with hundreds of tributaries snaking through her limbs.

Right before the huge figure could land a right hook on Tyler's face, Relic smashed his snare and crash, obliterating the cymbal in a spray of metallic shards and hot green light.

Relic was thrown off his drum stool, slammed against the wall as if the big guy attacking Tyler had decked him. Through the ringing in his ears, he could hear the partygoers, some groaning and some crying out in pain. Dozens of questioning voices cried out:

"Was that a gun?!"

"Ah! My arm!"

"Whaaa! This dope is the shit, dog!"

"I'm tripping straight balls!"

Relic regained his senses and looked out over his drum set, seeing his peers get to their feet and nurse cuts and bruises. He was relieved to see that nobody was severely hurt, but Tammy started screaming then.

"My parents are going to fucking KILL ME!"

Strong hands grabbed Relic's arm, hoisting him to his feet. He turned to see Bree breathing heavily.

"You alright?" She started to feel around his body, looking for any injuries.

"I'm fine," he said, his blurry gaze drawn back to those yellow-eyed creatures lurking in the woods. "Something—"

Relic was cut off by a strong hand grabbing his genitals. "Are you sure?" Bree asked huskily, leaning in to kiss him.

Recoiling in surprise, Relic put his hands on her shoulders, but he had no chance of pushing her away. Bree looked at him, genuinely confused by his reaction. But her eyes had that strange yellow glow that Relic saw coming off other figures getting to their feet—Nick with his necklace, Tyler with his shoes, and Trent with his furious eyes and a chunk of broken cymbal lodged in his skull.

Bree's hand went to work on him, as if she hadn't read the room or the look on his face.

"Bree!" Relic shouted, his attention torn between his overly stimulated girlfriend and the towering maybe-undead form of Sebastian's spurned lover. "You need to get off that shit!"

Suddenly, her powerful arm moved from his crotch to his neck, and he was lifted up against the wall. Bree's eyes were now a fiery green—the way his sticks looked when Relic turned them into eldritch weapons—and her face was a mask of fury.

"How do you know about that?!?!"

Relic choked out a pathetic groan as he reached both hands up to try to loosen her grip.

Almost immediately, Bree's hand relaxed and Relic was dropped back down onto the stage. "Oh my god..."

Coughing, Relic got to his feet, backing away from Bree in case she was ready to kill him. But she looked horrified, staring at her hands as if they were someone else's.

"Relic," she began, "I-I don't know what happened..."

Before Relic could respond, he saw the forms emerging from the woods through the glass doors behind Bree, probably a dozen hunched shapes—skrimkins, he could tell now. One of them was already in mid-air, and within a second or less it would smash through the sliding door.

Some supernatural energy allowed Relic to grab a pair of drumsticks from the bag on his floor tom and push Bree aside just as the glass exploded inward; more shrieks from the partygoers accompanied the inhuman growl from the creature scrambling in the shards of broken glass on the basement carpet.

Relic deftly spun a stick, lit it with green eldritch fire, and jammed it downward into the little thing's weird-shaped skull. It twitched once and then its body immediately began disintegrating, filling Relic with that emerald mist that was both refreshing and repugnant.

Bree gasped behind him, but Relic was focused only on keeping the creatures out of the basement. He leapt through the shattered door and met their charge, sweeping his sticks left and right, spraying yellow blood all over the lawn as he hacked and slashed and feasted.

Behind him, there were sounds from inside the house, but part of Relic knew those gasps and groans were directed toward the menacing presence of Sebastian's ex-boyfriend—the one he had brought to homecoming last year that looked like a professional wrestler—and not the massacre happening in the back yard. As one of the critters managed to slip through Relic's slashing sticks, its claws raked his back and he fell to a knee. Two other skrimkins took the opportunity to leap for his neck and Relic felt blood washing his collar.

The piercing nails were torn from his neck before they did too much damage, and Relic peered through his clenched eyes to see Bree standing over him ripping a skrimkin's head from its body. Instead of turning into that green mist, the thing's remains fell to the grass in a heap while Bree snatched up her next victim.

"Help!" someone shouted from the basement.

"Someone call the cops!"

Relic got back to his feet in time to cut down the last skrimkin. "Go help Tyler," Relic said. "I'll check the woods to make sure there aren't any more."

Giving Relic a look that said she wanted to say something, Bree hesitated a moment.

"I'll be right behind you, babe, I swear," Relic assured her, hoping to assuage any fear she may have about what happened between them on stage.

With a curt nod she turned and ran back inside.

Relic turned toward the woods and fell flat onto his face. His ankle groaned in pain. Looking down, he saw that there was a writhing root wrapped around it, pinning his ankle in an awkward, twisted position.

"Those were mine," a menacing voice said. Relic heard screeching tires in the distance as he looked toward the voice from the woods.

Shrubble Von Hellspawn strode forward as if he were a titan and not a three-foot-tall goblin—the hexlord towered over Altar Stone's drummer.

"This was my feast, you little bastard. I would have spared you and your friends—saved you, in fact, from these hateful little vermin." Shrubble kicked the head of the skrimkin that Bree killed, then held his staff forward as a sickly yellow magic began to emanate from it. "All you had to do was let me have them." The head began to crumble into that green energy and flowed into Shrubble instead of Relic.

A strange relief filled Relic, not wanting any more of that energy. He heard a car door shut from the front of the house, followed quickly by another.

"Relic!" Steven Meyers sounded like he was running toward the other side of the house.

Relic gripped his stick and sat up, cutting the root from his ankle. "I thought you needed to kill me," Relic said as he stood up. The magic from Shrubble's staff seemed to wane as the green fire of Relic's sticks intensified. "Isn't that why you came after me before?"

Shrubble hesitated, looking at Relic with a cocked head. Then he smirked. "That was before you knew what you were—before I knew what you were. But now I see, you're not the Chosen. You're...something greater..." Then, the hexlord's staff went out and he knelt.

"Holy shit, it worked!"

Ricky Warren appeared from the woods, looking past Relic toward the house. "He's here, isn't he?!"

Relic looked over his shoulder to see a distinct lack of activity in the basement. As if everyone had fled. Looking back to Ricky, he nodded toward Shrubble, who was still kneeling like some worshiping statue. "Who, him?"

Ricky's eyes were wild, searching all over the back yard as if someone were hiding in the shadows. "Nah, man. The dragon."

"Relic!"

Now Relic turned to see his father and Gate turning the corner of the house near the shattered sliding door. Gate stopped short, holding out his arm to direct Steven toward the eerily silent basement.

Turning to Ricky, Gate asked, "What'd you do, Ricky?"

"I saved them!" Ricky exclaimed happily. "I laced their weed with a Nexaphane cocktail—remember? With the Luneral Dirge guys? They started hearing the same voice you heard, Stick...like you wrote about in your journal? The modified Nexaphane lets you hear the dragon, but mixed with the weed..." Ricky slapped his hands together. "Night night, kiddos."

Relic imagined all his friends and classmates in the basement, each of them sprawled lifelessly from exposure to whatever Ricky had cooked up.

"You drugged all of them?" Steven asked, moving toward the door. But he was stopped short by a familiar voice.

"Clever."

Gate and Steven stepped away from the door then.

Becca Reynolds crushed broken glass under her bulky skater shoes, her eyes were two molten red orbs that seemed to smoke in her head. She smiled at Relic.

"Adratheon," Ricky breathed.

Relic heard the unmistakable click of a gun's hammer being drawn back. He turned to see Ricky standing where Shrubble had been—the hexlord had taken the opportunity to vanish apparently—a pistol aimed at Becca.

"Wait!" Relic screamed.

Ricky looked at him, confused. "Dude, this is our chance."

Becca kept laughing behind him and Relic turned to see his dad and Gate stepping back from the girl as if she were radiating some sort of painful energy.

"You can't kill her," Relic said, looking back to Ricky.

"Son!"

Time slowed as Relic turned back to his dad, but what he saw was an enormous visage of Adratheon towering over Tammy's house. Becca's body was levitating about three feet off the grass, her limbs dangling limply. Steven and Gate had dropped down to their knees, covering their ears against some phantom noise.

Adratheon appeared as a gargantuan, draconic head, like some ancient god descending from the cloudy autumn sky. He had eyes that matched Becca's burning orbs and its fanged maw hung open in a mocking laugh.

"Listen to him, son," that daunting hallucination instructed. "Let her die and you can have all my power—then hunt down that cowardly hexlord and claim what's rightfully yours."

Relic tried to turn away from that terrible face, but he couldn't. Time remained frozen around him, and red energy began coalescing around Becca, her arms raising like some hot, hardcore Jesus. Her eyes spat fire now.

"It can all be yours, son," Adratheon spoke again, and the "son" echoed painfully in his ears: "Son....son..."

"Son!"

Steven Meyers' voice broke the illusion and snapped Relic back to the present.

"Stop him, son!"

Relic spun, sticks burning with green fire, and leaped into the air. Ricky tried to adjust his aim as Relic screened his view of Becca, but before he could get a clear shot, one of Relic's sticks connected with the pistol and a loud metallic clang made Ricky scream and fall back.

The gun fell to the lawn in two smoking pieces and Ricky cursed as he cradled his hand.

"What the fuck is going on?"

Relic turned to see Becca staring at him in confusion, her eyes back to normal. She pointed at his sticks. "How are you doing that? And how'd I get out here?"

Dropping his sticks, which extinguished when they hit the grass, Relic walked past her as if in a daze.

Bree, Tyler, Sebastian, and Nick—along with several other teens—appeared in the jagged frame of the broken basement door, rubbing their heads, eyes, jaws, or anything else that they may have bumped when they passed out.

"Relic," Steven said.

Turning to his father, Relic said, "I'm not doing this anymore, Dad." Looking at Altar Stone, he added, "I quit."

INTERLUDE 2

SINS OF THE FATHER

June 16th, 1998

B arry Richardson waited impatiently. He was annoyed that Marshall Crane had sent him to such a scummy part of town, but if this guy was anywhere near as good as promised, then it would be worth the trouble.

The shoebox on his lap was revolting to him, but again, if it would deliver what was promised—what his son had promised him—then he could stand being seen with such a thing. Not that anyone of note would see him in this dilapidated waiting room.

"Mr. Richardson," a croaky voice called from behind the gay hippie beads that hung in the room's only open doorway. Barry scowled at those rainbow things; those *things*—combined with the Barbie shoes on his lap—made him feel the need to stop by a bar on the way home and maybe catch a game.

Those *things*. Looking at those things while holding those shoes...

The sudden mental image of himself bending over a cheap motel bed while some well-hung stranger shoved himself into his ass made Barry quiver slightly as he stood up, in a way that made him wish he had more time to dwell on that sick fantasy.

You fucking faggot, Barry thought as he walked toward the colorful beads. *You like it when you get huge guys ramming themselves into your hiney, don't you, queer-ass faggot?* He pushed the shoebox through that clacking curtain, not wanting to use his hands to touch anything in this place if he could help it. One of the stringed beads rolled against his hairy middle finger and his cock hardened.

Homo.

"Mr. Crane explained your request," the voice said from the smoky darkness that Barry entered. "Can you perhaps elaborate?"

Barry grunted. "Can you perhaps show yourself?"

A match lit, casting the dark room in a hazy glow. Barry saw a workbench between himself and a plain old man. He wore a name tag that said *Hanks* which was pinned to a gray, sooty apron. The walls were covered in pegboards that held all manner of tools: oddly shaped hammers, various pliers, knives, and rolls of leather.

"You always work in the dark?" Barry asked, setting the shoebox on the workbench between them.

Hanks adjusted his glasses as he regarded Barry. "It's better if I'm not distracted by what I see. Breaks my concentration."

Okay, fruitball, Barry thought, opening the shoebox. "These are the fetish—fetishes? Whatever, this fetish comes in a pair. They don't come in size elevens, so I just need them to fit my son's feet."

"That won't be a problem," Hanks said, getting up and moving slowly to the workbench. He regarded the shoes without touching them. "But I will need to be convinced that these will serve the intended purpose."

"Isn't that your job?"

Hanks removed his glasses, and suddenly Barry felt like he was looking into his father's judgmental eyes. Even though the man had been dead nearly a decade, Walter Richardson seemed to have been resurrected and was now looking at his middle-aged son with that same disapproving glare.

"The fetish will require a bond with the bearer and the maker," Hanks explained. "The High Warden surely provided the necessary instruction on the matter."

Barry was well past annoyed at this point. "Yeah, that's why I'm here, freakshow. We did the little seance, robes and all, and now we," he motioned between himself and Hanks, "*make* the fetish. Go on, hex these things."

Hanks pointed to Barry with a withered finger. "You are the maker, Mr. Richardson. The hex comes from you. I'm just the fabricator."

Barry hung his head, sighing, then looked up at Hanks. "Buddy, I'm not into all this cryptic bullshit. Marshall made some promises and I'm playing along, but I'm not about to do any of that fruity mojo shit here. Hail, Adratheon or Valaina, or whoever the fuck's calling the shots today. Just make it happen."

Hanks seemed unbothered. "You seem to believe your son will bond with this fetish out of spite for you. That is your intent, and that is what the cult requires. But what do you require, Mr. Richardson? What is your bond?"

"My bond is my foot in your ass, old man, if you don't get this done. We good?"

Hanks just stared.

Sighing again, Barry crossed his arms. Something gleamed in the old man's eyes that once again made him feel like he was a kid quivering under the disapproving gaze of his father. Finally, Barry conceded.

"I need my son to hate me. More than I hated my old man."

"Why?"

Twenty-six years ago, Barry bites Kevin's neck, his thick fingers gripping the man's muscled back while his other hand grips something even firmer. Moments later, their coach would walk in and make sure they're both kicked off the college football team for apparent drug use.

Barry felt his chest tighten. "My dad failed me. And I can't fail Tyler."

Sixteen years ago, Barry's thick hand is pushing down on the back of a twenty-year-old stud's head, which was bobbing up and down below Barry's desk just as his wife opens the door to his office and gasps.

Hanks regarded Barry before giving a curt nod.

"They'll be ready Tuesday. Make sure you bring the cash balance when you pick them up. Praise Valaina."

Barry almost made it out of the stuffy shop before he started weeping. But after he slapped himself across the face, the old well dried up again.

July 5th, 1998

Ricky Warren checked the gun's magazine, making sure all the bullets were loaded correctly. His dad's old Colt 1911 was well-kept, so Ricky hadn't tried firing the thing yet, he just knew it would work.

It had to work.

Sitting in his older brother's crappy car, he couldn't seem to get his hands to stop shaking despite how warm the night was. His teeth chattered.

Not for the first time since he returned to Laramie, Ricky wished he had some more blow.

Watching Steven Meyers' crummy apartment, there was still no movement. The guy seemed to sleep all day; fucking bum. While he had plenty of fond memories of Stick Meyers, Ricky wouldn't call the man a close friend. Band-mates were weird things—in a lot of ways, they were like family, but in other ways they were almost strangers that you happened to see occasionally at the office.

Right now, Steven Meyers seemed like an absolute stranger to Ricky. But he was still unsettled by the thought of killing him. And yet...

He had seen firsthand what the dragon was capable of.

Ricky first heard Adratheon's name in Sweden during the second Wacken Open Air. Unknown Oath was a last-minute addition to the bill, thanks to some clever maneuvering by their manager, Devon, but if Ricky had known what would happen there, he never would have boarded that flight.

Before Unknown Oath's set, Ricky had been getting blown by a gorgeous Japanese girl who had flown all the way from Tokyo for the chance to see Blind Guardian, and Ricky had promised to get her backstage if she gave good head.

She did indeed give good head, and he led her to Blind Guardian's tent. Unfortunately, the band wasn't around and the girl cursed at him a bunch in her native tongue before slapping him.

Up until that point, Ricky had thought the whole situation was fairly comical and would make a great story. Unfortunately, the slap was so sudden and powerful enough to send him sprawling toward his own band's smaller tent, and he knocked loose the first of Stick's journals that would end up wrecking his life.

The small notebook contained lyrics for *The Rest of the Wicked*, in which his drummer had been writing a huge, confounding epic that contained—among other things—the seeds of Adratheon's eventual seduction of Ricky Warren.

Presently, Ricky snapped the magazine back into the gun as he saw the door to Steven Meyers' apartment swing open. In Ricky's mind, dragon wings unfurled. He grabbed the door's handle, but froze when he saw father and son step out into a clear summer night.

Relic Meyers looked almost exactly like Stick Meyers back in the 70s and Ricky lurched toward the steering wheel to hold back a sudden sob.

His mind raced back to Sweden, after their set. Normally Ricky would be in full mayhem mode, partying until passing out at three or four in the morning. However, two babes had been all over him backstage, so he took them back to his room at the hotel and ended up breaking his record of three times in a single night.

The impressive act exhausted him, and he had slept through the entire next day. But his slumber was not peaceful. His dreams were oppressive, and though he had no exact memory of their contents, he recalled the feeling of losing a piece of his sanity when the entity said its name: Adratheon. When he finally woke up, the stench of the room was overwhelming. And after his eyes focused, he saw the bodies of both girls sprawled across him.

In pieces.

As he scrambled from that grotesque bed, he distinctly remembered the queasiness that came with picking up a detached human leg and tossing it limply aside. Everything that happened afterward was a blur, but Devon had made several calls and the incident was buried. But it lived rent free in Ricky's memory.

As Ricky's attention returned to the present, he felt the same panic and disassociation he had felt that horrible morning, and he began gasping for breath. Looking down at his dad's old gun, he suddenly felt like he had no idea why he had it.

What the fuck am I doing?! he asked himself. *I'm just going to kill this guy?!*

Ricky pulled open the glove compartment and slipped the gun in, shaking his trembling hand as if to get the filth of the thing off him.

As Steven and his son got into the van that had once taken Unknown Oath toward their doom, Ricky swore that he wouldn't do this terrible thing. Despite all the horrible things he had read by Steven Meyers' own hand, he wouldn't just murder the guy in the hopes that he might be able to stop whatever this Adratheon thing truly was from destroying the world.

No. Ricky knew he had to be sure. Steven had mentioned his original journal in his notes, and something told Ricky that it would certainly be here in Laramie.

In fact, it was probably right under his kid's nose.

Ricky started the car, swearing he wouldn't just shoot another person in the hopes it would kill the dragon.

Not unless he was sure.

August 1st, 1998

Guy Valentine watched his daughter sleeping. It was a rare sight; he had suspected that, like him, she only needed the occasional nap as opposed to losing six to eight hours on boring rest. And since she was on that Rothen shit—*You really think I didn't know, girl?*—he supposed she probably needed even less sleep than him.

He held the fetish in his hand, rolling the ring between his skeletal fingers. Not for the first time, he wondered if he even needed to curse his child. Wasn't she already cursed enough? Hell, if she only knew who her mother was...

Closing his fist around the ring, Guy slunk back into the deep shadows of his apartment, silently closing Delilah's bedroom door. Creeping back toward the master bedroom, he saw his dinner was asleep as well.

Cordelia Nelson was a slut and her blood had the taste of sweaty dudes, but Guy was grateful for her warmth as he slid into his cold bed. The chill of the world hadn't normally bothered him, it was just his existence now; cold solitude. And it was true that warmth really had no effect on his own body, with icy undead energy ensuring he remained eternally frigid. But he could still feel it.

Laying there, he looked at the black ring that he had intended to gift to his daughter, having to hope that she would actually wear the thing and help the cult awaken the curses. Instead, Guy Valentine slid the thing on his own crooked index finger. It fit snugly, but his emaciated digit served as a fine replacement for a hale teenager's.

Guy's smile was wicked, without an ounce of charity. "You never said we couldn't curse ourselves, Crane."

Cordelia moaned at that and rolled over, her small breasts pushing against his arm and awakening more than one appetite within him.

Exposing his fangs, Guy felt dark magic flicker within him. It wasn't like Valaina's mind control, forcing him to be her minion—this was something he had summoned. It was as if Guy Valentine were finally in control of his own destruction.

Fully aroused now, he pushed Cordelia's legs open and pierced her below the waist and just above the collar bone. Giving a gasp of pleasant surprise, she wrapped her legs around Guy's cold, skinny waist as he gave and took from her, gave and took, gave and took.

When Guy had drunk his fill and Cordelia's sex had drunk its own, the ring around the vampire's finger began giving off a faint yellow glow.

A song played in Guy's head—one that he both despised and loved, never truly able to break free of its melody.

The curse has come...from far beyond...

August 18th, 1998

The Cult of Valaina convened around the table. High Warden Marshall Crane assumed his position behind the ornate lectern that allowed him to loom over the other cultists.

Hooded and robed, their identities remained shrouded, but Marshall knew each of them all too well. They had come to him eager for answers and thirsty for power.

Looking at Barry Richardson's broad form, Marshall knew the power that man sought was the power to control and contain. That one sought only to suffocate his true nature in order to become something he wasn't. This made Barry a perfect follower, and Marshall considered the man his most loyal subject, even if he didn't realize it.

Next to Barry was the much smaller frame of Lana Sinclair, who foolishly thought the cult's power could bring her redemption; if she were lucky, it would maybe allow her to forget all she had done and seen. Marshall allowed her to think whatever she desired would come forth, as he needed her influence over Laramie's youth. But he could tell she was their weak link, and supposed she would not survive the upcoming trials.

And then there was Guy Valentine: a risky venture indeed, but Marshall Crane knew that nothing was gained without the appropriate level of risk. Giving a vampire any control over hexcraft was probably not the wisest move Marshall could have made, but he was convinced he would need the man on his side in what was to come.

Ricky Warren... *What was I thinking?* Marshall asked himself, not for the first time. However, the man's commitment to taking down Adratheon was unwavering, and his ability to gain confidence with Relic's little friend was quite impressive. He would just have to keep an eye on that one...

Sandra Reynolds, who Marshall admittedly knew the least about, was obsessed with getting her daughter back on the right path. Perhaps she had thought if Jesus couldn't do it, maybe this Valaina could. Marshall took advantage of that, as well as the Reynolds' ample cash flow.

Marshall began the ceremony, with each member explaining their hexbonds—the fetishes they distributed—and swearing their oaths to Valaina that they would return her father's power where it belonged.

Under our control, Marshall thought with a hidden smile, raising his hands to begin the ritual.

CHAPTER 21

"We need three more burgers and a chicken patty," Dina called, having to shout over the raucous noise out in the dining area.

"On it," Relic called, smashing two more patties next to the one that was already cooking on the flatiron. Hot grease splattered on his hand and he recoiled, shaking it off as he moved toward the freezer to grab some frozen chicken to drop in the fryer.

"I'll cover the grill," Rook said, wiping his huge hands on his apron. "Go wash that and put some ointment on it so it doesn't blister."

Relic shook his head, picking the metal spatula back up. "I'm alright. My hands are too callused to blister."

From the corner of his eye, Relic thought his boss might reply to that, something clever or funny to lighten the mood. But he refrained, and just moved to dress the buns. There was a clatter from the walk-in followed by a muffled curse.

"Your buddy is pretty clumsy," Rook shouted. "Think he'll last back here?"

Relic laughed. "Nick's a bass player, what do you expect? I'm sure he'll get the hang of it though."

As if on cue, Nick pushed the walk-in door open and came out with two huge metal, rectangular pans. "Hey, Rook, that shelf in the cooler might need fixed. That's like the third time it shifted down."

"Weird that it only started happening when you started, Weber," Rook chided, but his tone was pleasant. "I'll check it out when we close."

Nick grabbed the extra spatula and joined Relic on the grill. "Hey, man, did you hear about Becca?"

The name conjured up an image in Relic's mind that he had tried to forget, of Habitual Void's singer levitating in Tammy Beck's back yard on Halloween, a freaking dragon's head looming behind her. It had only been a week ago, but the memory felt like it had been haunting him his entire life.

"What about her?"

Nick leaned closer. "Apparently she, like, ran away or something. She wasn't at school for the last few days."

Now that Relic thought about it, he hadn't even noticed her absence from school—probably because he thought he was just doing a great job avoiding her.

"You think she ran away?" Relic asked, scraping one of the burgers from the grill. It seemed unlikely she actually remembered anything that happened at the party—nobody seemed to—but if she did, then it would make more sense that she wanted to get out of town. Unless...

As Nick gave his theory on the topic, Relic completely tuned him out as he considered the possibility that Adratheon had somehow fully taken control of Becca. He hadn't had a serious conversation with his father about anything that happened at the party—despite Steven's constant requests to do so—but now Relic felt like he had to have that discussion.

He wasn't really even sure what Becca was to him; he had considered her a bully and a rival at the start of the semester, but then she exposed him to the new Rhapsody album and seemed to be genuinely hyped about his band at Tammy's house. He wasn't sure if he could call her a friend, but at the same time he didn't want to just ignore the fact that she might be in danger—did he?

It's not my problem, Relic thought stubbornly. *Let someone else deal with it.*

Nick nudged him.

"Huh?" Relic realized one of the burgers was burning. He had been just staring at it in a trance.

"Yo, Earth to Relic!" Rook shouted from the kitchen door. "Take a break! Your girl's here."

Nick nudged him again. "I got this, man. Tell Bree I said hey."

Relic wiped his hands on the greasy apron around his waist and untied it, making his way to the front. Rook held the door for him and said, "I'll send a couple burgers your way." He snapped his thick sausage fingers and added, "Plain with cheese."

Grinning, Relic gave him a thumbs-up.

"Hey, babe!" Bree smiled while leaning over the counter, boosting herself up on her elbows. Even though she said the night before Tammy's party was the last time she used the VANDAL stuff, her shoulders and arms still looked buff.

"Hey, babe," a gruffer voice from nearby called. "Do I have to be as pretty as her to get my food?"

"Oh, pipe down, Earl!" Dina snapped. "You literally just told me your order! Hey, Bree! You're looking ripped, girl. I'll have to come work out with you."

Relic swung around the counter, put his arm around Bree's waist, and gave her a kiss.

She held his gaze with a smile. "Got time to chat?"

Nodding, Relic motioned to the kitchen. "Yeah, Rook's making us some food. Let's go grab a table."

"Got one," Bree said, motioning to their normal booth. Tyler had one arm around Sebastian and waved to Relic with his other hand. He looked happier than Relic had ever remembered seeing him, despite the remains of the black eye Trent had given him at the party.

"How's Nick liking it back there?" Tyler asked when Relic and Bree scooted into the seat across from him.

Relic shrugged. "I'm sure he'd rather be out working his old job, but he's here at least."

"That's cool you got him a job," Sebastian said. "I know his dad was out of work for a while, but apparently he just started a new job at the Easton plant—I think Rothen just bought it."

"Yeah," Bree said, raising a finger, "I told my mom to hook him up. She got him a supervisor job so he doesn't have to walk around."

Wow, Relic thought. He hadn't even heard about that. He knew Nick's dad was struggling after the injury, but he was pleasantly surprised to hear that Bree managed to help him out.

"So," Tyler said, pulling his arm over Sebastian's head to put both his hands on the table in dramatic fashion, "you guys going to the show?"

Bree groaned.

"What show?" Relic asked, feeling out of the loop.

"Nick's show," Sebastian said, "with Bag of Sax. Their bassist Shannon switched over to guitar and Nick's playing with them again. Habitual Void is supposed to be playing too, right?"

"What about Becca?" Relic asked. "Nick said she was, like, missing or something..."

Tyler waved a pointing finger at Relic as he scrunched his face up, searching his memory. "Yeah, I think I heard something about that."

"Did they get a new singer?" Bree asked. She turned to Relic as if just remembering a detail. "Oh, remember that cop? Hayes? At the hospital. I heard Becca's mom hired her as sort of a private investigator to help find her."

"Man, now I feel like I *have* to go," Tyler said. "I could give or take hearing Bag of Sax fumble through punk covers, but now I'm curious if Becca shows up."

"Two boring ass burgers with only cheese," Nick said, appearing suddenly. He placed Relic and Bree's food on the table, pulled a chair up, and spun it around to sit on it backward. "So what's happening? We getting the band back together or what?"

"Dude," Bree began.

"Kidding," Nick said, putting a friendly hand on Relic's shoulder.

"We're talking about coming to see your new band's show," Relic said, taking a bite out of his burger, chewing before asking, "Did you know Habitual Void was playing?"

He gave a startled look, searching each person's face at the table for some explanation.

"Nick!" Rook called from the kitchen. "Get back on the grill!"

Pushing away from the table, Nick pointed at them. "To be continued."

"You really want to go?" Bree asked Relic softly while Sebastian and Tyler were discussing something else. "We don't have to."

Relic turned to look at his friend bickering with Rook in the kitchen, probably backtalking the boss like an idiot. Grinning, Relic said, "Yeah, we should go."

Despite the levity, Becca still floated in his mind, staring at him with those fiery red eyes.

"Isn't it kind of early to Christmas shop?" Steven asked as they perused the various weights and fitness trinkets that adorned the shelves of Crane & Co. "Also, don't chicks like getting jewelry and shit?" He picked up a twenty-five-pound dumbbell, struggling to curl it.

Relic smiled at that. "Well, last year I kind of waited until the last minute and had to rely on outside help to find a good gift. Just wanted to get a head start. I got her a necklace last year, so trying something new. All she seems to do these days is play guitar and lift weights."

"Yeah, I'm afraid I'm not much help there," Steven said, setting the weight down. "I used to buy your mom stupid gifts. One year I got her this extendable spoon—the thing must have been like fifteen feet long if you pulled it out all the way."

Laughing, Relic asked, "Why?!"

His dad just shrugged, frowning slightly. "I liked seeing her laugh."

The look on his face made Relic immediately and desperately sad. Wanting to change the subject, he asked, "Hey, do you know a lady named Mindy Hayes?"

"The cop?" Steven snorted. "Man, I forgot about her."

"Well, she's not a cop anymore. She got let go."

Steven nodded. "Oh yeah, Keith mentioned that. Sounded like she was overreaching a bit."

Relic explained the situation with Becca. His dad made a motion for him to quiet down when he mentioned Adratheon.

"Let's talk about this later, Relic, alright?"

"There a problem?"

Father and son turned around to see Marshall Crane smiling at them as he adjusted a rack of weight-lifting gloves. He wore an elegantly tailored suit which seemed ridiculous in a store that sold gym clothes.

"No," Steven said sternly, "we're fine, Crane. Just looking around."

Regardless, Marshall approached them, hands held behind his back. "It seems our paths keep crossing, doesn't it? Although, this time, it appears both of you have been hiding things from me when I seem to recall—when you needed *my* help—I was much more generous in offering my aid."

Annoyed with the man's tone, Relic spoke before his father could. "What do you want?"

Looking from Relic to Steven, Marshall pursed his lips. "You knew about the hexlords, didn't you?"

"Yeah," Steven said, without hesitation.

"How did you find out?"

Relic looked at his dad, wanting to know as well.

Steven looked over his shoulder as he rubbed his forehead. "You know, Crane...I appreciate you helping my son out when he was trying to find me. Really, I do." He stepped toward the man, menace in his eyes. Relic was legitimately afraid of his father then. "But you have no idea what you've done—what kind of position you've put my son in. I'm not going to answer your questions and I'm not going to help you try to rebuild the institution that is responsible for all this shit."

Marshall's lips tightened under his mustache, but he didn't reply.

"Now," Steven continued, "perhaps you can help my son—what kind of gift would a fifteen-year-old weightlifter appreciate? His girlfriend is tough to shop for."

Unblinking, Marshall said, "Do not buy her a gift here. Immediately take yourself to a shop that contains the pampering paraphernalia that a woman would require after her workouts."

Steven nodded. "Thanks."

Relic followed his dad to the parking lot, but waited until they were in the van before he asked, "Can you at least tell *me* how you know?"

"Same way you knew," Steven said, putting his keys in the ignition. "You told me you hear voices—those dreams you have. I had the same thing. Adratheon was relentless, wouldn't leave me alone."

"So did he tell you that his daughter was possessing Mom then? Did you know what was going to happen?"

"No!" Steven exploded, gripping the steering wheel suddenly with white-knuckle fists as if to keep himself from strangling his son. He jerked his head toward Relic and in a calmer, restrained voice said, "No. Of course I didn't."

Relic felt tears coming. "Well, then maybe you can explain it, Dad." His voice cracked with emotion and he waited until he calmed himself enough to add, "Maybe you can tell me how you let this happen to Mom. And me. I mean... What am I, Dad?!"

Breathing steadily, Steven said, "You're my son, Relic. You're Mom's son. Whatever else doesn't matter."

"Yeah...I guess it doesn't matter that I'm the offspring of some hellbent demigod banging his daughter..."

Steven, hands still gripped on the steering wheel, breathed deep and raggedly before saying, "If I had known about your mom's family's past, I never would have..." He trailed off, closing his eyes.

"What do you mean about *her past*?" Relic asked, wiping the tears from his eyes—sudden curiosity had replaced the emotion in his voice. "Didn't you guys know each other since middle school?"

With his eyes still closed, Steven shook his head slowly. "It's not my place to tell, Relic. After everything...please don't ask me to betray your mom's trust."

Something sparked within Relic then, an anger that he had tried to keep quelled ever since he had to start explaining his father's absence to people. "What about *my* trust, Dad?! It seems like every day I find something else that you're hiding from me! I nearly died trying to get you out of there, and I never once gave you crap for bailing on me and Mom! I saved your life, Dad!"

Steven's head snapped up then, his eyes narrowed in a way that Relic had never seen—they reminded him of Becca's burning red eyes when Adratheon had possessed her. "I didn't want to be saved, Relic! I did what I did so you wouldn't have to deal with this!"

Both of them glared at each other for a long moment, each daring the other to speak first.

Finally, Steven gave in, his face softening. "Relic...I'm so happy to be able to be here with you—you need to understand that. You're like..." his voice cracked. "Dude, you're like the only thing that could keep me here. But when you get older, you might understand that it's not always about yourself...you know? Even if I thought I deserved happiness, you and your mom's happiness would mean more than that. And that's why I did what I did, and why...maybe, there's a piece of me that's angry at you for taking that away from me." He looked out the window longingly. "It was like my only chance at redemption."

Relic felt the tears rolling down his cheeks, his own glare replaced by a blank stare. "I'm sorry, Dad. But maybe this whole redemption thing isn't about hiding yourself away, hoping you can keep the danger away from the people you care about—maybe it's about helping fight it."

Steven peered at his son from the corner of his eye, the shadow of a smirk pulling the corner of his mouth. Almost immediately, Relic understood how much those words applied to his own life; breaking up Altar Stone and trying to ignore what might be happening with Becca.

"You're an insightful dude," Steven said, leaning back in the driver's seat, the tension in the van easing with his relaxed posture.

Relic cocked his head as he wiped the tears from his face. "I'm probably more insightful when I know what the hell is going on."

Steven nodded at that. "Alright. Look, what I'm about to tell you is something you found out from some public record, alright? It's not even a big secret really, but your mom doesn't necessarily go around announcing it to the world."

Relic nodded.

"Okay, well, you know her maiden name, right?"

Relic shrugged. "Monroe?"

Steven nodded. "Well, sometime in the 1940s it became Monroe. Her family's name was originally...Moreau."

The world darkened suddenly, and Relic felt like he was sinking into a swallowing, blackened abyss. His pulse quickened and machine gun-like visions of Cecily Moreau weeping in his dreams assaulted his mind.

"Madeline Moreau..." Relic heard himself say. *The only survivor of the massacre at Wane Street Manor.*

"That was Mom's great-great-grandmother," Steven said calmly, seeming to not even notice Relic's panic attack brewing, "making Mom a fifth-generation descendent of Cecily Moreau: the Widow."

Relic couldn't speak. Suddenly, his lineage actually made sense—not in the "whew, what a relief!" type of way, but in the "oh shit, we're actually in this together?!" type of way.

"Lana and I had no idea," Steven continued. "When we found Gustave's old musical scores and notes in that hidden study at the old Crane Estate... Man, Relic, we were just stupid kids, convinced there was some hidden magic in the world, you know? We never imagined we'd set that bitch free."

Relic felt himself nodding, but breathing was becoming harder and harder. The van felt stuffy and suffocating as Cecily's miserable face kept haunting his mind.

"And when the Widow latched herself to Mom...after what she made her do... Man, I honestly thought your mom would have thanked me for leading the Widow as far away as possible."

Lead Her Astray, Relic thought, wanting to almost laugh hysterically at the blatant nature of Unknown Oath's debut album title. But the madness had not yet overtaken him that much.

"Is she safe now?" Relic asked, finally controlling his breathing as he understood the gravity of what his dad was saying. "Since the Widow is gone?"

Steven motioned back to the Roanoke Mall. "Believe it or not, Marshall's cult is probably the best way we can ensure that. They want her trapped in Alternus for good, so they can channel her power—out here, they have no control over her or her curses. But..."

"But?"

Steven looked at Relic. "Adratheon was part of me for years, son. In a way, he's still a part of me, almost as much as he's a part of you. These *things* leave a taint behind, connecting me, you, and Mom to that place. What I know, he knows..."

Relic understood that, just as he understood that he was foolish to think that he could just walk away from this and let someone else deal with it.

A long silence followed in which Relic made a firm decision.

Suddenly, he thought of an awesome Christmas gift for his girlfriend.

"Hey, where's the best place we can get some shirts made?"

Steven recoiled in confusion, but after seeing the look on Relic's face, he smiled. "I think I know a guy."

Later that night, Steven dropped Relic off at home, their plan set in motion. Walking in the front door, Relic found Calvin and Dina cuddling on the couch in the dark living room, the glow of the TV casting the scene in serene bluish colors.

"Hey, pal," Calvin said warmly. Relic smiled and waved.

"Find anything good for Bree?" Dina asked, sitting up and grabbing a handful of popcorn from the bowl on the table.

Taking a moment to look at his mom, Relic thought about everything the woman had gone through. Having learned about her difficult lineage, he felt more love and respect for her than he ever had. And with how content she looked right now, he knew that the decision he made on the ride home was the right one.

Relic moved to take a seat on the end of the couch, taking a drink of his mom's Diet Coke before answering. He felt the need for dramatic suspense.

"Yeah, I think so. Dad has a buddy that makes custom t-shirts, so I'm going to get a bunch of Altar Stone shirts to sell at the concert."

Dina gasped, grabbing her son's shoulder. "You guys are going to play?!"

Smirking, Relic grabbed a handful of popcorn. He put his feet up on the coffee table and stole a glance at his mom's shocked face. "Is that alright?"

Smacking him playfully on the shoulder, Dina grabbed his head and hugged it. "Oh, let me be there when you tell Bree, alright?"

He tried to say, "Sure, Mom," but it came out as, "Sherma," with her arm hooked around his jaw. But he didn't break out of her embrace.

CHAPTER 22

R elic was surprised to see Becca Reynolds show up to English class the Friday before Habitual Void's show. He was actually early for a change, sitting at his desk as the rest of the class filtered in. Becca walked in soon after, immediately catching his eye with a smile and a nod.

He held up both his hands in a shrugging gesture. "Where you been?"

Sitting in the empty desk behind him, she pushed her hair out of her eyes and told him quietly, "I tried ditching town."

"Why?"

She looked at the ground, her expression uncharacteristically morose. "It's a long story, but my mom got involved in this weird cult." Becca looked over her shoulder to make sure no one else was listening before looking back to Relic. "I have a feeling you know about this stuff, but she won't tell me about what she's been doing." Shaking her head, she added, "Whatever it is...I think it's...doing something to me..."

Relic considered his words for a moment. "Like what happened at Tammy's party?"

Becca scoffed. "You mean that laced weed your bassist gave out? No, but he should be glad we just passed out and didn't all die, that idiot. No, I mean...remember what I wrote? That thing you read about that Adratheon guy?"

Relic nodded, not able to forget it.

"I started having more of these weird...like, hallucinations? Ever since my mom started going to those meetings."

Relic thought back to the party before the skrimkin attack—the yellow energy coming from Tyler's shoes and Nick's necklace. "Did your mom...give you anything? Maybe at the start of the school year?"

Frowning, Becca reached into her pocket.

"Alright," Mr. Hackley said as he walked into the room, setting his bag on the desk, "who's ready to talk about *The Great Gatsby*?"

Becca got up and went to her desk, leaving Relic to wonder what had latched Adratheon to her.

After class, Relic was bum rushed by Bree, who was still in way too good of a mood since he told her Altar Stone was officially back together. It was an infectious mood though, and Relic returned her affections, allowing Becca to escape before he could ask about whatever her mom had given her.

"I think I need to go talk to Gate," Relic told Bree as they went to her locker. "Did you want to come, or should I just catch you at lunch?"

"Should I come?" Bree asked, cocking an eyebrow. "Like, is this something...serious?"

Relic shook his head noncommittally. "I don't know. I just talked to Becca, and I'm wondering if Marshall's cult is like...I don't know...*cursing* the bands or something. You know Tyler's voice? And then something was up with that Habitual Void song at Tammy's..."

Bree jammed a thick chemistry book into her backpack. "Yeah, it sucked balls—that's what's wrong with it."

Snorting, Relic shut her locker for her. "I just want to know if that kind of stuff happened with Unknown Oath. Dad tells me the cult is sort of on our side in a way, but I get the feeling they're also causing some of this shit."

"Like Shrubble," Bree said. They shared a look then and, with a mutual nod, silently agreed to consult a true professional on the subject of occult activity in Laramie: the school janitor.

Gate was refilling chemical bottles as he listened to their news. "If her mom's part of Crane's cult, then you better keep an eye on her band," Gate said. "I don't have to tell you how instrumental music can be in—Shit...that's a pun, isn't it?"

Relic motioned for him to continue.

"All this shit started with music, man," he continued, screwing the cap back on a bottle. "But as we know, music can also undo said shit. I think it's best if Altar Stone keeps close to Cranial Choad."

Bree laughed. "Habitual Void."

Gate flashed his gap-tooth grin. "I like mine better."

"So," Relic said, turning to Bree, "we should have them play the wedding show with us?"

Snapping his finger and then pointing to Relic, Gate nodded. "Now you're thinking. You think we liked playing with Unkind Ways back in the day? Hell no, but your dad had to keep an eye on that tool, Valentine. So we always had to suffer through their sets."

Relic nodded, scratching the back of his head as he looked at the ground, wondering how to broach the next subject.

"Something else bothering you, kid?"

He turned to Bree. "Any chance you'd be willing to talk to Becca? I think she's also got lunch now."

Groaning, Bree rolled her eyes. "Yeah, I can. Want me to go now?"

Relic nodded, motioning to Gate. "Yeah, I'll be right behind you." After she kissed him and left, Relic turned back to the janitor. "You know about Adratheon, right? About...me?"

Gate lowered his eyes for a moment, but looked up to reply. "Just found out before Halloween. I'm sorry, kid. I had no idea things were that messed up."

"Yeah," Relic said. "Well, I didn't tell my dad about this yet, but remember how the Widow, like, sucked up that wendigo last year? Gaining its power or whatever? Well, I did that with a chupacabra before Halloween. And I think Adratheon wanted me to do that to Shrubble—you know, the hexlord."

Gate's eyes widened slightly. "Shit. Yeah...that can't be good."

"You think there's a way I could defeat the hexlord and somehow...I don't know, *catch* that power? I felt myself absorbing that chupacabra, and I think I know how I did it, even though I didn't want to." Relic made a containing motion with his hands. "What if we, like, I don't know...trapped it in something, you know?"

Nodding, Gate raised a finger to indicate an idea. "I know what you need, kid." He went to his desk and opened the drawer, pulling out a small square package. Gate tossed it to Relic, who caught it one-handed.

Holding it up, Relic turned a revolted expression toward Gate. "A condom?!"

Gate repeated the containing motion that Relic had made. "Trap that shit."

Relic tossed it back to him, instinctively wiping his hands on his shirt. "Why is that in your desk, man?"

Catching the prophylactic and ignoring Relic, Gate said, "The thing about a condom, man, is you still get the job done, but avoid any potential risks. You need to be able to suck off Shrubble—"

"Gross, dude."

"—while not taking on his power, but also keeping something else from nabbing it. Get the job done and avoid any risks; those risks being Adratheon getting his power back and wrecking Laramie and maybe the whole world."

Relic nodded. "Yeah, pretty much. So, you got any ideas?"

Gate held up the condom. "I did all the hard work, man. Can't you figure out the rest?"

"Great, thanks." Relic turned to leave.

"Hey, kid," Gate called. When Relic turned, the janitor tossed the condom back to him. "I've seen the way your girl looks at you. Better hang onto that."

Saturday night was the Bag of Sax/Habitual Void show and Relic took an early shift at Rook's so he could walk over to The Voodoo in time to catch it. Part of him was a bit sour going to see his peers' bands while his own band had yet to even play an actual, full gig. But when Tyler, Sebastian, and Bree surprised him by coming to the diner for a pre-show meal, it felt much more like a band activity.

"I hope your ex-boyfriend isn't at this show," Tyler said, dunking his fries in cheese sauce.

"He was never my boyfriend," Sebastian said, disgusted. "We just hung out a few times—trust me, I'm never meeting someone from an online chat room ever again."

"Was he even really in high school?" Bree asked, stabbing at her salad. Relic had noticed that since she quit taking that VANDAL stuff, her appetite seemed to be much less...ravenous.

Sebastian shrugged. "Honestly, I have no clue. I think he drove to my place a couple times, but my mom called the cops when he wouldn't leave me alone. When I first met the guy, he seemed super normal—albeit he looked like he could have wrestled on *Match Night Mayhem*."

They all laughed. Tyler put an arm around Sebastian and kissed the top of his head. It was then that Relic heard a familiar voice over the din of Home Plate's rush hour. He turned in the booth and saw a waitress moving away from Mindy Hayes, who was sitting at a table alone. She looked like she hadn't slept in days.

Feeling possessed, Relic got up and went to her table. She looked up, startled, but then relaxed when she recognized Relic. "Hey, Meyers. I forgot you worked here—I think I saw you in the back the last time I was in."

"Sorry to bug you, but...you were hired by Becca's mom, right? Mrs. Reynolds?"

Mindy looked around, making sure no one was listening in on their conversation. Satisfied, she said, "That's not something I'd typically discuss...but yeah. I had to track her down. Found her at a motel near the city limits, out near Dayton."

"How much do you charge?"

Cocking an eyebrow, Hayes asked, "You missing a daughter, Meyers?"

"I want to find out who made a pair of custom shoes..."

They arrived at The Voodoo just as Bag of Sax was setting up. Paying the three-dollars-a-head cover charge, Altar Stone sans bassist joined the small crowd that was waiting for the show to start. Immediately, something caught Relic's eye near the stage.

An upturned water cooler bottle was sitting on a chair with a crudely written sign reading *The Relic Meyers Cymbal Fund*. Relic felt a strange flutter in his chest then and Bree gripped his hand tighter; the flutter intensified when he saw just how many bills were shoved into that bottle.

"Hey!" Nick leaped off the two-foot-high stage and completed Altar Stone's lineup. "You guys made it!" He noticed them staring at the makeshift fundraiser set up. "Oh yeah, it's not much yet, but once the show starts we should draw some more people in—I think you'll have more than enough for a new cymbal...maybe one of those A Customs you were eyeing at the shop."

"Dude," Relic said, his voice slightly choked, "you didn't have to do this."

"Yeah, I did, man." He pulled at his collar, showing that he wasn't wearing that hemp necklace anymore. "After Tammy's party, Ricky told me about that necklace he gave me...said it was something called a fetish? Anyway, I swear, man, when I was wearing that thing, all I cared about was getting people to like me."

Relic noticed a faint yellow mark on Nick's skin where the necklace had been—but maybe that was just his mind allowing him to see the supernatural stain.

"The only reason I rejoined Bag of Sax—oh, I quit by the way, this is my only show, Sharon's switching back to bass—the only reason I agreed to play with them is because I thought I'd be able to...sell more product. It was Dustin that broke your cymbal...but don't blame him. I let him play when they didn't have a place to practice."

Any anger Relic would have felt over the betrayal was replaced by a deep appreciation that he had his friend Nick back, free from the grip of the cult's hex.

Nick looked back over at the jar of money. "So, yeah, I did need to do it."

Relic let go of Bree's hand so he could hug Nick.

"Not again," Nick groaned, just before the rest of the band joined in.

After Bag of Sax finished their soundcheck, Relic finally caught a glimpse of Becca helping Jay J. carry his drums in and Relic went to help them.

"Hey, man," Relic said to Jay J. "I wanted to let you know...I was kind of misinformed about something." He pointed to the cymbal fund bottle and explained the situation.

"Oh, dude," Jay J. said with wide, understanding eyes, "I'd be pretty pissed off too if someone messed with my drums without asking. Just know that I'd never do that, man."

"I'm not sure you could handle his set anyway," Becca joked and turned to head back out for another load.

Relic caught up with her and when they were alone on the sidewalk outside, he reached out and gently grabbed her arm. "Hey, wait."

She turned to him, curious and maybe a bit excited by his touch.

He let go of her and stuck his hands in his pockets, wondering how to explain. "Is there...is there any way you guys could, like, not play 'Adratheon's Lair' tonight?"

Surprisingly, Becca's face didn't change—Relic had expected shock or anger or something, but she just looked at him as if he asked her a perfectly normal request. "Why?"

He sighed, looking up into the darkening sky. "You know those things we see and hear? Like the thing you wrote about in class? That song did something like that to me at Tammy's."

Her sharp facial features seemed to soften then, as if she truly cared about Relic's wellbeing. Part of him wanted to suspect that the girl had a crush on him, but that just seemed extremely unlikely.

Then, her trademark smile returned, coy and kind of resentful. "So you didn't like it, huh?"

Relic laughed. "Honestly, I don't even remember it. I felt like I sort of blacked out right when it started and then snapped back out of it right when you guys finished."

Her smile faded then, and before she turned away to get more gear, she said, "That's too bad, man. I wrote it for you."

CHAPTER 23

The Christmas season crept up on Altar Stone, and they had only finished three out of the four songs they wanted to write for their concert in March. Both "Night of the Harrow" and "Bane of the Worthy" were about as solid as they were going to get, and Tyler had written the majority of a song with Sebastian about the group's D&D campaign called "The Keys of Transience" that Relic was massively stoked about.

However, he and Bree had been stuck on finding a hook for their Rhapsody-inspired epic that Relic had tentatively called "The Witchlord's Banishment," based on a short story he had started writing after finishing *The Sword of Shannara* by Terry Brooks.

Not even a few months ago, the thought of reading utterly disgusted him, and now here he was wanting to write a story—hell, he even had the occasional thought that he might someday write a whole novel. He might have jokingly asked himself, "What have I become?" But in light of recent events, he chose not to prod that bear.

"Maybe we should just learn another cover," Bree suggested, rolling her pinky over her guitar's volume knob to kill the low distortion coming from her practice amp. "Trying to force ideas out never seems to work."

Relic scribbled out a lyric on his notebook, deciding that "the Witchlord's might can't stand against our light" sounded a wee bit too corny for him. He rolled over, smacking out a rhythm on his chest. "Yeah, I was just really hoping to have more originals by now."

Bree set her guitar aside. "Maybe we just need to dry hump and watch some wrestling."

Relic laughed. "After that dinner? Man, I feel like I'm going to pop."

"That's the idea," Bree said as she stood up and stretched.

The phone rang.

Relic rolled over to answer it. "Hello?"

"I found him."

Motioning for Bree to hold on (even though she hadn't even been doing anything), Relic started to get up. "Yeah?"

Mindy Hayes sounded tired on the other line, as if she hadn't slept since Relic managed to get the two hundred and fifty dollars she required for the retainer. "Thomas Hanks. Six fifty-nine Chestnut Avenue, West Laramie. He's got a little workshop—no sign or anything, looks like just a run-down house in a pretty low-key neighborhood."

"Did you say Thomas Hanks?" Relic asked with disbelief. "As in...Tom Hanks?"

Mindy snorted. "That's him. Obviously not the actor. I'd advise against approaching this guy, kid. I get the sense that he's hooked up with some rough clientele, if you catch my meaning."

Relic didn't feel the need to tell her that he would in fact be approaching the man, so instead he thanked her and said he'd let her know how it all shakes out.

"Seriously, Relic," she added before hanging up. "I just sat outside that place and watched the guy's movements a little, but I got a real bad feeling about the whole situation. Whatever he's involved in can't be good."

Relic told her he understood and then hung up.

"What was that?" Bree asked.

Relic motioned for her to hang on as he picked the phone back up and dialed his dad's number.

"Hey, Dad? Remember when you didn't tell me that you let an evil demigod possess you and bang his daughter that was possessing Mom? Well, you owe me a big favor and I need a ride."

On the way to Hanks' address, Relic explained his idea to his dad and Bree; both of them whole-heartedly rejected the concept.

"You want to hire the guy who cursed your band?" Steven asked in disbelief. "You should steer way clear of guys like this, dude, trust me. What incentive will he have to help you?"

Bree leaned her head between father and son from the van's middle seat. "Your dad's right, Relic, I don't feel good about this. Like, at all."

"If there's one thing I've learned about being the son of a sinister dragon," Relic began.

Steven tried to interject: "You're not the—"

But Relic quieted him with a raised hand and coy grin. "It's that I need to trust my instincts. Dad, you know how this is—I mean, you got the dreams and visions and crap, right? Something tells me this is how we beat him, alright? So just freaking get us to Tom Hanks!"

Steven pulled the van up alongside the house, leaning over Relic to inspect the place. "So this is where he works?"

"Apparently," Relic said, opening the van door to the sound of nocturnal insects. "You guys wait here."

"Fuck that," Bree said. "I'm not letting you go in there alone."

"It's fine," Relic assured her. "I'd rather you both be out here—that way, if I'm not back in ten minutes, I'll have enough backup ready to help me out of a jam, alright?" He leaned back in the car to give Bree a kiss, holding her gaze as he said, "I'll be fine, seriously."

"Ten minutes," Steven said, checking the time on the van's dash.

Relic walked up to the front door and knocked. Shortly after, there was some rustling and the click of a deadbolt unlatching. The door swung inward to reveal a very plain old man in a pair of thick-framed glasses.

"I'm not open, son," he said.

"Hi, Mr. Hanks," Relic began, not really sure how to begin this discussion. "I was wondering if you could tell me why you cursed my singer with those Barbie shoes you made."

There was a long moment when the man didn't react, but then he pulled the door open farther to reveal his hunched, aged body clothed in a short-sleeved blue work shirt and a greasy apron around his waist.

"You're not one of Marshall's, are you?"

Relic shook his head. "I'm Adratheon's son."

The man visibly reacted to that. But instead of replying, he just turned back toward the darkness behind him and motioned for Relic to follow. So he did.

There was a strange waiting room inside and Hanks flipped a switch, creating several strands of light from behind a beaded curtain.

"Come on back and let me know what I can do for you," Hanks said. "It's not every day I get royalty in my little neck of the woods."

Relic cringed at that; being considered "royalty" because of his hideous lineage was rather repulsive to him, but he used it to his advantage in this case and passed through the colorful beads.

The workshop beyond was fascinating to Relic, so many strange tools and materials that he assumed were used to fashion items of terrible power. But the shoe-making instruments specifically drew his eye, confirming that he was indeed where he needed to be.

"So," Hanks asked, taking a seat behind his workbench and facing Relic, "how can I help you, son?"

Relic had asked Delilah about this next part, confirming his own existing suspicions. "You make fetishes for Marshall Crane and his cult."

"I do," Hanks said, unbothered that Relic had this information.

"So you know how to create items using Alternian magic, yeah?"

This time, Hanks just nodded.

"Assuming you have the cult's interests in mind, it seems to me that you would want to make sure Adratheon never came into power here in our world, right?"

This time, Hanks seemed to recoil from the question, but once more he nodded. "That wouldn't be good for anyone on Earth."

"Well, I have an idea to prevent him from doing so, but I need something to trap the power that he's trying to recover from his hexlords."

"You need a talion," Hanks said; it wasn't a question.

"What's a talion?"

Hanks stood up again, coming toward Relic. "It's an instrument of retributive magic. You know the saying 'eye for an eye,' yes? A talion is an artifact that embodies this sentiment. However, a talion isn't a judge—it cares nothing about morality or intent. It simply exists to strike a balance."

"A balance," Relic repeated, considering if this was the answer he needed.

Then, Hanks leaned over toward Relic, his face hard and almost angry. "But know this, son. Forging a talion comes with a cost—you put yourself into this as much as your father, so it will lash out at you just the same as it would him. A talion does not play favorites."

Relic tried to puzzle that out. "So, you're saying if I trap his power, neither of us can really get to it. And if we try to, it'll suck for either of us?"

Hanks snorted, his face easing slightly. "Suck. Yeah, that's about how it works."

"Can this talion be...anything?"

Shrugging, Hanks gave a little nod. "Within reason. Did you have something in mind?"

Relic did indeed have something in mind.

The week before Christmas, Bree became more anxious than she had ever been. Still stuck trying to finish "The Witchlord's Banishment" for Relic as a surprise Christmas gift, she was going crazy most nights sitting at the computer and trying to program MIDI drums on Guitar Pro with Sebastian's help. There seemed like so much to still do.

Her new friend from school, Abigail Diamond, was a pretty awesome artist and had agreed to do an art piece of Relic's Witchlord so Bree could make an actual album and have something to give him for Christmas. But until she had the art printed off, she couldn't put the thing together, and the waiting was driving her crazy.

Also, there was still the last half of the song she had to get right.

"Yo," Tyler said, snapping his fingers. "You there, Thompkins?"

Bree blinked and looked up. Tyler was on his bed, holding the hot pink Jackson guitar he'd bought with the money from hawking the Don Mattingly baseball card he swiped from Carl Sinclair's place. "If I can't wear the shoes anymore," he had told Bree when he first showed her the axe, "then I'm going to make damn sure my dad never forgets giving me them."

"Yeah, sorry," Bree said presently. "Still distracted trying to figure out Relic's new song."

"Why don't you play it?" Sebastian asked from behind Tyler. He was lying in bed during the guitar lessons, his face buried in a D&D book. "Maybe we can help."

Tyler strummed his guitar clumsily, making a faint discordant rattling sound. "Yeah, dude. I'm a pro now."

Bree smiled. "You don't need to be a pro to play this one, it's mostly just tremolo picking under my leads." She showed him the main riff and Tyler began to mimic it; Bree was impressed that he mostly had it down. She must be a better teacher than she thought.

Sebastian rolled off the bed and grabbed Tyler's toy Casio keyboard. He sat on the floor between the two and for the next hour they almost fully relieved Bree's anxiety by finishing the next Altar Stone song together. Part of Bree wanted to get down on herself for not being able to finish writing it on her own for Relic, but the chemistry she felt with Tyler and Sebastian dulled that part enough that she could easily ignore it.

When she got home that night, still charged from the guitar lessons that had evolved into a productive songwriting session, Bree quickly transcribed her ideas on her dad's computer. Even though she cringed at the sound of those MIDI instruments, it was enough to lock the ideas down so the band could eventually record the song properly.

The thought of being in a studio with her friends someday was getting her giddy, and by the time she finished her work, she was itching to hit the weights and take advantage of this vigorous energy building in her. As she was getting into her gym clothes, she heard an unexpected knock at the door.

"Relic's not home," Delilah said before Bree had even finished opening the door. "You know where he is?"

"Hey to you too," Bree snapped, still adjusting her top. "I think he went with his mom to one of Calvin's family Christmas things. Somewhere out in Remington."

Delilah mouthed a curse, but only let out an audible hiss before inspecting Bree's gym clothes. "Can you put on a jacket? I could use a hand."

"If you need a *hand* hand, you might want to remember that I'm not touching that VANDAL shit anymore."

Evaluating her again, Delilah gave a puzzled look. "You think you'd need it anymore? You're jacked, dude. Besides, we're not looking for a fight. My dad's been gone for almost three days now." She shook her head, looking at the ground. "It's not like I need him around—he left me enough money to get groceries and stuff for like the next three years, but his blood bags keep coming around asking where he is. Something's up."

"Well, what do you need me for?" Bree asked, but she was already curious enough to come along regardless—snooping on the cult would be just as thrilling as lifting weights, and she could use the fresh air.

"Just need another set of eyes, even if you just hold back and let Relic know whatever happens. Something tells me they're going to try that ritual again. Now that the fetishes are gone, they must have something else serving as Valaina's anchor. I doubt my dad will be able to feed us any more intel, so we'll have to get it ourselves."

Having no real reason to refuse, Bree threw on a pair of pants, grabbed a jacket, and followed Delilah down their normal route to Sanctuary. Unfortunately, any excitement Bree was hoping for was dispelled by the view of Marshall Crane's mansion, which looked dark and abandoned.

Feeling disappointed, Bree asked, "Are they meeting somewhere else?"

"I don't know," Delilah replied, still walking determinedly toward the house. "But this is better. If Marshall's out of town, maybe we can find some clues."

Suddenly, the promise of excitement wasn't as appealing to Bree. "You want to break in?!"

Delilah snorted. "It's not really breaking in if you know all the codes."

"You don't think he's changed them?" Bree asked, not truly believing a nefarious cult leader would slouch on the security of his not-so-secret lair.

"Only one way to find out," Delilah said.

Whether it was the antsiness inside Bree driving her to follow Delilah, or maybe just the fear of missing out on whatever the investigation led to, she kept pace with the dhampir who headed toward the back of the house.

It turned out, Marshall Crane didn't seem to think his adopted daughter would dare return to his home uninvited; after Delilah typed in the code on the digital keypad above the knob on the back door, a victorious click released the lock.

"Doesn't he have, like, cameras and stuff?" Bree asked nervously.

Delilah shook her head. "Cameras leave evidence and can apparently get hacked by internet nerds. Marshall is pretty old-fashioned when it comes to not wanting to be documented by technology."

They slipped in through the door and quietly shut it behind them. Bree nearly gasped seeing the interior of Marshall's mansion—it was like something from a movie. Even the back passage was like a fancy hotel entrance; compared to the Thompkinses' mud room, it was the very definition of extravagance.

"This way," Delilah whispered, motioning down a hall toward a set of paned double doors. Those doors were dark wooden frames with small glass windows set in them. As they approached and the artificial candle lights in the house reflected on one of those small panes of glass, Bree saw one of those rectangular portals fracture in her mind—a small crack in the center that spider-webbed out in jerky, stop-motion patterns.

Bree stopped mid-step, feeling like someone just gut-punched her.

Come on, Bree told herself, *not now...*

Delilah came back, gently taking her hand. "I have some extra doses..."

Bree yanked her hand out of the girl's grip, flashing an angry scowl. "No. I'm fine." That seemed to steady her resolve and she got a grip on herself.

They crept into the study where Bree saw faint flickering light illuminating the room; it was coming from—

"Is that a secret fucking bookcase passage?" Bree whispered. "What, does this guy think he's Batman?"

"He's rich enough," Delilah remarked, moving toward the passage that was lined with old-fashioned stone walls curving down a spiral staircase. "He must have fled in a hurry if he left this open."

Bree hesitated. "Dude, we're not going down there, are we?"

Delilah didn't even respond, disappearing down the eerie stairs. Bree was well past regretting coming along on this excursion, but she felt like she couldn't turn back now, so she reluctantly followed.

"Dad?!"

Delilah's voice was a choked, gasping surprise echoing up the stairwell.

Bree hurried down the rest of the stairs, hearing a groggy voice respond.

Delilah sounded more distant now. "What are you—"

"No! Get out of here, girl!"

Bree rounded the final few steps and saw Delilah pulling out one of her knives from the hidden sheaths in her jacket. Guy Valentine sat in the middle of an arcane chamber. The dancing lights of several candelabras revealed walls of inset shelves stuffed with dusty tomes, a purple rug below, and cloth hangings above depicting some winged female form. There seemed to be no ceiling in this room—only dancing shadows above.

"Hang on, let me cut these ropes," Delilah said. But Guy struggled away from her, trying to use his shoulder and head to repel her. His black spidery hair whipped out urgently.

"No! I said get out! It only wants me!" Bree saw now that Guy had been badly beaten, his lip swollen and split, blood splattered on his black leather jacket.

Something smashed upstairs and Bree jolted, moving away from the passage.

"Go!" Guy said. "I wore the ring! It knows what I am! Just go!"

There was a strange rumbling below, sending tremors through Bree's already shaking legs. "What is it?!" she whispered. But she already knew.

Shrubble Von Hellspawn descended the stairs, carrying his crooked staff that now ended in a sharpened point. His eyes were a fiery yellow and a cloudy green aura followed him, as if his stench was solidifying.

Delilah pulled out her other knife, stepping in front of her reluctant companion. The act seemed to awaken something in Bree, and she clenched her fists, ready to beat the shit out of this crusty little goblin.

"Let them go!" Guy shouted. The rumbling below intensified. "You can't eat them, you tree fucker. You can't defy Adratheon by eating little girls. Come suck on my cursed Alternian—"

Delilah charged Shrubble then, both of her knives igniting with green magic. Before Bree could even react, something smashed up through the stone floor below and pulled her hard against the wall. Her head rang and her vision blurred as the wind was knocked out of her. When Bree regained her senses, she felt the familiar earthen ropes binding her limbs.

"—dick!" Guy finished. "Come on! Get over here!"

Bree saw Delilah across the room, also restrained by writhing roots that shared the same smoky green aura that wafted off Shrubble. The smell of rotting leaves and muddy water assaulted Bree's nostrils, almost making her pass out just from the overwhelming stench.

"I think," Shrubble said, walking slowly toward Guy on his crooked feet with toes that ended in hooked talons, "these younglings seem to attract all you festering little wretches. Why would I harm them?" He raised his staff as he neared the thick wooden chair that held Guy. "They will undoubtedly release the other hexlords, and then, one by one, I can consume them—how shall the great Adratheon hope to repel his own scion, imbued with the very power he so foolishly locked away from himself?"

"Wait!" Delilah screamed, coughing against the acrid cloud that thickened around her. "Dad! Don't let him!"

Guy was laughing, mocking Shrubble as he approached. "It's alright, girl. I want this—Marshall wanted me to hex you, but I knew how this would all end.

You're better than me, Delilah, and your mom deserved better. Find her and tell her I did at least one thing right, yeah?"

Bree heard Delilah's coughing turn to sobs, and Bree felt her insides twist as she looked on, helpless. She pulled against the vines that constricted her, but it seemed to only make them tighten—Schwarzenegger wouldn't be able to break these things.

"Dad," Delilah managed to say between coughing cries. "Don't..."

Shrubble pulled his staff back, the sharpened point aimed for Guy's heart. The vampire was still laughing like a lunatic, sticking his emaciated chest out in a welcoming posture.

"Don't worry, girl," he shouted between laughs. "I'll make sure my essence rots this piece of—"

In a flash, Shrubble jammed the staff through the vampire's heart.

Delilah's shriek should have pierced Bree's ears, but she almost didn't even hear the sound of it over Guy's wailing death cry. Through the green haze consuming her, Bree saw Guy's body convulse wildly, the movement seemingly turning his flesh into that incorporeal energy that Bree saw Relic absorb from the chupacabra.

That energy swirled around Shrubble, who leaned his wretched little head back as it flowed into him. The hexlord made an exulting sound that disgusted Bree, and she felt her consciousness fading, as if the green stuff coming off the vines was poisoning her.

The last thing she heard as her senses faded to black was Delilah's defeated, heartbreaking sobs.

CHAPTER 24

O n Christmas Eve, Relic and Bree were attending to their holiday tradi-
tion: watching *Scrooged* in Relic's basement while eating greasy takeout
food. The main difference this year was the sporadic making out and fondling,
which was a definite perk for Relic—not just in a horny way, but it also told him
that Bree was seemingly over whatever had been bothering her lately.

Last week, things had been weird. Bree kept telling Relic she was sick, missing
practices and D&D night (which they had to have at Relic's house instead), but
every time he saw her, she looked fine. When he would call her, she only spoke
briefly before making some excuse to get off the phone. Part of him felt guilty,
thinking that he almost preferred her on the VANDAL serum that had made
her a sex-crazed She-Hulk.

But now they were relatively back to normal, just in time for Christmas. Relic
was presently struggling with Bree's bra strap under the hideous Christmas
sweater she had worn over as a joke, but before he could figure the damn thing
out, Bill Murray shouted one of their favorite lines from the movie and Bree
pulled away to quote it.

She mouthed "Why do you keep calling me Dick?!" along with the star of the
movie and immediately afterward gave Relic a look of surprise.

"Oh!" Rolling off him, she went to her guitar case.

"No, Bree!" As he propped himself up on the couch with his elbows, Relic's
voice assumed the quality of a teacher disciplining his student. "It's not jam
time. It's titty time."

Bree laughed, opening her case. "I don't want to jam, I want to give you your
Christmas present." She pulled out an almost identical gift that she got him last

year. "But in true failure fashion, I didn't do the joke gift again—maybe we just cut that from our traditions?"

Relic rolled off the couch. "Deal...because I forgot about that." They both laughed as he went into the laundry room to get her gift. He hadn't wrapped the huge cardboard box, but he did put a little green bow on it. As he hefted it around the corner, Bree's eyes went wide from the couch where she sat.

"Uh...was there a price limit?"

Relic snorted a laugh. "Whatever it was, I demolished it." He set the thing on the floor so Bree could reach it. "But it's also not really just for you. It's also kind of for me. And Nick. And Tyler. And Sebastian."

Bree's mouth fell open in elated surprise. "No way!" She handed him the present. "This too. And it's also kind of *from* you to the band...in a way."

Cocking an eyebrow, Relic took it. "Well, that's just not fair..." Without waiting for her approval, he tore it open. It took him a moment to fully realize what he was looking at, because at first he thought it was just a used CD, devoid of that glorious wrinkled shimmer that came with shrink-wrap.

But when his eyes finally focused on his band's logo at the top of the stunning fantasy artwork, his mouth fell open. The song he had begun composing with Bree, based on the first real story he had written only a couple scenes for, was visualized as an actual album cover.

Altar Stone's name was emblazoned in green letters above a scene of the cloaked Witchlord striding through an iron gate, and the song's title was elegantly written along the bottom of the cover: "The Witchlord's Banishment."

"Holy shit, Bree," Relic said as he turned the jewel case over, revealing the cover piece extending to the back, with the silhouettes of the five mysterious heroes that had rooted out the corrupt Witchlord. The song title was repeated again, and below it the credits said *Music by Altar Stone* and below that: *Concept and Lyrics by Relic Meyers.*

"Holy shit," Relic repeated, his vision blurring from the tears in his eyes. He lowered the gift to his lap, feeling his hand starting to shake. Turning to Bree, the joy on her face was almost more amazing than the gift. "You just put my present to shame, dude..."

Bree bit her lip to keep from laughing as she leaned in to kiss him with both hands on his face, wiping a tear from his cheek with her thumb. "There's more," she whispered, pointing to the case.

Letting out a defeated groan, Relic opened the thing, revealing a CD with the cover art printed on it. "How'd you do that?!" Relic popped the disc out, inspecting it.

"Dad's company has this sticker printing thing. But that's still not all." She coyly pointed toward the boombox on the small shelf near the wall—near where his drums would usually be if they weren't at school.

Confused, Relic got up to put the disc in. "Don't tell me someone else already wrote a song with the same name..." He imagined Bree finding a song by some obscure power metal band that shared a similar concept to his story.

"Excuse the shitty MIDI sounds," Bree said, pulling her legs up to sit cross-legged on the couch. "But hopefully you'll still get the idea..."

Not even fully sure what a MIDI sound was, Relic pressed play. The digital music sounded like something from an old video game, but the recognizable melody and rhythm made Relic's heart skip a beat. He turned to Bree, stunned.

"You finished it?!"

Bree smiled widely. "The band did...well, Nick didn't really do anything, but you got him slaving away at Rook's covering your shifts, so I gave him credit anyway."

As the music continued, Relic hurried over and dropped to his knees in front of his insanely perfect girlfriend and took her hands. "You're incredible, Bree. Like...seriously, insane—blowing all the expectations of girlfriends and guitar players away."

As they kissed, the song continued. Relic leaned back, "And this song—it's amazing, like freaking Rhapsody level... Are those strings?!"

Bree nodded, grinning so hard her face was reddening. "Sebastian helped me figure out tabbing on GuitarPro. It's freaking tedious, but should help with songwriting until we can start demoing stuff and eventually get in a studio."

Relic looked at the big cardboard box. "You can't open that now. I need to, like, rob a bank, or murder someone...I don't know." He looked back at her, shaking his head. "It's not fair, man."

Shoving Relic away, Bree scooted over to tear the tape off the box.

"Seriously, it's nowhere near this level," Relic warned, feeling severely insecure with what he had previously thought was a cool gift.

"No way!" Bree cried, pulling out one of the shirts. She held it up, covering her disgusting Christmas sweater, her mouth a wide O of surprise. "Our own shirts?!" She pulled her sweater off, revealing an exquisite bra that may have been worn for his benefit, but in Bree's excitement she must have forgotten to reveal it properly. She pulled the Altar Stone shirt on and stood up. "We have shirts! Dude, we can sell these at the show!"

Laughing, Relic got to his feet and the two made out well past the end of "The Witchlord's Banishment" and the credits of *Scrooged*.

Breathless afterward, Bree pushed Relic's face away far enough so they could hold each other's gaze.

"We should promise each other something, Relic."

Taken slightly aback, Relic frowned and nodded. "Okay."

Looking down at the Altar Stone logo on her shirt and the Altar Stone guitar pick necklace from last Christmas, Bree said, "We should promise that we'll both be as devoted to this band as we are to each other." She stared deeply into Relic's eyes, almost making him uncomfortable. "Because think of everything that's happened...not just with us, but Nick, Tyler...Sebastian's still kind of new, but I feel like Altar Stone is doing something bigger than just making music, you know?"

Relic nodded, knowing exactly what she meant. "I'm sorry I said I quit before. It was just, with everything..."

She nodded, putting a hand on his cheek. "I know. I don't blame you. I just want us both to promise that we stay as committed to it as we do to each other. Because," she kissed him lightly before adding, "I love you, Relic Meyers."

He smiled. "I love you, too, Bree Thompkins. And I think it's safe to say..." he motioned to the gifts, "we both really love Altar Stone."

Bree smiled, and kissed him much less softly then.

Delilah had felt like she might finally actually fall asleep when the knock came.

Figures, she thought, getting off the couch in the same clothes she wore for the past two days. She was done crying, but it seemed she was far from done mourning her father; and in Delilah's case, mourning involved being a complete bum and not showering.

She went to the door, and as she opened it, Steven Meyers was the last person she ever expected to see standing on the other side.

"Hey," Delilah said.

Relic's dad had his hands in his tattered jeans and he wore a red mechanic's jacket over a faded Iron Maiden shirt. He didn't smile at Delilah, but his face was kind and understanding. "Hey."

Delilah stepped back into the apartment and opened the door farther, crossing her arms against the chill. "Did you want to come in?"

He nodded and stepped into the gloom.

Delilah shut the door and moved the stack of empty pizza boxes that were on the living room floor to the small kitchen table. "Sorry, I haven't really gotten around to cleaning up."

Steven paced toward the curtained window, not speaking.

Uneasy, Delilah took a seat on the sofa, having no clue what this visit could be about.

"You know," Steven said, peeking out the window through a small gap in the curtains, "your dad had this apartment when you were still with your mom. I came here a couple times, mostly looking for a fight. But when I needed him, he was here."

"Needed him?" Delilah asked. "I thought you guys hated each other."

Steven laughed, turning to face her. "We did—we were both very stupid kids. But like I said, when I needed him, he was there."

Delilah felt a tightness in her throat and she tried to swallow it down. "What did you need him for?"

Taking a seat in the chair next to the sofa, Steven leaned forward with his elbows on his knees. "You and I never really talked about everything that happened—I also never thanked you for helping Relic when he needed you. But I think it's past time you knew what kind of man your dad was."

Delilah said nothing, but her throat continued to constrict her breathing.

"When I came back here in '94," Steven continued, "to try and put everything to rest—try to make things right. It was your dad I had to rely on. He knew what I was up against and he had the connection I needed to open the nexus."

He laughed softly, eyes distant. "He didn't owe me anything, so don't think he was being heroic or something on my account. The thing is, he was doing fine here—laying low, feeding off plenty of willing victims, and really managing his condition. Also, he knew what I intended to do—that song...once he became a vampire, like, fully—our song was like nails on a chalkboard to him."

Steven shook his head, leaning back, but still looking off into the past. "Some Alternians are drawn to it, like, to worship it or something. But it pained your dad to hear it. And still, he knew I intended to play it—endlessly, if needed—to keep my family safe. Which meant in order to help me, he'd have to hear that song over and over and over again...just, like, existing in total agony..."

Delilah didn't really understand. "So, why would he help you?"

His eyes met hers then, and there were tears in them. "Because of you. He said he couldn't stand the thought of Adratheon or his spawns coming after *my girl*." Steven's voice broke slightly then, before adding, "That's what he always called you...my girl."

The tightening in her throat broke then as she gasped out a sob, covering her face so this man she hardly even knew wouldn't see her sorrow. But almost immediately afterward, she felt his gentle hand on her shoulder, and she clutched at it desperately.

She knew she smelled awful and part of her still felt like she hardly even knew who Guy Valentine truly was, but that didn't stop the agonizing sadness that swept over her. So she clutched Relic's dad as if he were her only chance of survival.

He patted her head like no father figure had never done for her and said gently, "I think I might...I might know why he died—why Marshall wanted him dead. I think he knew how to cure you."

She pulled away in disbelief, but when she saw his face, hope took root in her like a cruel virus.

He gave her a slow nod. "But we have to find your mother first."

CHAPTER 25

The next couple months flew by for Relic, with only the occasional distractions from preparing for Altar Stone's first real show.

Despite the lame new principal—a drill sergeant-type dude named Mr. Stacy who had replaced the chronically ill Lana Sinclair, who Relic suspected was actually dead—school had become much more bearable. Relic's social life was still better than it had ever been, and Shrubble remained dormant for now, according to all of Delilah's reports. Becca had even confirmed with Relic that the weird Adratheon dreams and visions had stopped.

Relic got the sense that Laramie's never-ending ebb and flow of strange activity was certainly on the ebb side. Unfortunately, that meant it could start flowing at any minute. To shield himself against those flows, Relic had taken to carrying around his dad's old journal, referring to it often as if it were a bible.

If he were being honest, the real reason he carried that journal was because he felt like he was in *Indiana Jones and the Last Crusade*, constantly flipping through its small, scribbled pages as if it held the location of the Holy Grail.

By the time the week of the wedding/concert arrived, Relic and Delilah had tracked several potential sightings of Alternians back toward the Crane Estate. Two days before Hanks was set to have the talion ready (which happened to be the exact day of the concert), Steven had driven the two monster hunters back to the poisoned well.

"This has to be it," Relic said, absently twirling his sticks as they inspected the tracks leading to the well.

"It's gotta be like the Widow," Steven said, squatting to put two fingers in the stamped mud that formed an alien footprint. "She kept getting drawn back to the nexus below the school—it's like an outlet or something, for them to recharge their batteries."

"I bet this is where Shrubble came after the first time we fought him," Relic thought aloud. "Which means, if we can't finish him at the concert, we'll need to beat him here."

The ground seemed to rumble, then and the three of them stepped away from the well. Something belched from the depths, a croaking, ancient-sounding groan, and Relic looked to his dad for some sort of explanation.

There was something other than surprise on Steven's face, but Relic couldn't quite discern the look.

"What the hell was that?" Delilah asked.

"We should go," Steven said, backing up farther. "That song you wrote about the harrow, Relic...I'm having some serious déjà vu."

Relic followed his dad, letting his gaze linger only momentarily on the rusty farm equipment that still rested near the well. This time last year, he didn't even know what a harrow was, and he wished it had stayed that way. Seeing it now stirred the same uneasy feeling he'd had when he woke up to find song lyrics written in his own hand, yet with no memory of writing them.

When they got back into the van, Steven backed it up, speaking to Relic while looking out the cracked rear window. "I remember before Oath even played 'Alternus,' I kept hearing weird sounds from the old boiler room where you guys practice." He shook his head as if trying to get something out of his face. "No one else seemed to hear it, but it was almost like the Widow *felt* something coming then—like she was preparing to open the nexus there."

"Are you saying there might be another nexus here?" Relic asked.

Steven shifted into drive, shaking his head. "I don't think so. These hexlords shouldn't have that kind of power. What I *am* saying is that if Shrubble's coming back here, it means he might not have all of his power yet. If he can only take so much power from the well at a time, it means he must be trying to gain strength from other Alternians so he can draw the rest out. He needs to keep feeding—*we* have to feed him, fatten the bastard up—then we have to put him down here after the show, after he's hopefully eaten enough to draw out the rest of his power." He gave Relic a dire look. "Which you need to then take from him before Adratheon can."

Relic and Delilah shared a look.

"Well," she said soberly, "at least my dad might not get in the way this time..."

Having only been to two other weddings in his life, Relic clearly wasn't a connoisseur when it came to matrimony festivities. However, he felt like his mom and Calvin's ceremony was pretty damn good—not too lengthy or religous-y, and the reception afterward had decent food.

"You got somewhere to be?"

Relic, who had been staring at the watch his dad had gotten him for his birthday, looked up at his mom. Dina Meyers looked like she had stepped out of a Hollywood movie screen. Her dress was simple and her hair was up, with only a few curls framing a face Relic had never seen look so lovely...or so happy.

Smiling at her, he shook his head. "Was just hoping Dad would be here by now."

Dina's smile faltered a little as she pulled out one of the chairs at Relic's empty table. They both seemed to turn to the dance floor at the same time where Bree was dancing to Cher's "Believe" with her dad—both of them looked highly ridiculous.

"Can I tell you something?" Dina said, just loud enough to be heard over the music. "I honestly didn't expect your dad to RSVP at all. This would...it all might be too much for him, you know?"

Relic nodded, not wanting to tell her he was more concerned with his dad getting there with the talion in time for the thing to be properly consecrated at the show. Hanks had told them that the only true way to bind the thing to both Relic and Shrubble was to imbue it with the energy created by playing the song live.

In truth, Relic was still internally trying to forgive his father, so the man's comfort or emotional health weren't top priorities for his son.

"I still think he should be here," Relic replied absently.

Dina scoffed. "Steven barely made it to his own wedding. I had to send Gate out to find him. Your dad's never been known for his punctuality."

Bree slid into the chair next to Relic then, breathless and smiling. "I'd ask you to dance," she said to Relic, putting her chin on his shoulder, "but I hate rejection."

"I think he's starting to crack, Red," Dina laughed. "We both got him out there for at least one slow dance today. Progress is progress!"

Relic turned to kiss Bree on the cheek and said, "I seem to recall playing *Resident Evil* when you said you wanted to check this place out..."

Her eyes went wide and she smiled. "Dude...who would have guessed a year later we'd be playing a show in this place with our own band?"

He got up, extending Bree a hand. "Shall we?"

"Stay out of trouble, you two," Dina warned playfully, getting to her feet. "And, Relic," she pointed to his watch before adding, "maybe get your dad one of those for *his* birthday."

Relic and Bree left the ballroom and went to the stairs in the main hall. There were three upper levels to Wane Street Manor, but the third was off limits, as was the basement.

While they ascended the stairs, Relic admired Bree's green dress, which hugged her muscled body well. Not for the first time today, he imagined what their own wedding might be like someday. It was no longer some sort of hypothetical thing for him—they would certainly get married, and there was a strange mix of fear and comfort in that thought.

"This place looks too clean," Bree said when they reached the landing. "It's almost like a hotel or something."

Relic looked down either hall at the top of the stairs; each direction looked identical, with both passages containing four doors set into the walls (two on either side of the hall), ending at a closed mahogany double door.

Russell Thomkins was right, the place gave off a Spencer Mansion vibe that made Relic feel like he was in *Resident Evil*. Part of him even considered pushing a cabinet holding a vase of fake flowers to one side to see if a handgun magazine might be hidden underneath it.

"Should we split up?" Bree asked, raising a mischievous eyebrow. "Otherwise, nothing interesting will happen, right?"

Scoffing, Relic played along. "Which one you taking?"

Bree turned and went down the hall to the left of the stairs. Relic took the other one, opening the first door he came to. It was a nursery with an elegant hooded cradle from some long-lost era. There were plaques set up around the room describing different historical aspects of the decorations.

It's a freaking museum, Relic thought. His interest in interior design was not ravenous enough for him to read any of the tidbits, but he did approach the cradle as if he somehow knew Cecily Moreau was waiting to show him something.

The familiar sepia tone haze fell over the room then, and Relic saw a child in the cradle sleeping peacefully. It had to be Madeline Moreau, his great-great-great grandmother; the only child of Gustave and Cecily who would survive Adratheon's failed escape plan.

Being a boy of fifteen with no younger siblings, Relic had been mostly unaffected by babies and smaller children throughout his life. They were, if anything, annoyances. Loud at restaurants and movie theaters, messy, and criminally uninteresting. However, as he stood above the phantom vision of his ancestor, Relic somehow associated the slumbering thing with his adult mother.

For his whole life, Relic depended on his mother for everything, and she managed to provide despite her circumstances. He knew it wasn't easy for her, but she made it work, and he stood here now because of her. He felt the nasal sting of tears coming while he considered the cruelty of their ancestry.

The child in his vision would have her whole world destroyed, her siblings slaughtered by the mother that was transformed into a murderous specter by the whims of a trans-dimensional tyrant. And if that wasn't bad enough, Dina

Monroe would have to give birth to and sacrifice her life caring for an offspring of the very tyrant who had brought so much suffering to her ancestors.

"Do you understand now?"

Relic didn't have to turn around to see the ghost of Cecily Moreau standing behind him; he could feel the icy shroud hanging over her, now enveloping him as well.

"You wrote the song, didn't you?" His voice was thick with sorrow. "While I was in the Between...that's how you kept the cult from giving Adratheon's power to Valaina, right? If the hexlords had still been asleep in their cradles, there would be nothing stopping Valaina from draining them."

"He needs to die," Cecily simply said, stepping forward to better see her daughter. "You think if the cult had their way, they'd do anything to put an end to Adratheon? They don't care if it's him or Valaina trapped in Alternus, they just want their power. But the cruelty will only end with Adratheon's demise."

Cecily's ghostly hand caressed the incorporeal vision of her only surviving heir. "You have the power to stop all this—now, before he even has the chance to reclaim his power, or the cult siphons any of it to the monster that destroyed my family."

Her words felt like heavy loads placed on Relic's shoulders, as if he didn't already have enough to worry about. That weight was so real that he hardly even noticed Bree's hand on his shoulder, which somehow didn't even startle him when he did feel her presence.

"Is there like a ghost baby in that cradle?"

Relic laughed loudly and suddenly at that, morbidly entertained by the accuracy of the question. He turned to see her surprised face. "Sorry, that was..." he considered telling her, but then went with, "that would just be super creepy."

She smiled, seemingly pleased that she managed to conjure up something that would spook him. "The other rooms are pretty boring too. Just some plaques talking about how the original house was decorated. I didn't find a single ink ribbon."

Relic turned back to Madeline's cradle, but his phantom ancestors were gone. He felt a void in their absence, replaced by the sudden need to take action.

"You know," he said to Bree, "I never told you about what I saw in the restroom at Rook's..."

Turning to face her, Relic told Bree about the strange encounter with the interdimensional being who had helped sire him. When he was done, Bree crossed her arms over her elegant dress and sighed deeply.

"That's heavy, man..."

Relic looked back at the cradle, imagining it held the child that he and Bree might someday bring into the world. That image came with equal parts hope and terror, and Relic knew he had to take drastic action. Now.

"I'm starting to think this might be our best chance, you know?"

He felt Bree's questioning gaze on his back. It was almost as if he could hear her thoughts in here—but maybe it was just Cecily feeding him Bree's thoughts to embolden him.

Our best chance at what? Actually playing a show?

I think he's hearing things again...

Why can't we just have one normal goddamn day?!

Relic turned to her then, but the face he expected to see was much different than the one staring at him.

"We'll stop him," Bree said with a determined nod. "Your plan will work."

Smiling, Relic returned the nod. *No it won't,* he thought. *Because I have a new plan now...*

CHAPTER 26

"Are you sure about this?" Becca's face was devoid of any snark or mockery for a change. Relic thought she actually looked quite scared, but she did her best to hide it. The rest of Habitual Void were on stage setting up for their opening set.

"Yeah," Relic said, as casually as he could. The gravity of what he asked of her was not lost on him, but he spoke with the ease of telling her to swap one screamy song for another. In reality, he was asking her to summon Adratheon again.

Only this time, Relic would kill him. No more waiting and no more dealing with his stupid hexlords.

"Didn't you say you, like, blacked out last time we played it?" She looked over her shoulder, making sure no one else was listening before turning back to him and leaning closer. "I know something happened at the battle last year—when you guys played that Unknown Oath song."

Normally, Relic might have been taken back by that. But knowing that this girl had also been hearing Adratheon's voice, she'd be crazy if she hadn't already made at least some conclusions about what was happening in Laramie.

Relic just gave a slight nod.

Becca looked like she had expected the confirmation. "So, our song...it's like what people say happened with your dad's band? The music, like, does things?"

Nodding again, Relic pointed to his head. "Those things you hear—all that Adratheon shit? I'm going to stop that. I just need your help."

Becca returned the nod and shrugged. "Alright, just don't blame me when everyone passes out again from bad weed."

Smiling at her, Relic thought to himself, *Come and get it, dragon daddy.*

Bree changed out of her dress and into her stage gear, which consisted of black leather pants adorned with many buckles, a tight yellow top that exposed her shoulders and most of her arms, and the black combat boots that added enough height so she would stand almost as tall as her bandmates.

As she admired herself in the mirror, the bathroom behind her seemed to blur slightly, turning a hazy yellow. She tried to blink it away, but it didn't work. Turning, the place looked as it had before—a renovated public bathroom like you might see at a fancy restaurant; it might have once been a small washroom for wealthy nobles in the 1700s, but now it was just a ritzy place for people to shit.

Bree turned back to the mirror expecting the illusion to be gone, but she gasped and jumped back from the mirror when she saw the new reflection.

A ghastly dead woman in an elegant gown stared back at her, the mutilated body of Bree's boyfriend on the floor behind her. The haunting figure had a long, bloody kitchen knife in one skeletal hand, and her other hand reached out to Bree as if inviting her into the nightmare.

The figure mouthed something that Bree couldn't hear as blood thundered in her ears, but it looked like the ghostly woman found whatever she was saying highly amusing. The shadowy silhouettes of robed figures appeared behind her, arms raised as if in reverence of this monstrous woman.

Despite not hearing the words, Bree understood the message: "Join me."

Bree knew she was looking at the Widow—*No, Valaina,* she thought, knowing the Widow was dead. Relic had told her the Widow was destroyed when they sealed her away, Cecily Moreau's spirit separated from the cruel entity that they now knew to be Adratheon's spawn—Relic's-sister-slash-half-mother-slash-ugh barf.

Valaina could still retain Cecily's form though, if what Bree saw was at all real—*Is anything about her real? Is Laramie even real?!*—and the woman's beauty was truly terrifying to behold; nothing like the monstrous image Bree had pictured all those times last year when she tried to imagine what the Widow truly looked like.

The mirror shattered then, and the trauma Bree thought she had overcome came rushing back to choke her. Something wrenched her throat and tendrils of icy dread unraveled within her.

A voice pierced the suffocating void closing in on Bree then, and it was soft and pleasant—a promise from the relentless shattering glass. "Join me, my Chosen. Or he will certainly suffer."

Just as it seemed Valaina would breach the cracked, reflective glass separating their worlds, Bree blinked and gasped.

"You need a minute?" Becca asked, her reflection in the complete-ly-not-haunted mirror looking at Bree strangely. "I can wait."

Bree shook her head, feigning a laugh. "Pre-show jitters, I guess." She gath-ered up her things with shaky hands and jammed them back in her yellow gym bag. "You ready?"

Entering a stall and shutting its door, Becca's voice echoed as she relieved herself. "I think so. Relic wants us to play that song he told us *never* to play, so I guess it should be interesting."

Something struck Bree then, and she paused while reaching for the bathroom door. Stepping back toward the stall, she asked, "That song... Did you happen to write it—this will sound weird, but did you write it in your sleep?"

There was a flush followed by some rustling as Becca pulled up her pants. Opening the stall door, Valaina's horrid visage smiled at Bree, this time rotting and terrible and in the flesh. Bree once more gasped and recoiled.

Becca laughed as her own face returned. "Goddamn, you're jumpy. But, yeah...it was weird. I woke up with a pen in my hand—I think I had fallen asleep while working on it, then woke up and realized I had finished it without even remembering. How'd you know?"

There was a strange cackling in the far reaches of Bree's mind, like a witch whose well-laid plans had just come to fruition.

By the time Habitual Void was about to take the stage, Relic was still staring at his watch backstage, wondering where the hell his dad was with the talion. He was cutting it way too close. A shadow fell over him then.

"You got somewhere to be, man?"

Relic turned to see Nick staring down at him, his wide-collared black shirt revealing a neck unencumbered by a fetish, which settled Relic's nerves. Unlike the show at The Voodoo when he was getting high with his friends, he already had his bass on, working out his fingers as he quietly played through a song.

Spinning on his drum throne to face him, Relic shook his head, tapping out his own rhythms on his thighs. "Just hoping my dad doesn't miss our opening song."

"Don't worry, man," Nick said, nodding toward the crowd that was growing by the minute. "I got Tammy to set up a tripod with her dad's digital camera. Has a zoom lens thing and everything. We'll have some great footage."

Something about documenting the night made Relic nervous, but he supposed if things went smoothly, there'd be nothing left to worry about. He could end it all with one fell swoop.

"Relic!" Bree's voice sounded frantic.

Shit, what now? He turned to see her motioning to come out to the back hall that ran behind the stage. Once they were alone, she began in a low voice, "Why'd you tell Becca to play that song again? Didn't it freak you out at the party?"

Afraid if he explained too much to her she might try to rationalize his plan, and they just didn't have time for that, he shook his head. "It's fine, I talked to my dad," he lied. "It was just that weed everyone was breathing in." He told that part easily, as it wasn't completely false. "I think it might work well for us, you know? That song was super bad, so it'll make us sound that much better."

Bree's face didn't seem to buy his bullshit.

"Alright, metal fans," the DJ—hired by Relic's mom for both the reception and the concert—boomed through the manor's sound system, "are you ready for some entertainment brought to you by the brand-new power couple, Mr. & Mrs. Calvin Greeeeeeeen?!"

There was a roar of applause, and Relic pulled Bree closer. "Seriously, it's nothing, Bree. Trust me."

Her face cracked then and he felt slightly guilty. *She does trust me,* he thought miserably, *and I keep fucking lying to her.*

But again, if things went well, she'd surely forgive him afterward. If not, well, Relic supposed none of this would matter anyway.

"Please welcome," the DJ continued, his voice tinny and hollow on this side of the stage, "Laramie's own hardcore heathens, Habitual Void!" There was a surprising wave of applause that Relic hadn't expected.

"Wow," he said, smiling at Bree. "Sounds like we got a good turnout."

She grinned back, putting a hand around the back of his neck. "Dude, the place is packed." After kissing him, she asked, "Are you ready for this?"

No, he thought, but said, "Bet your sweet ass, Thompkins." He slapped it for emphasis and to convince her he wasn't going through an existential crisis—also, just because he liked touching her ass.

Raising a disciplinary finger, Bree scowled. "Not until after the show, rock star."

"Relic!"

His dad's voice jerked Relic's gaze toward the door they had come through. Steven Meyers hobbled toward them, the talion covered in a black cloth under his arm.

"Cutting it close, Dad!"

Steven took a deep breath, shaking his head. "Don't start, man. Hanks was still working on the damn thing until like twenty minutes ago. I gunned it here and had to run a bunch of red lights." He handed the talion to Relic, as if presenting a knight with his sacred armaments. "You play that Rhapsody song and make sure the crowd digs it, the old man said it would seal the deal."

The mention of Rhapsody jolted Relic's attention away from the talion. "Did you get my CD back from him?"

His dad laughed. "I'll buy you a new one, man. Just make sure you know what you're doing here. I gotta get out there and find a good spot so I don't miss Altar Stone bringing the house down."

Overcome with emotions, given he was about to finally play a concert with his dad in attendance, Relic wrapped his arms around his father, hugging him tighter than he'd ever hugged anyone. Steven returned the embrace and Relic thought he felt the man's chest heave as if he were sobbing.

Relic left the talion by his drums and went to the balcony alone during Habitual Void's set. The view up there was phenomenal, and he felt fortunate that none of the attendees below opted to enjoy its vantage.

He didn't want to risk anyone else's life.

Putting his drumsticks in his back pocket, Relic pulled his father's journal from the large side pocket of his cargo shorts.

"Make a pit!" Becca screamed into the mic, her band kicking off their first song. Relic was surprised he didn't hate the opening riff, which had more weight than most of their syncopated chugs—could almost be a metal song.

Relic flipped to the page where he suspected his dad had originally summoned Adratheon—the page titled "Dealing with the Dragon." Habitual Void reached the breakdown of their first song as Relic studied the words so he could properly recite them when the time came.

Did my dad actually write this nonsense? he wondered, struggling to pronounce all the names. Sol Saradys? Anathu? Who the hell were the Lorenguard and what did they have to do with Adratheon?

Relic supposed he didn't actually need to know these things, but his curious mind couldn't help but wonder what it all meant. Given this was all so tied to his own legacy, maybe someday he might learn more about his bloodline. But right now, he just needed to end it.

Similarly, Becca's band needed to end this damn song; Relic was starting to get nervous, and he didn't want to turn back now. He knew he could do this.

"This next one," Becca said, as Clayton's guitar still held out the final notes of the previous song, "I wrote in my sleep at the Jack Stanley Motel after watching *The Motel Maniac*."

The crowd roared at that, and Relic's interest was piqued as well. He remembered hearing that Becca had tried running away from home and was found staying in a motel, but he never would have guessed it was the Jack Stanley—that place had a nasty reputation, and Relic honestly didn't even know it was still in business. Also, she had played the song at the party before she ran away...

"This one's called, 'Adratheon's Lair'!"

Once more the crowd went nuts and something shifted inside of Relic, making him momentarily question what he was doing. But as if in response, he heard Cecily's voice again, urging him that now was the time.

As the music started, Relic read the incantation aloud.

"Lord of Neveren and First Scion of Sol Saradys," he began, speaking just loud enough to hear over the awful music—Becca's voice suddenly sounded like she was singing the words Relic recited. "Hear my call in your Tower of Woe, where your first son, Anathu, betrayed you. Hear my call across the plains of Revery, which you conquered when the Lorenguard dethroned the Burning One."

Relic heard clawed steps coming up the stairs outside the balcony doors, echoing ethereally from the Between. His heart began racing as he hoped no one down below could hear those distant sounds; any intrusion could interfere with his whole slaying the dragon thing.

"Attend me, from your grim and desolate fortress within Alternus," Relic finished, his fervor rising as the doorknob separating him from Adratheon rattled. "By your draconic name do I swear to abide by the terms of our dealings."

He closed the book and stood up as the door swung open. "Adratheon, I request a covenant."

Devon Andrews adjusted his tie as he stepped out onto the balcony with Relic, the ballroom in the Wane Street Manor fading away into the green smoke of Relic's dreams. The dragon's smile spoke more of boredom than pleasure, but he regarded Relic kindly enough. "Son." The word made Relic flinch, despite expecting it. "I didn't think you'd be ready to come to me yet."

Relic slowly turned sideways so he would be able to subtly grab his drumsticks. "What can I say? I've always been impatient." Looking around, he realized he must have fallen unconscious, entering the dream world of the Between to meet with Adratheon, just like his father had all those years ago. "Where are we?" He knew, but wanted to get the man—or dragon—talking.

Devon laughed then and Relic noticed instead of the fine loafers this guy wore last time they had met, his legs now ended in the same clawed feet Relic had seen in Rook's bathroom back in August.

"Don't pretend you haven't lurked in the Revery, son." Devon motioned to the smoky beyond. "I see all here—I rule here."

"Good," Relic snapped, "you can stay out of my world then. Keep your foggy kingdom here and leave us alone." He realized that his hand had frozen in place, fear keeping him from reaching his weapons; he forced his hands to move again.

Adratheon snapped his fingers and the sounds of the show below—music and crowd—turned to a quiet, distant fuzz. "I've always detested music," the dragon said, ignoring Relic. "Even the bards of Lorendale managed to hold some sway over me. It's quite the obnoxious form of expression."

"That's ironic," Relic said, still inching his fingers toward the weapons in his back pocket. "Considering you guys need it and all."

Devon's smile widened as he reached the balcony's rail, peering over now. "Quite. Almost as ironic as how you need me, yes? Need me to die so you can—What?" He turned back to Relic, leaning casually with his elbows on the railing. "Claim my power for yourself? Give it to your spiteful bitch of a sister—she's a terrible lay, son! Take my word for it, don't give in to whatever wiles she attempts on you, no matter what form she takes."

"You're fucked up, man." His finger touched the nearest stick and he slowly crept his other fingers over their reassuring shapes.

Devon/Adratheon pushed himself away from the railing, holding up a finger as he paced back toward Relic, his demeanor unaffected by the boy's hostility. "Or perhaps, like your other—lesser?—father, you would also like to strike a deal with me? Though, I must warn you, Relic: I have become quite hesitant to make pacts—the whole track record isn't great."

Relic spared a moment to ponder for the first time what kind of a deal his father made with this creature, but as Devon—no, Adratheon—stepped within reach, Relic assumed his best comic book vigilante voice to say, "I got your pact right here."

In a blur, he yanked a drumstick free, set it aflame with Alternian energy, and drove it downward into the bastard's heart—if he even had one.

Apparently, he didn't.

Relic looked up into Devon's amused face. The stick had pierced his chest and the smell of burning hair and flesh wafted into Relic's nostrils. Yet Adratheon smiled at him with Devon's annoyingly handsome face.

"Don't you think," Devon said, reaching up a hand to put two delicate fingers on Relic's wrist and guide the enchanted stick out of his chest, "if my own spawn could kill me, your sister would have done so by now?"

Nearly overcome with despair, Relic felt numb as he watched his drumstick's magic fade away in his hand. He felt so sure this would work; everything felt like it had aligned. *Why am I even here?!* The question came to him like a sudden punch to the gut. He had a plan tonight, and on a whim he thought he could undercut all of that—bypass all the mini-bosses and go for the endgame right away. Had all those video games taught him freaking nothing?

"You seem demoralized, my boy," Devon said, pacing back to the balcony's railing. "If it's any consolation, you're only about the millionth little cretin to try to end my existence. My fifty-second son, Anathu, now he was a real pain in my ass..."

Relic let his hand holding the useless stick drop to his side slowly as he accepted his failure. He felt his presence in this place already faltering, the real world calling him back—Habitual Void's song must have been almost over by now.

As the scene became hazy, Relic asked the most pressing question on his mind. "What deal did you make with my dad? What did he promise you?"

Devon turned to him, his smile almost sympathetic. "His firstborn."

The green smoke consumed them both then, and the last thing Relic saw in the Between before returning to the concert was the memory of his father—decked out in his cult robes—casting a curse on his young, sleeping son.

CHAPTER 27

Relic avoided walking through the crowd on his way back toward the stage, not wanting to cross paths with Steven Meyers—afraid of what he might say to the man who promised his firstborn son to a devil.

As he came down the stairs, he saw his mom and Calvin—changed out of their fancy wedding attire—making their way across the foyer toward the ballroom.

Dina gave him a startled look. "Hey! Aren't you supposed to be going on stage soon?"

Seeing his mom after having failed to take vengeance on the entity that had essentially cursed Dina Monroe's family tree, Relic felt a strange rekindling within him. It reminded him that he hadn't really failed her—he hadn't even played yet.

There was still time.

"Heading that way," he said with a smile. "Oh, I forgot to mention: after the show, the band is having a little celebration over at Dad's."

Dina took Calvin's hand. "I don't care what you do, hon, we'll be on our honeymoon."

Calvin chuckled. "Yeah, a luxurious and exotic stay at the Crosstown Suites!"

They all three laughed as the music in the ballroom began to fade out.

Calvin motioned toward the closed doors. "Altar Stone's about to rock, right?"

Nodding, Relic turned back to his mom, the meeting with Adratheon still obviously on his mind. "I forgot to ask: Did that Devon guy ever come around again?"

Dina looked at Calvin. "It's funny you ask that…"

Calvin patted his pocket. "Yeah, he just gave us a pretty insane check. We just bumped into him a second ago—did you not see him? Looked like he came down those stairs right before you."

Relic didn't have much time to dwell on that revelation.

"Meyers!" Nick's head poked out through the side doors leading to backstage. "We're about to set up, man!"

The stage curtains were closed as the house sound crew set up mics and Altar Stone convened at the side of the stage. They each anxiously observed their gear all set up now, waiting for them to invoke the rites.

"You feelin' good?" Nick asked Tyler, not unkindly.

Nodding, Tyler turned from Nick to Sebastian. "Yeah. Feelin' real good."

Smiling at that, Relic tucked his sticks into his back pocket as he retrieved the long package his dad had brought. "Get ready to feel even better, man." Bree stepped aside, holding her guitar up by the neck to allow Relic to display the long cloth-wrapped object.

"What's this?" Nick asked, leaning over Sebastian's shoulder to get a better look. "Pre-show gifts?"

"Something like that," Relic said, pulling back the cloth to reveal the talion.

"Holy crap!" Sebastian gasped. "Is that, like, *the* Emerald Sword?"

Relic dropped the black cloth to hold the gleaming sword out for the band to see. He wasn't sure if Hanks had somehow forged it himself, or just modified a sword, but the thing was a work of art. The long, grooved silver blade looked sharp on either edge, and Relic handled it carefully, using his open palm to support it. The emeralds set into either side of the sword's crossguard were almost the size of eggs.

Each member of Altar Stone stared at it in silent wonder.

"Yeah," Relic finally answered, holding the thing out for Tyler to take. "Until you start playing guitar live, I figured it might be cool if you had something to hold."

His friend looked up at him in disbelief, as if he couldn't imagine wielding something so majestic. Relic recognized the look—it reminded him of the time he had first shown Tyler the Rhapsody album at school, and the time Tyler rolled his first critical hit in D&D, obliterating an orc shaman's skull.

"No way," Tyler said. "You want me to hold this while I sing?!"

"Can you?" Relic asked, suddenly worried that the entire plan hatched by himself, Bree, his dad, Gate, and Delilah hinged on someone imbuing the sword with the energy from their performance.

Tyler's face changed from shocked wonder to a cocky grin. "Of course I can, I just—this thing looks expensive."

"Is it sharp?" Nick asked.

It better be, Relic thought, *I need to lop Shrubble's ugly head off with it after the show.* "Yeah," Relic said, turning from Nick back to Tyler. "So don't go spinning it around and shit. I just thought you'd hold it up during 'Emerald Sword,' then I'll come grab it and set it behind the drum riser." This part was crucial, as he didn't want someone running off with the only neutral thing that could capture Adratheon's power.

Tyler reached out slowly and gripped the sword in his powerful hand.

"This is going to be badass," Bree said with a laugh. "People are going to wig."

"You all ready?"

The band turned to see one of the sound guys motioning toward the stage with his thumb.

"Yeah," Tyler said, turning with the talion in a double-handed grip, the blade leaning against his shoulder. "We're ready."

When the curtains pulled open, the DJ's voice called out, "Let's make some noise for Altar Stoooooone!"

Relic was blinded by stage lights that flashed rapidly as he counted off on his hi-hats: one—before he got to two, the roar of the crowd nearly bowled him over. He could barely make out the silhouette of Bree, who had turned around to look at him with shocked eyes. Time slowed to a crawl.

Two—

He could see Tyler out of the corner of his eye, waiting in the wings to make a dramatic entrance before the first verse hit.

Three—

Nick had both fists raised in the air, basking in the love that the huge audience—*Where did all these people come from?!* Relic wondered—gave in deafening torrents.

Four—

Finally, Relic turned to the newest member of Altar Stone, who dressed the part, wearing a long black cloak that his D&D sorcerer would have definitely worn. His face was stretched back in unadulterated excitement as he prepared to hit the song's first chords.

Sebastian's synthesized horns swelled right before Relic and Bree kicked the song off. Something exploded in Relic, an energy beyond anything he had ever experienced. Watching Bree shred that opening riff while he provided punctual cymbal accompaniments on the new crash cymbal Nick had gotten him, Relic couldn't imagine a happier time in his life.

He could barely hear his rapid-fire double bass come in with the song's first downbeat pattern—the crowd was worked up into a frenzy, hearing something that was so beyond what any of them had probably expected coming to a metal concert in Laramie, Indiana.

After the song's bridge (where Sebastian nailed the synth lead), Tyler stalked onto the stage wearing the white leather jacket he and Sebastian had found at a Goodwill. His attire and confidence made him look like a modern high fantasy lord. He held the talion high with one hand as he pumped his fist with the other arm.

Relic felt like his head would split in half with how wide he was smiling. He kicked into the hardest part of the song for him: the verses. But when he heard Tyler perfectly sing the opening line with his own unique voice about crossing the valleys to search for the third key to open the gates, he felt so invigorated that even if his legs had cramped while trying to maintain a blistering 180 bpm sixteenth-note double bass pattern, he probably wouldn't have even noticed.

The band played the song flawlessly, and the crowd reacted more powerfully than Relic could have ever imagined. When the chorus hit and Tyler sang about "winning" the black lord, Relic felt something stir in his gut—something that made him instantly visualize the chupacabra's power that he absorbed in the fall. That oppressive sensation he experienced back then, the one that his mind tried to reject but some primal thing deep within him grasped desperately for, came back now, making his legs stiffen.

He could feel the muscles he had developed over his shins cramping now as he reached the halfway point of the song.

No, he thought, gritting his teeth and once more trying to repel that alien ecstasy that could only be Adratheon's power within him. *Come on, Relic! You've played this song at least twenty times! Don't blow it now!*

But the talion flared to life then, just as Tyler decreed that he would search for the Emerald Sword, hefting the blade above his head. The tightness within Relic burst free at that moment, relieving his cramps just as Bree hit the huge chords and Sebastian conducted his digital symphony with his fingers.

The crowd roared their approval as the emeralds set into the sword's crossguard flashed and a fiery green aura exploded around the talion. Relic's eyes went wide as he crashed along with the orchestral hits, almost not believing this whole thing was actually working. His eyes darted between the crowd and his band members, but it was as if none of them saw what he saw.

Relic was scared he was hallucinating, but with that strange knowing he felt in his core, he refused to believe his eyes were deceiving him.

Even though the audience certainly reacted to the weapon's consecration, it was as if only Relic saw the true magic the crowd helped Altar Stone conjure up. Whether or not that was accurate, when Bree kicked into the song's solo, Relic didn't even care. His legs were loose again and he got to finish playing one of the most badass songs he had ever heard with his best friends, all while a crowd of rambunctious, unknowing sorcerers cheered them on.

The remainder of the band's set consisted of a few other covers, as well as their original songs "Bane of the Worthy," "The Keys of Transience," "The Witchlord's Banishment," and the specifically chosen closer, "Night of the Harrow."

Relic said that song would summon Shrubble, and Delilah had no reason to believe otherwise. Even out in the alley, they could hear the PA blaring the first part of the song. Delilah wished she could have the same passion as Relic and Bree when it came to heavy metal, but it just felt so abrasive to her.

In that regard, it wasn't surprising to her in the least that it had such an effect on these blood-thirsty monsters.

"You ready back there?" Gate asked, looking into the rearview mirror through a cloud of cigarette smoke.

Delilah turned in the passenger seat to watch the things squirm in the back again. There were seven skrimkins reaching their sharp little claws out, trying to swipe at their two captors through the tight net. Their chattering was like a mix of snakes hissing and annoying bird chirps, and Delilah was ready to be rid of the wretched little things.

The echoes of the Altar Stone song were reaching a crescendo then, and Gate rolled his window down to toss out his smoke. "Well...the kid was right..."

Delilah looked beyond the little monsters and saw the distinctive green glow approaching the dead skrimkin they had left by the manor's back door.

"There he is," she said, climbing back over the struggling skrimkins so she could throw the van's rear door open. She threw aside a piece of canvas to reveal another dead skrimkin. She picked it up by its limp neck and pulled out one of her knives to start butchering it just as Shrubble began his feast.

"Hey, Shrubs," she shouted, her voice piercing the muffled music in the alley. "You were right! These things just seem to keep following me!" She sliced off the creature's arm and dropped it out the back of the van; it flopped into a puddle. "But I think I might just take these to Relic back at the well, just to watch the two of you slimeballs fight over Adratheon's scraps!"

Shrubble's staff emitted an explosive green pulse of magic then. The naked trees at either end of the alley that hadn't yet gotten their spring leaves were drawn toward his power, like great skeletal hands with hundreds of reaching fingers.

"Go!" Delilah shouted, and Gate floored it, jerking the van forward so suddenly that Delilah was almost thrown out the back. Fortunately, her reflexes allowed her to grab hold of the closed door.

The sounds of Altar Stone faded beneath the creaking of the animated trees reacting to Shrubble's command. Delilah carved off another piece of the skrimkin, ignoring the threatening chatter and reaching claws from the live ones in the net.

"Don't worry," she scowled at them, seeing her father's final gasps reflected in each of their disgusting yellow eyes. "You'll get your turns."

The van sped down Wane Street, leaving a trail of dead Alternians in its wake on its way to the poisoned well.

And the hexlord took the bait.

Chapter 28

During the final chorus of "Night of the Harrow," Tyler once again brandished the talion over his head as he chanted the anthem:

"From the cradle down below
A wretch comes forth
Through seeds we've sown
Blood stains the harrow
That cursed the dawn
And now we are left in the dark alone."

The lyrics Relic had written (or Cecily had written) became a sonic chant over the beating heart of the chorus' driving rock beat. This time, Relic saw many eyes in the crowd go wide when the sword produced emerald flames at the exact time his sticks ignited.

Relic surprised himself when that happened, gritting his teeth as one of those enchanted sticks crashed his new Zildjian A Custom cymbal. Fortunately, the thing didn't shatter like his old one at Tammy's party, but he struggled to keep the final beats of the song while extinguishing his sticks.

It was no good though: he couldn't dispel anything. The magic was untethered that night in Wane Street Manor.

As the band held out the final chord of "Night of the Harrow," Relic stood up to wash his cymbals using small, quick strikes with sticks that trailed fading green fire. Relief mixed with extreme exaltation as his drumsticks returned to normal and the house went wild for his band's finale.

The stage lights flashed wildly, probably convincing the rest of the band and audience that the Alternian magic was just clever theatrics. Bree and Nick looked to him for a cue when to hit the final notes and, when he gave it, the band finished their performance just as they had begun: perfectly in sync.

A voice came over the PA: "Give it up, folks—give it everything you got—for the one and only, Altar Stone!"

They certainly did.

Relic joined his friends at the front of the stage to soak in the applause. He saw familiar faces in the crowd: Howard Sloan was pointing out to some nearby nerds that he knew Relic, Steven Meyers was raising his fist and screaming in the front row, Dina and Calvin were clapping wildly not far from his dad, even both Bree's parents (still in their wedding attire) screamed for an encore.

But Relic knew they couldn't do that, as much as he might want to.

"Dude," Tyler said, having to yell in Relic's ear over the noisy applause. "Something's up with this sword, man. You didn't tell me it lights up and shit."

Relic laughed and took the talion. It felt right in his hand, like he already knew how to use it, as if he had been born with it in his grip. *That's good,* he thought, *I'm going to have to use it soon...*

"Should we play another cover?" Nick asked, yelling into Relic's other ear. "I hear a bunch of encores out there!"

Relic shook his head, turning to Bree. She caught his look and nodded, still smiling wildly.

"Leave them wanting more," Bree shouted, nodding for them to get off stage.

"What if we want more?" Sebastian replied, his voice louder than Relic had ever heard him speak.

They all laughed as they left the stage, the applause still at a fever pitch.

Steven Meyers hustled out the manor's side entrance, avoiding any acquaintances that might want to chat. There was a chill in the air that he didn't like, and his eyes darted up and down the eerily empty street. As he got to Gate's old Cavalier parked along the side of Wane Street, he heard footsteps behind him.

He turned to see a familiar character—one that he hadn't seen since he was twenty-two, which was the last time he watched Constrained Media's cult classic slasher *The Motel Maniac.*

Standing at least seven feet tall, the gangly man wore the iconic bloodied janitor coveralls that clashed with his elegant (but torn and ratty) bellboy jacket. His face was obscured by that papery shower cap pulled over his features, displaying only the angry face crudely drawn on with childlike marker strokes. In his hand was the knife that had the *Do Not Disturb* tag dangling around its bloodied blade.

"Oh, come on!" Steven moaned just before the second hexlord slashed at him.

Relic and Bree urged the rest of the band to go mingle with the crowd and to check on Tammy, who had agreed to run their merch booth during the show.

"Sell some shirts!" Relic called after them as he hefted the talion and motioned for Bree to hurry up. After she got her guitar back in its case, they ran out the back door. Relic felt an eerie chill in the air, which didn't seem natural. But he ran with Bree toward the corner of Wane Street and McCormick Avenue where they had agreed to meet Steven.

"Where is he?" Relic cursed as they reached the car, seeing no sign of his dad.

"Relic..."

He turned to see Bree pointing at the ground and his racing heart hit the brakes.

Near the front tire there was a splash of fresh blood next to a set of car keys.

Relic jerked his head up, running toward the intersection. "Dad?!" Looking in all directions, there wasn't any sign of danger or even movement. A car drove by, laying on its horn as it steered clear of the stupid teenager in the middle of the road. But no sign of his dad.

"Dudes!"

The new voice gave Relic hope, but when he turned and saw Ricky Warren approaching, he felt a different sort of concern. However, the man's expression was one of elation.

"You guys destroyed, man! Altar Stone fucking rules!" He walked like he was drunk, holding out his gesticulating arms as if he were trying to balance some huge piece of furniture. "That was seriously incredible!" His face changed suddenly when he got close enough to see the talion. "Dude, that sword is righteous." He held up his fist and began singing Rhapsody: "For the king, for the—"

"Have you seen my dad?" Relic asked frantically, moving back toward the car to rejoin Bree as she investigated the scene. "He was supposed to meet us here."

"Nah, man," Ricky replied, following. "That's your pops though: always seems to have something cooking, ya know?"

Bree picked up the keys and held them out to Ricky. "Can you drive?"

Relic opened his mouth to object, but they had to hurry. Ricky, who had almost shot Becca Reynolds, wasn't at the top of Relic's list of trustworthy companions. Also, the dude looked drunk. But they had to get to Romney and they couldn't bring someone else into this whole thing.

"Come on," Relic said, motioning for Ricky to take the keys as he went around to the passenger seat.

Ricky snatched the keys. "Let's roll, baby! You guys mind if I roast a bone?"

Delilah tossed the last piece of the skrimkin into the dirt road leading into the Crane Estate. In the distance she could see the green haze of Shrubble's presence; the hexlord seemed to be either running super fast or was propelled by some force. Delilah gritted her teeth, thinking that she had been fueling whatever force that was by feeding the bastard a seven-course meal.

The van lurched to a stop and Delilah fell forward into the puddle of yellow ichor on the van floor. "Ugh," she groaned. "Thanks for the warning, Gate!"

The janitor came to help her out of the pungent, sludgy remains of her butchery.

"What do we do now?" Gate asked. "Hide or something?"

Delilah shook her head while also shaking the filth off her hands as she looked out into the darkness. "He'll just sniff me out at this point."

"Well, hopefully Relic gets here soon with that scallion or whatever," Gate said, digging another cigarette out of his pack. "I hate waiting around."

Allowing herself a laugh, Delilah corrected him. "Talion."

As if the word were an incantation, the ground shuddered under their feet and both of them reached out for each other to retain balance. A groaning sound came from the side of the old house, and they both went to see as massive tentacles burst up from Shrubble's well, throwing stones and dirt in all directions. Glass shattered as the windows on the house and the van were hit by flying debris.

Gate and Delilah took cover behind the van, but the dhampir allowed herself to peer around the vehicle's grille so she could see those monstrous things unravel like some great sea creature. They were tangles of great roots, groaning and creaking as they moved like boneless appendages, reaching to grab, choke, break, and pulverize.

"Well," Delilah said, drawing her knives, "at least we won't be bored while we wait."

"Can you go any faster?"

"My man," Ricky said to Relic, laughing in disbelief. "We're going seventy-five in a fifty-five. You got enough to cover a speeding ticket? I sure don't!" He hiccuped and seemed to almost lose his grip on the wheel, swerving to correct himself. "Besides. I don't have my license."

"Jesus, man," Bree groaned from the back seat. "One of us should have just drove."

Relic sighed, tapping his feet nervously. "Just hurry up. It's getting late."

"What's the rush, Relly Belly?! You're supposed to party after a show like that, not haul ass into the middle of—Where is it we're going again?"

"Turn here!" Relic shouted, pointing to the familiar dirt road that led toward the estate.

"Look out!" Bree shouted.

Relic jerked his head and saw the obstacle that apparently Ricky's inebriated vision hadn't registered yet, because he didn't slow down. The Cavalier took the turn fast enough to peel out and send a spray of gravel, leaving the drunk driver no time to hit the brakes before plowing into a tree in the middle of the dirt road.

The placement of that tree was the subject of several profanity-riddled queries that raced through Relic's mind before the collision, but even as the front of the car smashed inward and the back of the car kept sliding around to send them spinning, he knew the answer to all those questions.

Shrubble Von Hellspawn laughed in Relic's mind as his head smashed painfully against the passenger window. The car kept spinning or rolling (he couldn't tell) and his body was pressed hard against the seat belt. He closed his eyes against the violent ride, hoping each bump would be the last.

Finally the car settled, and Relic opened his eyes, his head throbbing and his knees sore from banging against the dash. He turned to see Ricky slumped against the steering wheel, a trickle of blood matting his long hair against his brow, then twisted to check on Bree. But she seemed one step ahead of him.

"You alright?" she asked, gasping as she struggled to get her seat belt off. She looked virtually unharmed, which relieved Relic, but when he realized how *empty* he suddenly felt, he turned panicked eyes to the vacant space between his legs.

The talion was gone.

Relic scrambled out of the car.

"Is he dead?" Bree asked, but Relic couldn't even interpret her words as he stumbled around the crash site looking for the emerald sword. There was a distant groaning that shook the ground itself, making Relic's sudden vertigo worsen. He focused his eyes and saw a green haze in the distance, and against that smoky horizon he saw—

"Are those fucking tentacles?!" Bree stepped up next to him. "Holy shit, Relic. You gonna fight that with a sword?"

"If I can find it!" Relic said, turning to continue his search. "Check there! I don't see it in the ditch over here."

He heard Bree run to the other side of the car. "There it is! The tree has it!"

Relic climbed over the car's hood and saw what she meant. The tree *did* have it. One of the branches was wrapped around its jeweled crossguard like a skeletal fist with a hundred fingers and it slowly pulled the blade into its massive trunk.

"No!" Relic screamed as he grabbed the sword's grip, standing on the roof of the car and pulling with all his might. But the soles of his wrestling shoes squealed as he was pulled along with the sword into a great gaping maw that now opened up to swallow them both. Just as Relic's hands were about to get digested by the thing, he felt the sword begin to give.

He turned to see Bree next to him, her muscled arms swelling and shaking as she gnashed her teeth and dragged the talion back out of the tree's mouth. Together they kept drawing the sword farther and farther from the void that was this creature's maw, and finally Relic was able to feel the weapon's power within his grasp.

In his mind, he visualized waking up that power in his drumsticks, setting them aflame. While he had often wondered if he could perform that act with something other than objects he so closely identified himself with, he had never truly attempted.

Now he did.

The emerald in the crossguard seemed to glimmer slightly, but then the sword was jerked back toward the tree's widening, thorny gullet. More branches had joined this desperate tug of war.

"It's slipping," Bree growled through clenched teeth.

Relic saw her veiny biceps, looking like they were about to explode like overfilled water balloons. He couldn't believe how powerful she looked—he couldn't believe how hopeless this situation would have been if he hadn't brought her along.

That realization triggered something in him, and he thought of their Christmas Eve promise. All Bree's talk of devotion was like a bright green spark down in his bowels, and it lit the fuse that allowed him to imbue the sword with his innate eldritch power.

The Emerald Sword earned its namesake, its blade exploding with vibrant green light, charring and withering the animated branches. Relic and Bree pulled the talion free then, like a joint King Arthur yanking Excalibur from its stone.

"You did it," Bree gasped.

But as Relic watched Shrubble's minion shrink away from the Alternian magic they wielded together, he just said, "That was all you, babe."

CHAPTER 29

Bree and Relic were both panting heavily as they neared the estate's toppled archway, which now blocked the driveway leading toward the house. They narrowly dodged a huge root tentacle that slammed down near the van, the aftershock causing Bree to grab onto Relic's shoulder for purchase.

"Gate! Delilah!" Relic motioned for Bree to stay behind him before he gripped the talion with both hands. He couldn't see the hexlord anywhere through the gathering green smoke pluming from the broken earth. "Where is he?"

"Over here!" It was Delilah.

They followed her voice toward the house, their pace hindered by lack of visibility and the gaping fissures that continued to belch eldritch mists into the night. There was a glow of vile magic coming from below, providing them some light to see where they needed to avoid stepping. It was clear to Relic now that Shrubble had finally been able to draw out the rest of his power; the air was palpable with it.

Relic heard the sounds of conflict up ahead: Delilah grunted and Gate cursed, the thick sounds of flesh hitting flesh punctuated by inhuman growls and shrieks. *What the hell are we running into?* Relic thought, but the weight of the sword and the feel of Bree's occasional hand on his shoulder gave him enough courage to reach the house's ruined front porch.

"Welcome, kids!"

Bree gasped as Relic looked toward the bizarre figure standing where the house's front door used to be, which was now broken in three pieces on the porch. It was a gangly old woman, slightly hunched in a rotting blue dress that a 1950s housewife might wear. Her apron was covered in filth.

The back of the woman's dress was torn open, and several contorted arms jerked wildly from her deformed hunchback, each of those limbs wielding a cleaver, meat tenderizer, or some other deadly kitchen utensil.

The woman held a tray of what Relic hoped were just rotten, slimy sausages, because the alternative might have been too much for him to bear. She raised the tray to offer them one of her snacks.

"You kids just can't seem to get enough of my delectable dicks," the witch cackled, the tray shaking in her wobbly hands. "Come on—"

The porch shook then as a huge tree tentacle thing fell limply on the roof, rolling over Relic and Bree's heads to flop on the ground dead.

"—in and slurp these suckers down before the little scamps inside eat 'em all up." She turned then to go back into the house, and Relic could see the whole of her horrid back. A curved spine separated two pools of wrinkled flesh that stretched occasionally against several writhing skulls, mouthing curses through their elastic holds. The arms flailed around as if they wanted to kill Relic and Bree, but the teens just exchanged disgusted looks and decided not to accept the woman's invitation.

"Back here!" Delilah called.

Relic pushed Bree against the porch as a smaller tendril of Shrubble's animated vines reached up out of clay soil that might once have been a garden. He swung the talion down awkwardly, and when it cut the thing in two there was a deafening screech from somewhere below.

He felt that one, Relic thought gladly.

Bree kicked half the dead thing away from her. "This is fucking insane, dude."

Gate appeared from the gloom then, blood streaking down in his face from a cut along his hairline. "Where's your dad, kid?!"

Relic shook his head. "I don't know. Ricky got us here. Where's Shrubble?"

Gate's eyes were watching something on the ground. Relic turned to see the thing he had cut in half begin to deteriorate, its essence swirling into a mist and winding its way upward into one of the talion's emeralds.

Laughing, Bree grabbed his shoulders. "It works!"

"This way!" Gate led them around the corner, leaping over a legless skrimkin who clawed at them desperately. Relic rammed the sword into the thing's head, watching it mistify (*Yeah!* he thought. *Mistify would have been a badass band name!*) and get sucked into the green gem. He could feel the power, but it was different now—distant and removed, but no less potent.

"Come now," a voice that could only be Shrubble's taunted from the mist, "don't you want to join your precious father?" Something struck like lightning then, and Delilah cried out in pain. The light from the cracks below intensified at the same time, creating silhouettes in the mist: Shrubble raising his staff and Delilah, arms wide and ensnared, held captive.

Just as Relic was about to burst into a run toward the hazy scene, there was a scuffle behind him and Bree shouted, "Relic, help!"

Turning, he saw Gate swarmed with skrimkins—nearly a dozen of them. Bree began yanking them off, tearing off heads and limbs as if she were pulling out weeds. Relic raised the sword to help, but it was suddenly caught on something. Looking up, he saw one of the huge tentacles wrapping around the blade like a snake. The bark on the thing sizzled against the weapon's touch, but kept wrapping its bulk around the emerald sword.

Something pulled his gaze back to Shrubble and he saw those narrowed lantern eyes peering straight at him through the fog. The hexlord smiled wickedly.

"You won't need this down in the cradle," he whispered, but Relic could hear him perfectly. Then, the little goblin gestured with his staff and the appendage tore the talion from Relic's grip and launched it toward the house. The shattering glass told him it had landed somewhere inside.

"Bree!" He quickly pulled out his drumsticks and spun them to life. "The sword! It's in the house!"

Bree wrenched the final skrimkin off Gate and helped him up. "We're on it!" The bloodied janitor limped toward the front porch as Relic slashed at Shrubble's tentacles with his more familiar weapons, cutting his way to rescue his ex-girlfriend.

Ricky rolled painfully out of the car, his head pounding and his left leg in agony. He wasn't sure, but he thought it was broken. When he had come to, it had been pinned under the wrecked door and he had probably hurt it more by dislodging the thing. Moving it was incredibly painful and he didn't even try to put any real weight on it yet.

The weird sound of huge trees being cut down drew his gaze toward a strange green glow on the horizon. His only guess was that it was either a rave of some sort, with the lights flashing behind moving objects, or some bizarre fireworks display. But his vision was still blurry, so he couldn't be sure.

"Little assholes trying to get me killed getting to their little afterparty," Ricky moaned, getting up on his good leg. Something shifted in his pants, and he realized his new pistol—a more modern Beretta which he had been keeping tucked into the back of his pants under his jacket—had fallen into his briefs during the wreck. He shifted it back into place as he hopped on one foot up the road.

"Better at least have some beer waiting for me."

His left leg seemed to function a little more now, assuring Ricky that it probably wasn't broken. As he got in sight of the old farmhouse, he could almost walk normally.

"I've been here," he thought aloud, realizing now that it wasn't his vision that was blurry, but that the place seemed shrouded in some thick fog.

"Welcome back," a creepy voice whispered.

Ricky spun around, instinctively drawing the gun from his pants. He pointed it at nothing. All he saw in the distance behind him was more fog—he couldn't even see the wrecked car anymore or that huge tree.

Was there a fucking tree in the middle of the road? he suddenly wondered, as if just remembering it.

"You fucking twerps," Ricky spat, limping on toward the house. "What if I'm an undercover cop, huh? Here to bust up your underage drinking orgy?" He scoffed at the idea. "Damn kids..."

It wasn't until the ground violently shook and Ricky nearly stumbled into the grass that he began to think that something was truly not right. That was when he fully remembered.

"We're at the goddamn Sinclair place?!" He struggled to his feet just as he heard a girl shriek.

"Gate!" The dire plea awoke something in Ricky.

Now, Ricky Warren would never have considered himself a heroic man, but maybe it was the gun in his hand, suddenly giving him the impression that he was Martin Riggs and Roger Murtaugh needed his help, or maybe it was the familiar taste in the atmosphere reminding him why he came back to Laramie in the first place. Whatever it was, Ricky scrambled heedlessly toward the house, almost oblivious to the octopus legs flailing around in the sky.

The girl screamed again, and Ricky was almost full-out sprinting when he reached the porch. Once there, the sight stopped him dead in his tracks.

Relic's buff girlfriend was fending off a crazy grandma that tried to shove a slimy hot dog into the girl's mouth, while Ricky's former bassist struggled to pull a knife out of his chest while also blocking a meat tenderizer from caving in his skull; both implements were wielded by several extra arms growing out of granny's back.

Despite everything that Ricky Warren had witnessed in his life, he was at a complete loss for words. He simply raised the gun, aimed between the two struggling companions, and fired into Grandma Sinclair.

The gunshot managed to startle Relic, even as he was carving through a supernatural tree tentacle with magic drumsticks, but Delilah's scream kept him focused on the task. After dealing with three writhing appendages, Relic reached the well where Shrubble waited.

"Relic, no!"

Before Relic could look toward her to see what she warned him about, his feet froze and he was almost thrown forward from his momentum. Looking down after regaining his balance, he saw his feet getting sucked into some sort of swampy quicksand. He was trapped.

Shrubble cackled, holding out his staff as the fingers on his other hand began working some kind of hex on Relic. *Fucking spellcasters,* he groaned, trying to force his legs out of the muck. But it seemed like the more he struggled, the more stuck he was getting. He threw the stick in his right hand like a knife, but it ricocheted off some sort of barrier that glimmered around the hexlord.

"Daddy's not here to save you this time," Shrubble said in his rat-like voice. Relic didn't know if he was referring to Adratheon, Steven Meyers, or Guy Valentine (in Delilah's case), but it kind of covered all the bases.

"Come here," Relic threatened, jamming his remaining stick in the solid ground so he could pull himself out. "I'll show you a daddy, bitch." But as Shrubble's magic continued to work, that pool of sucky earth widened and his stick came loose.

"Oh, I can see your daddy," Shrubble replied, stepping closer and raising his staff. "He waits for me in the Between. He depends on me, trusts me." His voice became a wicked cackle as he stepped within reach of Relic's stick. But before Relic could slash at the creature with a carefully aimed stroke that would have taken its head off, he felt blinding pain in his chest.

Relic looked down to see Shrubble's staff, sharpened like a stake, jammed into the right side of his chest. It seemed surreal, like the impaled body wasn't his and he was just getting queasy looking at someone else getting stabbed. But when his own blood started darkening his shirt, the true agony of the wound coursed through him and he screamed in pain.

"Relic!" Delilah cried, her voice strained as she struggled against her bindings.

He dropped his stick to grab the staff, trying to force it back out of his body. But the thing burned his hands and he had to let go. It was then that he felt the power leaving him. Through watery eyes, Relic saw Shrubble's wicked, wide-eyed expression—he was in ecstasy. It was then that Relic knew.

Shrubble was sucking him off.

After Ricky emptied his pistol's magazine into the roasted wiener cook, Bree left him to guard Gate on the porch as she made her way through the disgusting house looking for the sword. There were all kinds of strange sounds coming from below, either from the basement or somewhere beyond, but she focused, knowing that Relic needed her.

Four skrimkins scrambled toward her from different parts of the house, but she made short work of each of them, pounding them into mush, refusing to be distracted from her goal.

She found the blade in the kitchen, but before she could bend down to grab it, Relic screamed in agony outside and she froze. There was a single pane of glass sitting in the kitchen's back door and it stared at her, daring her to make a move toward the talion. In that filthy, spotty piece of glass, she saw a different kitchen reflected: her kitchen, where Relic screamed on the floor as a werewolf mauled him.

And Bree stood frozen, terrified to do anything but watch.

Swallowing, Bree shook her head. *Not now not now not now,* she panicked. *Come on, you can do this.* She closed her eyes and clenched her bloodied fists, telling herself people could die if she didn't get her shit together. And when she opened them, her eyes fell on her salvation.

Delilah's pouch was sitting discarded at the other end of the kitchen, near another broken window. She scrambled for it, opened it, and pulled out three vials of VANDAL serum.

"Better not take any chances," she said, jamming them one by one into her ass. She exhaled deeply after each shot, as if orgasming, knowing that nothing would be able to stop her now.

She grabbed the sword, unknowingly awakening its power just like she had with Relic's drumstick, and kicked the back door open.

As Shrubble drained him of the Alternian magic he had consumed, Relic felt like long hairs were being pulled out of him slowly, one at a time. He felt the chupacabra's essence being dragged out of him through the staff, clawing at his innards to keep from joining Shrubble's growing legion.

"Adratheon would want me to kill you," Shrubble said between groans of pleasure. "He doesn't want any more of his spawn trying to usurp him, but as a usurper myself...well, I might have some use for you down below. When I kill the other hexlords and take their power, I can put you back in my cradle and you can be one of my hexlords." He laughed wildly at that notion. "Along with your father—both your fathers!—and your mother." His laughter became maniacal. "And your sister!"

The fantasy Shrubble spun seemed to distract him, his eyes growing distant as he continued rambling about his brilliant scheme. Relic clenched his eyes and tried to focus on undoing whatever was happening. Having no idea how he actually used his drumsticks as eldritch knives, he hoped he could also randomly know how to cast some sort of counter spell now that his oppressor was distracted.

Through his painful, violent connection with the hexlord, Relic felt something then. A subtle release, as if he had just taken a piss or something. Opening his eyes again, Relic saw the cause and it wasn't anything he had done. Behind Shrubble, Bree was using the talion to cut Delilah free from her bindings.

Relic tried to hide his relief, which wasn't too difficult as Shrubble continued to drain him. His pain-addled mind began to wonder if this ritual (or whatever it was) would take everything, including all the Adratheon parts of him.

He strangely found himself hoping so, even though that would mean he could no longer fight.

As if that sudden hope were a burning coal in his guts that Shrubble had accidently touched, the hexlord pulled his staff out of Relic and spun around to face the interlopers.

Relic gasped in relief, watching helplessly as Bree charged toward the hexlord with the talion held in a double-fisted grip. Shrubble raised his staff and blocked the blow, sending the sword sprawling from Bree's hands.

He wanted to scream out a warning, telling Bree to get away from him. But his voice wouldn't work as his body caved in on itself. His fading vision could see the two of them clash, with Bree grabbing onto Shrubble's arms to wrestle the staff from his hands. Behind them, Delilah kept the grasping tentacles at bay with her knives.

"Bree," Relic gasped, still trying to pull his weakened body out of the sucky mud. He couldn't get free, feeling powerless as he watched his girlfriend battle his sworn foe in his stead. Delilah leapt at the hexlord with both her knives downward, but a huge muddy fist burst up from below, punching the dhampir back into the mist.

Bree followed suit and uppercutted Shrubble, sending the smaller figure flying through the air. Unfortunately, he landed near his staff and rolled over with it back in his grasp. Bree charged him, but fell to her knees as he aimed his staff at her and afflicted her with some sort of hex that caused her limbs to contort. Relic felt like he was about to get one foot free, losing his shoe as he wiggled in every direction to escape his muddy confines.

"Bree! Get away, please!"

It was then that she turned toward him, her eyes burning yellow orbs.

"No," Relic mouthed, as if frozen in that moment of realization: it wasn't just Bree looking at him, she was something more now. "No, Bree. Don't."

He watched, heart pounding, as Bree pushed herself up from the ground, her fists clenched tight. Something shifted in the air around her—an unseen force, raw and volatile, surging back toward Shrubble. The hexlord flinched, his staff snapping backward as if the magic had been ripped from him and forced back into its source. He barely had time to react before Bree lunged. Relic saw the brief flicker of panic in Shrubble's glowing eyes before Bree's fist connected with his face, the impact landing with a sickening crunch that sent the creature hurtling backward.

Relic could see the talion, only a few inches from his grasp. "Bree, wait!" But he knew it was useless; he could hear the meaty sounds of his guitar player absolutely pummeling the pathetic creature, punch after punch that sounded nothing like the movies. This was primal aggression, rage made physical.

Finally, Relic wrapped his hand around the grip of the talion, and just the feel of it in his grasp seemed to loosen the hold Shrubble's muddy trap had on his legs. He squirmed free and got to his feet.

But when he turned to put an end to the hexlord, he saw that his girlfriend already had.

And all the power Shrubble had consumed during his short stint in Laramie was now flowing into Bree Thompkins, who stood over the hexlord with bloodied fists, her body heaving with deep breaths of expended fury.

"Bree..." Relic didn't know what to say; he just stared at his girlfriend, the unsated talion falling from his hands as he fully comprehended his failure.

As the mists began to recede, Delilah appeared, looking half-dead on her feet. As tentacles flopped over lifelessly around her, she regarded Relic. "I should have known." Her voice was much more jovial than Relic expected. "Valaina wouldn't have chosen her own brother or son." She laughed then, without humor, and walked over to stomp on what remained of Shrubble's head.

After that grisly display, she turned to Bree and held one of her knives out to her, hilt first. "I guess you're one of us now."

Relic's heart sank as Bree turned to look at him with eyes that were entirely hers now. Looking into those eyes, Relic could feel her fear and confusion having just discovered she was Valaina's Chosen. He shook the mud off his hands and went over to hug her, feeling tremendous power flowing through the girl he loved.

"Holy shit," Ricky said, helping Gate limp toward the teens that stood over a slain hexlord. "I think they're cooking dicks in that house, guys."

CHAPTER 30

T he band agreed to meet at Rook's the next afternoon to recap their show. Since Relic would have to work afterward and it was a fairly central location for them all, it seemed the best place to hang out.

The bizarre mixture of fear, excitement, victory, and crushing defeat the night prior almost led to Relic and Bree having sex for the first time, but they settled for a shower and a few episodes of *Mr. Bean* before passing out together from exhaustion. Relic wasn't even surprised that the wound on his chest, which had seemed to stop hurting after Bree killed Shrubble, had healed overnight; only a small puckered scar remained.

They arrived at Rook's early to meet with Mindy Hayes shortly after lunch.

"You were smart not to call the police," she said, stirring some sugar into her coffee. They were one of three occupied tables at the diner, but the other two parties were on the other side of the restaurant, giving them plenty of privacy. "Who knows what they would run with if Steven Meyers was reported missing again."

"Can you help us find him?" Relic asked anxiously. He had called his dad's apartment about a dozen times, and they went over there in the morning just to be sure. There was still no sign of him.

"There was blood," Bree added. "Maybe he went to the ER or something?"

Mindy nodded. "I already checked with the hospital. No official record he was admitted." She took a sip of her coffee, set the mug down, and then leaned forward to regard them both. "But I spoke with a paramedic who said he saw an eighties rocker guy with long hair come in, blood on his jean jacket. So I think he was definitely there."

"Did you ask anyone else?" Relic prodded.

Mindy shook her head. "After the whole Valentine situation, I'm not taking that chance again. Speaking of which—think your friend Delilah would talk to me? I haven't been able to track down her dad, and she might be able to help us, given her own circumstances."

Relic and Bree exchanged a nervous look then and Relic quickly added, "I'll ask her."

Nodding, Mindy took another sip of her coffee before scooting back in her chair. "This stinks of Rothen," she said under her breath. "I'll let you know what I find out. Get back to me about Valentine's kid."

After their private investigator was gone, Relic and Bree moved to their booth in somber silence. Both of them were contemplating everything that happened since the show and what it all meant for them going forward.

Relic broke the silence. "Maybe we should talk to your mom." She turned to him and he added, "I'm not paranoid about Rothen like Mindy is, but maybe she could know something about my dad. He wouldn't just disappear like this, you know?"

Bree nodded, looking at the table. "I'm kind of scared to even talk to her after... Well, you know what Delilah's been saying, about the cult and Rothen being at odds over that whole DeMono Tech thing." She looked back at Relic. "If I'm really this Valaina's Chosen thing...like, does the cult worship me now? And how do you think my mom would react?"

Relic widened his eyes and sighed, not having an answer for either. Things were really getting complicated. Fortunately, the door chimed then and a familiar voice bellowed, "Altar Stone!"

Bree and Relic turned to see Nick, who walked in raising two metal horns, his face absolutely jubilant. It was infectious, and Relic and Bree returned the greeting with horns of their own.

"Where the hell did you guys go last night?!" Nick slid into the seat across from them just as the door chimed again and Sebastian came in with Tyler.

"What happened?!" Tyler demanded, letting Sebastian scoot into the booth next to Nick while he grabbed an extra chair to join them. After slapping Relic's open palm in greeting, Tyler pointed to Bree. "You guys disappeared! You missed all the praise. We also sold out of those shirts."

"If we need some more," Sebastian said quickly, pointing to Relic, "my cousin runs a little shop over by the mall. Could probably get some cheap."

"We'll need 'em," Nick said, putting his palms on the table dramatically, "because this summer... Guess what?"

The band members exchanged questioning looks.

"What?" Bree finally asked.

"I turn sixteen," Nick said, nodding and smiling. "And you know what that means, dudes. Altar Stone Midwest tour!"

Tyler snapped and pointed at him. "Yes! We get a couple more songs written and, Relic, can I keep using that sword? You gotta show me how it works, because I don't know how it was lighting up and stuff."

"Wait wait wait," Bree said, holding up her hands. "We're not doing any tours until we have something recorded. We need a demo to sell at shows, right? Not just shirts."

Relic watched all this with a smile on his face, relieved that, despite the looming threats that awaited them, he knew he could face it with his band. He put his arm around Bree then, drawing her gaze to his.

Adratheon's son and Valaina's Chosen smiled and kissed. Maybe they were destined to be sworn enemies and maybe they would die miserably in a potential apocalyptic, interdimensional war, but for now, they were madly in love and playing in the most badass band they could imagine.

There were much worse ways to face the end of the world.

Or, even worse, junior year of high school.

Epilogue

Steven Meyers jerked awake, his head darting in either direction as he looked for the Motel Maniac. But he was in what looked like a hospital recovery room, only much nicer. Even in his groggy state, he could tell from the nature of the place that he was in a Rothen facility.

As he pushed the sheets off, he saw he was in a hospital gown, only again, much nicer. He winced against the pain in chest near his right shoulder where the Motel Maniac had stabbed him. Steven might have thought it strange that he was stabbed in the exact same spot as his son would later be impaled by Shrubble's staff, but for now he was just pissed that he let that bastard get the jump on him.

The door to the room beeped then, and the metallic handle clicked open as Lydia Thomkins strode in, still wearing her elegant dress from the wedding.

"Hang on," she said, holding a hand up. "You've been sedated, Steve. Just wait until all your senses are back."

"Why'd you bring me here?!" he demanded. "My son was waiting for me. What time is it?!"

"It's over," Lydia said, holding up both hands now in an effort to calm him. "Everyone's fine. Relax." She stood at the foot of his bed. "You passed out from blood loss at the ER, but after what happened upstairs, I had the Corps bring you back here."

"Why?!" Steven asked, recoiling as he yanked the IV from the back of his hand. "And what do you mean upstairs? Are we below Wane Street Manor right now?" His heart began racing, afraid of what this all might mean. "You brought *me* down *here*?! Are you crazy?!"

Lydia just smiled. "How else were we going to open the nexus?"

Less than twenty minutes later, Steven, dressed in tactical gear and sporting a headband to keep his hair back, was led two floors down into a part of the facility that was still under construction. He didn't have much time to consider what the hell he was doing, feeling like if he didn't act fast, things would only get worse for Relic.

He wouldn't fail his son again.

"You'll be reporting to our top soldier," Lydia explained calmly, as if she were just escorting a new intern to their first day on the job. "Captain Jacy Narvaez served as a special operative for the CIA before we recruited her to the Corps. Just follow her lead and you should be in and out."

Steven laughed at that, knowing the last time he went to Alternus the gap between "in" and "out" was just a few years of torture. Regardless, he got off the elevator and followed Lydia down a nondescript hall that ended in a set of heavy double doors. Lydia slid her card through and opened them. Steven gasped.

The room beyond was out of a nightmare—more specifically, *his* nightmare. A circular chamber housed a gaping hole in the earth that undulated like some sort of breathing asshole with teeth. Five soldiers were checking their submachine guns and other equipment as they turned to regard their boss and newest recruit.

"Captain Narvaez," Lydia said, almost ignoring Laramie's slimy rectum that kept puckering as if trying to suck on a giant straw just out of its reach, "this is Steven Meyers. Your mission depends on him, so if you lose him, don't even consider coming back." She turned to Steven then and he saw something strange pass over her face.

Is that actually compassion, Lydia?

"Understood," Jacy said, and then eyed Steven as if he were nothing more than a piece of equipment. "Welcome to the Corps."

Another soldier with the name *Reverend* on his uniform handed Steven an MP5. "Safety's on," he said. "Probably won't need it, but you might feel better carrying it."

Looking at Lydia, he wanted to once more say how crazy this was. But before he even had the chance, she turned on her high heels and made for the door.

"We have thirty-six hours to find Valaina before that thing closes, Stick," Lydia said over her shoulder. "You're the only one that knows where she is."

As if in response, the dimensional rectum belched and began undulating more rapidly.

"Time to go," a third soldier said, her voice calm and calculated. Steven turned to watch her attach a black nylon rope to a clip on her belt. Her name tag read *Rio* and her dark almond eyes regarded Steven coldly. "Strap in, Meyers."

A younger soldier who looked like he might have just graduated high school patted Steven's shoulder. His tag said *Kane* and his jaw worked on a piece of gum as he smiled and said, "Loved your drumming on *The Rest of the Wicked*, dude. Stay close to me, I'll bring you back in one piece."

"Masks on," the last soldier called, his tag identifying him as *Lock*. He snapped a flare and dropped it into the gaping maw. "Looks like more gas is coming."

A pungent stench filled the chamber then, and Jacy held out a gas mask for Steven. "They don't call us the Rotten Corps for nothing," she said, this time smiling just before sliding on her mask. Steven had just enough time to admire how hot the woman was before he slipped his own mask on.

The team descended into the abyss and Steven felt a strange calm steady his gloved hands as he slid down the rope.

He may be going to hell again, but at least this time he would do so with the crystal-clear vision of the man his son had become. While whistling "Emerald Sword" in his mask, Steven Meyers followed the Rotten Corps into Alternus.

Please consider reviewing this book by scanning the code below:

As an indie author, reviews are the best way to support my books so I can keep writing more.

Thank you!

ABOUT THE AUTHOR

Brady J. Sadler is the drummer and founder of the Indiana-based fantasy metal band, Lorenguard. Since abandoning the not-so-prestigious life of a mediocre percussionist for an amazing band—playing an obscure style of music in America—Brady has become a prolific tabletop game designer and author.

He lives in Indiana with his loving family and a couple hateful cats.

You can keep up with him at www.bradyjsadler.com.